Praise for *New York Times* bestselling author Lenora Worth and her novels

"This heartwarming romance
will draw readers in."
—*RT Book Reviews* on *A Certain Hope*

"Lenora Worth's *A Perfect Love* is a
beautiful testimony to the true meaning
of family and forgiveness."
—*RT Book Reviews*

"*A Leap of Faith* is a sweet
and enchanting romance between
two flawed but redeemable characters."
—*RT Book Reviews*

"Her best story yet, it is filled with
spiritual depth and hidden meaning."
—*RT Book Reviews* on *Heart of Stone*

LENORA WORTH
A Certain Hope

❦

A Perfect Love

Love Inspired

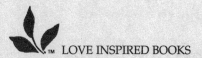 LOVE INSPIRED BOOKS

Recycling programs
for this product may
not exist in your area.

ISBN-13: 978-0-373-65147-4

A CERTAIN HOPE AND A PERFECT LOVE

A CERTAIN HOPE
Copyright © 2005 by Lenora H. Nazworth

A PERFECT LOVE
Copyright © 2005 by Lenora H. Nazworth

www.LoveInspiredBooks.com

Printed in U.S.A.

CONTENTS

Books by Lenora Worth

LENORA WORTH

has written more than forty books for three different publishers. Her career with Love Inspired Books spans close to fourteen years. Her very first Love Inspired title, *The Wedding Quilt,* won *Affaire de Coeur*'s Best Inspirational for 1997, and *Logan's Child* won an *RT Book Reviews* Best Love Inspired for 1998. With millions of books in print, Lenora continues to write for the Love Inspired and Love Inspired Suspense lines. Lenora also wrote a weekly opinion column for the local paper and worked freelance for years with a local magazine. She has now turned to full-time fiction writing and enjoying adventures with her retired husband, Don. Married for thirty-five years, they have two grown children. Lenora enjoys writing, reading and shopping… especially shoe shopping.

A CERTAIN HOPE

Now faith is the substance of things hoped for,
the evidence of things not seen.
—*Hebrews* 11:1

To the Ricks family—Barbara, Bob and especially Jordan. You all hold a special place in my heart.

Chapter One

You've got mail.

Summer Maxwell motioned to her cousin Autumn as she opened the letter in her computer. "Hey, it's from April."

Autumn hurried over to the teakwood desk by the window. The Manhattan skyline was etched in sun-dappled shades of steel and gray in front of them as together they read the latest e-mail from their cousin and roommate, April Maxwell.

I'm at work, but I'll be leaving for the airport in a few minutes. I'm so nervous. I'm worried about Daddy, of course. And I'm worried about seeing Reed again. What if he hates me? Never mind, we all know he does hate me. Please say prayers for my sweet daddy, and for safe travel. And that my BMW makes it there ahead of me in one piece.

"That's our April," Summer said, smiling, her blue eyes flashing. "Her prayer requests are always so practical."

"Especially when they come to that car of hers," Autumn said through the wisp of auburn bangs hanging in her eyes. "She's not so worried about the car, though, I think. She's got a lot more to deal with right now, and that's her way of dealing with it. She's not telling us the whole story."

Summer tapped out a reply.

We're here, sugar. And we will say lots of prayers for Uncle Stuart. Tell him we love him so much. Keep in touch. Oh, and let us know how things go with Reed, too. He doesn't hate you. He's just angry with you. Maybe it's time for him to get over it already.

Summer signed off, then spun around in her chair to send her cousin a concerned look. "Of course, he's been angry with her for about six years now."

Reed Garrison brought his prancing gray-and-black-spotted Appaloosa to a skidding stop as a sleek black sports car zoomed up the long drive and shifted into Park.

"Steady, Jericho," Reed said as he patted the gelding's long neck. He held the reins tight as he walked the horse up to the sprawling stone-and-wood ranch house. "I'm just as anxious as you, boy," he told the fidgeting animal. "Let's go find out who's visiting Mr. Maxwell on this fine spring day."

Reed watched from his vantage point at the fence as a woman stepped out of the expensive two-seater convertible. But not just any woman, oh, no. This one was very different.

And suddenly very familiar.

Reed squinted in the late-afternoon sun, then sat back to take a huff of breath as he took in the sight of her.

April Maxwell.

It had been six long years since he'd seen her. Six years of torment and determination. Torment because he couldn't forget her, determination because he had tried to do that very thing.

But April was, as ever, unforgettable.

And now she looked every bit the city girl she had become since she'd bolted and moved from the small town of Paris, Texas, to the big city of New York, New York, to take up residence with her two

cousins, Summer and Autumn. Those three Maxwell cousins had a tight bond, each having been
named for the seasons they were born in, each
having been raised by close-knit relatives scattered
all over east Texas, and each having enough ambition to want to get out of Texas right after finishing college to head east and seek their fortunes.
Not that they needed any fortunes. They were all
three blue-blooded Texas heiresses, born in the
land of oil and cattle with silver spoons in their
pretty little mouths. But that hadn't been enough
for those three belles, no sir. They'd wanted to
take on the Big Apple. And they had, each finding
satisfying work in their respective career choices.
They now roomed together in Manhattan, or so
he'd been told.

He hadn't asked about April much, and Stuart
Maxwell wasn't the type of man to offer up much
information. Stuart was a private man, and Reed
was a silent man. It worked great for both of them
while they each pined away for April.

Reed walked his horse closer, his nostrils flaring right along with Jericho's, as he tested the
wind for her perfume. He smelled it right away,
and the memories assaulted him like soft magno-
lia petals on a warm summer night. April always
smelled like a lily garden, all floral and sweet.

Only Reed knew she was anything but sweet.

Help me, Lord, he thought now as he watched her raise her head and glance around. She spotted him—he saw it in the way she held herself slightly at a distance—but she just stood there in her black short-sleeved dress and matching tall-heeled black sandals, as if she were posing for a magazine spread. She wore black sunglasses and a black-and-white floral scarf that wrapped like a slinky collar around her neck and head. It gave her the mysterious look of a foreign film star.

But then, she'd always been a bit foreign and mysterious to Reed. Even when they'd been so close, so in love, April had somehow managed to hold part of herself aloof. Away from him.

With one elegant tug, she removed the scarf and tossed it onto the red leather seat of the convertible, then ran a hand through her short, dark, tousled curls. With slow, deliberate steps he was sure she'd learned during her debutante years, she did a long-legged walk across the driveway, toward the horse and man.

"Hello, Reed."

"April." He tipped his hat, then set it back on his head, ignoring the way her silky, cultured voice moved like rich honey down his nerve endings. "I heard you might be coming home."

Heard, and lost more sleep than he wanted to think about right now.

"Yes," she said, her hand reaching out to pat Jericho's muzzle. "I drove from the Dallas airport."

"Nice rental car."

"It's not a rental. It's mine. I had it shipped ahead so I'd have a way to get around while I'm here."

Reed didn't bother to remind her that they had several available modes of transportation on the Big M Ranch, from horses to trucks and four-wheelers to Stuart Maxwell's well-tuned Cadillac. "Of course. You always did demand the best." *And I wasn't good enough,* he reminded himself.

"I like driving my own car," she said, unapologetic and unrepentant as she flipped a wrist full of black-and-white shiny bangle bracelets. They matched to perfection the looped black-and-white earrings she wore. "I hope that won't be a problem for you."

"Not my problem at all," Reed retorted, his gaze moving over her, a longing gnawing his heart in spite of the tight set of his jaw. "Looks like city life agrees with you."

"I love New York and I enjoy my work at Satire," she said with a wide smile that only illuminated her big, pouty red lips. Then she glanced around. "But I have to admit I've missed this ranch."

"Your daddy's missed you," Reed said, his tone going low, all hostility leaving his mind now. "He's real sick, April."

She lifted her sunglasses. "I know. I've talked to the doctors on a daily basis for the last two weeks."

In spite of her defensive tone, he saw the worry coloring her chocolate-brown eyes and instantly regretted the reason she'd had to come home. But then, he had a lot of regrets. "Seeing you will perk him up, I'm sure."

She nodded, looked around at the house. "Nothing has changed, and yet, everything is changing."

"You've been gone a long time."

"I've been back for holidays and vacations. Never saw you around much." The questioning look in her eyes was full of dare and accusation.

But he wouldn't give her the satisfaction of knowing he'd deliberately made himself scarce whenever he'd heard she was coming home to visit. Until now. Now he didn't have a choice. He couldn't run. Her daddy needed him here.

He shrugged, looking out over the roping arena across the pasture. "I like to go skiing for the winter holidays, fishing and camping during the spring and summer."

"Still the outdoorsman." She shot him a long, cool look. "That explains your constant absences."

"That and the fact that I bought up some of the land around here and I stay pretty busy with my own farming and ranching."

"You bought up Maxwell land," she said, her chin lifting in that stubborn way he remembered so well.

"Your daddy was selling, and I was in the market to buy."

She looked down at the ground, her fancy sandal toeing a clog of dirt just off the driveway. "He wouldn't want anybody else on this land. I'm glad you bought it."

For a minute, she looked like the young girl Reed had fallen in love with. From kindergarten on, he'd loved her—at first from a distance, and then, up close. For a minute, she looked as vulnerable and lonely as he felt right now.

But that passed. Like a light cloud full of hope and sunlight, the look was gone as fast as it had come. When she looked up at him, the coolness was back in her dark eyes. "I expect you to take care of this land, Reed. I know I can count on you to do that, at least."

"Thanks," he said, and meant it, in spite of the accusing tone in her last words. "You know I'd never do anything to hurt your daddy. He taught me a lot and he's given me a lot—me and my entire family, for that matter."

"Y'all have been a part of this land for as long as I can remember," she responded, her eyes wide and dark as she stared up at him.

Reed wondered if she was remembering their times together. He wondered if she remembered the way he remembered, with regret and longing and a bitterness that never went away, no matter how sweet the memories.

"I'll be right here, as long as Stu needs me," he told her. He would honor that promise, in spite of having to be near her again. He owed her father that much.

"I guess I'd better go on inside then," she said, her tone husky and quiet. "I dread this."

"Want me to go in with you?" Reed asked, then silently reprimanded himself for offering. He wouldn't fall back into his old ways. Not this time.

"No. I have to do this. I mean, he called me home for a reason, and I have to accept that reason."

Reed heard the crush of emotion in her voice

and, whether out of habit or sympathy, his heart lurched forward, toward her. "It's tough, seeing him so frail. Just brace yourself."

"Okay." She nodded, turned and walked back by the stone steps to the long wraparound porch, headed for her car. Then she turned back, her shiny gamine curls lifting in the soft breeze. "Will we see you at supper?"

"Probably not." He couldn't find the strength to share a meal with her, not tonight.

"Guess I'll see you later then."

"Yeah, later."

Reed watched from across the fence as she lifted a black leather tote from the car, her every step as elegant and dainty as any fashion plate he'd seen on the evening news. But then, April Maxwell herself was often seen on the evening news. She worked at one of the major design houses in the country—in the world, probably. Reed didn't know much about haute couture, but he did know a lot of things about April Maxwell.

His mother and sisters went on and on about how Satire was all the rage both on the runways and on the designer ready-to-wear racks, whatever that meant. April was largely responsible for that, they had explained. Apparently, she'd made a good career out of combining public relations and fashion.

She was just a bit shallow and misguided in the love and family department. She'd given up both to seek fame and fortune in the big city.

And he'd stayed here, broke and heartbroken, to mend the fences she'd left behind. Well, he wasn't broke anymore. And he wasn't so very heartbroken, either.

Why, then, did his heart hurt so much at the very sight of her?

She hurt all over.

April opened the massive wooden double doors to her childhood home, her heart beating with a fast rhythm from seeing Reed again. He looked better than ever, tall and muscular, his honey-brown hair long on his neck, his hazel-colored cat eyes still unreadable. Reed was a cowboy, born and bred. He was like this land, solid and wise, unyielding and rooted. After all this time, he still had the power to get to her. And she still had regrets she couldn't even face.

Before she could delve into those regrets, she heard footsteps coming across the cool brick-tiled entryway, then a peal of laughter.

"Ah, *niña,* you are home, *sí?*"

April turned to find one of her favorite people in the world standing there with a grin splitting his aged face.

"*Sí*, Horaz, I'm home. *¿Como está?*"

"I'm good, very good," Horaz said, bobbing his head, his thick salt-and-pepper hair not moving an inch.

"And Flora? How is she?"

"Flora is fine, just fine. She is cooking up all of your favorites."

"That sounds great," April said, hugging the old man in a warm embrace, the scent of spicy food wafting around them. She wasn't hungry, but she'd have to hide that from Horaz and Flora Costello. They had been with her family since her father and mother had been married more than thirty years ago. And after her mother's death when April was in high school, they'd stayed on to take care of her and her father. She loved them both like family and often visited with their three grown children and their families whenever she came home, which was rare these days. The entire Costello clan lived on Maxwell land, in homes they'd built themselves, with help from her father.

"You look tired, *niña*," Horaz said. "Do you want to rest before supper? Your room is ready."

April thought of the light, airy room on the

second floor, the room with the frilly curtains and wide, paned windows that allowed a dramatic view of the surrounding pasture land and the river beyond. "No, I don't want to rest right now. I want…I want to see my father."

Horaz looked down at the floor. "I will take you to him. Then I will instruct Tomás to bring in the rest of your bags."

"Yes, I left them in the trunk of the car." She handed him the keys. "And how is Tomás? Does he like high school?"

"He's on the football team," Horaz said, grinning again. "My grandson scored two touchdowns in the final big game last fall. We won the championship."

"I'm glad to hear it," April said, remembering her own days of cheerleading and watching Reed play. He'd been a star quarterback in high school and had gone on to play college ball. Then he'd gotten injured in his senior year at Southern Methodist University. After graduating, he had come home to Paris to make a living as a rancher. She had gone on to better things.

Not so much better, she reminded herself. You gave up Reed for your life in New York. Why now, of all times, did she have to feel such regrets for making that decision?

"Come," Horaz said, taking her by the arm to guide her toward the back of the rambling, high-ceilinged house.

As they passed the stairs, April took in the vast paneled-and-stucco walls of the massive den to the right. The stone fireplace covered most of the far wall, a row of woven baskets adorning the ledge high over it. On the back wall, over a long brown leather couch grouped with two matching comfortable chairs and ottomans, hung a portrait of the Big M's sweeping pastures with the glistening Red River beyond. Her mother had painted it. The paned doors on either side of the fireplace were thrown open to the porch, a cool afternoon breeze moving through them to bring in the scent of the just-blooming potted geraniums and the centuries-old climbing roses.

As they neared the rear of the house, April felt the cool breeze turn into a chill and the scent of spring flowers change to the scent of antiseptics and medicine. It was dark down this hall, dark and full of shadows. She shuddered as Horaz guided her to the big master bedroom where the wrap-around porch continued on each side, where another huge fireplace dominated one wall, where her mother's Southwestern-motif paintings hung on either side of the room, and where, in a big bed handmade of heart-of-pine posts and an intricate, lacy wrought-iron headboard that reached to the ceiling, her father lay dying.

Chapter Two

The big room was dark, the ceiling-to-floor windows shuttered and covered with the sheer golden drapery April remembered so well. When her mother was alive, those windows had always been open to the sun and the wind. But her mother was gone, as was the warmth of this room.

It was cold and dark now, a sickroom. The wheelchair in the corner spoke of that sickness, as did the many bottles of pills sitting on the cluttered bedside table. The bed had been rigged with a contraption that helped her weak, frail father get up and down.

April walked toward the bed, willing herself to be cheerful and upbeat, even though her heart was stabbing with clawlike tenacity against her chest. I won't cry, she told herself, lifting her chin in stubborn defiance, her breeding and decorum that of generations of strong Maxwell women.

"Daddy?" she called as she neared the big bed in the corner. "It's me, Daddy. April."

A thin, withered hand reached out into the muted light. "Is that my girl?"

April felt the hot tears at the back of her eyes. Pushing and fighting at them, she took a deep breath and stepped to the bedside, Horaz hovering near in case she needed him. "Yes, I'm here. I made it home."

"Celia." The whispered name brought a smile to his face. "I knew you'd come back to me."

April gasped and brought a hand to her mouth. He thought she was her mother! Swallowing the lump in her throat, she said, "No, Daddy. It's April. April…"

Horaz touched her arm. "He doesn't always recognize people these days. He has grown worse over the last week."

April couldn't stop the tears then. "I…I'm here now, Daddy. It's April. I'm April."

Her thin father, once a big, strapping man, lifted his drooping eyes and looked straight into her face. For a minute, recognition seemed to clarify things for him. "April, sweetheart. When'd you get home?"

"I just now arrived," she said, sniffing back tears as she briskly wiped her face. "I should have been here sooner, Daddy."

He waved his hand in the air, then let it fall down on the blue blanket. "No matter. You're here now. Got to make things right. You and Reed. Don't leave too soon."

"What?" April leaned forward, touching his warm brow. "I'm not going anywhere, I promise. I'm going to stay right here until you're well again."

He smiled, then closed his eyes. "I won't be well again, honey."

"Yes, you will," she said, but in her heart she knew he was right. Her father was dying. She knew it now, even though she'd tried to deny it since the day the family doctor had called and told her Stuart Maxwell had taken a turn for the worse. The years of drinking and smoking had finally taken their toll on her tough-skinned father. His lungs and liver were completely destroyed by disease and abuse. And it was too late to fix them now.

Too late to fix so many things.

April sat with her father until the sun slipped behind the treeline to the west. She sat and held his hand, speaking to him softly at times about her life in New York, about how she enjoyed living with Summer and Autumn in their loft apartment in Tribeca. About how much she appreciated his allowing her to have wings, his understanding that she needed to be out on her own in order to see how precious it was to have a place to call home.

Stuart slept through most of her confessions and revelations. But every now and then, he would smile or frown; every now and then he would squeeze her fingers in his, some of the old strength seeming to pour through his tired old veins.

April sat and cried silently as she remembered how beautiful her mother had been. Her parents had been so in love, so perfectly matched. The rancher oilman and the beautiful, dark-haired free-spirited artist. Her father had come from generations of tough Texas oilmen, larger-than-life men who ruled their empires with steely determination and macho power. Her mother had come from a long line of Hispanic nobility, a line that traced its roots from Texas all the way back to Mexico City. They'd met when Stuart had gone to Santa Fe to buy horses. He'd come home with several beautiful Criollo working horses, and one very fiery beauty who was also a temperamental artist.

In spite of her mother's temper and artistic eccentricities, it had been a match made in heaven—

until the day her mother had boarded their private jet for a gallery opening in Santa Fe. The jet had crashed just after takeoff from the small regional airport a few miles up the road. There were no survivors.

No survivors. Her father had died that day, too, April decided. His vibrant, hard-living spirit had died. He'd always been a rounder, but her devout mother had kept his wild streak at bay for many years. That ended the day they buried Celia Maxwell.

And now, as April looked at the skeletal man lying in this bed, she knew her father had drunk himself to an early grave so he could be with her mother.

"Don't leave me, Daddy," April whispered, tears again brimming in her eyes.

Then she remembered the day six years ago that Stuart had told his daughter the same thing. "Don't leave me, sugar. Stay here with your tired old daddy. I won't have anyone left if you go."

But then he'd laughed and told her to get going. "There's a big ol' world out there and I reckon you need to see it. But just remember where home is."

So she'd gone on to New York, too eager to start her new career and be with her cousins to see that her father was lonely. Too caught up in her own dreams to see that Reed and her daddy both wanted her to stay.

I lost them both, she thought now. *I lost them both. And now, I'll be the one left all alone.*

As dusk turned into night, April sat and cried for all that she had given up, her prayers seeming hollow and unheeded as she listened to her father's shallow breathing and confused whispers.

Reed found her there by the bed at around midnight. Horaz had called him, concerned for April's well-being.

"Mr. Reed, I'm sorry to wake you so late, but you need to come to the hacienda right away. Miss April, she won't come out of his room. She is very tired, but she stays. I tell her a nurse is here to sit, but she refuses to leave the room."

She's still stubborn, Reed thought as he walked into the dark room, his eyes adjusting to the dim glow from a night-light in the bathroom. *Still stubborn, still proud, and hurting right now,* he reminded himself. He'd have to use some gentle persuasion.

"April," he said, his voice a low whisper.

At first he thought she might be asleep, the way she was sitting with her head back against the blue-and-gold-patterned brocade wing chair. But at the sound of his voice, she raised her head, her eyes widening at the sight of him standing there over her.

"What's the matter?" she asked, confusion warring with daring in her eyes.

"Horaz called me. He's worried about you. He said you didn't eat supper."

"I'm not hungry," she responded, her eyes going to her sleeping father.

"Okay." He stood silent for a few minutes, then said, "The nurse is waiting. She has to check his pulse and administer his medication."

"She can do that around me."

"Yes, she can, but she also sits with him through the night. That's her job. And she's ready to relieve you."

April whirled then, her eyes flaring hot and dark in the muted light from the other room. "No, that's *my* job. That should have been my job all along, but I didn't take it on, did I? I…I stayed away, when I should have been here—"

"That's it," Reed said, hauling her to her feet with two gentle hands on her arms. "You need a break."

"No," she replied, pulling away. "I'm fine."

"You need something to eat and a good night's sleep," he said, his tone soft but firm.

"You don't have the right to tell me what I need," she reminded him, her words clipped and breathless.

"No, I don't. But we've got enough on our hands around here without you falling sick on us, too," he reminded her. "Did you come home to help or to wallow in self-pity?"

She tried to slap him, but Reed could see she was so exhausted that it had mostly been for show. Without a word, he lifted her up into his arms and stomped out of the room, motioning with his head for the hovering nurse to go in and do her duty.

"Put me down," April said, the words echoing out over the still, dark house as she struggled against Reed's grip.

"I will, in the kitchen, where Flora left you some soup and bread. And you will eat it."

"Still bossing me around," she retorted, her eyes flashing. But as he moved through the big house with her, she stopped struggling. Her head fell against the cotton of his T-shirt, causing Reed to pull in a sharp breath. She felt so warm, so soft, so vulnerable there against him, that he wanted to sit down and hold her tight forever.

Instead, he dropped her in a comfortable, puffy-cushioned chair in the breakfast room, then told her, "Stay."

She did, dropping her head on the glass-topped table, her hands in her hair.

"I'm going to heat your soup."

"I can't eat."

"You need to try."

She didn't argue with that, thankfully.

Soon he had a nice bowl of tortilla soup in front of her, along with a tall glass of Flora's famous spiced tea and some corn bread.

Reed sat down at the table, his own tea full of ice and lemon. "Eat."

She glared over at him, but picked up the spoon and took a few sips of soup. Reed broke off some of the tender corn bread and handed it to her. "Chew this."

April took the crusty bread and nibbled at it, then dropped it on her plate. "I'm done."

"You eat like a bird."

"I *can't* eat," she said, the words dropping between them. "I can't—"

"You can't bear to see him like that? Well, welcome to the club. I've watched him wasting away for the last year now. And I feel just as helpless as you do."

She didn't answer, but he saw the glistening of tears trailing down her face.

Letting out a breath of regret, Reed went on one

knee beside her chair, his hand reaching up to her face to wipe at tears. "I'm sorry, April. Sorry you have to see him like this. But…he wants to die at home. And he wanted you to be here."

She bobbed her head, leaning against his hand until Reed gave in and pulled her into his arms. Falling on both knees, he held her as she cried there at the table.

Held her, and condemned himself for doing so.

Because he'd missed holding her. Missed her so much.

And because he knew this was a mistake.

But right now, he also knew they both needed someone to hold.

"It's hard to believe my mother's been dead twelve years," April said later. After she'd cried and cried, Reed had tried to lighten things by telling her he was getting a crick in his neck, holding her in such an awkward position, him on his knees with her leaning down from her chair.

They had moved to the den and were now sitting on the buttery-soft leather couch, staring into the light of a single candle burning in a huge crystal hurricane lamp on the coffee table.

Reed nodded. "It's also hard to believe that each of those years brought your father down a little bit more. It was like watching granite start to break and fall away."

"Granite isn't supposed to break," she said as she leaned her head back against the cushiony couch, her voice sounding raw and husky from crying.

"Exactly." Reed propped his booted foot on the hammered metal of the massive table. "But he did break. He just never got over losing her."

"And then I left him, too."

As much as he wanted to condemn her for that, Reed didn't think it would be kind or wise to knock her when she was already so down on herself. "Don't go blaming yourself," he said. "You did what you'd always dreamed of doing. Stuart was—is—so proud of you. You should be proud of your success."

"I am proud," she said, her laughter brittle. "So very proud. I knew he was lonely when I left, Reed. But I was too selfish to admit that."

"He never expected you to sacrifice your life for his, April. Not the way I expected things from you."

"But he needed me here. Even though she'd been dead for years, he was still grieving for my mother. He never stopped grieving. And now…it's too late for me to help him."

"You're here now," Reed said, his own bitterness causing the statement to sound harsh in the silent house.

April turned to stare over at him. "How do you feel about my being back?"

Her directness caught him off guard. Reed could be direct himself when things warranted the truth. But he wasn't ready to tell her exactly how being with her made him feel. He wasn't so sure about that himself.

"It's good to have you here?" he said in the form of a question, a twisted smile making it sound lightweight.

"Don't sound so convincing," she said, grimacing. "I know you'd rather be anywhere else tonight than sitting here with me."

"You're wrong on that account," he told her, being honest about that, at least. "You need someone here. This is going to be tough and I…I promised your daddy I'd see you through it."

That brought her up off the couch. "So you're only here as a favor to my father? Out of some sense of duty and sympathy?"

"Aren't those good reasons—to be helping out a friend?"

"Friend?" She paced toward the empty fireplace, then stood staring out into the starlit night. "Am I still your friend, Reed?"

He got up to come and stand beside her. "Honestly, I don't know what you are to me—I mean, we haven't communicated in a very long time, on any level. I just know that Stuart Maxwell is like a second father to me and because of that, I will be here to help in whatever way I can. And yes, I'd like to think that we can at least be friends again."

"But you're only my friend because you promised my father?"

"Since when did this go from the real issue—a man dying—to being all about you and your feelings?"

"I know what the real issue is," she said, her words stony and raw with emotion. "But since you practically admitted you're doing this only out of the goodness of your heart," she countered, turning to stalk toward the hallway, "I just want you to know I don't expect anything from you. So don't do me any favors, okay? You're usually away when I come home. You don't have to babysit me. I'll get through this somehow."

"I'm sure you will," he said, hurt down to his boots by her harsh words and completely unreasonable stance. But then he reminded himself she was going through a lot of guilt and stress right now. It figured she'd lash out at the first person to try to help her, especially if that person was an old flame. "Guess it's time for me to get on home."

"Yes, it's late. I'm going to check on Daddy, then I'm going to bed." She started for the stairs, but turned at the first step, her dark head down. "Reed?"

He had a hand on the ornate doorknob. "What?"

"I do appreciate your coming by. I feel better now, having eaten a bit." She let out a sigh that sounded very close to a sob. "And…thanks for the shoulder. It's been a long time since I've cried like that."

He didn't dare look at her. "I'm glad then that I came. Call if you need anything else."

"I will, thanks." Then she looked up at him. "And I'm sorry about what I said. About you not doing me any favors. It was mean, considering you came here in the middle of the night just to help out. That was exactly what I needed tonight."

Reed felt his heart tug toward her again, as if it might burst out of his chest with longing and joy. He wanted to tell her that he needed her, too, not just as friend, but as a man who'd never stopped loving her.

Instead, he tipped his head and gave her a long look.

"I'll be here, April. I'll always be right here. Just remember that."

Chapter Three

April pressed the send button on the computer in her father's study, glad that she had someone to talk to about her worries and frustrations. Then she reread the message she'd just sent.

Hi, girls. Well, my first night home was a bad one. Daddy is very sick. I don't think he will last much longer. I sat with him for a long time—well into the night. Then Reed came in and made me eat something. Okay, he actually carried me, cave-man-style, into the kitchen. Still Mr. Know-It-All-Tough-Guy. Still good-looking. And still single, from everything I can tell, in spite of all those rumors we've heard about his social life. He was very kind to me. He held me while I cried. And I cried like a baby. It felt good to be in his arms again. But I have to put all that aside. I have to help Daddy, something I should have been doing all along. Today, Reed and I are taking a ride out over the ranch, to see what needs to be done. I hope I can remember how to sit a horse. Love y'all. Keep the prayers coming. April.

That didn't sound too bad, she thought as she took another sip of the rich coffee Flora had brought to her earlier. She'd told Summer and Autumn the truth, without going into the details.

Oh, but such details.

After the devastation of seeing her father so sick, April hadn't wanted to go on herself. But Reed had made her feel so safe, so comforted last night. That wasn't good. She was very weak right now, both in body and spirit. Too weak to resist his beautiful smile and warm golden eyes. Too weak to keep her hands out of that thick golden-brown too-long hair. Too weak to resist her favorite cowboy. The only cowboy she'd ever loved.

You're just too emotional right now, she reminded herself. You can't mistake kindness and sympathy for something else—something that can never be.

Yet, she longed for that something else. It had hit her as hard as seeing her father again, this feeling of emptiness and need, this sense of not being complete.

Thinking back on all the men she'd met and dated in New York, April groaned. Her last relationship had been a disaster. All this time, she'd thought she just hadn't found the right one. But now she could see she was always comparing them to Reed.

That had to stop. But how could she turn off these emotions when she'd probably see him every day? Did she even *want* to deny it—this feeling of being safe again, this feeling of being back home in his arms?

No, she wouldn't deny her feelings for Reed, but right now, she couldn't give in to them, either. They had parted all those years ago with a bitter edge between them. And he'd told her he wouldn't wait for her.

But he was still here.

He's not here because of you, she reminded herself. He's here because he loves your daddy as much as you do.

She couldn't depend on Reed too much. She had to get through this one day at a time, as her mother used to tell her whenever April was facing some sort of challenge.

"One day at a time," April said aloud as she

closed down the computer. But how many days would she have to watch her father suffering like this?

"Give me strength, Lord," she said aloud, her eyes closed to the pain and the fear. *"Give me strength to accept that with life comes death. Show me how to cope, show me how to carry on. Please, Lord, show me that certain hope my mother used to talk about. That hope for eternal life."*

Turning her thoughts to her father, April got up to take her empty coffee mug into the kitchen. She wanted to watch to see how the nurse fed him, so she could help. She wanted to spend the morning with him before she went for that ride with Reed. Actually, she didn't want to leave her father's side. Maybe she could stall Reed.

He'd called about an hour ago, asking if she wanted to check out the property. Caught off guard, and longing for a good long ride, April had said yes. Then she'd immediately gone to check on her father, only to find the nurse bathing him. April had offered to help, but the other woman had shooed her out of the room. At the time, a good long ride had sounded better than having to see her father suffer such indignities. But now she was having second thoughts.

"Finished?" Flora asked, her smile as bright as

her vivid green eyes. Flora wore her dark red hair in a chignon caught up with an elaborate silver filigree clip.

April put her mug in the sink, then turned. "Yes, and thanks for the Danish and coffee. You still make the best breads and dainties in the world, Flora."

"Gracias," Flora said, wiping her slender hands on a sunflower-etched dish towel.

"And how you manage to stay so slim is beyond me," April continued as she headed toward the archway leading back to the central hall.

"Me, I walk it all off, but you? You need to eat more pastry," Flora said, a hint of impishness in her words.

April turned to grin at her, her eyes taking in the way the morning sunlight fell across the red-tiled counters and high archways of the huge kitchen. Even later in the year, in the heat of summer, this kitchen would always be cool and tranquil. She'd spent many hours here with her mother and Flora, baking cookies and making bread.

"I guess I walk mine off, too." April shrugged, thinking how different life on the ranch was from the fast pace of New York. Here, she could walk for miles and miles and never see another living soul, whereas New York was always full of people in a hurry to get somewhere. Wanting to bring back some of the good memories she had of growing up here, she said, "Maybe I'll make some of that jalapeño bread. Remember how Daddy used to love it?"

"Sí," Flora said, nodding. "He can't eat it now, though, *querida.*"

"Of course not," April said, her mood shifting as reality hit her with the same force as the sunbeam streaming through the arched windows. "I'm going to talk to the nurse to see what he can eat."

Flora nodded, her brown eyes turning misty with worry. "He is a very sick man. I keep him in my prayers."

"I appreciate that," April said. "I guess our only prayer now is that God brings him some sort of peace, even if that means we have to let him go."

"You are a very wise young woman."

"Mother taught me to trust in God in all things. I'm trying to remember that now more than ever."

"Your *madre,* she loved the Lord."

"Yes, she did," April said. Then she turned back to the hallway, wishing that she had the same strong faith her mother had possessed. And wishing her father hadn't ruined his health by drinking and smoking.

As she entered his room, she heard him fussing with the nurse. "I don't…need that. What I need…is a drink." Stuart's eyes closed as he fell back down on the pillow and seemed to go to sleep again.

The nurse, a sturdy woman with clipped gray hair named Lynette Proctor, clicked her tongue and turned to stare at April. "Man can barely speak, and he still wants a drink." She gave April a sympathetic look. "His liver is shot, honey. Whatever you do, don't give him any alcohol."

"I don't plan on it," April retorted, the woman's blunt words causing a burning anger to move through April's system. "And I'd like to remind you that this man is my father. You will show him respect, no matter how much you agree or disagree with his drinking problem."

Lynette finished administering Stuart's medication, checked his IV, then turned with her hands on her hips to face April. "I apologize, sugar. My husband was an alcoholic, too, so I've seen the worst of this disease. That's one reason I became a nurse and a sitter. I feel for your daddy there, but I just wish…well, I wish there was something to be done, is all."

"We can agree on that," April said, her defensive stance softening. Then she came to stand over the bed. In the light of day, her father looked even more pale and sickly. "This isn't the man I remember. My daddy was so big and strong. I thought he could protect me from anything."

"Now it's your turn to protect him, I reckon," Lynette said. "Do you still want to go over his schedule?"

"Yes," April said. "Show me everything. I'm going to be here for the duration." She stopped, willing herself to keep it together. "However long that might be."

Lynette touched a hand to her arm. "Not as long as you might think, honey. This man ain't got much more time on this earth. And I'm sorry for your pain."

"Thank you," April said, wondering how many times she'd have to hear that from well-meaning people over the course of the next weeks. *How much can I bear, Lord?*

Then she remembered her mother's words to her long ago. *The Lord never gives us more than we can bear, April. Trust in Him and you will get through any situation, no matter the outcome.*

No matter the outcome. The outcome here wasn't going to be happy or pretty. Her father was dying. How could she bear to go through that kind of pain yet again?

She turned as footsteps echoed down the hallway, and saw the silhouette of a tall man coming toward her.

Reed.

He'd said he'd be around for the duration, too.

April let out a breath of relief, glad that he was here. She needed him. Her father needed him. Maybe Reed's quiet, determined strength would help her to stay strong.

No matter the outcome.

Reed listened as the very capable Lynette told them both what to expect over the next few weeks. It would get worse, she assured them. He might go quietly in his sleep, or he might suffer a heart attack or stroke. All they could do was keep him comfortable and out of pain.

With each word, told in such clinical detail, Reed could see April's face growing paler and more distressed. He had to get her away from this sickroom for a while, because he knew there could be many more days such as this, where she could only sit and watch her father slipping away.

When Lynette was finished, Reed motioned to April. "He's resting now. Good time to take that ride."

At the concern in her dark eyes, he whispered,

"I won't keep you out long. And Lynette can radio us—I have a set of walkie-talkies I bought for that very reason."

"I'll take my cell phone," April replied, watching her father closely. Then she turned to Lynette and gave her the number. "Call me if there is any change, good or bad."

"Okay," Lynette said. "He'll sleep most of the afternoon. He usually gets restless around sundown."

"We'll be back long before then," Reed said, more to reassure April than to report to the nurse.

Seeming satisfied, April kissed her father on the forehead and turned to leave the room. Once they were outside in the hallway, she looked over at Reed. "I don't think I should leave him."

He understood her fears, but he also understood she needed some fresh air. "A short ride will do you good. It'll settle your nerves."

"Just along the river, then."

"Whatever you say. You're the boss."

April shot him a harsh look. "Don't say that. I'm not ready to be the boss."

"Well, that's something we need to discuss," Reed replied. "A lot of people depend on this land for their livelihoods." He hesitated, looking down at the floor. "And…well, Stu let some things slip."

"What do you mean, let some things slip?"

"Fences need mending. We're got calves to work and brand. Half our hands have left because Stu would forget to pay 'em. Either that, or he'd lose his temper and fire 'em on the spot."

April closed her eyes, as if she was trying to imagine her father roaring at the help. Stuart had a temper, but he'd always handled his employees with respect and decency. When he was sober, at least.

"You keep saying 'our' as if you still work here."

Reed placed his hands on his hips, then raised his eyes to meet hers. "I've been helping out some in my spare time."

Groaning, she ran a hand through her bangs. "Reed, you have almost as much land now as we do. Are you telling me you've been working your ranch and this one, too? That's close to fifteen hundred acres."

"Yeah, pretty much. But hey, I don't really have anything better to do. Daddy helps, too. And you know Stu's got friends all over East Texas. Your uncles come around as often as they can, to check on things and help out. Well, Richard does—not so much James. But they have their own obligations. We've all tried to hold things together for him, April."

She let out a shuddering breath. "I'm just not ready for all of this."

"All the more reason to take things one day at a time and get yourself readjusted."

"There's no way to adjust to losing both your parents," she said. Then she hurried up the hallway ahead of him, the scent of her floral perfume lingering to remind him that she was back home, good or bad.

Reed watched as April handled the gentle roan mare with an expert hand. "I see you haven't lost your touch."

April gave him a tight smile. "Well, since you told Tomás to bring me the most gentle horse in the stable, I'd say I'm doing okay."

"Daisy needed to stretch her legs," he replied.

"I still go horseback riding now and then."

"In New York City?"

She laughed at his exaggerated way of saying that. "Yes, in New York City. You can take the girl out of the country—"

"But you can't take the country out of the girl?"

"I guess not." She urged Daisy through the gates leading out to the open pasture. "Who's that other kid with Tomás?" she asked as the two teen-agers waved to them from where they were exercising some of the other horses.

"That's Adan Garcia. They're best friends and they play football together. He helps Tomás with some of the work around here. Just a summer job."

"Why is he staring at us?" she asked. "He looks so bitter and…full of teenage angst."

Reed shrugged. "Guess he's never seen a woman from New York City before. Maybe that ain't angst, just curiosity about a 'city girl.'"

"Will you please stop saying that as if it's distasteful?"

"Not distasteful. Just hard to imagine."

"You never thought I'd make it, did you?"

"Oh, I knew you'd give it your best."

She kneed Daisy into action, tossing him a glare over her shoulder.

Reed followed on Jericho, anxious to know everything about her life since she'd been gone. "So what's it like in the big city?"

She clicked her boots against Daisy's ribs as they did a slow trot. "It's exciting, of course. Fast-paced. Hectic."

"Your eyes light up when you say that."

"I love it. I enjoy my work at Satire and it's fun living with Summer and Autumn."

Reed turned his head to roll his eyes. What kind of name was Satire, anyway? But right now, he didn't need to hear about her fancy threads workplace. So he asked the question that had been burning through his system since she'd come home. No, since she'd left. "And how about your social life? Dating any Wall Street hotshots or do you just hang with the Hollywood types?"

She slanted him a sideways look. "Honestly, I rarely have time to date."

His gut hurt, thinking about all the eligible bachelors in New York. "I don't believe that."

"Okay, I've had a few relationships. But…I've found most of the men I date are a bit self-centered and shallow. They're so involved in their careers, they kind of rush their way through any after-hours social life. I don't like to be rushed."

That made him grin. In his mind, she'd just described herself. Her new self. But then, maybe he'd misjudged her. "You never did like to be rushed. Maybe the city hasn't changed you so much after all."

"No, I haven't changed that much. I know where I came from. And besides, most of my colleagues tease me about my Texas drawl."

Reed could listen to that drawl all day long.

"You have that edge in your voice now. That little bit of hurried city-speak."

"City-speak?" She grinned. "I can't imagine what you're talking about."

"Oh, you know. Fast and sassy."

As they walked the horses toward the meandering river, she gazed out over the flat grassland. Red clovers and lush bluebonnets were beginning to bloom here and there across some of the pastures. "Well, fast and sassy won't cut it here, unless I'm roping cattle. But at least I can apply my business skills to detangling some of the mess this ranch is in."

"How long do you plan on staying?"

Her eyes went dark at that question. "I…I told my supervisor I'd be here indefinitely. I have three weeks of vacation time and she agreed to let me use my two weeks of sick days. I've never abused my benefits at Satire, so she knew I was serious when I came to her asking for an extended leave of absence."

"And when…things change here, you'll go back?"

"That's the plan."

Reed didn't respond to that. But his silence must have alerted April.

Pulling up, she turned to stare over at him from

underneath her bangs. "You do understand I have to go back?"

He nodded, pushed his hat back on his head. "I understand plenty. But tell that to your daddy. He has other plans, I think."

She shook her head. "I'm not even sure he realizes I'm here."

"Oh, he knows. It's all he's talked about for the last week. Every time he'd wake up, he'd ask for you. I kept telling him you were on your way. I think he's been waiting for you to get home just so—"

She looked cornered, uncertain. "Just so what? What do you mean? That he's going to give up and die now? After seeing him, I've accepted that, Reed."

"Yeah, well, that's something we can't help, but there's more to it."

Her eyes widened with fear and confusion. "Why don't you just explain everything, then? Just give me the whole story."

Reed didn't want to have to be the one to tell her this, but somebody had to. Stu had revealed it in his ramblings and whispered words. And Reed had promised the dying man he'd see it happen. "April—your father—he thinks you've come home for good."

Chapter Four

"Home for good?"

April stared over at Reed, a stunned wave of disbelief coursing through her system.

Reed nodded, looked out over the flowing river. "He has it in his head that you'll just take over things here. I mean, it's all going to be yours, anyway. It's in his will. And Richard and James both know that."

"My uncles have agreed to this?"

"They'll get their parts—a percentage of the oil holdings and mineral rights, things like that. But for the most part, the land and the house will belong to you."

April swallowed the pain that scratched at her throat. "I thought...I just figured he'd dele-gate things to Uncle James and Uncle Richard.

I thought I'd get only my mother's part of the estate." She shuddered, causing Daisy to go into a prance. "Honestly, Reed, I've tried not to think about that at all."

"Well, start thinking," he said, the words echoing out over the still pasture. Then he waved a hand in the air, gesturing out over the landscape. "Pretty soon, all of this will be yours, April. And that means you'll have a big responsibility. And some big decisions."

She didn't want to deal with this today. "Could I just get settled and—could I concentrate on my father, just for today, Reed? I'll worry about all of that when the time comes."

"Okay," he replied, his tone as soft as the cooing mourning dove she could hear off in the cottonwood trees. "I won't press you on this, but I just thought you should know."

"I'm not sure what I'll do," she admitted. "I just don't know—"

"We'll work through it," he said, a steely resolve in his words.

"You don't have to help me, Reed." She could tell he didn't want to be tied down to the obligations her father had thrust onto his shoulders. And neither did she.

"I don't mind," he said, turning to face her as he held the big Appaloosa in check.

"Well, maybe I do," she retorted.

And because she felt herself being closed in, because she felt as if she were back in college and Reed was telling her what was best for her all over again, she spurred Daisy into a fast run and left Reed sitting there staring after her. She had to think, needed to feel the spring wind on her face. This was too much to comprehend all at once.

Way too much for her to comprehend. Especially with Reed sending her those mixed messages of duty and friendship. She didn't want his pity or his guidance if it meant he was being forced to endure her. She could handle anything but that. So she took off.

Again.

Reed caught up with her at the bend in the river where a copse of oak saplings jutted out over a broken ridge. Just like April to take off running. She'd always run away when things got too complicated. She was doing the same thing now that she used to do whenever they'd fought. She'd get on her horse and take off to the wild blue yonder. Sometimes she'd stay gone for hours on end, upsetting her parents and the whole ranch in general with her reckless need to be away from any kind of commitment or responsibility.

Well, now she was going to have to stop running.

"April," he called as he brought Jericho to a slow trot beside her. "Slow down and let's talk."

"I don't want to talk," she said over her shoulder.

But she slowed Daisy anyway. Even April wouldn't run a poor horse to the grave.

Reed pulled up beside her as they both brought the horses to a walk. "Let's sit a spell here by the water. Then we'll head back and I'll point out some of the most urgent problems around here."

"I think I know what the most urgent problem is," she retorted as she swung off Daisy. "My father is dying."

Reed allowed her that observation. He knew all of this had to be overwhelming. He hopped off Jericho and stepped over to take Daisy's reins. "I understand how you must be feeling, April. That's why I'm here to help."

She turned on him, her brown eyes burning with anger and hurt. "But you don't want to be here. I can see that. I don't want you to feel obligated—"

Reed tugged her close, his own anger simmering to a near boil. "You don't get it, do you? I *am* obligated. To your father, and to you. What kind of man would I be if I just walked away when you both need me?"

"You mean, the way I walked away, Reed? Why don't you just go ahead and say it? I walked away when my father needed me the most. I was selfish and self-centered and only thought of myself, right?"

He nodded, causing her to gasp in surprise. "I reckon that about sums things up," he said. "But if you aim to keep on punishing yourself, if you aim to keep wallowing in the past and all that self-pity, then maybe you don't need me around after all. You seem pretty good at doing that all on your own. That and running away all over again."

He handed her Daisy's reins and turned to get back on Jericho, to wash his hands of trying to be her friend. He could just concentrate on being nearby when the time came. He could hover around, checking on things, without having to endure the double-edged pain of seeing her and knowing she'd be gone again soon.

"Reed, wait."

He was already in the saddle. It would be so easy to just keep going. But he didn't. He turned Jericho around and looked down at April, his heart bolting and bucking like a green pony about to be broken. Just like his heart was about to be broken all over again.

"I don't want to fight you, April. I just want to help you." He shrugged. "I mean, don't we have that left between us at least? When a friend needs help, I'm there. It's just the way it is."

She stared up at him, her brown eyes soft with a misty kind of regret, her short curls wind-tossed and wispy around her oval face. She was slender and sure in her jeans and T-shirt, her boots hand-tooled and well-worn.

"It's just the way *you* are, Reed," she acknowledged with her own shrug. But her eyes held something more than the regret he could clearly see. They held respect and admiration and, maybe, a distant longing.

He still loved her. So much.

"I need…I do need your help," she admitted. "I don't think I can handle this on my own. You were here when my mother died. Remember?"

"I remember," he said, nodding. He remembered holding April while she cried, right here on this spot of earth, in this very place, underneath the cottonwoods by the river. They'd watched the sun set and the stars rise. They'd watched a perfect full moon settle over the night sky. And he'd held her still. Held her close and tight and promised her he'd never, ever leave her.

Would he be able to keep that promise this time?

Reed knew he could keep his promises.

But he also knew April hadn't learned how to do the same.

But he got down off his horse and took her hand anyway. He didn't dare hope. He didn't dare think past just holding her hand. "I'll be right here," he told her.

"Thank you." She smiled and took his hand in hers, a tentative beginning to a new truce.

They stayed there, in what used to be their special spot, for about an hour. April had called the house twice to check on her father, so Reed decided maybe he'd better get her home. At least he'd been able to fill her in on some of the daily problems around the ranch. They'd somehow made a silent agreement to concentrate on business. Nothing personal.

"How about we head back?" Reed asked now. April seemed more relaxed, even though he could tell she was concerned over this latest news of her becoming full owner of the Big M. "I'll show you the backside of the property. Should be home just in time for vittles."

That made her laugh at least. "You truly will always be a cowboy, won't you, Reed?"

He nodded, flipping his worn Stetson back on his head. "I was born that way, ma'am."

She laughed again at the way he'd stretched out the polite statement. "I hear you bought one of our guest houses for yourself."

"Yep." He got back on Jericho, noting the animal was impatient to get moving again. "A right nice little place. Three bedrooms, two baths, oak floors, stone fireplace and a game room that begged for a new billiards table."

April slipped back on Daisy with ease. She always had been a grand horsewoman.

"I'm glad someone is occupying that house. It always seemed silly to me to send guests to another house when we have so much room in the big house."

"Ah, but that's the way of the Texas cattlemen. Showy and big. The bigger, the better in Texas."

They trotted along at a reasonable pace, back over the rambling hills of northeast Texas. Reed took in the dogwoods just blooming in the clumps of forest at the edge of the vast pastureland, their blossoms bright white amid the lush green of the sweet gums and hickory and oak trees. Here and there, rare lone mesquite trees jutted at twisted angles out in the pasture, like signposts pointing toward home.

"It's funny how small our apartment is in New York, compared to all this vast property," April said.

"I would have thought you'd feel stifled there amid all the skyscrapers and traffic jams," Reed said, then wondered why he'd even made the comparison.

"I did at first," she replied, the honesty in her eyes surprising him. "The city took some getting used to. But now…well, I like being a part of that pulse, that energy. In a way, New York is as wide-open and vast as this land. You just have to find the rhythm and go with it."

"Too fast-paced for me," Reed said, thinking they were straying back into personal territory. To lighten things, he asked, "How do Summer and Autumn like it?"

"They love it, too," April replied, laughing. "We all joke with our friends about how we left small towns with such big, famous names—Paris, Athens, and Atlanta—only to wind up in the biggest city of all—New York."

"I guess your friends do get a kick out of making fun of our slow, country ways."

"No, we don't allow that," she quickly retorted,

an edge of pride in her tone. "Reed, you never did get that we loved our lives here in East Texas, but we all felt we had to get away, in order to…to become independent and sure-footed."

That statement had his skin itching, as if barn fleas had descended on him. "Seems you could have done that right here on the Big M."

"No, no, I couldn't," she said, giving him a slanted look. "I felt stifled *here,* Reed. I feel free in the city."

"Well, that just doesn't make a lick of sense, April."

"I know," she replied, her head down as Daisy picked her way over a bed of rocks and shrubs. "It's hard to explain, hard to reason, but Daddy depended on me so much. I couldn't replace my mother, Reed. And I knew he'd never marry again. I had to get away."

Hearing the fear in her words, hearing that soft plea for understanding, Reed got it for the first time. April hadn't been running from him, necessarily. She'd been trying to spread her wings and get out from under the grief her father had carried in every cell of his being. "It must have been hard for you, having to see him that way, day in and day out."

"It was. So when Summer and Autumn jokingly suggested we all head east, I jumped at the chance. I was the one who convinced them to just try living in New York with me for a while."

He wanted to ask her why she'd turned to her cousins instead of him, the man she supposedly loved. But he guessed staying here with him would only have moved her from one dependent man to another. Maybe she was afraid because of what she'd seen happen to her father. Reed told himself he wouldn't have smothered her, but in his heart he knew he certainly would have cherished her, and he probably would have been overly protective.

Instead he only nodded. "New York—about as far away from East Texas as a body can get. And you've all been there ever since."

"Yes, although I think they'd both like to come home more than me, truth be told. They don't say that, but I've gotten hints that Summer has been thinking about that for a while. She had a very bad relationship end recently and I think she's longing for the safe structure of her hometown and her family. Or at least the structure her grandparents gave her, growing up."

"Why didn't she come home with you? She could visit Athens easily."

"Work. She's a counselor at our neighborhood YWCA in New York. She loves her work, but it's so easy to become burned out, dealing with inner-city families on a daily basis. Their lifestyles are sure different from what we're used to."

"I can only imagine," Reed replied. Then he asked a question that he hoped April wouldn't take the wrong way. "Do y'all have a church in New York?"

April quickly nodded. "Oh, yes. We all attend a lovely brownstone chapel not far from our apartment."

"I'm glad to know you kept the faith, even in big ol' New York City."

She gave him a measuring look. "Preaching to me, Reed Garrison?"

"No, just checking to make sure you haven't completely changed on me."

"I'll have you know there are lots of Christians in the big city."

"Glad to hear it."

She gentled Daisy to a slow walk. "Reed, I've never lost my faith in the Lord. Summer and Autumn and I all know that God is in control of all things. We don't hide our Christianity. We celebrate it. That's why Summer just broke things off with her boyfriend. He resented her faith, used it to taunt her. She wouldn't allow him to undermine something so important in her life. None of us would do that."

Reed nodded, sensing from her strong tone that maybe April had been through a similar situation. But he refused to ask her about that. "Summer always was the most sensitive of all of you."

"Yes, and Autumn is the most practical. Which leaves me, the shallow one, right?"

He turned to face her, then reached across to hold Daisy's rein. "I never said you were shallow, April. I might have thought that at one time, but now—"

"Maybe now you're finally seeing the real me, at last."

Reed was just about to comment on that and tell her that he'd like to get to know the real her, when suddenly Daisy whinnied and started kicking her front legs in the air. "Whoa, there, girl," Reed said, glad he still had a grip on the mare's reins.

"What on earth?" April said, settling the horse down with soothing words and a tight tug on the reins.

Reed dismounted and stared down at where Daisy had landed. "Glass," he said, shaking his head.

"Daisy must have stepped in it," April replied, hopping down to stand beside him. "Is she hurt?"

Reed calmed the animal, then stood facing Daisy. He moved his hands down the mare's front right leg to the fetlock, then leaned in to support the animal as he pulled Daisy's right front foot up. "Yep. Got a chunk of bottle glass embedded, right there." He pointed to a tender spot just inside Daisy's shoe. "No wonder she got spooked." Then he motioned toward Jericho. "I've got a farrier's knife in my saddle bag. If you don't mind getting it for me, I'll try to see if I can clean her foot at least."

April did as he asked, quickly finding the instrument and bringing it to Reed. She watched as he moved the knife around Daisy's hoof and shoe. As Reed worked, a rounded piece of thick gold-colored glass fell out from Daisy's hoof. "Looks like the chunk hit her right against the frog, then got stuck near the shoe. She's gonna be bruised for a few days."

"We need to get her home and let someone look at this."

Reed nodded his agreement. "I can put some duct tape over it for now. Then I'll call the vet."

April searched his saddlebag for the tape. "You travel prepared, Mr. Garrison."

"Yes, ma'am. You never know what you'll need out here alone. Have to take care of our horses."

April gave him a proud look. "I feel good, knowing you've been watching out for things around here. I'm sure my father appreciates it."

"Just doing my job," Reed replied, embarrassed and touched by her compliment. He'd jump through fire to help Stuart Maxwell. And his daughter.

"I guess we'd better walk her home," April said, patting Daisy on the nose. "It's gonna be okay, pretty girl."

Reed glanced around. "Looks like someone has been camping out here. And maybe drinking something stronger than a soda. They must have had a good time, breaking up all these empty bottles."

"Trespassers, just one more thing to worry about," April said. Then she glanced up at him. "I'll need to ride home with you."

Reed heard the hesitancy in her words. "Well, if you'd rather walk—"

"No, no. It's a long way. I don't mind riding shotgun."

His gazed moved over her face. "Are you sure?"

"Of course I'm sure. How many times have we ridden double over the years?"

Reed remembered those times. Too vividly. "Well, let's get going," he said, the edge to his voice making him sound curt. "We'll have to go slow for Daisy's sake."

When he had April settled behind him in the saddle, he tried to ignore the sweet smell of her hair and the way her hands automatically held to him. Instead, he concentrated on the mess they'd just left.

"We'll have to find out who's been having field parties out in our back pasture," he said over his shoulder. "Probably kids out for kicks."

"Yes," she answered, her tone so soft, Reed almost didn't hear it.

He had to wonder—was being this close causing her as much discomfort as it was him?

Discomfort and joy, all mixed up in the same confusing package. But then, that described his feelings for April exactly.

Lord, I need your help. I need to show restraint and self-control. Please help me to do and say the right things. Lord, just help me out here in any way you can.

The spring wind whipped across the open pasture in a gentle whispering, as if in answer to Reed's silently screaming prayers.

Chapter Five

While Reed took care of Daisy's foot with a medical boot until the vet could get there, April immediately went to see her father. As she left the warm sunny day outside and waited for her eyes to adjust to the dark recesses of the back part of the house, she said a prayer for her father.

"Lord, he never...my father never went to church with my mother. Show him the way home, Lord. Don't let him go without accepting You into his heart."

Lynette Proctor stepped out of the bedroom. "Oh, I thought I heard a voice out here. Are you okay, honey?"

April looked at the husky nurse, wondering if she could trust the woman. "I was saying a prayer for my father."

"Oh, how sweet." Tears pricked at Lynette's brown eyes. "If it makes you feel any better, I read to him from the Bible every night. I don't know if he can hear me or not, but I read anyway. Helps to pass the time, and it sure can't hurt for both of us to get a lesson."

"I appreciate that," April replied. "And I'm sorry about yesterday."

Lynette ran a work-worn hand over her clipped gray hair. "What in the world are you talking about?"

"I was rather rude to you—"

"Think nothing of that, sugar. You wouldn't believe what I've seen. Death brings out a lot of emotions, both good and bad. And when it's like this, where we have to wait—well, I've seen catfights right over a dying soul, people arguing over the will already, things like that. Family is very important, but some families just don't realize what they've got until it's too late."

April looked into the darkened room. "We've only got each other, my father and I."

Lynette's big eyes widened. "Oh, I wouldn't say that. Your father has had a host of friends coming and going since word got out that he's in a bad way. They say a man can tell how rich he is by his friends. He might be dying, but he was a very wealthy man, friend-wise. He can't take all his millions with him, but he sure can take those kind words and the way his friends have held his hand and told him how much they love him. He can take that to his grave."

April felt hot tears filling her own eyes. "Thank you, Mrs. Proctor. That's very reassuring."

"Call me Lynette, honey." Then she pulled an envelope out of her pocket. Oh, I almost forgot. Flora told me to be sure and give you this."

April took the cream-colored envelope, recognizing the fancy paper and the engraved address. "An invitation to the Cattle Baron's Ball. Daddy always loved this event when my mother was alive."

She thought back over the pasture full of longhorns she and Reed had seen while riding the land. The lanky herds of spotted cattle had milled around, getting fat off the bounty of the lush range, their droopy eyes and elegant long horns giving them a distinctive, sullen look. Reed had pointed out Old Bill, their senior sire bull, and several calves who'd been born recently. The Big M was famous for its quality, pure-bred longhorns. Just one more thing that tradition demanded of April. She'd have to keep that going long after her father was gone.

"I suppose I'll have to get used to attending such events," she said, wishing her father could guide her on what to do.

Lynette squinted at her. "Well, Flora said something about your attending in honor of your father."

April frowned and shook her head. "Oh, I couldn't. Not with Daddy so sick."

Lynette patted April's hand, then shrugged. "Just passing the message on. Flora really wanted you to have this. Maybe you should talk to her about it."

"I will," April said, rubbing a finger over the envelope. "And I'll send my regrets."

So many regrets, April thought as she went into her father's bedroom and sank down in the chair next to his bed. Stuart was sleeping, his breathing labored and irregular. The doctors had explained his condition, and how he would slowly deteriorate, but April still had a hard time accepting that the frail figure lying in this bed was her father.

"Hi, Daddy," she said, her voice squeaky and husky. "It's April. I went for a ride with Reed." She reached over to grasp her father's hand, noticing the bulging veins and the age spots covering his hand. "We have such a beautiful place here, Daddy." She looked at his hand and felt it move slightly. Maybe he could hear her. "I don't know what to do, Daddy. I'm not sure I'm up to the task of running the Big M. But I won't ever let it go, I promise. Somehow, I'll find a way. I promise you that."

Tears spilled from her eyes as she realized the implications of the promise she'd just made. Leaning over, April laid her head on her father's soft, clean-smelling cotton blanket. "Don't leave me, Daddy. If you'd only get well, I'd do anything. I know I left you once, when you begged me to stay. And now...it's too late to change that. But...if we just had one more chance."

Holding her father's hand tightly with both of hers, April sobbed, her grief and her regret so overwhelming that she didn't think she'd make it through the next few weeks.

Then she felt Stuart's hand moving beneath hers. Surprised, she raised her head. "Daddy?"

With a ragged effort, her father tugged his hand away from her grasp. Disappointment surged through April's system. Was he turning away from her pleas?

But Stuart didn't turn away. Instead, he opened his eyes and reached up to her face, his bony fingers trailing through her dark curls like wisps of smoke. "Love you, Sweet Pea," he managed to say, the words coming long and hard and labored. "Trust you." Then he dropped his hand and fell back asleep.

April stayed at his bedside, a smile on her face in spite of the tears she shed.

Reed sat at the big oak desk he'd bought from an antique store in Dallas. He'd put it in the roomiest of the extra bedrooms of what used to be the Big M guest house. This room had a view of the rolling green pastures and the well-stocked fish pond at the back of the property. He could see the big house from here, too. He could see the arched double window of April's upstairs bedroom, located right over the swimming pool. That window caused memories to come swirling back, like moondust caught in spiderwebs.

Maybe he was caught in a web, too. A web of need and longing for something that could never be. He turned to the big collie lying at his feet. "Well, Shep, old boy, she's back and I'm in big trouble. Any suggestions?"

Shep yawned, stretched his front paws across the Aztec-style rug covering the hardwood floor and grunted a reply.

"You're no help," Reed retorted. "No help at all."

The phone rang then, making Shep bark and Reed jump. "Man, I gotta get a grip."

"Reed, it's Richard Maxwell. I was just calling to check on things at the Big M."

"Hello, Richard," Reed said, glad to hear from Stuart's brother. "I guess you've heard April's home?"

"Yeah, the girls e-mail back and forth. They're pretty worried about her and Stu. How's she taking things?"

"Not too good. She's devastated about her father, of course. And she's not sure about the future."

"Who is, these days? How's my brother?"

Reed filled Richard Maxwell in, wondering why the man hadn't called April directly. But then, the Maxwell brothers had come to depend on Reed lately to give them the truth, straight-up, about the ranch and their brother. So Reed told Richard the truth. "I don't expect him to last much longer, Richard."

"We're making arrangements to come over," Richard told him. "I tracked James down and he and I hope to be there by the weekend. And I might tell the girls to come on down, too."

"That would be good. I know Summer and

Autumn would be a big help to April. You know how close they all are."

"I sure do," Richard said, laughing. "Three peas in a pod, that's what we've always called them."

"It's hard on April, being here alone," Reed said.

"She's not alone, boy. She has you. You always could talk her down—and we all know how high-strung she can be at times."

"I hear that," Reed said, a smile creeping across his lips. "I'm just not sure I can be of much help—"

"You're solid, Reed," Richard replied. "Stuart knows that. That's why he's set such high store in you."

"I appreciate the vote of confidence," Reed replied, not feeling confident at all.

They talked a few more minutes about the day-to-day operations of the ranch, then Richard said goodbye. Reed didn't mind that Stuart's brothers were keeping close tabs on things at the Big M. He wouldn't have it any other way. After all, a lot was at stake here. The livestock, the land, the oil leases, the acreage, the house and surrounding buildings—it all added up to a big amount of responsibility and a huge amount of revenue. But it was more than the wealth. The Big M was home. It always would be home.

At least, to Reed.

But would April want to make it home again?

That question nagged at Reed as he worked at his computer, filing away bills and keying in information on the spring calving season. It was a busy time, both for him personally, with his spot of land and his own growing herd, and for the Big M.

"I sure don't need any…"

Distractions. He was going to say distractions. But April Maxwell was much more than a distraction. She was like that piece of glass that had found its way into Daisy's foot. April was embedded inside Reed's heart. And he had the big bruise to prove it.

Reed sat, watching the sun set over the hills. He sat there and prayed for guidance and strength as he stared up at those windows—windows that shielded the woman he loved.

"Hi, girls."

April typed the greeting to her two cousins back in New York. She knew that they'd read the e-mail together, as they did each night when they all gathered around the computer, taking turns checking their personal messages, then sharing the really good ones with each other.

What would she do without Summer and Autumn? She was the oldest by two years, but her cousins were both very sensible and mature. Summer was more temperamental and subject to fiery outbursts of temper, while Autumn was always calm and in control. But they both felt the Maxwell loyalty just as much as April did. She had to wonder how different their lives might be if she hadn't dragged them to New York with her all those years ago.

Wishing they were both here, she continued her update.

Daddy is about the same today. But he did something so very sweet. I was talking to him, crying, wishing he'd just get up out of that bed. And he heard me! He touched his hand to my face and told me he loved me.

It was so special. My daddy never was one for words, you know. I don't remember the last time he said that to me. It took all of his effort, but now I know he has forgiven me for leaving him. I should have never done that. I love my life in New York with y'all, but now I'm wishing I'd just stayed here and worked somewhere closer to home—Dallas had a lot of potential. I knew that. Houston, even. Why did I have to go all the way across the country? Okay, I did it because Reed was pressing me to settle down. He got too close, too fast. I needed to be independent. I felt closed in by so much grief and pain. I guess I was afraid to let go of my heart after losing Mother. I can see that now. Funny how time causes us to look back and just all of a sudden see things so much more clearly.

I know what you're saying to each other—that it was our plan, our dream. We had to stick together. We had to show our formidable fathers that we could strike out on our own, just as they all had. Even now, all these years later, it's so hard to admit that we were all running from something.

We succeeded, but is it enough? Is it enough that I left Reed and my daddy behind? Is it enough that Summer had to go through that terrible relationship with Brad Parker in order to realize her real worth? Or that she still can't make a commitment to anyone because of how her parents left her on her grandmother's doorstep? Is it enough, Autumn, that you always have to have concrete proof of anything—that you can't go on faith alone, even in your love relationships, even in knowing that Summer and I love and support you, no matter what? No wonder none of us can find a man. We've set our sights way too high and we've forgotten what really matters. I guess all of this has got me thinking about things—how do we know we've made the right choices in life? Have we really listened for God's voice, or have we just listened to what we wanted, what we thought we needed, whether it hurt others or not?

I walked away from Daddy's grief and Reed's overbearing love. Summer, you've been turning to the wrong men all your life because you don't want to be abandoned ever again. And yet, they've all let you down, especially Brad. And Autumn, well, girl, you have to have too many details, too many charts and graphs in life. We all need to loosen up and turn back to the Lord. We need to go on faith and let it all work itself out.

Oh, I didn't mean to preach. Really I didn't. I'm just so confused right now. Did I tell y'all I went riding with Reed this morning? Did I tell y'all that I think I still love him?

I have to turn in soon, but I want to go and sit with Daddy for a while. Don't take what I said the wrong way, please. I'll be okay. We will always be okay, because we have each other. I wish y'all

were here, but I know you have work to do—
other obligations.

Other obligations kept me away from home for
so long. Now, I have only one obligation. I have
to get through watching my father die. Summer,
maybe you should call Uncle James. He is your
father, after all. Maybe you could make amends,
make your peace with him. Before it's too late.

"Wow." Autumn Maxwell turned to her cousin
after she finished reading the e-mail from April.
"I've never heard April talk like that. She must
really be depressed."

Summer shifted on the deep-cushioned red
couch they'd found at a second-hand store in Soho.
"Yeah, to even suggest I get in touch with my
daddy. She's obviously not thinking very clearly.
She knows where I stand on that issue."

"But…she's looking at it from a different angle
now, honey. Uncle Stuart is dying. April's thinking your daddy, or even mine, could die, too. And
with so much left unsaid."

Summer tossed back her long blond hair.
"Some things are better left unsaid. You know
that, Autumn."

"But I'm beginning to wonder if that philosophy is so wise," Autumn replied, hoping she sounded encouraging. "What would it hurt—"

Summer hopped off the couch, her black yoga pants dragging against her bare feet. "It would hurt *me,* so let's change the subject, please."

Autumn sent her cousin a questioning look, but all she got in return was Summer's retreating back and the slamming of her bedroom door.

Autumn sighed, and turned back to the computer.

Hi, April. I don't think Summer's ready for any sage advice just yet, sweetie. But I understand how you must be feeling. It must be so hard to watch your father die. I am sending you hugs and prayers. And I promise, if you just say the word, we will both come home, whether Summer wants to do so or not. She might not want to face her parents yet, but she will do anything to help you get through this. Promise.

Now, tell me all about your ride with Reed. I want details, good and bad. And I want to know the exact minute you realized you still loved him. I want to know what that must feel like. I've never been in love, you know. I have to live vicariously through you, I reckon.

So, tell me everything. Is Reed as good-looking as ever? Or even better?

April had to laugh at her cousin's inquisitive nature. Autumn was all business during the day. She was a CPA at an exclusive Manhattan firm—a firm that her powerful father had managed to get her an interview with, an interview that Autumn had protested at first—that independence thing again. But Autumn had taken things from there and she'd fought hard to make her father proud. She worked long hours, as well as most weekends, and she barely had a social life. But Autumn said she liked things that way. April believed that Autumn secretly wanted to break loose and live a little, but she just didn't know how. Autumn was the quintessential good girl, right down to her oh-so-proper white cotton PJs. But Autumn was also a very good listener. Her cousin could be very precise in getting to the heart of a matter.

And right now, April's own heart was being torn apart by her father's sickness and the sure acceptance that she still loved Reed Garrison.

It's a long story, she typed. I hope you're not sleepy tonight. And yes, Reed is even more gorgeous than he was when I left him. He's mature and a bit weathered, but still very attractive.

And there's more. Daddy wants me to take over the Big M. On a permanent basis. That would mean I'd have to stay here. Near Reed. I don't know if I'm ready for that responsibility. I need advice, cousin. Good advice.

I don't know what to do.

April signed off the computer and stood up to look out the windows of her room. She looked toward the east. She could see the dark shape of the brick guest house Reed now lived in. It was so like Reed to buy a house that had a clear view of the Big M's main house. It was so like him to stand guard over this ranch.

She saw the light from a single lamp burning into the night, and she wondered if Reed was down there, looking up at her window. She wondered if he was thinking about her right now.

April turned from the window and crawled into the crisp, sweet-smelling sheets of her bed, secure in the warm feeling of knowing Reed was nearby.

Ever watchful.

He'd always been right here, waiting.

But how long could a man wait for a woman who was so frightened of giving her heart away?

Chapter Six

"Vandals?"

Reed nodded at his father's one-worded question.

"Yep. It's been happening a lot lately."

Sam Garrison held tightly to his stallion's reins, then glanced down at the leftover campfire. "Charred beer bottles. Cigarette butts. Kids, maybe?"

"Has to be," Reed responded, walking Jericho toward the broken fence wire near the main highway. "They must be sneaking in off the main road. Probably parking their cars in that clump of trees just around the curve to the Big M."

"How much damage have you found so far?" his father asked, squinting underneath his worn straw cowboy hat.

"April and I saw the same thing about two days ago, on our ride around the property near the river. Daisy got a sliver of glass from that little campfire. She's still bruised. Stepped on some broken, burned-out bottle glass. Now this. I'd say some of the locals are having field parties on Big M property."

"Did you ever do things like this when you were young, son?" Sam asked, a grin splitting his bronze-hued face.

"Did you?" Reed countered, his own grin wry. Then he shook his head. "I didn't have to trespass, remember? I was lucky enough to live on the Big M."

Sam tipped his hat at that comment. "And lucky enough to be just about the same age as the heir apparent."

"I don't recall mentioning April," Reed said, his grin dying down into ashes, just like this campfire had.

"Didn't have to mention her. She's written all over your face."

"It shows that much?" Reed asked, dropping his head down in mock shame.

"Son, I'm not a rocket scientist," Sam said, "but your mama and I know you still love April.

Your mother thinks that's why you've never found anyone else."

"In spite of Mom's efforts to hook me up with every single lady at church and beyond?"

"Yep. Your ma loves you and…well, she wants some grandchildren. So do I. You know, we ain't getting any younger."

"Look mighty fit and young to me," Reed said, hoping to sway the conversation away from April.

But he should have known better. His father was as shrewd as they came, a real cowboy poet of sorts, a literary man who could quote Emerson and Thoreau and could still ride a horse and herd cattle better than any other man on the Big M.

"I'm fit, all right," Sam replied, slapping a hand to his trim stomach. "But fit don't cut it when a man's wishing for the next generation to carry on."

"I'm carrying on for you just fine, I thought," Reed said, frowning.

"That you are. Working the Big M and your own place. Makes a man proud. But…you're kind of stubborn in the love department. You ought to go after that girl, show her that you were wrong all those years ago."

"Me?" Reed shouted the word so loudly, Jericho did a little prance of irritation. "Me?" he repeated with a low growl. "Maybe your memory is getting rusty, Daddy. April was the one who had to get away from this place and away from me. I couldn't very well hightail it to New York and kidnap her. I don't want a woman who won't come willing to me."

"Then make her *want* you, boy," his father said. "I had to do that with your mama."

"Oh, really. And here I thought she was the one who caught you."

"I let her think that, of course. But your mama was as prim and proper as they come. Still is. Had to woo her all kinds of ways. By the time I got through courting her, she was as strung up as a baby calf on branding day."

"Not a pretty picture, Pa," Reed said, shaking his head as he chuckled. "Don't think Mama would appreciate being compared to a calf."

"Well, she's certainly called me a stubborn old bull a few times," his father countered in a testy tone. Then he tilted his head. "Besides, we were talking about your love life, not mine. Mine's been just fine for close to thirty-five years."

Reed pinched his nose with two fingers, willing the tension in his head to go away. "Whereas mine is nonexistent, right?"

"Got that right, yes sir."

"Would you listen if I told you with the utmost respect to kindly stay out of my business?"

"Probably not." Sam waved his hand in frustration. "You need to get on with it or get over it, son."

"I'm trying," Reed said in a ground-out tone that made him sound more mad than he really was. "I'm trying."

Sam shook his hat and put it back on. "Tough times, these. Hard to watch one of my best friends dying right before my eyes. And one of the finest men in all of Texas, at that. Guess I shouldn't be pushing you back toward April. That girl's got enough to worry about without having you underfoot."

"That's why I'm trying to play it safe," Reed said, glad his father understood that at least. "I can't push her or rush her, Daddy. Not now, when she's so scared and hurt. I tried that the last time, and she bolted like a scared pony. She's...well, I've never considered April as fragile, but right now, that's exactly what she is. I don't want to be the one to break her."

Sam urged his horse forward. "Then be gentle, son. Show some understanding. You always did go in with guns blazing, in any situation. Might want to curve that domineering gene you obviously inherited from your ma's side of the family."

"Yeah, right," Reed said, smiling at his father. "You can blame it on Mom, but we both know you're as mulish and demanding as they come when you want to be."

"Who, me?" His father feigned innocence by rising his bushy brows and scrunching up his ruddy nose.

"Guess I got it double," Reed reasoned as he followed his father back toward home.

"You could say that," Sam agreed, his laughter echoing out over the pastures and trees.

Reed loved his parents with a fierceness that made his heart ache, and he loved what they had between them, that strong sense of loyalty and friendship that had been tempered by faith and family, through hard times and good times. He wanted that kind of love, that kind of commitment for himself.

And he wanted it with only one woman.

As they neared the lane leading back to the big house, Reed couldn't help but look up at that arched window. He hadn't talked to April today. He'd wanted to give her some time with her father. Time alone. Precious time. He'd wanted to give her so much, but he'd held back.

He was learning restraint, at long last. He was learning patience, at long last. He was learning what his wise father had been trying to tell him. That old cliché was true. Sometimes, in order to win back something you loved, you had to let it go. Well, he'd tried that route. And he'd learned to be patient the hard way through all those years. It hadn't brought April back. But she was back now, under sad circumstances. And this time, he wouldn't make any mistakes. He'd be patient, he'd be gentle, he'd be steady and sure. Reed wouldn't use her grief and despair to bring her back to him. That would be wrong, so wrong. But he'd be nearby if she needed him.

Lord, let it be right. Let it happen in your own good time, as Mama would tell me.

Grief was no way to start a relationship, or to bring April back to his way of thinking.

So he'd keep on waiting. And hoping. It was the only thing he could do.

Laura Garrison busied herself with setting the table in the kitchen of the big house. April helped her, putting out silverware and tea glasses, glad for the quiet strength Reed's mother possessed.

"I'm so glad you came by," April said, remembering all the times Reed's mother had been a guiding force in her life, especially after April's own mother had died. "And I insist that you and Mr. Sam stay and help me eat all this food."

"I wouldn't mind visiting with you," Laura said, her big brown eyes lighting up. "That is, if you're up to company."

"I could use the company," April admitted. "I've spent all day with Daddy, reading to him, talking to him. Sometimes, he opens his eyes and…it's almost as if he's smiling up at me. Other times, he just sleeps."

Laura finished basting the baked chicken. "The rolls are almost ready," she said as she came to help April with the salad and vegetables. "I hate that you're having to go through this, sugar. Stuart has always been our rock, strong and steady, a good leader with a heart of gold."

"That heart is old and worn-out now," April said, her hands gripping the cool tiles of the counter. She'd sent Flora and Horaz back to their house to rest and enjoy their own dinner. They needed a good night's sleep and some peace and quiet. Sam Garrison was sitting with her father while she and Laura prepared dinner. "Everyone here is so devoted to him. That has brought me a lot of comfort."

"We all love your daddy," Laura said, her shiny

bob of brown hair flowing across her forehead with a defined slant. "And we all encouraged him to give up that bottle. But he just didn't have the strength. It's been hard on all of us. That's why I wanted to come and see you. We're all in this together, April."

April reached out to hug her friend. "Thank you so much. And please, stay for dinner and…why don't you call Reed, too? It'll do me good to have y'all for company. I can't stand the loneliness."

"Are you sure?" Laura asked.

April knew what she was asking. Did she really want Reed there?

"I'm sure." April nodded. "You don't have to walk on eggshells around me, Miss Laura. Reed and I, we've made a truce of sorts. Now is certainly not the time to bring up past hurts and regrets."

"*Do* you have regrets?" Laura asked, her eyes clear and full of understanding. Then she put a hand to her mouth. "I'm so sorry. I shouldn't have asked that."

"It's okay," April replied. "And the answer is yes. I regret that I was selfish enough to leave my father when he really needed me to stay. And I regret that I hurt Reed."

"You had to do what you thought best," Laura said with a shrug.

It was so like Reed's mom not to pass judgment. But April knew Laura Garrison loved her son first and foremost.

"I had to get away, yes," April said, hoping to explain. "I had to grow and expand my horizons, so to speak. But mostly, I knew I could never make Daddy happy. Not in the way my mother made him happy. And I've never admitted this, but I was so afraid I'd never be able to make Reed happy, either. I...I didn't think I could settle down and be a ranch wife. I'm not like you, Miss Laura."

Laura's chuckle surprised April. "Honey, do you really think any woman is prepared to be a ranch wife? It's a hard job. Being a wife and a mother are hard jobs, no matter where you live. But if you love someone enough—"

"You make sacrifices," April finished. "I wasn't ready for that sacrifice."

"Well, you know, Reed could have met you halfway."

April shook her head. "What? Should I have made him move to New York with me? I hardly think Reed would have been happy living in the big city."

"No," Laura agreed. "But he could have fought harder to…to try a long-distance relationship."

"It would never have worked," April replied, sure as rain that Reed would have been miserable. "I couldn't ask that of him."

"You never tried," Laura pointed out with a soft smile.

"I didn't want to force him to wait for me."

"Honey, he's still waiting," Laura said. "Think about that. And if I know my son, I think he'll keep on waiting, because he's not going to get between you and the grief you're feeling right now."

That revelation hit April with all the force of being thrown from a horse. *Was* Reed truly still waiting for her? She'd wondered that so many times, had even hoped that might be the case. Then another thought even more formidable hit her.

Was she still waiting for Reed, too?

That question nagged at April all through dinner. Reed's parents were pleasant and upbeat, keeping the conversation light. They talked about the warm spring weather, about the alfalfa growing in the pastures, about the livestock moving through the fields and paddocks. They talked about April's job in New York and asked questions about life in the big city.

And while they talked, Reed sat silent and still, a soft smile flickering across his wide mouth now and then. He toyed with his tea glass and ate his chicken with the relish of a hearty appetite, his eyes settling now and then on April.

Each time he looked at her, something shifted and slipped inside her, like river water gliding over a rockbed. She thought back over the years she'd been away and wondered how she'd ever managed to leave him. Was it the grief eating away at her? Or was it the regret?

I have to be sure, Lord, she thought. *I have to be sure that if I decide to stay here and do my father's bidding, that it's for all the right reasons. I don't want to hurt Reed again. And I can't take any more hurt myself. Help me, Lord. What is Your will in all of this?*

"Ready for some dump cake?" Laura asked now.

"I'm always ready for cake," Sam replied, winking at April.

Laura got up, but Reed put a hand on his mother's arm.

"I'll get it, Mom. Coffee, too?"

"Sure," Laura said, the surprise in her voice sparkling through her eyes.

"Want to help me?" Reed asked April.

She glanced up at him, wondering what he was up to. But his eyes held only a warm regard that made her feel secure and safe. "Yes. I'll bring the coffee if you get the plates for the cake."

"I think we can handle that," Reed said. She saw the warning look he sent to his two curious parents. "You two behave while we're getting dessert."

"Us? We'll just sit here and let your ma's fine cooking settle while you young folks do the rest of the work," his father replied, his eyes twinkling.

"They are so cute together," April said, not knowing what else to say.

The laughter and whispers coming from the table across the arched, tiled kitchen washed over her like a familiar rain. She loved Reed's parents and had always wished her own parents could have had such a solid, stable, long-term relationship. Instead, Stuart and his Celia had had more of a roller-coaster ride of intense love and obsession, followed by bouts of anger and fire— Until death had ended it all, leaving both April and her father shocked and devastated.

She could see now that her mother's sudden

death had been at the core of her fears. She was beginning to realize that maybe that was the main reason she'd been so afraid to give in to her love for Reed. That was why she'd run away. She couldn't deal with something so rich and intense just after losing her mother. What if she lost Reed, too?

You did lose him, she reminded herself as she gathered coffee cups and cream and sugar onto a long porcelain serving tray adorned with sunflowers and wheat designs.

"You look mighty serious there," Reed said over her shoulder, grabbing the coffee carafe before she could put it on the tray. "I'll take this over, then come back for the cake and plates."

April watched as he set the coffee carafe on the table. He had that long-stride walk of a cowboy, that laid-back easy stride of a man comfortable in his own skin.

And he looked good in that skin, too.

Stop it, she told herself as she looked away from Reed and back to the heavy mugs she'd put on the tray. When Reed came back to the counter, she looked up at him, then asked him in a low voice, "Why have you never married?"

From the look in his eyes, she wished immediately she could take that question back. But it was out there now, hovering over them like a swirl of dust, stifling and heavy.

If the question threw him as much as it had her, he hid it well behind a wry smile. But he didn't miss a beat in answering. "I reckon I'm still waiting for the right woman to come along," he whispered.

"Think you'll ever find her?"

He leaned close, the scent of leather and spice that always surrounded him moving like a wind storm through April's senses. "Oh, I found the right woman a long time ago. But I'm still waiting for her to come around to my terms."

April's heart banged hard against her ribs. Her hands trembled so much, she had to hold onto one of the mugs in front of her. "What...what are your terms, Reed?"

His voice whispered with a rawhide scrape against her ear. "I only have one stipulation, actually. I want that woman to love me with all her heart. I want her to love me, only me, enough to stay by my side for a lifetime and beyond."

April looked up at him then and saw the love there in his stalking-cat eyes—the love and the challenge. "You don't ask for much, do you, cowboy?"

"Doesn't seem like much if you look at it the right way."

Then he turned and sauntered back to the table where his parents waited in questioning wide-eyed silence.

And April was left to look at the scene with a whole new perspective. And a whole new set of fears.

Chapter Seven

April came into the kitchen the next morning only to find Flora slumped in a chair, crying.

"What's wrong?" April said, rushing to the woman's side. "Is it—is it my father?"

She'd sat with him late into the night, pouring her heart out to him, telling him that she still loved Reed, only now she didn't think she deserved to be loved back. Telling him all about her fears and her reservations, her hopes and her dreams. She'd checked on him just minutes ago and Lynette had assured her he was sleeping.

"No, no, *querida*," Flora said, reaching up a hand to April. "It's not your papa. It's…" She waved the other hand in the air. "It's Tomás. That boy is giving us so much trouble lately."

April breathed a sigh of relief only to see the

concern in Flora's rich brown eyes. "What's Tomás doing that's so bad it would make you cry?"

Flora shook her head. "He shows no respect. His parents—they both work all day long—they let him run wild. No restraint. And that Adan— *élse malo*—he's mean, very mean. He's going to get in big, big trouble, that one." She lapsed into a string of Spanish, then went back to wringing her hands.

From what April could glean from Flora's rantings, she gathered Tomás and Adan had taken Horaz's pickup for a joyride and had been stopped by the sheriff for speeding. There was a hefty ticket to pay. And Horaz would probably have to be the one to pay it, since Tomás's parents were heavily in debt from overextending themselves.

"I'm sorry, Flora," April said, patting the distraught woman on the shoulder. "Do you want *me* to pay the fine?"

"No," Flora said, getting up to wipe her eyes on her gathered apron. "That wouldn't help. The boy needs to learn how to fix his own problems. He will work it off. His grandfather will see to that, even if my son thinks Tomás can do no wrong. No wrong for big football star."

April knew enough to understand the implications of that. High-school football was a very popular sport all over Texas. And Tomás was a gifted athlete, she deduced from everything she'd heard since coming home, which meant his other, less noble traits would sometimes be overlooked for the sake of winning the game. Unless he pushed things too far. "If Tomás rebels against authority too much, he might get kicked off the football team next season."

"Sí, sí," Flora replied. "This is what I try to tell my son. This is what Horaz tries to explain to Tomás. Heads of wood, those two. Heads—stubborn heads. *Loco.*"

April smiled at Flora's sputtering condemnations in spite of the seriousness of the situation. "I could try to talk to Tomás," she offered.

Flora grabbed April's hand. "You have too much—too much to worry with. Tomás, he is my responsibility. Mine and his grandfather's, since we've been put in charge of him for the summer. His own parents are too busy to see the problems." Another harsh string of Spanish followed.

"I love Tomás, too, remember?" April replied, remembering how she used to take the young Tomás horseback-riding when she was a teenager. "What if I get Reed to talk to him? He looks up to Reed, or at least he used to when he was little."

Flora's eyes lit up. "*Sí,* Reed. Everyone looks up to Reed. And Tomás has heard the stories of Reed Garrison. Now there was a football star, that one. He never gave his parents any trouble. And he was the best in his day."

"Yes, he was," April replied, her memories of crisp autumn nights so real she thought she could smell the smoke from the bonfires, hear the words of the high-school song. And she could clearly see Reed's smiling, loving face from the crowd of padded players on a green field. He'd always searched for her in the cheerleading line, giving her a wave for promise and hope.

What had happened to that promise and hope?

"Will you ask him?"

Flora's plea brought April back into the here and now, all the memories gone in the blink of an eye.

"Of course," April said, wanting to reassure Flora. But just thinking of having to face Reed again after he had thrown down the gauntlet last night made her want to run and hide away in her room.

But April was done with running and hiding. Her father wasn't going to get out of that death-bed. Reed wasn't going to back down. She had to stand up and take responsibility for her actions and her mistakes. It was up to her now to make sure the Big M kept on going. And if that meant she'd have to counsel one of their own—she and Reed together—then so be it.

At least dealing with Tomás would take her mind off her father and her feelings for Reed.

"I'll call Reed right now," she told Flora. "Just let me have a cup of coffee first."

Flora hopped up, her hands fluttering in embarrassment. "I'm so sorry. I should have—"

"Don't be silly," April said, waving the woman back down. "I'll get both of us a cup of coffee. And maybe some of that wonderful cinnamon coffee cake you always have stashed around here."

Flora smiled at that. "Better with melted butter on it. You can slip it into the microwave. Or I can do that."

"You sit," April commanded. "I'll take care of breakfast."

She wasn't sure if she could actually eat, but if Flora's cooking didn't entice her, nothing would.

She thought about Reed again. She'd thought about Reed for most of the night. She wondered if her father had heard her talking about him last night, had understood how strong her feelings were. How scared she was to make that final step toward Reed, that step that meant family and home, total commitment, total surrender.

She had a feeling Reed wouldn't want it any other way, and why should she blame him for that? She longed for that kind of love herself, even if she was terrified to try it.

On the other hand, what about her job at Satire? She had responsibilities there, too. And she loved what she did there, the things she'd accomplished. She was good at her job. How could she walk away from something that she enjoyed, a career that gave her contentment and a measure of accomplishment? A career, she reminded herself, that oftentimes took control over her entire life, leaving her alone at the end of the day. When she looked back, if she hadn't had Summer and Autumn there with her in New York, she probably would have been lonely and miserable, in spite of the friends she'd made at work.

No, April told herself with a fierce denial, coming home has just brought too many things to the surface. I can't just abandon my career. I can't do that.

Bringing the coffee and food to the table where Flora sat, April put her own turmoil to rest for now and managed to smile over at the other woman. "I guess being a grandparent is just as hard as being a parent."

Flora nodded, took the coffee with a *"Gracias."* "You think once you raise them, everything will be okay. It's never okay. You worry." She pressed a hand to her heart. "You worry here, you hold them close, here, always."

"I guess my father worried about me, even when he knew I was doing all right in New York."

"Sí. He always talked about you. Very proud, that one. Always longed to see you. Especially when—"

She stopped short.

"Especially when he was drinking?" April asked, finishing Flora's unspoken thoughts.

Flora nodded, tears brimming her eyes again. "A good man, a very good man. But the drink—it made him say things he couldn't take back. Very sad."

April felt that sadness down to her very bones. So much time wasted, so much love lost. She didn't think she wanted that kind of love, the kind that made a powerful, virile man turn into a wasted-away skeleton of himself.

Did she love Reed too much? Could she ever accept that love, with all the stipulations it required?

Then she remembered Reed's words to her last night. *I only have one stipulation.... Doesn't seem like much if you look at it the right way.*

I don't know the right way, Reed, she thought. I don't know how to look at love without seeing the pain involved.

She glanced over at Flora and found the woman's eyes closed and her lips moving. "Flora?"

"I pray," Flora said, her eyes still closed. "I pray for you and Mr. Stuart, and Reed and my Horaz. And especially for my Tomás." Then she opened her eyes and smiled. "God has already answered part of that prayer. You and Reed, you will see to my grandson, *sí?*"

"Sí," April replied, lifting her eyes to the heavens.

"I hear you, Lord," she said out loud.

Flora smiled and took a long sip of her coffee.

April wanted to see him.

Reed let that bit of information settle into a simmering stew inside his gut. It hurt to think about her. The physical pain of loving her was getting to him. It had been okay when she was off far away, across the country. Time, bitterness and distance had faded his pain, and the soft rage he'd felt at her leaving, into a kind of mellowed photo album of memories. Memories he'd hidden away until now.

And he hadn't helped matters by challenging her last night. He'd practically asked her to stay, right there in the kitchen, with his well-meaning parents watching in rapt awe. He'd almost blown it. Again.

"I'm needing some guidance here, Lord," he said aloud as he pulled his rumbling pickup into the sprawling side yard of the big house. *"I've got a nice, easy thing going here. I have my bit of land now, a place to call my own. I've worked hard these last few years. You have blessed my life, Lord. Only one thing was missing."*

And that one thing was now waiting for him out by the crystal-blue waters of the swimming pool. Ending his prayers on a silent plea for strength and restraint, Reed opened the wrought-iron gate leading to the back of the property. He found April waiting for him right where she said she'd be. For once.

She was wearing a golden-beige sleeveless pantsuit of some sort. Linen, his mother might say. Soft linen that flowed around her like a summer wind. Her jewelry reflected the same gold of her clothes, simmering and rich against her porcelain skin.

Reed had to stop and take in a breath. She

looked like some noble ancient princess, sitting there on the chaise. Until he looked into her dark eyes.

"What's wrong?"

April gestured to the cushioned chair beside the umbrella table. "We need to talk."

Oh, boy. He didn't like that look in her eyes. The last time she'd told him they needed to talk, she'd already packed her bags for New York and just wanted to tell him goodbye.

He sank down in defeat, took off his hat and said, "So, talk."

"It's about Tomás," she said, letting out a breath with each word.

"Tomás?" Confused but relieved, Reed leaned forward. "What's up with Tomás?"

She handed him a glass of lemonade, then settled back on the chaise. "Flora is very upset with him." She told him the whole story then. "She wanted me to ask you to try to reason with him, tell him to take it easy and be careful. You know, a kind of man-to-man talk."

"Why me?" Reed asked. "And why do you look so sad and serious?"

She shrugged, causing her chunky jewelry to settle back around her neck. Reed eyed the pretty stones and glowing gold. "Everyone around here looks up to you, Reed. Flora thought you'd be the natural choice for the job. And if I look sad, well, I am. But that's not something for you to worry about. Flora needs your help right now."

He got up and paced around the rock-encrusted pool deck. "That's me. Good ol' Reed. Salt of the earth. The go-to man." For everyone except her, of course. Shrugging, he started to leave. "I'll talk to Tomás. He's supposed to be helping me with some fence work today anyway. Give us a chance to have a nice long chat."

"Are you angry at me?"

She was right behind him, so close he caught the whiff of her floral perfume. "No," he said with a long sigh. "I'm not angry at anyone. Just tired and confused, is all. And sad, just like you." He turned to face her, looked down at her dark curling hair, her big brown eyes, and her beautiful mouth, and felt the flare of that old flame, burning strong inside his heart.

Then he did something he would later call very stupid. He kissed her, right there in the broad open daylight, by the swimming pool, with the many windows of the long, rambling house open for all inside to see. It was a stupid move because he'd steeled himself to go slow, to take things easy. He didn't want to spook her.

She didn't seem spooked in his arms.

She kind of melted against him, her hands touching his hair as a soft sigh drifted between them. Her sigh. Or maybe it was his. Reed couldn't be sure. But he was very sure of one thing. And that one thing made his hard heart turn to mush.

April still loved him, too. This he knew with the instinct of a man who always knew what he wanted, even when he wasn't sure how to go about getting it. He aimed to find the right way to go about winning April back. For good.

With that declaration pumping through his head, he let her go and stared down at her, hoping he didn't seem too triumphant. "That…that wasn't supposed to happen," he said with a ragged breath. "I mean, we were discussing this situation with Tomás, right?"

She managed to nod. "Right. I'm not sure how—"

"I know how," he interrupted, one finger tracing a wayward curl of rich brown hair that had managed to find its way across her cheek. "One look, April. That's all it takes. One look and I remember everything. And I want to hold you, and protect you and kiss you."

He saw the fear rising up in her eyes like a mist coming in over the river. "We shouldn't—"

"I know. It's the wrong time. It's not fair to either of us. But there it is. We kissed each other, and, unless I'm mistaken, you enjoyed it just as much as I did."

She lowered her head, staring at the gently moving water in the serene pool. "Reed, we need to concentrate on my father right now. And all the problems on this ranch. The vandalism, and now this with Tomás." Then she looked back up at him. "But I've learned something, coming home. This place doesn't just run itself. A million little problems crop up each day. And I want to thank you for always…for helping my father through all of this. I know it hasn't been easy for you. You could have left—"

"I wanted to stay," he said, the old anger coming back to numb the joy he'd felt at having her back in his arms. "I will stay. No matter what happens. *This* is my home. This will always be *my* home. Is that clear, April?"

His own anger was reflected back at him through the haze of anger in her eyes. "Very clear, Reed." Then she turned to head back inside the house. "Just talk to Tomás. Flora and Horaz don't need to be worrying about him right now."

"Yes, ma'am." He tipped his hat and headed back to the gate.

So much for thinking she still loved him. She did, he knew that. But she wouldn't admit that to him, or to herself, either. She'd watch her father die, bury him, then she'd go right back to New York. Running scared again.

And she'd leave Reed here waiting, all over again.

Chapter Eight

You've got mail.

Summer called out to her cousin. "Hey, April's sent us an update. Want me to read it out loud?"

"Sure," Autumn said, distracted by the mound of paperwork in front of her. Tax time. It was a killer, but it paid the rent. And being a CPA for one of the largest accounting firms in New York meant she was right in the thick of things. Just the way she liked it. She liked numbers and charts. She liked proof. Everything had to add up, make sense. Only two more days of this intense tax season frenzy, and then she could relax a bit. Not that she ever actually relaxed.

"Go ahead, I'm listening," she called to Summer.

"Okay."

"'Daddy is about the same. Uncle Richard called Reed the other day, then called me. He hopes to come and visit this weekend. He said I should ask y'all to come home, but Autumn's surely busy right now. Maybe in a few weeks, if Daddy can last that long. If not, well, I guess y'all will have to come when things change, when he's gone. He looks so frail, so old. How did I let things get this bad?'"

Summer stopped reading. "No mention of *my* daddy, huh? No mention of Uncle James and Aunt Elsie. Of course, they're probably off on the yacht, unaware of anyone else but themselves."

"Your bitterness is showing," Autumn called.

"You think?"

"Just read me the rest, so I can get back to work."

Summer turned back to the computer.

"'Reed kissed me this morning.'"

That brought Autumn careening across the big lofty living room so fast, the magnolia-scented candles Summer always kept lit flickered from the stirring of air. "What?"

"Says so right here," Summer replied, pointing at the words on the screen. "Reed kissed April."

"Oh, my." Autumn sank down on a cushioned

polka-dot footstool near Summer's chair. "What else does she say?"

"'We were by the swimming pool. It was mid-morning. He kissed me right there in the sunshine. And it felt as if we'd never been apart. I don't think this is smart right now, even if it felt so right. I have to think about Daddy. And did I tell y'all that Daddy thinks I'm home for good, that he expects me to stay here and run the Big M?'"

"Makes sense," Autumn murmured. "She will inherit it after he's gone. I mean, Daddy and Uncle James will get their parts, but they both gave up running the Big M long ago. And Uncle Stuart is the oldest. She's his daughter. Makes sense to me that he'd leave the majority of the ranch holdings to his only heir."

"Shouldn't we be jealous or something?" Summer asked.

Autumn slapped her on the arm. "Of what? Our parents have just as much loot as Uncle Stuart. And we're not hurting, either."

"I was just teasing," Summer said, sticking out her tongue. "I don't want any of it, anyway. Besides, my parents are too busy spending their part to worry about actually thinking about *my* future."

Autumn scowled at her cousin. "You need therapy."

"I don't need some overpaid shrink to tell me that my parents don't care about me," Summer retorted. "Now, can we get back to worrying about April?"

"Sure," Autumn replied, more worried about Summer. She had a chip on her shoulder that seriously needed shaking. But Autumn wouldn't be the one to do it. "Go on," she said, nudging Summer. "Keep reading."

"'I don't know what to do. I planned to return to New York and Satire. I've built up a career there and I have a good chance of getting a promotion when we break into ready-to-wear this fall.'"

"Head of ready-to-wear marketing," Summer said, nodding. "She'd be so good at getting Satire's ready-to-wear off the ground. Trendy new threads and upscale department stores—stock should go right through the roof. Glad I invested early."

"It would mean lots of traveling to all the various stores," Autumn said. "All over the country and around the world. And I'm the one who told you to invest early, so you're welcome. We both should make some money off this one."

"How can she run the ranch and do that, too?" Summer shot back, ignoring her cousin's other remarks.

"What does she say?"

"'I don't think I can do both—run this place and keep my job, let alone get a promotion.'"

Summer jabbed the computer. "Told you."

"Just keep reading," Autumn said, scanning the words on the screen. "I've got to get back to work."

Summer turned and started reading again.

"'I'm in such a fix. But all of that aside, I have to be near Daddy right now. I talk to him every night, tell him all the things I wished I'd said before. I'm not sure he can hear me, but it feels so good to pour my heart out to him. Why did I wait so long? Why did I let myself fall back in love with Reed? I've realized that all this time, he's been waiting for me to come back, and now that I'm here, it's for all the wrong reasons. I'm home to watch my father die. So Reed is being kind and patient and undemanding, but I've also realized that maybe, just maybe, I've been waiting for Reed all these years, too. I guess I always thought he'd come for me, you know? That somehow, he'd come to New York and tell me he wanted me back home, with him. Isn't that silly?'"

"She's completely stressed," Summer said, finishing the e-mail. "Maybe I should go there, be with her. She's getting too caught up in memories of her first love. That's dangerous. She shouldn't get her hopes up."

Autumn stared at her cousin. "What's wrong with a little hope? Uncle Stu is dying. And she still loves Reed. What's wrong with hoping that they might actually get to be together?"

Summer jumped up, headed for the kitchen. "I just wouldn't pin too much hope on a happily-ever-after," she called over her shoulder. "She's been through enough."

Then she came back to the sofa with a container of yogurt. "Maybe I should just go there and help her get her head straight."

"You could go to *lend her your support*," Autumn said, "not shatter her illusions. You have gobs of vacation time accumulated." She started back toward her desk. "Then as soon as tax season is over, I could come, too. If—"

"If it's not too late," Summer finished. "I'll see what I can arrange at work. Take a few days. I could use a vacation anyway."

"That's an understatement," Autumn replied. "But if you go and your parents do show up, don't make a scene, all right? It's not the time to make a big deal out of past hurts, Summer."

"Yes, ma'am," Summer said, saluting her cousin, her frown pulling her oval face down.

"You're so calm and collected, Autumn. How do you do that?"

"Do what?"

"Always stay in control. I mean, I blow up, shout, fight, pout. But not you. Always got it together."

"You make that sound like a sin."

"It is, if you can't ever let go and just—react."

"I don't recall reading about that in the Bible."

"I do," Summer countered. "Something in Psalms, about asking the Lord to cleanse us from our secret faults."

"I don't need cleansing and I don't harbor any secret thoughts. I'm just fine."

"Well, I guess I do—harbor secret thoughts, that is," Summer replied, her eyes downcast. "I guess I got me a lot of cleansing to do. I cry out, just as King David did, but sometimes I don't think the Lord is listening."

Autumn touched her cousin's arm. "Well, just don't do it when you get to the Big M. I mean, don't cry out at your parents or raise a ruckus. Ask God to ease your famous temper. April needs us to be strong and supportive."

"If I go, I won't make a scene, I promise," Summer replied.

Autumn hoped her volatile cousin meant

that. It would be bad if Summer lost her cool while Uncle Stu lay dying.

"You know Mr. Stuart is dying, right?" Reed asked Tomás as they rode the fences the next morning.

Tomás held on to the dash of the hefty red pickup with one hand while he worked on adjusting the radio dial to a hard-rock station. "Yeah."

Reed pushed the boy's hand away and turned the radio off. "And you understand that we all need to rally around the family right now, not cause any hassles?"

Tomás glanced over at him, his dark eyes slashing an attitude a mile wide underneath the fringe of his silky black bangs. "You mean, like I shouldn't get speeding tickets and cause an uproar with my grandparents?"

"Yeah, I mean that," Reed said with a sigh. "Want to talk about it?"

"I wasn't going that fast."

"You just got your license. You might need to take it easy until you're a little more experienced."

"I *am* experienced, Reed. I've been driving all over this ranch since I was twelve."

Reed nodded. "I did the same thing. Best place to learn to drive. But driving on these dirt lanes is a whole lot different from driving out on the high-way or up on the Interstate. I'd hate for something to happen to you or your buddies. And I don't think Adan's parents would approve of this kind of behavior, either."

"We're okay, Adan and me. Or we would be if everybody would just leave us alone."

Reed stopped the truck near a sagging barbed-wire fence, then got out. "It's our job to hassle you, man. Keep you in shape. We wouldn't want the star of the football team to get in trouble."

"I'm covered there," Tomás said with a twist of a grin as he slammed the truck door. "Coach understands me."

"I'm sure he does," Reed said, wondering when things had changed so much in high-school sports. His coach had kept a tight rein on all the players—curfew, good grades, no late-night shenanigans, no drugs or liquor. A long list of no-nos. Nowadays, it seemed as long as a boy could throw a ball or run fast, he could get away with indiscretions of all kinds. "Listen," he said as he and Tomás rounded the truck, "we all care about you. If we didn't care, we'd just let you run loose."

"My parents let me do whatever I want," Tomás retorted. "*They* trust me."

Reed stared over at the young boy. Tomás was

handsome in a dark, brooding way. A way that could lead to trouble down the road. And from the pained expression on the boy's face, Reed decided Tomás wished his parents did care a little bit more. A whole lot more.

"Do your parents know about the ticket?"

"Yeah, sure. No big deal."

"Uh-huh." Reed could only guess what his own father would have done in the same situation. It would have been a *very* big deal. "Well, your grandparents think differently. So…Horaz is giving you yard duty on top of your other chores."

"What?" Tomás threw down the coil of wire he had gathered from the back of the truck. "I have to mow that big yard? That is so *not* fair."

Reed shrugged. "Life is so not fair at times. But you have to roll with the punches. You got the speeding ticket. Now you get to do the time."

"But Grandpa said he'd help me pay it."

"Yes, and because he's doing that, he expects you to work off some of the price."

"That's just not right."

"Neither is going sixty-five in a thirty-five-mile-per-hour zone. Can't have it both ways, Tomás."

"My dad says I can have it all, if I just keep playing football. He says one day, I can own a ranch like the Big M."

"Your dad is proud of you, I reckon," Reed replied, shaking his head. "But first, get a good education, and stay out of trouble. I sincerely hope you become a success in football, Tomás. College and pro. But don't count on that. Have a backup plan."

"Did you?" Tomás asked, his expression clearly stating the obvious. Reed had had the same dream and it ended when he messed up his knee.

The boy's pointed question should have hurt, but Reed knew in his heart he was content with his lot in life. He could deal with it. Well, almost. "As a matter of fact, I did have a backup plan," he told Tomás. "I always wanted to have my own spot of land, right here near the Big M. And now I do."

"Yeah, and look how long you had to work to get that," Tomás remarked, his tone smug and sure.

Reed grabbed Tomás by one of his thick leather gloves. "Hey, I'm proud of my land. I worked hard to get it. I wouldn't have it any other way. And you'd better learn right now, son, there aren't any shortcuts in life."

"You sound like my *abuelo*. But then, both of you have spent most of your lives catering to the whim of the big man, right?"

Reed wanted to smack the kid, but he held his temper in check. "We weren't catering to anyone's whims, Tomás. We were making a living—an honest living. Your grandparents have had a good life here on the Big M. Stuart Maxwell has made sure of that. And he's always helped my family, too. Don't bite the hand that feeds you, and don't ever disrespect Stuart Maxwell again."

Tomás looked down, his sheepish expression making him look young and unsure. "I just want a better life, Reed. I just want more."

"We all want that, kid. But…just make sure you go about getting the good in life in the right way. Remember your roots, your faith in God. Remember where you come from. Don't do anything stupid, okay?"

Tomás looked doubtful, then shrugged. "Yeah, sure. I'll be careful."

"I hope so," Reed said. He'd have to pray that Tomás had listened to him. Really listened.

April tried to listen to what the preacher was saying in church the next Sunday. But her mind wandered off in several different directions, maybe because Reed and his parents were sitting right behind her. She could almost feel his catlike eyes on her.

He'd been standoffish and quiet since their kiss. He'd been avoiding her. He came by and called to check on her daddy and give her updates on the

ranch. That was something at least, since he could send any one of the many hands they had on the Big M to do that job.

But then, Reed had always been a meticulous details man. He'd always been thorough in anything he did—from playing football to starting a vegetable garden to dating the rich girl from the big house. In fact, she had to remind herself, he'd been so complete in his love for her, in what he hoped their future would be like, that he'd spelled it out in detail for her over and over again.

And she'd let him believe she wanted the same things.

She looked up at Reverend Hughes. What had he just said? His mercy endures forever? Did God show mercy to those who turned from him? Would God show mercy to her dear, dying father? Would God show her that same mercy?

I was scared, Lord. I was so scared.

She could understand now. Her heart and her head had matured a hundred times over. If she had married Reed back then, she would have made his life—the simple life he'd always wanted—miserable.

Because I was miserable.

Why couldn't she just be happy? Why had she gone so far away to find her own brand of happiness?

Because I was scared. I'd lost my mother. I'd watched my father deteriorate into a mire of grief. Even going away to college hadn't helped. The weekends at home only brought the pain back into a sharply focused kaleidoscope of anger and grief.

That grief had been so overwhelming, so thick with despair, April had felt as if she were drowning. And she felt that same pulling feeling now, which was why she'd taken a precious hour away from her father to come to church.

I had to get away, to find some peace, some space.

Back then, and now, for just a little while.

But she didn't want to repeat the same mistakes, follow the same path again. *Not this time, Lord.*

All those years ago, she'd hurt Reed. And she'd never wanted to hurt Reed. She loved him. Loved him still.

I need Your mercy, Lord.

April thought about her father. Asked God to show all of them his tender mercies. She had to take it one day at a time. That was all she could do at this point. She couldn't think beyond her father and what lay ahead— Even if she did feel Reed's eyes on her, willing her to think of him and their future.

* * *

When April got home an hour later, Flora greeted her in the kitchen. "I just got here myself. Lunch is in the oven, *querida*. Oh, and you have a message from a Katherine Price. Phone was ringing when I came in. Lynette can't hear it back there. We've got that phone turned off, so we don't disturb your father."

"Katherine called?" April took the note Flora had scribbled. "Urgent."

"Sí," Flora said, taking off her church hat so she could serve up the pot roast she'd left in the oven on warm. "Is she someone from your work?"

"My supervisor, the CEO of public relations," April said, reaching for the phone. "She's probably wondering why I haven't called in to work."

"You have enough to worry about."

"Yes, but I also have responsibilities back in New York. Although I pretty much cleared my desk before I left."

"You should eat first," Flora said, concern marring her tranquil eyes.

"I will later. You and Horaz go ahead. Are any of your family joining you for Sunday dinner today?"

"No," Flora said with a sigh as she tied her apron. "My son, Dakota—you remember him—

he took his wife on a weekend to Dallas. Left us in charge of Tomás, of course."

Her fingers on the phone, April asked, "Did Reed talk to Tomás?"

"*Sí,* but the boy was very angry still. Blamed us for his troubles. He's not happy to be doing yard work."

April had to smile at that. "It's going to get hot out very soon. But then, Tomás should be used to sweating, what with football practice all the time."

Flora nodded. "He's just not used to authority. *Obstinado,* that one."

April shook her head. "I hope things get better. Now, you get your lunch ready while I make this call."

She left Flora humming a gospel tune. Heading out onto the long tiled verandah by the swimming pool, April dialed Katherine Price's home number.

What did her boss want on a Sunday afternoon?

Her stomach twisting in knots, April waited for the phone to ring. Just one more thing to deal with. She didn't need problems at work while she had so much going on here at the Big M.

But then, she'd already decided she couldn't handle both.

She once again prayed for that mercy Reverend Hughes had talked about. Mercy, and strength. She needed both for the long days ahead.

Chapter Nine

"April, darling, how in the world are you?"

Hearing the lilt in Katherine's voice made April breathe a sigh of relief. If her boss was in a bad mood, she wouldn't have called April "darling."

"I'm okay, all things considered," April replied into the phone. "I got your message. Is everything all right?"

"First, how's your father?"

April could envision the sophisticated leader of Satire public relations and marketing worldwide sitting on a chaise lounge on the sprawling balcony of her Park Avenue apartment, sipping an espresso and eating biscotti. But she was touched that Katherine had thought of her father before rushing headlong into business.

"My father is about the same, Katherine. The

doctor comes by each day and tells us there is nothing else to be done. He hasn't opened his eyes for days now."

"You poor dear," Katherine said. "I wish there was something *I* could do."

April couldn't take any sympathy. She'd fall apart and she didn't want to do that in front of fashionable, together Katherine Price. "You can tell me what's happening at Satire. Why you called with an urgent message."

"Oh, right. Well, darling, you know we're in the midst of getting prepared to launch the ready-to-wear this fall. And of course, you've done such a great job with the preliminary marketing. You left things in good shape and the marketing and public relations departments are following your guidelines to the letter."

"But?" April asked, hearing the worry in Katherine's voice. "Is there something else that needs to be done?"

"Well, darling, you know I wouldn't ask if it weren't really important."

"Just tell me," April said, dread making her words sound sharp.

"Darling, is there any way you can fly back to New York for a couple of days? It's just a glitch or two with one of the department stores. They're trying to renege on the original contract. They want to cut back on their advance orders for the fall line."

"The contracts are ironclad," April replied, thinking there was no way she could leave her father right now. It was ironic how her whole perspective on work had changed.

"We know that, April," Katherine said through a long-suffering sigh. "But the store in question is giving us grief. Frankly, I think they're about to declare bankruptcy and they're trying to clean house, so to speak, before this goes public. That's why we need you here to negotiate—through our lawyers, of course. You always know what kind of spin to put on this type of crisis."

A crisis. Katherine Price, the head of PR for one of the most successful fashion houses in the world, thought that one department store trying to go south was a crisis.

April wanted to tell her that she now knew what a real crisis was like, but it wasn't Katherine's fault that her father was so ill. "Which store is it?" she asked, wondering how she was going to take care of this without going back to New York.

"It's Fairchild's," Katherine replied. "You know they've already had to restructure and lay off employees nationwide. They were banking on Satire to help them get back in the thick of things—they haven't had a winning label in their stores for a very long time now, just mediocre stuff all around—but it looks as if someone within their ranks got cold feet about overextending the stores with this massive order."

"Would that someone be Danny Pierson, by any chance?" April asked, the pieces of the puzzle beginning to come together in her mind.

"Why, as a matter of fact, he's the one who called me personally," Katherine said, surprise echoing out over the phone line. "Is there something about him I should be aware of?"

"Only that I dated him last year and it ended rather badly," April replied. "He didn't take the breakup very well."

"Oh, my. How long did you two date?"

"About six months," April said, remembering what a pompous control freak Danny had been. "He…made certain demands I couldn't meet."

"And now he's making those same demands on Satire," Katherine said. "Darling, you know not to mix business with pleasure. How could you let this happen?"

April held a finger to her forehead and pushed at the bangs covering her eyes. "I didn't let anything happen, Katherine. He didn't work for

Fairchild's when we were an item. He went with them right after the beginning of the year, this year. And I'm sure he's just now discovered our contract with them. I can't imagine he'd be doing this to get back at me, though. He could jeopardize not only Fairchild's reputation, but his own."

"Then you agree you should come back and handle this?" Katherine asked, her tone firm.

"I didn't say that," April replied. "I think all we have to do is tell our lawyers to meet with Fairchild's and explain how things stand. That should get Danny to back off."

"And what if he doesn't? Darling, you know how important this ready-to-wear launch is. We've been working on this for eighteen months straight."

"I realize that," April said, "but, Katherine, I can't leave my father right now. He's…he's not going to last much longer."

Silence. Then a long sigh. "I understand. And you have my utmost sympathy, dear. But we need someone who can sweet-talk the powers at Fairchild's. And that would be you."

"What if I call Danny?" April asked. "Maybe I can nip this in the bud before it goes any further."

"You'd be willing to do that?"

"I can try. It's a start, at least. And I'll call all

my contacts at Fairchild's and find out if this is something Danny just cooked up, or if it's really serious."

"Well, I guess if that's the best we can do right now—"

"I'll take care of it," April said, her insides recoiling at the idea of having to deal with slimy Danny Pierson again. But then, it was part of her job to negotiate tricky situations with clients. And there was a lot riding on this deal, as Katherine had reminded her. "I have Danny's number in my business files. I'll call him first thing tomorrow."

"Thank you so much," Katherine replied. "And keep me posted on this."

"I will, of course," April said. "I'll get this cleared up. Don't worry."

"I know you will. And darling, I really am so sorry about your father."

"Thank you," April said.

When she hung up the phone, she turned to find Reed standing in the doorway.

He looked sheepish. "Sorry, I didn't mean to listen in. Flora told me you were here in the den."

"It's okay," April said, raising a hand in the air. "Just a problem at work."

"You don't need a problem at work. You have enough to worry about right here."

"I know, I know. And I don't need everyone reminding me of that, either."

He stalked into the room. "Sorry. Is everything all right at work?"

"Just a little mixup with one of our clients. I'll get it straightened out."

"Do you need a break from all of this?"

"No," she said. "I'm afraid to leave the house. He's so frail and quiet." Right now, she really wanted to just run away from everything and everyone. Especially Reed. He was hovering and that made her nervous. "Did you need to talk to me?"

"No. Just wanted to check in. See how you're holding up."

"How do I look?" she asked, the words snapping out like a whip against hide.

"Like you need a break, just as I said."

He moved toward her, but she backed away. "I don't need a break. I'm fine. I just need to think about how to take care of this problem without having to go back to New York."

The silence between them told her he was weighing her words. Weighing and judging, she imagined.

"So you want me to go?" he finally asked.

"That's entirely up to you, Reed." She looked up at him, the hurt in his eyes making her wince at her harsh attitude. If she could be honest with him, she'd rush into his arms and beg him never to leave. But she wasn't ready to take that step. "I just need some time alone," she said.

"Okay. Mom wanted me to invite you over to supper tonight."

"I can't leave the house, Reed. You know how things are."

This time, he watched her back away again, then moved after her until he had her in his arms. "Hey, I do know how things are. We can have supper here again. Or we can just send something over, if you don't want company."

"I can't eat," she said, hot tears brimming in her eyes. "I can't think beyond his next breath."

"I know," he said, kissing the top of her hair. "I wish there was something I could do."

His gentleness almost did her in, but she took a calming breath and let out a shaky laugh. "Funny, that's what my boss just said, right after she practically ordered me back to New York."

Reed lifted her chin with a finger. "You're not going back right now, are you?"

Offended at his possessive tone, she pulled away. "No, of course not. But I'm going to have to make some calls, fight some fires. I still have a job—or at least I did when I left New York."

She could feel the condemnation again, see it in his eyes as he spoke. "Yeah, I guess you can't just forget about your work."

"No, I can't. But I'm not leaving my father." At his raised eyebrows, she added, "Does that surprise you, Reed? If so, then I guess you don't know me as well as you think you do."

He stepped back. "I thought I knew you, but the old April would probably have taken off by now. This April, the woman I'm looking at right now... I think she has staying power."

"Impressed?"

"No, proud," he said before turning to leave. Then he whirled at the arched doorway. "I am proud of you, April. You're doing the right thing."

Before she could think of a mean, smart retort, he left the room, the sound of his cowboy boots clicking with precision against the tiled floor.

"I don't know the right thing to do," April said, her plea lifting up to the heavens. "I don't know what I should do or say."

She silently prayed that God would give her the grace to do what she had to do. And that Reed would continue to be proud of her, no matter what decisions she had to make over the next few weeks.

He wasn't very proud of himself, Reed decided later that night. He was trying. Heaven help him, he wanted to do and say the right things when it came to April.

But the woman just brought out the worst in him.

As well as the best.

So the subject of New York City was definitely a sore spot between them. But then, Reed couldn't understand why anyone would want to leave a place like the Big M. The rolling pastures and hills, the trees and ponds, the rows and rows of crape myrtle growing all over Paris, the Red River nearby, all the work a big ranch required—all of this was his lifeblood. His family had lived and worked on this ranch for generations. He was as rooted here as the cottonwoods and the *bois d'arc,* or bow dark trees, as the locals called them.

He just couldn't understand why April didn't feel the same toward her home. What had driven her away from the place she'd always seemed to love.

Grief.

The one word echoed around him like a dove's soft coo. He remembered April telling him that her father's grief had stifled and scared her. But what about her own grief? Maybe she hadn't actually worked through her own pain after her mother's death.

No, instead she'd run from it. And she was still running. But she was being brave in coming back to her home, no matter the horrible memories and the sadness that seemed to shroud the big house these days. Maybe she was home in the flesh, but her spirit was somewhere far away. Her spirit was lost in maybes and what ifs and what-might-have-beens. Just as his own seemed to be, Reed decided.

When he coupled her immense grief back then with the fact that he had been constantly hovering with unsolicited advice and unwelcome demands, asking her about marriage and family, well, no wonder the woman had escaped. He shouldn't have pushed her so hard. But he'd wanted a future with her so very much. He still did. But she was grieving yet again.

The phone rang, jarring him out of the troubled thoughts that were pounding at his brain.

"Hello," he said, his tone full of irritation.

"Son, are you all right?" his mother asked.

"Just dandy. What's up?"

"I wondered why you didn't come by for dinner. You and April."

His mother's words were full of questions and implications.

"April wasn't in the mood for company, Mom.

And I don't think she's been eating very much at all, either. I think she's lost even more weight."

"That girl eats like a bird. Always did."

"Well, I guess her appetite is taking a hit these days."

"Did you offer to stay there at the house with her?"

Reed lifted his gaze to the heavens for support. "Mom, she didn't want me there."

"Oh, I think you're wrong there," his confident mother responded. "I think she wants you there, but she's afraid to voice that."

"Well, I can't second-guess her. Never could."

"The Lord has a plan for you two. I've always believed that."

"Well, then let's just let the Lord show us the way," Reed said, his tone lighter this time. He knew his mother meant well, and he loved her for caring. But he also knew that if he and April were ever to have a life together, then it would have to be something they both wanted, regardless of how strongly his mother felt about it.

It would be up to God to intervene.

Reed thanked his mother for calling, then hung up the phone. He was just about to go to bed when Shep started barking and pawing at the back door.

"Need a walk, old fellow?" Reed asked as he swung the door open.

He stepped outside and heard the noise at about the same time Shep took off toward the small storage shed behind the house.

Someone was out there.

Shep barked with renewed frenzy as he galloped toward the shed. Reed hurried after the dog.

"Who's there?" Reed called, hoping it was just an armadillo or a possum.

When he heard footsteps echoing out behind the building, he knew the intruder was human. He ran toward the shed, listening as Shep's angry, agitated bark filled the quiet night.

Reed reached the shed just as a shadowy figure cleared the wooden fence behind the shed. "Hey, you," Reed called, "too chicken to show your face?"

All he heard was the sound of hurried footsteps and then the roar of what sounded like a four-wheeler taking off. And Shep, barking at the fence.

When he was sure that the intruders were gone, Reed called to his dog. "Let's go get a flashlight, boy."

Reed got a high-beam light out of his truck, then inched his way around the outbuildings.

He saw footprints near the back of the shed, but couldn't find anything else.

Apparently, he'd caught the culprits just about to jimmy the locked door.

"I wonder what they thought they'd get out of there," Reed said to Shep. The dog barked back, still anxious to chase his quarry.

Reed thought about the equipment in the shed. The riding mower was stored in there, along with some tools and other garden supplies. He usually kept an empty gas can in there to use to refuel the lawn mowers. Maybe whoever it was wanted to get some free gas.

"Strange," Reed told Shep as they circled the yard. "We've never had burglaries or vandalism on this place before."

But someone was stirring things up now. The campfires in the pastures, the damaged and broken fences all along the highway, and now this.

Someone was trespassing on the Big M and on his land, too. And Reed aimed to find out who that someone was.

Chapter Ten

April finished helping Lynette turn her father, so they could change the sheets and give him a sponge bath. He hadn't responded to their touch or their words in days. He was beyond eating or taking in fluids. All the equipment and machines had long ago been removed from his room.

Now it was just a matter of time.

Tucking the fresh-smelling sheet over his clean pajamas, April leaned down to kiss him. "Okay, Daddy, you're all set for the day. You might have some visitors today. Uncle Richard's scheduled to arrive. He's going to stay a few days, help us out around here."

Stu's breath barely left his chest. His skin was wrinkled and spotted with age. His hair, once thick and crisp brown, now consisted of a few grayed wisps.

"He looks at peace, honey," Lynette said, shaking her head at April. "I think he's ready to make his journey home."

April hated hearing that, but seeing her father this way, she would almost welcome such peace for him. For his soul. "I hope…I hope he's having pleasant dreams."

Lynette came around the bed and patted her hand. "I reckon he's making his way to your mother's side right now. She'll be there to greet him, you know. Her and your grandparents, everyone who's gone on ahead of him."

April swallowed back the hot tears burning at her throat. "That should bring me some comfort, shouldn't it?"

"It should," Lynette replied. "But death is hard on the living. We have to stay behind, missing them. I guess you've missed your mother for a long time now."

"More than I can say," April replied, weariness overtaking her as she swayed against the bed.

She was so tired, she felt chilly and numb, and a bit disoriented. When she wasn't sitting here by her father's side, she barricaded herself inside his big office on the other side of the house, going through files and calling ranch workers for reports. The work was endless, and supervising it had taught her much more than she'd ever learned growing up here.

She'd also been in touch with her department at Satire, hoping to clear up the mess with Fairchild's. And she was still trying to reach Danny Pierson. She'd left her cell phone and home numbers with his secretary, but Danny was playing hard to reach. Why he'd pick now of all times to stall out on this deal was beyond April's comprehension. But Danny had always been a grandstanding, arrogant businessman. At first, his assertiveness and confidence had attracted her. Now they repelled her. There was healthy ambition, and then there was ruthless ambition. April appreciated the first but no longer wanted to be a part of the latter.

She decided she didn't have the energy to worry about that right now. Danny knew how to reach her, and he knew what she wanted to talk to him about. He'd always been good at tracking *her* down when he wanted something.

She turned as the door creaked open. Flora stuck her head inside. "I'm sorry to interrupt, April. But Mr. Reed needs to speak with you."

April nodded, then turned back to touch her father's hand. "I'll be back in a little while, Daddy."

She came out of the dark room, her eyes hurting at the brightness of the morning. She'd lost track of the days. They'd all started merging into one big dark vortex of longing and prayer, coupled with late hours of work and bedside visits. She rarely left her father's side, rarely left the house even to go outside, unless one of the workers needed her advice on something. She had to be there with him, coaxing him to go to her mother, telling him it would be okay, telling him that God would take him home.

Lord, let him find his way back to her and You.

She saw Reed at the end of the long hallway. "Hi," was all she could manage to muster.

"Hey there. You look exhausted."

"Thanks, so do you."

"Yeah, well, I guess neither of us is getting much sleep."

"I have my reasons, but what about you?" she asked, puzzled by the serious expression on his face. "What now?" she asked, sensing that something else had happened.

"The vandalism," he replied. "It's getting worse. Had someone snooping around my garden shed two nights ago."

"Really? Why didn't you tell me sooner?"

He looked toward the closed door of the bedroom. "You know why. Anyway, Daddy and I have been patrolling the ranch at night. We take shifts with some of the other hands."

"Thank you," April replied, not sure whether to be appreciative or angry that he'd taken matters into his own hands. "You don't have to do that, though. We can call the sheriff."

"I don't mind," he responded, scooting her out onto the dappled tiles of the long back patio. "C'mon. You need some fresh air."

"I think I've forgotten what that is."

"All the more reason to sit in the sunshine."

She did that, finding a wrought-iron patio chair to fall against. The soft floral cushions were warm and welcoming, just like Reed's gentle eyes. "Tell me all about this trespassing and vandalism."

"It's the strangest thing," Reed began, only to be interrupted by Flora at the door with lemon cookies and freshly brewed iced tea. *"Gracias,"* he told her with a big smile.

April didn't miss the smile or the way Reed had so thoughtfully asked for refreshments. "Thank you," she told him when Flora had gone back inside.

"Eat a cookie," he suggested, shoving one in her hand.

She took a bite, felt it begin to stick and grow

in her tight throat, then grabbed her glass of tea. "Talk," she said, motioning with her hand.

"Oh, as I was saying, they don't take anything on these nightly excursions. And they don't do much damage. Just seems to be kids having parties on our property. Now, why they'd want anything from me—that's what I don't get."

"Have you actually caught anyone?"

"No, no. We can't seem to place where they're coming in. They move around a lot, so it's hard to pinpoint 'em. But we always find traces, can tell that they've been on the property. They don't even try to hide the messes they leave."

"So what can we do?"

"Well, I'm going back out tonight. And I've told Richard all about it. He's going on rounds with me tonight, too."

April was too tired and worried to get mad that Reed was going over her head to her uncle. After all, she had no right to question his actions or his motives. Uncle Richard had been helping out with the daily routine of this ranch for several years now.

"Well, just be careful," she said, hoping her tone didn't sound too irritated. "I can't deal with something happening to you or Uncle Richard on top of everything else." She shrugged, threw down the cookie, and looked away from his questioning gaze. "I've got this problem at work I'm trying to deal with, and no one will return my calls on that. And Daddy is getting worse by the minute. I don't know—"

He shifted forward then, taking her hand. "You know you can lean on me."

She could only nod, staring out at the tranquil flow of the swimming pool. She blinked back tears. "Look at this place. It's so beautiful. The sun is still shining. The land is thriving, growing, changing, providing. This place provides for all of us. Why did it take me so long to understand that? And to see just exactly how much work goes into a place I've taken for granted all my life? Why now, Reed, when he's dying? Why couldn't I see what he saw, what you tried to show me?"

"Hush," Reed said as he dropped to his knees and put his hands on her face. "Hush, now. It's gonna be all right."

She pushed away from him and got up to pace. "It will never be all right again, Reed. My mother is dead. My father is dying. I've made such a mess of things. I don't have any immediate family left."

"You have me." He was there, urging her to be still. "Hold on to me," he said. "Hold on or hit me or scream at me. But don't push me away again, April."

She bit her lip, trying to hold back the pain. But she was so very tired. So she turned to him, fell against him, let him wrap her in that same warmth the sun was providing.

He felt as strong and formidable as this land. He felt like the earth and the sky and the wind all wrapped up in one comforting, gentle blanket of warmth. She wondered what it would feel like to have such assurance, such security with her always. To have Reed holding her at night when she was afraid, to have him there with her each morning with the sun shining so brightly. Could she even dream of such a hope?

I am with you always.

The words from the Bible verse echoed in her head.

The Lord was with her, April realized. But did the Lord have enough grace to give her a second chance?

Always.

She looked up at Reed, saw the assurance there in his eyes. "I need...I need you," she said, the words husky and thick with tears. "I need you, Reed."

"I'm here, darlin'. I'm right here."

She let him hold her while she cried. Then she raised her head and smiled as she sniffed back tears. "You were right. I did need some fresh air."

"Want me to come in and sit with you and your daddy for a while?"

She thought about that. She hadn't allowed others inside her father's room with her. She'd wanted to be alone. But this morning, she needed some company and some comfort. "Would you?"

"Of course."

She took his hand and turned toward the house. Then she turned around and grabbed her half-eaten cookie. "Thank you again," she told him as they went back inside. "For everything."

Reed squeezed her hand and guided her back to her father's side.

They sat there with Stuart until Flora came in to tell April that her Uncle Richard had arrived and lunch was ready in the kitchen.

"Thank you," April said, her voice hoarse, her throat tight. "We'll be there in a minute."

She turned to Reed. He'd sat here without complaining, without idle small talk. He'd barely said two words, but he'd held her father's hand the whole time. And her hand. He'd held her hand. He was holding it now.

"Will you stay for lunch?" she asked, wondering when she'd decided to quit fighting her feelings for him. Suddenly, instead of wanting to avoid him, she wanted him here beside her. Was it a sign of weakness or a sign of acceptance? She couldn't be sure.

"I'll stay," he said in a soft whisper. "It'll give me a chance to update Richard."

She nodded. "Let's go get Lynette to relieve us then. She's doing Daddy's laundry, I think."

"She's a good nurse. Goes beyond the call of duty."

"Yes, she is. At first, I wasn't so sure about her. But she's very devoted to Daddy."

"We all are," Reed added as they left the room. "I'll go find Lynette while you greet your uncle."

"Okay."

April watched as he headed toward the other end of the house, where the combination laundry room and mud porch was located behind the garage. She turned left into the kitchen.

"Uncle Richard!"

Her handsome uncle turned and gave her a bittersweet smile. "C'mere, girl, and give your ol' uncle a hug."

April rushed into his arms, her breath leaving her body in the big bear hug he gave her. Uncle

Richard smelled of spice and leather, which only reminded her of her father.

"It's so good to see you," she told him as she managed to extract herself from his embrace. "And you're just in time for lunch."

"Can I go in and see Stu first?"

"Of course." She glanced over at Flora, then back to her uncle. "But I have to warn you. He doesn't look the same as you probably remember."

"I understand," Uncle Richard said, his dark eyes going misty. "I'll be right back."

While he hurried toward the back of the house, April helped Flora put ice in the tea glasses. Together, they set the table and got the food dished up. Reed came in and poured the tea, as natural and comfortable here as he would be in his own house.

Uncle Richard came back a few minutes later, his eyes watery, shock creasing his tanned face. "Hate to see him like this. You know, he was always our big brother. We could turn to Stu for anything, anything at all, and he'd move heaven and earth to see that we got it. Just wish I could do the same for him now."

"I know." April glanced from her uncle to Reed, then pushed at the salt-and-pepper tuft of curls falling across Richard's forehead in a rakish style. "Have you heard from Uncle James?"

Richard shrugged, shifting his weight, and stomped his handmade snakeskin boots. "Your other uncle is not available right now. Taking a cruise down to the Keys on the Maxwell yacht. I've sent him word, but I've yet to hear back from him."

"Some things never change," April said, amazed that the middle brother of the Maxwell clan could be so shiftless and uncaring, considering they'd all been raised by wonderful parents with a strong set of values. Uncle James and his wife, Elsie, liked the good life. And they'd taken advantage of all the Maxwell holdings in three counties to make sure they had a grand lifestyle. While they'd lived that lifestyle, Summer had spent most of her time with her mother's parents, in a house that had been standing for over a hundred years. Even though her grandparents had loved her with a strong foundation of faith, Summer had an empty place in her heart, a place still waiting to be filled by her parents. An empty place and a bitterness the size of Texas.

"What exactly does James do?" Reed asked. "I mean, when he's not traveling around."

"He's supposed to be in charge of our oil leases," Richard said as they all sat down to eat. "But I have to stay on him all the time. I've got people in place to make sure things are handled, if you get my drift."

Reed nodded, shooting a glance at April. "April's been checking the books here at the ranch. Everything seems to be in order now. April's done a good job of catching things up. Stuart has a lot of people working on the details of the day to day activities."

Richard nodded his approval. "Stu always was thorough. Now, James…he just wants to keep having a good ol' time. I've tried to tell him his rodeo days are over and he's not getting any younger, but that boy won't listen to reason. He should be here with Stu."

No wonder Summer rarely talked to her parents. April remembered how they'd left Summer behind in the small town of Athens, Texas, time and again, so they could travel the world and be seen at all the right places, cashing in on the lucrative endorsements Uncle James had made during the heyday of his rodeo career.

How could they do that to their daughter? How could Uncle James stay away now, when his brother needed him?

"Do you think he'll come home at all?" she asked Richard after they'd said grace over the food.

"Who knows?" Richard said, shaking his head

as he took a corn pone from the basket Flora had put on the table. "Flora, honey, you've outdone yourself. Fresh peas and fried chicken, mashed potatoes. Gayle will have my hide for going off my diet, but I can't resist."

Flora beamed with pride. *"Gracias."*

"Flora, sit down and join us," April said, urging the woman down into a chair. "Where's Horaz today?"

Flora looked embarrassed. "In town with Tomás. Taking care of some business."

"Oh, okay." April figured that business had to do with the traffic ticket Tomás had been issued. "I hope everything works out."

"Sí," Flora replied as she absently dipped herself a big helping of steaming peas. Then she gave Richard a bright smile. "Teenagers."

"Tell me about it," Richard said, laughing. "These girls—remember them, Flora? Growing up here on the Big M and running loose all around half of Texas. We sure had our hands full, didn't we?"

"Sí," Flora said again, grinning. "And how is Autumn? She is a good girl, that one."

April smiled as she sampled the creamy mashed potatoes. Everyone loved Autumn, even if her cousin was a bit set in her ways and as straitlaced as an old shoe.

Uncle Richard chewed his chicken, then laughed. "Autumn is still Autumn. Born with a calculator attached to her hand. Always after the bottom line, that one. Have you talked to her lately, April?"

"Only on e-mail," April admitted. "I haven't made many phone calls to New York. I'm usually in with Daddy and I don't want to disturb him. But Summer and Autumn e-mail me daily, and me, them. They've offered to come down, but I told them not yet."

"Modern technology. I'll never get the hang of it," Uncle Richard said. "In fact, I'll let y'all be the first to know a big secret. I'm retiring in the fall."

April put down her fork. "You're closing the firm?"

"Nah, now, I'll never close Maxwell Financial Group. We've got clients all over Texas, honey. But I've hired me a hotshot financial advisor to take over. He knows all about computers and technology, and he's as sharp as a tack when it comes to making people money. The man is a genius."

"Have you told Autumn about this?" April asked, wondering how her cousin would take her father's retirement.

Autumn had always had this dream of one day returning to Atlanta, Texas, to work with her father. But her father probably didn't know about Autumn's dream, since Autumn refused to stray from her ten-year plan. And that plan included working in New York for a few more years.

"Not yet," Richard admitted. "Your Aunt Gayle knows, of course. And I've already put Campbell on the payroll—that's one of the reasons I was able to come here to be with y'all. Campbell can hold down the fort."

"You hired this…Campbell to take your place?"

"Not necessarily. He will be chief financial advisor, but I'll always be the boss, retired or not. Campbell Dupree understands how things work. He won't be any trouble for the family. None at all. He grew up in Louisiana, but he got a top-notch education at Harvard. He's traveled the world, got a real handle on how international finances work."

Richard said this with the kind of pride and confidence that April's daddy used to exude. The Maxwell men were nothing if not arrogant and self-assured. She had to wonder if Campbell Dupree fit that mold, too. And how Autumn would react to such a man taking over the family business.

"Maybe you should tell her, Uncle Richard,"

April said with a gentle plea. "I mean, she's going to be so surprised."

"Well, I don't know why. That girl knows I can't work the rest of my life. If James can travel the world without a care, then why can't I?"

"You deserve some downtime, that's true," April replied, "but Autumn—well, she cut her teeth at Maxwell Financial Group. She sat at your knee, right there in the company you built from the ground up, and learned everything she needed to know about money and finances."

"That's right and one day, it will all be hers," Uncle Richard reasoned. He dipped more peas and grabbed another corn pone.

"She might be upset that you've hired someone though."

"Now, why?" Uncle Richard sent April a sharp look. "Unless you're trying to tell me that Autumn might have wanted the job."

"Well, she's hinted that she'd love to one day move back home and—"

"Well, bless Bessy, why didn't the girl tell me that?"

"It's not set in stone," April said, hoping Autumn wouldn't be angry at her for spilling this secret goal. "I guess she's just afraid of...of disappointing you. You know, if something went wrong."

She glanced over at Flora and Reed, but found no help there. Flora kept her eyes glued to her plate and Reed tried hard not to look too curious and amused.

Uncle Richard stared across the table at her. "Autumn could never disappoint me. She's my baby. I'm so proud of her. You know, she's sent some big clients my way over the years. That girl's got contacts all over the world. She's about the only person who could match Campbell, I reckon."

"She's very good at her job, that's for sure," April said, pushing her fork around in her food.

"Well, Sam Houston and Custer, too," Uncle Richard said as he sat, shock-faced. "You just never know about people. I'll have to think about this and see what I can do."

"Well, you can't fire your new hotshot financial genius," April said. "That wouldn't be right."

"No, that wouldn't do," her uncle agreed. "The man's got an ironclad contract. But I might have another solution." He beamed at April, then winked. "A solution that just might be a win-win situation for all of us."

April wondered what her lovable but impulsive uncle had suddenly concocted for his only daugh-

ter. Maybe she should warn Autumn. Later, she
decided. Much later. Right now, she didn't have
time to get caught in the middle of a family squabble. And right now, Autumn was deeply and glee-
fully caught up in tax season.

She'd find the right time to explain things to
her stubborn cousin. But much later.

Chapter Eleven

"Did you ever find out what your uncle has cooked up?"

Reed asked April later that night.

"No. He's as stubborn and tough as an old barn-yard rooster, and just as unpredictable."

"Do you think Autumn's gonna pitch a fit about him retiring and hiring this new fellow?"

"Oh, yes," April said. "I guess I should warn her, but honestly, I don't have the energy right now to handle putting out yet another family fire."

"It's between them, anyway," Reed said. "Might be best to let Richard tell her."

"I thought about that, but I can't keep this from Autumn. We tell each other everything. I just have to find the right time to break it to her," she whispered back, careful not to bother her father.

Not that their quiet chatter could bother him. He hadn't responded to anything they said. His body was slowly shutting down. So now April could only wait and pray.

So many people had been by to see him. April had tried to keep a list of everyone, so she could thank all of them later.

"You have a remarkable family," Reed said, his words soft-spoken. "You know, when we were growing up, there was this one big old oak tree right near the back fence of y'all's yard. I used to climb up in that tree and watch—"

"You spied on me?"

He shook his head. "Not spying so much. Remember those grand parties your parents would have out on the back lawn?"

"Oh, yes. Mother loved entertaining, loved having a crowd here. Sometimes, she'd have the whole Cattle Baron's Ball committee here for a 'planning' party. They loved attending that big event, mingling with all the other ranchers and oil people. Of course, I had to decline Daddy's invitation to the ball this year, even though Flora said I should go in his place." April stared at her father, then asked, "So, you wanted to come to the parties?"

Reed nodded. "I wanted to be a part of something big like that. But it wasn't the glittery parties I wanted to see." He turned in the muted light, his gaze falling across April's face, washing her in longing. "It was you."

April felt the heat of her blush down to her toes. "But you saw me every day, Reed. We ran around this entire ranch like a couple of wild heathens."

"I know that," he said, and she could see the memories in his eyes. "But at those parties... you'd walk out, all dressed up in fluffy party gowns and I'd just about fall out of that tree." He shrugged. "I reckon somewhere around my fourteenth birthday, I started seeing you as a real live girl. I remember the party your parents had for you when you turned sixteen."

"You were invited to that party, Reed Garrison."

"I know I was. And I came."

"But you didn't stay," April said, the memories rushing over her, reminding her of that warm spring night years ago. She remembered seeing Reed in his church suit. He'd looked so uncomfortable, and so very handsome. And she remembered the way he'd looked at her. "I wore a white dress."

"It was the most beautiful thing."

"You wouldn't talk to me. I thought you were mad about something."

"I wasn't mad. I wanted to kiss you."

"But you were afraid?"

"Very afraid."

"You acted so funny, as if you had a frog in your throat."

"I did. I saw you through the open doors, and then you came down the back verandah stairs in that white dress and your mother's pearls. I'd already lost my heart to you, but that night, I knew something was different. That things would be different between us if I did kiss you."

"Oh, Reed—"

Stuart moaned, causing both of them to jump up as if they'd been caught.

"Daddy?"

April felt her father's hand squeezing hers. "I think he wants to tell us something, Reed."

"Stuart? It's Reed. What is it?"

Stuart moaned again, lifted his other hand.

"Daddy, do you hurt? Can I get you anything?"

Both Reed and April leaned forward, trying to hear the raspy words. But April heard only one word.

"Happy."

She looked up at Reed. "Did I hear him right?"

Reed glanced back down at Stuart with a frown. "You're happy?" he asked.

Stuart nodded, a slight movement of his head. He didn't open his eyes. "For you two."

Then he fell back into the deep sleep April had become so used to seeing.

Reed motioned April to follow him to the door. "Uh, April…I think he believes we're, uh—"

"Back together," she finished. "I didn't think he could hear anything we say, but I guess he can."

"And we've said a lot lately."

"But we never said we were back together."

Reed pulled her close, planting a soft kiss on her cheek. "Some things don't need to be voiced to be seen, April."

Shocked, she could only stare up at him. Could her father, as sick as he was, see what she couldn't admit with her own heart? "I don't know—"

"I do," Reed replied. "But I don't have time to go into this now, and besides, I can tell you're not ready for it yet. I have to meet Richard down at the stables. We're going out on patrol, remember?"

"Yes. Flora was supposed to wake him at ten. Is it that late?"

"Yes, it is. Why don't you go to bed and let Lynette take over?"

"I will in a little while. I'm just going to sit with him a little longer. See if he says anything else."

Reed gave her a soft grin. "Stuart believes in us, April. Maybe you should try doing that, too."

April watched him saunter up the hallway, her heart drumming a beat of longing and pride. Her father hadn't been able to talk to her very much, but he'd told her all the things that were important. He loved her, and he was happy to see her back with Reed. Her dying father believed she was home for good and everything was as it should be.

Why couldn't she believe that, too?

"I don't believe you finally took the time to call me," April said into the phone an hour later. "Danny, do you know what time it is here in Texas?"

"I know exactly what time it is," Danny Pierson said into the phone, his tone smug and pleasant. "That's because I'm sitting in a hotel in downtown Dallas."

"You're in Dallas?" April moved through the house, the mobile phone at her ear. She'd left Lynette with her father so she could take this call. "What are you doing there?"

"Checking up on our store at the Galleria," Danny said. "It's one of our top producers, you know."

"I've heard things weren't going so well with

Fairchild's," April shot back, unwilling to deal
with his spin on things.

"There are always rumors in our business. You
should know that, April."

"Why are you blocking our contracts with
Fairchild's, Danny? It's a bit late in the game to
shut things down now."

"I'm just concerned," Danny replied. "This is
a risky move for Satire. And it's even more risky
for Fairchild's. You know how exclusive our stores
are, April."

"Yes, I do. That's why I think this is a good
move. Satire will bring in hordes of customers.
You have to agree with that. Fairchild's certainly
knew that when these contracts were being nego-
tiated."

"Yes, but I didn't work for Fairchild's then. And
that was—well, that was when I thought I could
trust you."

"You can trust me now, Danny, past differences
aside. Don't do this. Just because *we* didn't work
out, don't make this personal."

"Is that what you think I'm doing?"

"That's it exactly," she said, fatigue making her
snap. "And I really don't have time to go into that
now. Just know that our contract is tight and you
can't back out on the deal now."

"Meet me in Dallas and we'll go over the details."

"I can't do that. My father is very ill."

"I'm sorry to hear that. Your family has quite an impressive name around these parts, highly respected. I know this is hard on you."

"Very hard. Which is why I don't need this problem with Fairchild's right now. Just back off and honor the original agreement, Danny."

"Only if you meet me to discuss it."

"I can't do that."

"Then I'll drive up to Paris. It's not that far from Dallas. I checked the map. Always did want to see that replica of the Eiffel Tower with the red cowboy hat on top you always talked about. Didn't you tell me it's near the Civic Center?"

"Don't come here," April said, panic bubbling through her system. "It's not a good time."

"But business is business and I'm sure you don't want this deal to go sour."

"Danny, my father is dying. Just do what you can to make this happen. I can't worry about this right now."

"We'll see," Danny replied, his tone less threatening now. "I understand about your father, April. I'll try to go back to the board of directors and see what I can do to clear this problem. But I'd like to see you."

"Another time," April said. "Just call me tomorrow with the details."

She hung up, then glanced out the big windows at the back of the house, a sense of dread filling her soul as the night grew dark and cloudy. She did not need Danny Pierson here, harassing her about business or personal matters. Not now.

So much to worry about. Her father. Reed and Uncle Richard out there hunting down trespassers. Danny and business pushing at her. So much to think about, to take care of.

"I need You, Lord. I need Your strength."

She waited, staring out into the dark night. But the silence of an empty, desolate house was her only answer. That and a distance rumble of thunder and lightning out over the trees to the west.

April turned from the darkness and walked down the long hall toward her father's room.

"Mighty quiet night," Richard said as he adjusted the black Stetson over his wiry salt-and-pepper hair. "Too quiet. But looks like a little bit of rain might blow in."

"Yep," Reed answered in a whisper. "Maybe if

a storm comes, our vandals will give up this game for tonight."

"I doubt that," Richard replied, chuckling. "If it's kids out for kicks, they won't know when to quit. Probably don't have sense enough to get in out of the rain."

"Until we catch 'em," Reed said. "Then they'll have more to worry about than wet clothes. Want some more coffee?"

"Nah. I'm getting too old for all that caffeine. I tell you, son, old age ain't no picnic."

"I hear that." Reed was silent for a while, then added, "Stu spoke to April and me tonight."

"He did? Well, that's something, I reckon."

"He said he was happy. For us."

Richard let out a grunt that merged with another rumble of thunder in the sky. "A dying man's last wish. He wants you and April together. He's always wanted that."

"He's not the only one."

"When are you gonna make that happen, son?"

"That all depends on April."

"How's that gonna work, with you here and her back in New York?"

"You think she'll go back?"

"Well, I'm thinking she has a life there. No

need for her to waste away on this old ranch, unless, of course, that's what she wants to do."

"It'll be her choice."

"So you'll let her go again?"

"I don't want her to stay here and resent me for it."

"What about if she stays here and loves you for it?"

"Now that would be a different matter."

"You need to learn the fine art of persuasion, Reed."

"I'm not a salesman like you, Richard. I don't have the right words."

"Oh, I think you do. I can talk a good game myself, as far as people's finances. But when it comes to understanding women—"

"Zero?"

"You got it. But I do know this. You have to persuade women sometimes. They want to be wooed. They want to know they're loved and treasured. They like security."

"You sound just like my daddy. He pretty much told me the very same thing. By my reasoning, April should see that she'd be secure with me."

"Women like that old-fashioned kind of romance," Richard replied sagely. "Why, I don't know. But Gayle is always telling me that. So

I romance her as often as I can, just to be on the safe side."

"April is a modern woman, Richard. She has a mind of her own. She's very independent. And very secure in her own way. I'm not so sure romance can compete with that."

"Maybe not. But I think she loves you just as much as you love her. She just needs some reassurance."

"Don't we all?"

"Yes, we do. That's why we have to keep the faith, through good and bad."

They fell silent again. Reed could hear the cicadas singing, the fluttering melody of the alfalfa swaying in the damp wind. He smelled a hint of honeysuckle, reminding him of April's sweet-smelling hair. He closed his eyes in a prayer— not his will, but God's plan.

And then he heard the snapping of trees, the crackle of heat against branches, and he smelled a different kind of scent, this one acrid and smoky. He saw the fire rising up out of the copse of bow dark trees nestled along the fence rail.

"Richard?"

"I see it. Somebody's gone and set fire to that wooden gate out there."

Reed hopped up. "With this wind, that could spread to the fields."

"I'm right behind you," Richard shouted as they rushed toward the growing fire.

Too late to worry about an ambush or a surprise attack. Whoever was doing this had grown bolder. And much more dangerous.

"Hey!" Reed called as two shadowy figures took off running through the trees. "Hey, stop right there!"

"Did you bring a rifle?" Richard shouted as he stomped at the fire. He took off the lightweight jacket he was wearing and hit at the trees.

"I did," Reed answered as he searched the trees. "But I left it in the truck. I didn't think things would turn this nasty."

"Go after them," Richard called. "I'll get this little brushfire out in no time."

"You sure?" Reed asked, stepping on embers and hitting at the fence with a broken tree limb.

"Yeah. It's almost out now."

Richard was right. They'd managed to subdue the fire that had been leaping up the fence and through the small trees. And thankfully, Reed felt a few big, fat raindrops hitting his hot skin.

Rain. God had sent rain.

* * *

I think it's going to rain.

April typed the words on her laptop, careful to keep an eye on the nearby bed and her silent, sleeping father.

She continued the e-mail to her cousins in New York.

Things are getting tough here. Summer, I appreciate your trying to get away, but I understand when things come up. You are needed at the center, so please don't worry about rushing down here. You both will be here soon enough, I know. And you'll be here when I need you. And I will need you. Reed has been so sweet. He sat with Daddy and me tonight. He sat and held my father's hand and prayed and talked to me in soothing, comforting words. I've changed since coming home. I now know that this is home. But I'm still afraid of making that final commitment— to Reed and the future he could offer me. I want to love him. I do love him. And I need him now more than ever. But I'm so tired and so afraid. I'm afraid to love him. Isn't that the silliest thing? I can see him reaching out to me, can feel his eyes on me. But it's as if I can't move toward him, as if something is holding me back. My heart is too heavy to hold all the feelings I have for Reed.

She stopped typing and closed her eyes to that heaviness for a brief moment. Then she finished the e-mail. I'll talk to y'all later. I'm going to sit here and wait for Reed and Uncle Richard to come back.

She shut the laptop and stilled, listening to the wind and the thunder, her gaze moving over her father's shadowy profile.

Then she closed her eyes again and fell asleep, her dreams lost in a gossamer time of happiness and laughter, a time of a young boy in his church suit and a young girl in her white dress and pearls, smiling at each other on a perfect spring night.

April heard the rain hitting the roof at about the same time she heard something crashing on the other side of the house.

Jumping up in disoriented, wide-eyed shock, she checked on her father, then stumbled across the room and creaked open the door of the bedroom. "Lynette?"

No answer. Flora and Horaz had gone home right after dinner. And April had sent Lynette to bed down the hall hours ago. Glancing back at the digital bedside clock, she saw that it was well past midnight.

She called out again, afraid Lynette had fallen. "Is anyone there?"

The rain came down in a wash of gray that danced across the yard like a sheet waltzing in the wind. The sky lit up with the glare of brilliant golden lightning and the banging of angry thunder. She watched it through the many windows around the patio, her breath coming in little shallow gasps as she stayed in her spot at the bedroom door.

Worried that something had happened to Lynette, April decided she couldn't just hover here like a ninny. She hurried toward the front of the house, hoping to find the nurse. "Lynette, are you all right?"

And that's when April saw the figure of a man standing at the other end of the hall.

Chapter Twelve

April squinted into the darkness, thinking maybe Reed and Richard had returned. But she could tell by the stance of the intruder and by the hooded jacket he wore to hide his face that this wasn't either of those two men.

The locked gun cabinet was behind the intruder, in her father's office, and her cell phone was upstairs in her bedroom. No help there. She didn't dare go back in the bedroom. The intruder might follow her there and hurt her father.

Trying to think which way to go and what to do next, April called out. "What do you want?"

"I won't hurt you," the man said, his voice shaky and raspy. "I just need to get some stuff and leave."

"What do you want?" April asked again,

moving back toward the front of the house. If she could run up the central hall to the front door, she'd be able to grab a phone or escape. But she couldn't leave her father alone.

"Just turn around and go back in your daddy's room."

Surprised, April realized this intruder knew the layout of the house—and apparently knew *her*. As her eyes adjusted to the darkness, she saw that the man was dressed in dark clothes, making it hard to even guess at his identity. "Who are you?"

"Just go back inside the room and you won't get hurt."

He had a Spanish accent.

April felt the hair on the back of her neck standing up. "What are you after?"

"Lady, you ask way too many questions." He waved his hand at her and advanced toward her. "I don't want to hurt you."

"Then just leave. Now." She hoped he didn't have a weapon. "No one will have to know you were even here. But you need to hurry. My uncle will be back soon."

He fidgeted and glanced around behind him. "I can't do that."

He sounded resigned to his dirty work.

And he sounded young and frightened.

April moved a step closer, determined to get him away from the back of the house and her father. She checked again, squinting in the darkness, but still didn't see any type of weapon on him. And then she looked around for one of her own.

Because she wasn't going to let whoever this was get away. Not without a fight, at least.

Reed ran through the rain like a man being chased by hounds. He could see one of the vandals just up ahead. Apparently, this time they'd hidden their means of escape near the very back of the property line, probably on one of the riding trails.

"Stop," Reed called, his words lost in the wind and the rain. "You'll only make this worse if you keep running."

Whoever it was kept right on running anyway. Reed hurried after them, his bum knee sending signals of protest with each step.

They were nearing the fence along the property line now. The pasture gave way to uneven, weather-worn gullies and terraces. Reed hopped over a muddy terrace, the rain falling in his eyes and blinding him. He winced as his leg twisted, but he didn't stop.

The lone figure hesitated just enough at the fence line to give Reed an edge. He surged forward with all the power of a linebacker, tackling the man in a groan of pain and exertion just as he tried to climb over the fence.

They rolled and tussled in the wet mud and grass, but Reed had more strength and muscle than the other guy. It took Reed only a few seconds to realize this wasn't even a grown man.

He was wrestling with a kid.

April said a prayer, hoping that her father would sleep through the ruckus and that Lynette was safe in her room. "Just take what you want and leave," she said, watching the shadowy figure for any signs of flight or fight.

"I don't want to hurt anyone."

The man—make that *boy*—seemed jittery and skittish, but then he was breaking and entering her house, so she figured that gave him the right to be a little nervous. It also gave her an edge.

"That's good that you don't want to hurt me." She stood perfectly still, her gaze fluttering over a huge clay vase sitting on a dark console in the center of the hallway. If she could get to that vase…

He didn't speak, didn't move.

"So are we just going to stand here all night?" she asked, her breath sticking in her throat.

"No, I don't think so."

"Good. Just turn around and leave the way you came and we'll call it even. Please, I don't want to disturb my father."

"I can't do that."

"Why not?"

The dark figure stalked toward her, his hand held out. "C'mon, my friend is waiting by the road. You'll have to come with me."

"Got you," Reed said as he landed his quarry flat on his back, mud and rain sliding off both of them. He held the captive down with both hands, his breath coming in a great rush of air. "Now you can explain what you're doing on Maxwell land," Reed shouted.

The kid kept his face turned away. And he wasn't talking.

Reed grabbed him by the chin, turned him around, and in a flash of lightning saw the face he would have least expected to be doing damage to the Big M.

"Tomás?"

The boy winced, closed his eyes, then moaned.

"Let me up, Reed. So I can explain. Before it's too late."

"What do you mean, too late?" Reed said, loosening his grip on the boy.

"The house," Tomás hollered. "They went to the big house. I don't want them to hurt April."

Reed held the boy by his shirt collar. "Who? Who's up at the house?"

"My friends. Two of them. They had this plan—to take money from the safe—that's all we wanted, just some money."

Reed's blood went cold as realization hit him. "So you planned this whole thing? You distracted everyone just so they could break in?"

"Sí," Tomás said, his voice shaky, his expression filled with shame and remorse.

"You messed with the wrong people, son," Reed said angrily. Then he yanked Tomás up and half dragged him along, mud sluicing at their feet as he hurried back to his truck. "You'd better hope it's not too late, Tomás. You'd better pray that nothing's happened at that house."

"I'm not going anywhere with you," April said, her pulse throbbing at an alarming rate in her ear. But she refused to be afraid. Suddenly, everything was very clear in her mind. This was her home, and that was her father lying in that bed. She'd been afraid of loving Reed too much; she'd been afraid of coming home to death and grief. But she wasn't afraid now. She wasn't about to let this little twerp get the best of her. "Did you hear me? I'm not leaving this house with you."

He shifted his feet, his gaze darting here and there. "Look, I don't want any trouble. We'll just drive you out to the highway and let you go."

"You said, there's someone with you?"

"He's waiting in the car. But I promise we won't hurt you. We don't want any trouble. We just wanted some easy cash. This was supposed to be easy."

She breathed a sigh of relief at his words, but didn't believe him. "Well, this is not easy for either of us, is it? My father is very ill, but then, you probably already know that. And yet, you still just wanted some easy cash? Does it make you feel good, breaking into the home of a dying man?"

"I'm sorry," he said, his head bent. "It wasn't supposed to be like this—"

April listened, her heart skipping and skidding. This was just a kid! And his voice seemed so familiar.

This new knowledge made her bold, took away some of her initial shock and fear. She stared at the stranger, thinking it was time to end this standoff. Making a split-second decision, she rushed for the table to grab the vase.

But the kid was faster. He ran smack into her and pushed at her grasping hand. April caught hold of the lip of the heavy vase, then aimed it for his head. He ducked, but not before she managed to lift the vase just enough to nick his temple with a hard blow. Screaming, he grasped at her hand, sending the vase crashing to the tile floor. The echo of the crash startled the kid, giving April time to push him away. Expecting him to come at her, she quickly grabbed a fractured piece of the broken clay to use as a weapon. But the boy backed away, then turned and ran up the wide hall.

And right into Lynette Proctor.

Reed and Richard both rushed inside the gaping door leading from Stuart's office to the back verandah.

"Somebody sure broke in," Richard said, his breath heaving, his hair plastered with rain and mud.

Reed pushed Tomás ahead of him, careful to keep a firm grip on the teenager's wet, dirty clothes. "Yeah, but then, our friend here had already told us that." He gave the frightened kid another shove as they entered the house. Tomás had talked a lot in his nervousness. And Reed still couldn't believe what the boy had told them.

But now, he saw it with his own eyes.

The office was ransacked, drawers left open and empty, files tossed to the four walls.

"I'll deal with this, and you, later," Reed told Tomás.

"Where is our help?" Richard whispered as they heard a commotion on the other side of the house. He headed for the gun cabinet.

"The sheriff should be sending someone," Reed said. They'd called 911 from the truck. He shoved Tomás at Richard. "Watch him."

Richard nodded toward the gun cabinet. "Don't you need protection?"

"I'll manage," Reed replied. He didn't want to accidentally shoot April or Lynette, or anyone else for that matter. "You just make sure Tomás stays put."

"Be careful," Richard said, his grip on Tomás's shirt collar making the boy grimace in pain.

Reed rushed out into the dark hallway, the sound of rain and thunder mingling with the sounds of angry voices emanating from the front of the house.

"April?" he called, a rippling fear causing him to see red. "April, are you all right?"

He ran to Stuart's room and was relieved to see that Stuart was sleeping and undisturbed.

But where was April? Where had that noise come from?

When he heard sirens out on the road, Reed sent up a prayer of thanks for that, at least. "April?"

"We're in here."

He followed her voice, hoping he wouldn't find something horrible in the next room.

He found them in the den. Lynette Proctor and April stood over the trembling figure they had cornered on a chair by the window.

"Are y'all all right?" Reed asked as he hurried to April.

"We're fine," she said, falling into his embrace and getting herself all wet in the process. "We're okay."

She sounded a bit shaken. Reed looked her over, taking in the fear and resolve in her big, dark eyes. "Are you sure?"

Lynette grunted, then held a hand toward the man in the chair. "We snared us a burglar. I tackled him right there in the hallway, after April tried to ping him with a vase."

"They tried to kill me," the teenager said, his voice shrill, his tone whining and afraid.

"You broke into my father's office," April shouted down at him. "You could have hurt someone, or worse, you could have gotten shot."

"If I'd had me a gun," Lynette said, her tone smug and firm, her eyes flashing. "I heard him rustling around in there. Left a mess, that's what he did."

Reed stared down at the dark-headed boy. "You're a friend of Tomás's, right? Adan? You're Adan."

The boy didn't answer. He just sat there glaring.

Richard came in then, pushing Tomás ahead of him. "Looks like we found our vandals." He thumped Tomás on the head. "Kid, have you lost your mind, trying to break into the Big M?"

Tomás crumpled into a heap on a nearby chair, then shot an accusing look at his partner in crime. "You told me nobody would get hurt."

"Nobody did," April said. "But you're both lucky we didn't shoot first and ask questions later."

"He was only supposed to take some cash from the safe," Tomás said, his defiance almost comical. Except this was no laughing matter.

"I couldn't find the safe," his friend wailed. "Then she came down the hall toward me." He pointed to April, then swallowed hard. "They're gonna put us in jail, Tomás." He lapsed into Spanish.

Reed thought he heard a very sincere appeal to God in there somewhere. "You need to pray, both of you." He turned to Tomás. "Tomás, why would you be a part of this?"

Tomás shrugged. "They dared me."

"They dared you?" Richard echoed, shaking his head. "Son, haven't we been good to you?"

Tomás glared up at him. "*Sí,* but…I feel like a loser. The hired help, getting handouts. Always only handouts."

April leaned close. "Tomás, your grandparents are a part of this family. We don't give handouts. We have loyal people on our land, people who work hard and make a good living. We consider all of them family, even you." She grabbed him by the arm. "Now tell me why you did this?"

"I told you—they dared me. I had to show them I wasn't scared. But…my ride left me out there in the pasture." He frowned at the other boy. "They were only supposed to take a little money."

Reed winced, shook his head. "You're gonna

have to tell the sheriff the whole story, Tomás. And I have to call your family."

Tomás groaned. "It started out as a game. A dare. We had some fun, hanging out in the pastures. Then we started leaving things here and there, just to—"

"Just to make us think it wasn't serious," Reed finished. "I guess that's why you tried to break into my toolshed, too, right? Just to throw us off?"

"We didn't mean any harm."

Reed glanced at April. "Until someone suggested robbing the big house, huh? Then you had to distract us one more time, so your friend here could do his dirty work, right?"

Tomás glared across at the other boy. "He said it would be for kicks, to get some cash, just for fun. He said no one would ever trace it back to us."

"Are you both dumb as dirt?" Richard asked, his hand holding onto Tomás's friend with a firm grip. "What's your name again, son?"

"Adan," the boy mumbled, his head down.

"Well, Adan, I hear the sheriff coming. Might as well give me your parents' number, so we can call them, too. And whoever was waiting to give you a ride out of here—well, I reckon they're long gone by now. We'll have to let their parents know. It's gonna take a while to straighten all of this out."

Reed looked at April again. "Are you sure—"

"I'm fine," she said. "Just a bit dazed."

"You sure didn't need this."

"No, I didn't. But at least now we know who was behind the vandalism."

He nodded. "Yeah, we solved it."

"Together," she said, her smile bittersweet.

"With me out there, chasing down a kid, and you in here, trying to—what was that Lynette said?—*ping* another one on the head with a vase." He felt the shudder passing through his body. "April, when I think of what could have happened—"

"It didn't."

"At least we got through this without too much trouble, and nobody seriously hurt."

"We're quite a pair."

"Yeah," Reed said, relief flooding through his system. "Quite a pair." He couldn't tell her that he'd been in a dark fear out there, wondering if she had been hurt. He couldn't show her just how relieved he really was. "Let's go let the sheriff in and get this night over with."

"Flora, we're not going to press charges," April said the next day.

Flora was inconsolable. "*Gracias,* April, *gracias. Lo siento. Lo siento.*"

"It's not your fault," April said, taking Flora into her arms. "It's going to be all right."

"What will become of my grandson?" Flora asked, her eyes watery and red-rimmed.

"Community service," April replied. "Reed and I thought it was the best way to teach these boys a lesson."

"They could have gone to jail," Flora replied, shaking her head. "*Por qué?* Why would Tomás do such a thing?"

April had wondered that herself during the sleepless hours of the long, rainy night. "From what we could gather, his friends pressured him. They saw an opportunity and they took it. They talked Tomás into creating a distraction, so one of them could sneak into the house and get whatever cash they could find. Cash and other valuables, according to the sheriff."

"There is no excuse for this," Flora said, wiping her eyes. "His parents—they finally sat down with us and Tomás and had a long talk. At least, that is something good."

"That *is* something good," April agreed. "Maybe now they will pay more attention to Tomás."

"He might not get to play football this fall," Flora said. "Serves him right, *el niño loco.*"

Reed came into the kitchen, followed by Horaz. "It's all taken care of," he told April.

Horaz took his wife into his arms, talking to her softly in Spanish.

"What was decided?" April asked.

"There will be a hearing, closed, because they're juveniles, of course. But from what we could gather and from what the sheriff could promise us, they'll probably have to pick up trash up on the main highway for the rest of the summer, then do volunteer work at the local food bank and a couple of other charities for a long time to come."

April nodded. "Do you think that's a fair punishment?"

Reed let out a frustrated breath. "I don't know. What they did was wrong, but in the end, nobody got hurt, thank goodness. They were more stupid and scared than dangerous. It could have been much worse."

"You're right. I don't know who was more scared last night, me or that boy."

"He came here with Tomás," Reed said, disgust evident on his face. "He had meals right here in the kitchen, swam in the pool, fished, rode horses."

"And saw a lot of things he could pawn or sell for profit," April reminded him. "Will they be on probation for a while?"

"I'd say a good long while," Reed replied. "And they're both off the football team for the next season."

"You tried to warn Tomás," she said, taking Reed's hand in hers.

"I should have done more."

"Reed, you can't take care of all of us. You're only human, you know."

"More human than I realized," he said. "My knee is still protesting my midnight run."

"I'm proud of you."

"Oh, yeah?"

She felt the heat of his gaze, the longing in his question. "Yeah."

"Proud enough to have dinner with me to-night?"

"I can't leave—"

"Here, in the dining room?"

She glanced around. "Do you think that's wise? I mean, after all the commotion last night?"

"Don't you think we deserve a nice dinner for our crime-solving abilities?"

That made her smile. "I don't know. I wouldn't feel right—"

"It's just dinner, April. Just you and me."

Confused, she stared up at him. "What do you have in mind?"

"Just some time together, alone. We'll be right here, if your dad needs us."

"Who's cooking?"

"Not me," he assured her. "And certainly not Flora. She needs some time off."

"I agree."

"My mom will provide the food."

"Reed, she's already done so much."

"She doesn't mind. It's part of her matchmaking skills."

That made her smile. "Everyone's determined to bring us together."

"And I'm the first one in line."

"Is that what this dinner is all about?"

"Maybe."

April smiled up at him. "Should I dress for this dinner?"

"Yes, ma'am. Dress up. Get all glamorous."

"For you?"

"Will you, for me?"

"I think I can find something in the back of my

closet, if I can just find the energy actually to get dressed."

"Good." He leaned forward and gave her a kiss on the forehead. "You rest up and I'll see you around seven."

"Okay."

April watched as he left the room, then turned back to Flora and Horaz. They both looked miserable and embarrassed.

"It's okay," she told them as she rushed forward to give them a hug. "I love you both so much. You know that, right?"

"*Sí,*" Horaz said. "We feel the same."

"Let's go visit Daddy," April suggested, needing to be near her father.

Taking them both by the arms, she led the old couple down the long hallway, refusing to let the scare they'd had last night bother her anymore.

She'd learned what really mattered, since she'd been back at the Big M. And right now, seeing her father and being with the people she loved was all that mattered.

And those people included Reed Garrison.

Chapter Thirteen

"Can you believe this?" Summer said as she finished reading April's latest e-mail. "Vandals and
a break-in at the Big M? That's just what April
needed."

"Doesn't sound too good," Autumn said absently from her paper cluttered desk. "I'm just
glad everyone is okay."

"Yes," Summer said as she shut down the computer and took her empty teacup to the sink. "I'm
surprised April didn't shoot that Adan."

"April hasn't been near a gun since she left
Texas," Autumn reminded her overly zealous
cousin.

"She still knows how to use one, though,"
Summer replied. "We all do."

"Don't remind me," Autumn countered. "I don't
like guns."

"Necessary in today's world."

Autumn glanced up at her cousin. "You must have had a bad day at work."

Summer ran a hand through her long hair. "Yeah, if that's what you call helping three more battered women find the strength to stay away from their husbands, then I guess I did have a pretty rotten day."

Autumn dropped her ink pen. "I'm sorry you didn't get to go visit with April."

"Well, work has to come first."

"You need a vacation, Summer."

"So they tell me." She shrugged. "Let's not worry about me. Just think—right about now, Reed is getting dinner ready for April. That's so nice." Then she let out a gasp that made Autumn jump.

"What?"

"I just remembered. Today is April's birthday."

Reed figured April had forgotten that today was her birthday. But he hadn't, which was why he'd tried so hard all day to get things in order for their special dinner.

The house was back to normal. Reed had hired two ranch hands to help him get the office cleaned up. Adan hadn't found the safe, which was tucked behind a small book cabinet, but he'd done a good bit of damage. His parents had readily agreed to pay for that. All three of the boys were put on probation and community service, their parents ordered to supervise them strictly. The driver had bolted and run, but his parents had been just as upset as Tomás's and Adan's, and the authorities agreed he was just as guilty. They'd been planning this all summer by deliberately messing up the land so everyone on the ranch would be distracted just enough to allow the break-in. And they'd waited for the perfect night to do it.

It had been calculated and perfectly timed, but they'd failed anyway, because they were young and hadn't thought of the consequences or all the things that could go wrong. Well, they'd be thinking about that for a long time to come now.

The judge had also suggested they all attend church on a regular basis. Reed didn't think that would be a problem.

He glanced around the formal dining room one more time, making sure everything was ready for his evening with April. When he thought about what might have happened last night, he thanked God for protecting April and Lynette and April's father. Things could have taken a bad turn, but that was over now and Reed was glad. He only wanted to give April some time away from all of it, a chance to put all the bad stuff out of her mind.

The long glistening pinewood table was set with the abstract sunflower-etched china and matching crystal. Two golden glazed hurricane lamps sitting on the massive sideboard sparkled with the fire of vanilla-scented candles. The big, glass-paned doors were thrown open to the tiled patio and the pool beyond, allowing the cool night breeze and the scent of fresh blooming jasmine and gardenias to waft through the big room. Soft, soothing Spanish guitar music played in the background.

"It looks real nice, son."

Turning to give his mother thanks and a hug, Reed said, "You go on home and rest now. I appreciate everything y'all did. And thanks for inviting Richard over for the evening so we could have dinner by ourselves."

"Anything to help April get through this." She kissed him on the cheek. "And to help you and April find your way back to each other."

"Think good food will win her over?"

"Couldn't hurt. That and my handsome son."

"Thanks again, Mom."

She'd had Reed's daddy grill them two juicy ribeye steaks, and she'd fixed fresh steamed vegetables and chocolate mousse, knowing April loved chocolate.

Reed watched his mom leave, then turned to check himself in the mirror over the long buffet. He wore a tuxedo—something his mother had suggested. His hair was combed and he smelled fresh and clean. "Guess I'll do."

"Oh, you'll do just fine."

He turned to find April standing at the arched door to the dining room; his breath caught in his throat as he took in the sight of her.

She wore a creamy satin sleeveless dress with a big collar that framed her slender shoulders and showed off her long neck. The dress flared out at her waist in a full-skirted halo that dropped almost to her ankles. She wore matching cream-colored shoes, and pearls on her ears and around her neck.

Reed had always loved April in her pearls.

"You'll do, too," he said, his voice husky and intimate. "Come here and let me look at you."

She whirled into the room like a ballerina, smiling over at him. "It was my mother's. I found it in the storage closet where Flora put all her clothes."

"Pretty as a picture," he said, holding her out away from him as he looked her over. Then he leaned close and gave her a peck on the cheek. "Happy birthday, April."

Her eyes widened, first in surprise, then in a dark sadness. "It is my birthday, isn't it?"

"Yes. That's what this party is all about."

Her eyes turned misty then. "Thank you."

Reed kissed her again, then gently touched her cheek. "No tears tonight, okay?"

"Okay," she said, the one word shaky.

He tugged her toward the table. "C'mon in."

She glanced around the room. "Reed, this is so nice."

"How's Stuart?"

"He's the same. Lynette promised to call me if anything changes, good or bad."

"So we can have an hour alone, just to talk?"

She nodded, glancing back out toward the hallway. "I have to admit, I feel a little guilty, all dressed up like this, with him so sick."

Reed came around the table to pull her close. "We're right here, sugar. Right here nearby. Your daddy wants you to be happy. You can take a little time to eat and relax."

"I hope so. I'm not sure I have an appetite, but everything sure looks good."

He smiled, touched a hand to her curling bangs. "We missed the Cattle Baron's Ball. It's tonight, in Dallas."

"You could have gone—to represent the Big M."

"Not without you."

"That's so sweet."

Reed tugged her close, taking in the scent of lilies and honeysuckle that seemed to float around her. "Right now, I don't feel very sweet. I feel selfish, because I just wanted some time with you all to myself."

"At least you're honest."

"I'm trying…and I'm trying to be patient."

She pulled away and turned toward the table. "Why don't we eat this wonderful food?"

"Okay." He backed off, knowing she was still skittish. Knowing and wondering when she'd just give in and love him the way he loved her. Or let him love her the way she should be loved.

"Let's say grace," April said, then she bowed her head and thanked God for the bounty of the Big M. *"And for keeping all of us safe. Give my father some peace, the peace that he needs right now. And help Tomás and his family, Lord. We ask this in Your name."*

"Amen," Reed said. "Here you go," he told her as he adjusted her chair. "Want some mineral water?"

"Sure." She watched as he poured sparkling

water from a green bottle chilling in the ice bucket. "Thanks."

He waited as she took a long drink. "Good?"

"Tingly. That hit the spot."

Reed fell for her all over again, simply because she seemed nervous and fragile. And she looked so young and pretty, just like on that night of her sixteenth birthday.

"Ever wish we could turn back the clock?" he asked.

She took up her knife and fork. "Of course. I wish I could make Daddy well, and…that Mama was here with us. I wish I could understand why death has to separate us."

Reed saw the sadness in her dark eyes. "I don't know how you handle it, knowing he's dying. I think about my parents and how much I love them. It's just hard to imagine, even when we know we'll see them all again one day."

"It is hard," she said, nibbling on her vegetables. "I haven't handled it very well. I want to blame God, you know. But I understand it's a part of life and no one's to blame. Death is just part of the journey. It's really another part of life, just in a different place."

"You're very wise to think that."

"My mother taught me to have faith, always."

"Do you have faith in me, April?"

He watched the play of emotions on her face, saw the joy, the fear, the pain, the hope. And waited for her answer.

"You've been so kind, Reed. So much a part of my life. I couldn't have made it this far without you here, helping me out. I didn't want to admit that, didn't want to look weak and helpless. But I've come to realize that turning to someone for help isn't a sign of weakness. It's a sign of strength, a sign of how much I do believe in you."

Reed leaned back in his chair. "Wow, that was some speech."

"But it wasn't what you wanted to hear?"

He threw down his fork. "You know what I want to hear, but I don't have the right to ask you that, not now, when Stuart is so sick."

April leaned forward and grabbed his hand. He saw the tears brimming in her eyes. "Are you willing to wait for me, Reed? Are you willing to give me some more time?"

Reed got up and pulled her out of her chair. "I've been waiting all my life. What's a little more time?"

Then he kissed her, to show her that he was more than willing to wait. But on his own terms.

"I want you to love me again, April. I just want that—whenever you're ready."

He saw in her eyes that she did love him. He felt in her kiss that she had always loved him.

Patience. He had to learn patience. But he'd been so very patient, for so long.

April looked up at him, touching his face. "I don't deserve you."

"You deserve to be happy. You deserve…whatever can make you happy. I hope I can help in that department. I promise I'll try."

"I just need to get through this. And then, I'll decide what to do…about everything."

That wasn't exactly what he wanted to hear. "About us, you mean?"

"Yes, about us. About the ranch. Everything."

Then she kissed him again, feathering his face with little butterfly touches. "Can we break into that chocolate mousse now?"

Reed had to laugh at that. "You're trying to distract me."

"Will it work?"

"No. I can't be distracted from getting what I want. You should know that about me."

"I do. It's one of the things I love—"

"One of the things you love about me?"

"Yes."

"I guess that'll have to do for now," he said as he handed her a dessert dish full of the creamy mousse.

She smiled and grabbed a spoon. "It's a start."

The dinner ended way too soon for Reed. They'd finally settled down to small talk and laughter. He loved the way April laughed. When she was truly happy, her whole face lit up, her creamy porcelain skin glowing with an inner light.

He wanted to make her laugh for all the days of their life.

"Thank you again," she told him as they carried their plates into the kitchen. "This evening was so lovely. And it did help me to relax. It was a very thoughtful birthday present."

"Good," he said. "Let's take a stroll around the backyard before we say good-night."

She raised her dark brows. "Okay."

"Don't worry. It's just a friendly walk—to fight off the calories in that chocolate mousse."

She laughed at that. "I guess that would be smart."

He took her out by the pool. "Look at those stars."

April followed his gaze, lifting her head to the

dark heavens. "A clear night, after all that rain last night."

Reed pulled her back against his chest, then wrapped his hands around hers at her side. "The good Lord always sends us signs of his beauty and his bounty, even after a bad storm."

"It was a bad night all the way around," April said, a long sigh leaving her body. "I still can't believe Tomás would be involved in such a thing."

"He's young and misguided," Reed replied, resting his chin on top of her silky curls. "And his parents have always allowed him to kinda run wild. They left things up to Flora and Horaz."

"And they tried, they really did," April added. "But Tomás isn't their responsibility, no matter how much they want to help him."

"I think things will change now. Some good should come of this bad. We've given those boys a second chance. I just hope they don't mess up again."

"I don't think Tomás will. At least he has all of us behind him." April turned to face him then. "You are a good man, Reed. You always look for the good in others, too. And you're always willing to give people another chance."

He touched his forehead to hers. "Hush, you're making me blush."

"I just want you to know—"

The ringing of the doorbell pealed through the house, stopping April in midsentence. "Now who could that be this late? Maybe Uncle Richard forgot his key."

She hurried inside, her skirts swishing. Reed followed her. "Hey, wait up." After last night's break-in, he didn't want her answering the door without him right there.

The bell rang again just before April opened the big door. "I'm coming." Turning to look back at Reed, she whispered, "Someone sure is impatient."

When she turned back to face the visitor, Reed heard her sharp intake of breath. Then he felt a definite chill as her body stiffened.

"Danny, what are you doing here?"

The man standing at the door had sandy-blond hair and an attitude, from what Reed could tell. Reed hated him on the spot. Something about the arrogant way the man slanted his gaze possessively over April brought out Reed's protective instincts.

And his jealousy.

"May I come in?" the man asked, waving a hand in the air. "The bugs in Texas are just as big as everything else around here."

April shot Reed a confused, shocked look. "Of

course. Come in." She motioned to Reed. "Reed Garrison, meet Danny Pierson."

"Reed?" Danny's icy-blue eyes glazed over as he stared at Reed. "Well, I've certainly heard a lot about you. You and April…grew up together, right?"

"That's right," April interjected before Reed could explain how things were. She gave Reed a warning glare as she closed the door.

"And who are you?" Reed asked, shaking the hand the other man extended. After all, his mama had taught him manners. But his daddy had taught him how to fight.

And he sure smelled a good ol' fight coming on.

Apparently, so did April. "Danny is—"

"Her ex-boyfriend," Danny finished. "But I hope to change that." He put an arm around April's shoulder, then smiled over at Reed. "Know what I mean?"

"I think I do," Reed said, a slow rage burning its way through his system. Then he glanced at April and saw the distress on her face. "Maybe you should have called first. This isn't a good time. April's father is ill."

"I'm aware of that." Danny scanned them both

with a puzzled look. "Is that why you're both so dressed up?"

Reed curled his fists at his side. "We were having dinner. A *private* dinner."

"Oh." Danny shrugged, tightening his grip on April. "Hope I didn't interrupt anything important. But April and I have some unfinished business."

Reed stepped forward. "I don't think—"

"Reed, it's okay," April said, coming between them. "Danny's company—Fairchild's Department Stores—is under contract with Satire. We just need to work out some of the details."

Reed glared at the other man as if he were a nasty bug. "Is *this* the problem you were telling me about?"

April nodded. "Yes. I mean, Danny and I have some problems to clear up. It's just business."

"Did you invite him here?"

"No, not really. But since he's here, I think I should talk to him."

"Yeah, man," Danny said, clearly triumphant. "We're just going to talk. About old times and a bright new future."

Reed felt the pulse throbbing in his jaw, felt the tension flaring through his head as he clenched his teeth.

"April, are you sure?"

"Yes," April said. Then she turned to Danny. "Why don't you wait in the den?" She pointed across the hall. "I'll just show Reed out."

"See you, Reed." Danny grinned, then turned to go into the other room.

April took Reed by the arm. "Can we talk?"

"About what?" he said as they went into the kitchen. "About that fancy city fellow coming here to win you back? April, I won't—"

"You won't what, Reed? Let him near me? Let him flirt with me?" Her eyes were snapping a dark fire, but Reed wasn't sure just which one of them she was mad at—the ex or him. Maybe both. "I'm a big girl, remember? I've lived out on my own for a very long time now."

He closed his eyes. "I don't need to hear the rest. You've had other relationships, same as me."

"Yes, but you've jumped to the wrong conclusion here, same as always. Danny and I are over. We've been over for a very long time."

"So what's he doing here?"

"He was in Dallas on business. When he finally returned my calls, he asked to come here."

"And you told him he could? I can't believe that! Your father—"

"Stop it," she said, her face flushed, her eyes black with rage. "Just stop it. And leave, now.

After everything…after all we talked about tonight, you still think the worst of me."

"April, I—"

"Just go, Reed. I can't take any more of this. Don't you see? No matter what we feel for each other, you will always, always think of me as the shallow little rich girl who broke your heart. You don't even believe what I've tried to explain to you. You think you know what's best for me. I can't go through that again."

Broken and baffled, Reed slowly nodded his head. "Well, neither can I."

He turned and stomped through the house to the open doors leading out to the pool. And he didn't look back.

He couldn't look back.

He'd just used up the last of his patience. There was nothing left. Nothing but an aching emptiness that was as vast and deep as the beautiful starry sky over his head.

"I guess nothing good is gonna come out of this particular situation after all, Lord," he said, his questioning prayer echoing out over the night.

When he reached his truck, he turned and looked back at the glowing lights from the house. And he felt like that teenager all over again, on the outside looking in.

Chapter Fourteen

April held her hands to her temples, massaging away the nagging headache that seemed to be coming on strong. This night had been just about perfect, but now it was going downhill very fast.

"Feeling bad?" Danny asked as she came back into the den.

April dropped her hands to stare at him. He looked every bit as handsome as she remembered him. But now she could see through all that charm. And besides, he'd ruined her night with Reed. She'd have to deal with *that* one later. Now she just wanted Danny gone. "I'm not feeling at my best, no. Danny, why did you come here?"

He shrugged and picked up a small crystal bowl from the coffee table, moving it from hand to hand. "I thought we had some business to discuss."

April grabbed the bowl before he managed to drop it. "The only business we have is this—we're over, through, finished. And you didn't have to create this little snag in the contracts between Satire and Fairchild's just to get back at me."

"Oh, you think that's what this is all about?" he asked, coming so close she could smell his expensive aftershave. That scent had at one time made her all giddy. Now she just wanted to be sick.

"Isn't it?" she asked. "I told you not to come here. My father is dying, this ranch is in a mess, and I don't need you to complicate things."

"Nothing complicated about me, babe," he said, one finger trailing down her face to her neck. "I just wanted to see you again."

"So you did plan this whole thing?"

He smiled, shifting closer. "Of course I did. The contracts are pretty standard, but I managed to find a couple of loopholes. So I used that as an excuse. That and a quick trip to Dallas. Then it made sense to swing by here and see you."

April backed away. "This is ridiculous. You're not only wasting my time, but you're using Fairchild's perks to take a side trip to Paris, Texas? Danny, not only is that risky, it's downright stupid. You could lose your job."

"I have the authority to do whatever I see fit regarding the Satire line. My employer knows what I'm doing."

"But I bet you put a really good spin on things, just as you've always done."

She turned, but he grabbed her by the wrist, twisting her back around. "Don't walk away from me, April."

"Let me go," she said, her resolve giving way to the warning moving through the pain of her headache.

"Oh, no. I didn't come all this way to be ignored."

"Danny, I don't know what you expected, but I can't help you. Not with the contracts, and certainly not with us. The contracts can't be changed without a big, ugly battle, and I'm not interested in anything you have to say regarding us."

"Without a big, ugly battle there, too, you mean?" he said, his eyes flaring a white-blue. "Is it because of *him?*"

April yanked her arm away, then rubbed the spot where he'd held her. "If you mean Reed, it has nothing to do with him. But it has everything to do with *you*. I don't feel the same about you as I once did."

"Oh, yeah, I remember. Because I'm ruthless and cutthroat and I don't play fair?"

"That and other things," she said, remembering his quick temper and his refusal to compromise on any issue at all, including her faith. "I think you just need to leave."

"Not yet," he said, coming toward her.

April turned just as he grabbed her around the waist. He tried to kiss her, but she pushed him away. "Danny, stop it."

"Oh, don't play that game."

He tried again, but April was too quick this time. She scooted around a high-back chair. "I asked you to leave and I mean it. Do you want me to report your behavior to the CEO of Fairchild's?"

"You'd do that, just to get even?"

"I'd do that just to get rid of you."

"You know, I can stall on these contracts, hold up the entire shipment of Satire ready-to-wear."

"You go right ahead," April said, weary with all his threats. Weary to her very bones. But she had more backbone now than she'd had when they were dating. "I'd like to see you explain that to the higher-ups. Fairchild's is already in a heap of trouble. It wouldn't do to miss this chance to make a comeback. I don't think it would sit well with all those people you're trying to impress. And I know how hard you try to impress, Danny."

She saw the anger flaring in his eyes. He came

at her, trying to grab her arms, but she was ready for him. April swung around and picked up the nearby cordless phone. "Just touch me again and I'll have the whole ranch down on your head."

He stepped back, hands up. "I guess I misjudged you, April. I thought you'd come begging."

"I don't beg anyone."

He stood silent, staring at her for a moment. Then he let out a defeated sigh. "Okay. I don't want a fight. I just wanted to put things right between us."

"Things will be fine if you leave now. But if you ever try to pull something like this again, Danny, I'll have to report you. And I don't want to have to do that."

He shrugged, checking the anger she could see pulsing in his jawline. "It would be your word against mine."

"Yes," she said, remembering how they'd been happy together at one time. But it had been a false happiness, and it hadn't withstood the test of time. Not the way her friendship, her love for Reed, had. Maybe God had sent Danny here for that very reason, so she could see what a real love between a man and a woman should be like, even with time and separation between them.

Why had she sent Reed away? He would have

made quick work of getting rid of Danny Pierson for her. But April knew it was better this way. This was her battle, not Reed's, no matter how much Reed would want to protect her. If she couldn't stand up to Danny, she'd never be able to face Reed or anyone else again. She wanted Reed's respect and she wanted him to see that she wasn't that spoiled socialite he'd accused her of being the day she left.

She looked over at Danny, feeling nothing for him. That, and knowing that her love for Reed could be a blessing instead of a fear, gave her the courage she'd never had before. "It would be your word against mine. But I think you know which one of us people would believe. After all, you haven't exactly been discreet and tactful in how you treat people."

"I guess I haven't at that." He slumped against a chair, scowling. "And you've been a model of propriety."

His sarcasm and criticism didn't sting the way they should have. April had been through so much since the last time she'd seen him. He had no idea just how strong she'd become. But he was about to find out.

"I don't have to justify myself to you, Danny. Now, I think it's time for you to leave—"

"April!"

Lynette's frantic call from the hallway stopped April in midsentence. She whirled and hurried down the hall. "What is it?"

But when she saw Lynette's tear-streaked face, she knew. She knew.

"Is he—"

"It's bad," Lynette said, taking both of April's hands in hers. "You'd better come. I'll call Richard, too."

April gave Danny a helpless look. "I have to go."

Danny nodded, his face going pale. "I understand."

April didn't have time to make sure he left the house. She rushed to her father's room, dread coursing through the erratic pulse beating its way through her system.

Reed entered the house from the back. The dining room was dark, but a light burned from the kitchen and the long hallway. He went into the kitchen and found Flora sitting at the counter, her hands clasped in prayer.

She looked up at the sound of his steps. "Reed! It's so sad. So sad."

Reed could feel the weight of death pushing

through the house. Just hours ago, he and April had laughed and talked, walked through the gardens. Then he'd gone and gotten all riled up and ruined things. Again.

He wouldn't hurt April again. And he wouldn't allow himself to be hurt again. He'd just about decided that maybe she would never love him the way he loved her, that maybe she'd changed but he'd stayed the same. He'd been in the same holding pattern since the day she'd left. Maybe she was right in getting angry with him each time he tried to step in and save the day.

But wasn't that what being a life partner, a helpmate, was all about? Shouldn't he be the one to always be by her side and hold her up in her time of need? He was just an old-fashioned country boy who loved a sophisticated, very modern city girl. But it wouldn't matter, if he couldn't make her love him back.

He might just have to accept that and let her be.

When Richard had told them it was near the end, Reed hadn't hesitated to come here and be nearby. Just in case she needed him.

"I know, Flora," he said now, taking the woman's withered hand in his. "It's tough. But you and Horaz, you know you mean the world to him, and to April. She'll need you both now."

"Sí," Flora replied, nodding. "Horaz is in the den with that other man. Waiting."

"What other man?"

"That stranger who showed up."

"Oh, Danny Pierson? He's still here?"

She bobbed her head again. "He said he no leave with April's father dying. He said he wanted to stay in case she need him."

"I'll take care of him," Reed said. Then he stalked across the entranceway, determined to throw that no-good out on his ear.

But the sight he saw made him stop and stare—and feel ashamed for his take-no-prisoners attitude. No wonder April had kicked him out earlier.

Horaz was talking quietly to Danny Pierson, talking and nodding his head, a gentle smile on his face. And Danny seemed to be listening. Gone was all the arrogance and the bluster Reed had witnessed on meeting the man earlier. Danny seemed intent on what Horaz was saying, his expression one of concern and respect.

Both men looked up as Reed entered the room.

"Hola," Horaz said, getting up to shake Reed's hand.

"Hey," Reed said, puzzled down to his boots. "What's going on?"

Danny stood then and extended his hand. "I'm

so sorry about April's dad. Horaz was just telling me about him. He sounds like a decent man."

"He is," Reed said, wondering if this night could get any more confusing. "And what are you still doing here?"

Danny raised a hand. "Hey, now, I know I came on a little strong before, but April set me straight. I was wrong to come here, but now that I'm here, well, I can't just leave her. I have to make sure she's okay."

"Do you even care about how she feels?"

"Of course I do," Danny said, sincerity making him look a whole lot younger than Reed had first believed. "I—I just wanted to see if there was any chance—"

"Not a chance," Reed said.

"She told me that." Danny let out a breath. "She's changed. She seemed more sure of herself."

"April has always been very self-assured."

Danny came to stand face to face with Reed. "Now that's where you're wrong. At times, she seemed very insecure to me. And she let me walk all over her. But she didn't do that tonight. Tonight she stood up to me and told me how things are. I thought I could just come in here and get her back with threats and my old condescending routine, but it didn't work this time."

Reed let that soak in, thought seriously about punching the guy, then asked, "And do you understand now? How things are?"

"I think I'm beginning to," Danny said, some of the old smugness coming out again. "It's you, man, all the way. I think it was always you. But, hey, I can't fight all that's going on here. I just didn't want to leave. Not yet."

Reed wanted to toss the man out the door, but how would that make him look? April was already steamed at him. He didn't want to make a scene, not tonight. Danny was right. April had changed, even if Reed still saw her as that beautiful sixteen-year-old socialite. She was stronger now, still determined, still beautiful, but a whole lot more courageous. Or maybe she'd been courageous all along and Reed just hadn't seen it. He'd always thought she'd been a coward for running from their love. But didn't it take courage to do what she'd done? To move across the country to a strange place and start a new life? Didn't it take courage and strength to leave everything and everyone she loved, in order to overcome her father's grief? And her own? She'd had to start over in order to become the best person she could be. But surprisingly, she'd never lost her faith in God in all that time.

Why was that so very clear to him now?

Reed suddenly realized that maybe he'd changed, too. Normally, he would have fought a cad like Danny Pierson with all his might, no questions asked. But in spite of his jumping to conclusions earlier tonight and making April mad at him all over again, Reed had shown restraint. He'd left quietly, if reluctantly.

If only he'd kept the faith, as April had done. He'd never given her the benefit of faith. He'd never actually believed in her. And that was part of the reason she hadn't turned back to him now.

"You want me to go?" Danny asked.

"Sit down," Reed told Danny. "I'm going back to check on her."

Danny sank back down in the chair then glanced over at Horaz. Horaz nodded and lowered his head, silent but sure.

Reed decided Danny was in good hands with Horaz, so he headed toward the back of the house, his footsteps sounding against the tiled floor. He dreaded going into that room, dreaded seeing April and her father. But she needed someone to be there with her. She needed someone to believe in her.

He wanted to be that someone. This time, he wouldn't let her down.

Chapter Fifteen

April stood over her father's grave, the mist of a silent rain falling in a gentle dance all around her. April didn't feel the cool mist or hear the soft rumble of thunder in the distance. She couldn't smell the sweet, clinging scent of so many flowers covered with the tears of rain. She was lost somewhere in the past.

She was remembering all the good times. She'd had a blessed life, growing up here on the Big M. She'd had parents who loved and cherished her. They'd given her the world. Her mother had taught her always to have a life of faith, always to put God first in all things, no matter how privileged their life had been. And even though she'd tried to do that, April had never understood the responsibility that came with vast wealth, or the obligations that came with a deep, abiding faith, until now.

Now, all of this belonged to her. And she didn't know if even her strong faith could sustain her.

She could feel the weight of that responsibility on her shoulders, could hear her mother's laughter, could see her father's brilliant smile.

"What am I supposed to do now, Daddy?" she asked, the chill of the spring day causing her to wrap her arms around herself. "I miss you already. I miss you so much and, now, I miss Mama all over again. I'm all alone."

"No, you're not."

She turned to find Reed standing there with a raincoat and an umbrella, his eyes washing over her in the same misty way the water was washing over the cemetery.

"We missed you back at the house," he said as he stepped forward. "Had a feeling you'd be here."

She turned back to stare down at the flower-covered grave. "I guess everyone thinks I'm incredibly rude."

"They all understand," he said as he draped the coat around her shivering body and held the umbrella over both of them.

He didn't speak again and April thanked him for that, her heart brimming with love for him and this land. If she could just let go enough to accept that love.

Finally, she cleared her throat and pushed away the tears. "Is the house still full?"

"Just the family now," Reed said, one arm holding her steady. "Summer and Autumn are doing a good job with supervising the food and the visitors. They were even nice to Danny before he left. But they were worried about you."

"I just needed some air." Then she sent him a soft smile. "You were nice to Danny, too. Thanks for letting him stay at your house."

"It was interesting—two of your exes talking about old times."

"I guess y'all compared notes?"

"No, I'm just teasing about that. I told him he was welcome to stay as long as he didn't mention anything about your time with him, or ask me anything about you and me now. He understood and he was a perfect gentleman."

"Imagine that. I think this trip has changed him."

"It's changed all of us."

"Yes, I guess it has."

She felt the tug of his hand against the coat. "Remember that verse from Isaiah? 'The grass withers, the flowers fade, but the word of the Lord stands forever'?"

She nodded, thinking these flowers were too beautiful ever to fade. But they would. They would.

"I've always loved that particular verse."

She let out a struggling laugh. "And why are you telling me this?"

He kissed the top of her head. "Just to remind you that some things withstand the test of time. That love surpasses pain and death. I understand that you're scared about a lot of things, but God's love and grace will get us through this, April."

She laid her head on his chest, seeking the warmth and security that he offered. "I know. That's what I keep telling myself. It's just so hard to understand, to accept. We should have had a good life together, my parents and I. I wanted them to see their grandchildren, to live to be very old. I wanted so much for them. Now that will never happen."

"They will see it all, April. They'll be watching over you."

"I have a lot to think about," she said. "Too much to think about."

"Take your time. The Big M is functioning. We all know what needs to be done."

"You've been taking care of things for a long time now, Reed. Thank you for that. And for being there the other night, when…when—"

"Shhh." He kissed her again, a soft whisper against her temple. "I'm not going anywhere."

"Uncle Richard will be a big help," she said, gaining strength with that reassurance. "I'm not so sure about Uncle James. He couldn't wait to leave today. Probably afraid Summer would light into him and her mother, the way she kept glaring at them."

"Yep." Reed became quiet again, then turned her to face him. "April, about the other night when Danny showed up—"

"Look, Reed, I was a bit stressed out that night. I mean, all that with Tomás, then Danny."

"I know. But there is no excuse for how I reacted to Danny Pierson being here. I'm sorry I jumped to the wrong conclusion. I seem to do that, where you're concerned."

"It's water under the bridge," she said. "We've been through worse."

"Yeah, like me always doubting you. I can see now why you bolted and went to New York. It wasn't just about your father's grief. It was because I was smothering and demanding, right? And

I never believed in you enough to show a little faith."

April raised her head to stare over at him. "Reed, none of that matters now."

"Yes, it does. It matters more than ever. I don't want that to happen this time."

April could feel the weight pressing at her heart. "Things are different now. I'm not that young girl who clung to your every word."

"No, ma'am, you are not that. You're a woman. But you're still the only woman I want."

April pulled away, her breath catching in her throat. "I can't think about this right now. I've got so much to consider, so many things to decide."

She watched as Reed stepped back. "Okay. I guess I thought that part had been decided—that you and me belong together."

"Belonging together and *being* together are two different things," she said. "I've got to decide what's best for my future. Do I stay here or go back to New York? I don't know."

She could tell that wasn't what he wanted to hear, but she wasn't going to fight with Reed right here over her father's grave. "Can we talk about this later?" she added.

He nodded, a gentle resolve in his eyes.

"C'mon. You're freezing. Want me to drive you back to the house?"

"I did walk," she said, shaking her head. "I took off before the rain came and I just sort of wound up here."

"We could take the long way home."

She raised an eyebrow. "Oh, yeah?"

"Let's go for a long drive around town."

"That sounds nice. I'm not ready to face everyone back at the house just yet."

"Okay, then. Let's go."

Reed drove his mother's car through Paris, Texas, past the Culbertson Fountain in the historic district. "Did you know this is considered the prettiest plaza in all the state of Texas?" he asked April, hoping to make her laugh.

She did laugh. But she still sat slumped over in her corner of the car. "Well, it *is* lovely."

He drove by the old railroad depot, then on past some of the old homes lining the streets. "This rain is nice. We needed a good rain."

"Yes, I guess we did."

"I called Mom and told her we were going for a drive, so no one would worry about you."

"Thanks."

"Want to see the Market Square Mural? That's always a crowd pleaser."

"Reed, I know what Paris looks like. No need to be my tour guide."

"Sorry. Guess you do remember some of it, even if you never took that fancy convertible of yours for a spin."

"I remember all of it." She smiled over at him. "Remember that summer my mother insisted we have our picture taken in front of the Eiffel Tower—our Eiffel Tower?"

He laughed, hoping she was at last beginning to feel better. "I sure do. She made me wear a red cowboy hat just like the one up on the tower. I think my mom has a copy of that picture somewhere."

"And I had on red boots. My mother wanted to do an abstract—with the picture all black and white, except for the hats and my boots. She said that replica was truly a Texas treasure and that the red hats and boots would represent the heart of Texas and us. And she said that we didn't need Paris, France. Not when we had Paris, Texas."

"Your mother was amazing."

"Yes, she was. So talented."

"You know, I have one of her abstracts hanging in the den at my house."

"Yeah?"

"Uh-huh. When your dad decided to sell me the guest house, he gave that picture to me as a house-warming gift."

"I haven't even seen your house."

"I know. One day, I'll give you the tour."

"One day."

Reed noticed the crape myrtles blooming all over the place. Along the roadsides, the red clover and Indian paintbrush were beginning to spring up. Out in the field, the bluebonnets tipped their heads to the rain.

"It's almost summer," he said. "Lots of work to do."

April sat up and looked over at him. "Stop the car, Reed."

Concerned, he pulled the car over at a small park. "You okay?"

She bobbed her head, then turned to look at him.

"I have to go back, you know."

His heart did a quick thud, then sank down. "To New York, you mean?"

"Yes. I have to take care of some things."

"Is that your way of telling me you won't be back here?"

"I don't know," she said. The honesty in her eyes hurt him. It was too bright, too expectant.

He turned toward her. "April, I know today was hard on you. The funeral, all the people, everything. You've got a lot of burdens to bear, and I don't want to be one of them. If you need to go back to New York, then I guess all I can do is kiss you goodbye."

"Just like that?"

"Just like that. What do you expect me to do, beg you to stay? You know I want that, but only if you want it, too."

"You'd let me go, and not condemn me or resent me?"

"I've never condemned you. I resented that we couldn't be happy together. But happiness has to come with certain sacrifices. I can see that now."

"But Reed, is it fair for you to sacrifice *your* happiness while you wait for me to decide about things?"

"I'm happy. I was happy."

"Until I came back."

He tugged her into his arms. "Listen, I love you. I have always loved you. You can see that. Anybody with two eyes can see that. I can't hide it. But…we've both changed. I've learned to be patient, but I've also learned to be less demanding and more understanding."

"So you won't be angry when I leave again?"

"I'll be hurt, but not angry. I wish…I wish I could just sweep you up and take you home to the life I've always dreamed about us having. But that wouldn't be right. It wouldn't be fair. You had to go away once. And now it's time for you to go away again. We both knew it was coming."

She hugged him close. "I won't neglect the Big M. I promise. I won't let anything happen to the ranch."

Reed held her tight, shutting his eyes to the reality of her leaving him again. "I know you won't. And we'll all be here to help."

"You've always been right here."

"Yes, ma'am." He held back the pain. Was he crazy to hold on to such an uncertain hope? To cling to that dream of having her as his wife? "Maybe it's time for me to throw in the towel, though."

She raised her head. "What does that mean?"

"Maybe it's time for me to accept that you might not feel the same way—about us, I mean."

She touched a finger to his lips. "Don't say that. I can't keep expecting you to wait. But I don't want to lose you, either. I don't know what's wrong with me."

Reed knew what was wrong. "You've just lost your father. You're dealing with so much pain and grief. I won't push you for anything else right now. But when you're ready, I'll be here. Right here. Will you remember that, and…just call me if you need me?"

She fell back into his arms, her tears pouring out like the rain shrouding them inside the car. Reed held her as she cried, the gray of the dreary afternoon turning to the darkness of a rainswept night. He held her and accepted that he might not ever be able to hold her again.

"Hold on, I'm coming."

April ran to the ringing phone, dropping bags as she went. It was one of her co-workers from Satire, wanting to see how she was doing and if she wanted to go out to dinner with the gang. In the couple of weeks she'd been back, she'd had all sorts of invitations.

"Thanks for the offer," April said, her eyes scanning the New York skyline. "But I'm just going to stay in tonight and catch up on some work."

"That's what you tell everyone who calls here," Summer said from the doorway after April hung up. "You should get out more."

April started putting away the groceries she'd

picked up around the corner. "I don't want to go out."

Autumn came out of the bathroom draped in her old terry robe, with a towel on her head. "Did I hear the phone ringing?"

"It was for April," Summer said, making a face. "She declined a fun night on the town, from what I could gather."

"I don't want to go out. End of conversation," April said, annoyed with her well-meaning but overbearing cousins.

"Have you heard from Reed?" Autumn asked as she fixed herself a cup of tea.

"No. And I don't expect to hear from Reed. Why should Reed call me? I left him. Again."

"You didn't leave *him,* technically," Summer pointed out. "You just left Texas. Again."

April turned to face her cousins. "Do y'all ever wish we could just pack up and go home?"

"I knew it," Summer said, stomping her sandal-clad foot. "You *want* to go home, don't you, sugar?"

April sank down on a high stool at the counter. "I think I've finally made up my mind. But I had a little help from a most unlikely source."

"Tell us," Autumn said, getting out two more tea bags and cups.

April pushed at her hair, tugging the silk scarf away from her throat. "Katherine fired me today."

"What?"

"Well, she fired me, then she offered me another position with Satire."

"Katherine is a strange bird," Autumn said, shrugging. "So what kind of other position?"

"Western region director of Satire ready-to-wear. I'd be based in Dallas."

Summer plopped on the couch. "As in Dallas, *Texas?*"

"Yes. That would be the one."

Autumn hopped around the counter. "That would mean you'd be near home, honey! Near—"

"Near Reed," April finished. "I'd be able to work *from* home, according to Katherine. It would involve some traveling and time spent in Dallas, but for the most part, I'd be able to work from the Big M."

Summer twisted her lips, a sign that her mind was racing. "Does Katherine know about this thing between Reed and you?"

"I told her some of it when I got back a couple of weeks ago." She shrugged. "Katherine knew something was wrong. She thought I was just depressed about Daddy, but when I started telling her, everything kind of spilled out."

"I think Katherine is compromising," Autumn said with a practical tone. "She doesn't want to see you go, so she's come up with a way to keep you and let you go home, too."

"Amazing," Summer said.

"Amazing," April repeated.

"Are you going to accept?" Autumn asked.

April sat there, her heart thudding a beat that told her at last she could have it all. "What if I do and…it's too late for Reed and me? I've held him away for so long. I was so afraid. And the funny part is, now I'm not afraid of loving him, but I *am* afraid to tell him that. Because I think I've waited *too* long."

"Oh, I don't think it will ever be too late for that, honey," Summer said. "That man is so in love with you."

"And I love him," April said, thinking the words sounded strange, being said out loud. "I love Reed."

"Well, amen," Summer shouted. "Admitting it is the first step, you know."

"The first step to what?" April asked, still scared silly.

"To being happy," Autumn finished. "Now, why don't you call Reed and tell him?"

"I can't do that yet," April said. "I have to find the courage."

"You could just surprise him and show up," Summer replied.

The thudding in April's heart changed tempo, began a new, hopeful beat. "Maybe I will."

"You ought to just call the woman," Richard said. "It's been over two weeks. Don't you worry about her?"

"Every hour on the hour," Reed admitted.

They were standing near the roping arena, watching one of the hands work with a feisty colt. It was a clear day with a powder-blue sky full of promise.

"I've talked to her, of course," Richard replied, his hands slung over the fence. "I'm kinda keeping things going until she can get back down here."

"Did she say she was coming back anytime soon?"

"I think she'll want to check on things from time to time."

"And that's why I'm not going to call her. I don't like long-distance, time-to-time relationships."

Richard let out a chuckle. "You two cut the

cake, you know that? You dance all around the issue here."

"Oh, and just what is the issue here?"

"That you love that girl and she loves you."

"Then why am I here and why is she there?"

Richard leaned close. "I don't know. But you're a Texan through and through, Reed. And Texans never back down from a fight."

"I don't want to fight with her anymore."

"Then don't. Just go and get her and bring her home."

"It's not that easy."

"How can you say that when you've never even tried?"

Reed stared over at April's uncle, his thudding heart changing tempo. It begin to beat with a little more strength and confidence. "You know, you're right. I've never been to New York City."

Richard slapped him on the arm. "Well, son, I'll fire up the company jet and you can be there by morning."

"Let me just go pack an overnight bag," Reed said. "This time, instead of letting her run away from me, I'm gonna run *to* her."

"Now you're talking."

Richard was right. Maybe if he went after April, she'd finally believe in their love.

* * *

"I need you to meet me by Central Park," Summer said.

April made a face at her cell phone. "Right now?"

"As soon as you can get there. I have a nice surprise for you."

"Summer, I told you I can't do lunch today."

"Just meet me," Summer said, impatience crackling through the line. "It's a beautiful day and you need some sun. And I need to talk to you."

"Where are you?"

"Fifth Avenue and 59th Street, at the fountain."

"Okay, that's not very far. I guess I can make it."

"Good. See you."

April hung up, let out a sigh toward all the files on her desk, then grabbed her purse. Summer seemed so insistent. Wondering what her cousin needed to talk to her about and what the big surprise was, April walked out of the building, then headed toward 59th Street. "This had better be good."

"This is going to be good," Summer told Reed just before she gave him a peck on the cheek. "You were smart to call me first, buddy. Because you know she'd just bolt again if you didn't have the element of surprise on your side."

"Are you sure?" Reed asked, glancing around the busy streets. His hotel was right up the street from April's office, but he'd called the apartment first and talked to Summer. Summer had cooked up this crazy meeting at the park. Now Reed wasn't so sure.

"Trust me," Summer said. "Now, she'll be coming from that way." She waved her hand, her bangle bracelets making a soft medley. "I'm going back to work." She started walking backwards in her high heels. "Don't mess this up, Reed."

Helpless, Reed watched her go, then glanced around the plaza and over at the hills and trees of the park. "Who knew something this big and green could be in a city?"

The fact that he was talking to himself didn't seem to bother the many people passing by. They all looked serious and businesslike, and they mostly ignored him.

So he waited, enjoying the warm sunshine and the blooming flowers and the brilliant summer-new trees.

And then he saw her.

April hurried up the street, her huge baby-blue leather tote bag slung over her arm, her short hair wafting out around her face. She wore a floral print dress with tight, elbow length sleeves and a full skirt that hit just below her knees. And she had on those infernal tall sandals like Summer had been wearing.

She looked so fresh and pretty, Reed had to glance around to make sure he wasn't dreaming.

He waited, watching as she looked toward the park. Watching as her expression changed from purposeful to surprised…to confused…to happy.

Maybe Summer was right. The element of surprise seemed to be working.

"Reed?" she said as she hurried across the intersection separating them. "How—"

"Don't ask," he said as he pulled her into his arms. "Just don't ask."

She didn't. She hugged him tight. "Can I ask *why,* then?"

"Because I love you," he said as he held her away. "Because I decided it was time for me to do the running." He kissed her forehead. "I've never gone chasing after a woman, and since you're the only woman I've ever wanted…well, here I am."

"You came for me." It was a statement filled with wonder and endearment. "You came here, for me?"

"Yes, ma'am. Why else would I be standing in the middle of Manhattan in the middle of May?"

"I was coming back, you know."

"Really, now?"

"Yes. I have a new job, in Dallas. I can work from home."

"And where would home be?"

"The Big M, with you."

"So I could have spared myself this trip to the Big Apple?"

"Oh, no. Seeing you here, well, that seals the deal. Now I know you really do love me."

"You doubted that?"

"No, but you doubted me. You coming here, I think it means you don't doubt me anymore."

"No, I don't."

"Good, because I'm not afraid anymore. I love you," she said.

Reed's heart beat faster with each impatient car horn, with each tread of feet against asphalt. "I love you, too."

"Want to go home now?"

"Not just yet," he said, holding her face in his hands.

"I want to see the rest of this big park. And your city."

"I'll be glad to show it to you. And then we can go home. Together."

"Together," he said. He kissed her, the certain hope of their love coloring his world with blessings and thankfulness.

* * * * *

Dear Reader,

Death is never easy to accept, but it is a part of life. As Christians, we are taught that this life is just a part of eternity. We know that a better life is still to come. But still, we weep when we lose a loved one. So we have to keep the faith and hold fast to that certain hope that will bring us eternal life.

April had to learn this lesson as she watched her father dying. She also had to learn that sometimes the things we fear the most are the very things that we need the most. She needed Reed's love, but she was afraid to embrace that love. She didn't want to be hurt. Reed was steadfast and strong, but he wanted her on his own terms. Together, they had to move toward a faith of things hoped for. They found that hope in their love for each other.

My hope for you is that your faith will always be strong enough to get you through the worst of times, and that it will bring you comfort and strength in all things.

Until the next time, may the angels watch over you always.

Lenora Worth

A PERFECT LOVE

There is no fear in love,
but perfect love casts out fear.
—1 *John* 4:18

To my niece, Jessica Smith, with lots of love.

Chapter One

This wasn't the best place in the world to have a breakdown, either in one's car or one's life.

Summer Maxwell was having both, however.

Wanting to say words her grandmother wouldn't appreciate, Summer kicked the front right tire of her late-model sportscar, then let out a frustrated groan as she looked up and down the lonely Texas back road. A sign a few feet from her car stated Athens, 9 Miles.

So close, yet still so far away.

"I just had to *drive* all the way home from New York, didn't I?" she shouted to the hot, humid wind. "And I just had to do it in this pitiful excuse for an automobile."

Summer eyed the faded red of the twenty-year-old Jaguar, wondering why she'd never bothered to buy a new car. Maybe because this one had belonged to her father at one time, and maybe because that was a connection she wasn't ready to give up, even if it wasn't always pleasant.

James Maxwell had given his only daughter the car when she'd graduated from high school, his silky, charming words making the deal all the more sweet since he'd missed the graduation ceremony. "Daddy wants you to have this one, honey. I'm getting me a brand-new Porsche. And your mama, she doesn't want this one. Guess that means I'll be buying her a Cadillac soon."

"Yeah, you sure did buy Mama a new set of wheels," Summer muttered as the gloaming of another hot Texas day brought a cool wisp of breeze floating over her. And James Maxwell hadn't even bothered to wish his daughter well as she headed off to college with her cousins, April and Autumn. No, her father hadn't bothered with much at all regarding his daughter. Maybe because he'd wanted a son so badly, to carry on the glory days of his rodeo career.

"Sorry, Daddy," Summer said now and wondered why she always felt it necessary to apologize for everything.

Her parents were globe-trotters, too tied up in each other and her father's rodeo and oil-industry endorsements to worry about their rebellious daughter. So they'd dumped her on her mother's parents for most of her life, while they enjoyed the good life that came with being oil- and cattle-rich Maxwells.

"I'm almost there, Memaw," Summer said as she lifted the hot hood of the car, then backed away as a damp mist of smoke poured over her. "Must be the radiator again."

Wishing she hadn't been so stubborn about *not* flying, or about *not* taking her cousin Autumn's sensible sedan, Summer looked up and down the long road. She could call her grandfather on her cell, get him to come and pick her up. That is, if her cell would even work in these isolated piney woods.

"Or I could walk," she reasoned. "Maybe physical activity would keep me from having that breakdown I so richly deserve."

Grabbing her aged baseball-glove-leather tote bag from the passenger's seat of the convertible, Summer tried her cell. Low power and even lower battery. No surprise there.

"Okay, I guess I get to walk nine miles along this bug-infested highway. Nice, Summer, real nice."

She was about to put up the worn black top of

the car and lock it, when she heard a truck rumbling along the highway.

"Oh, great. Let's hope you are a kind soul," she said into the wind. "'I have always relied upon the kindness of strangers,'" she quoted from Tennessee Williams.

And let's pray you aren't some psycho out on the loose. Not that she couldn't handle herself. She was armed with pepper spray and a whole arsenal of self-defense courses. She'd learned all about how to protect herself, working as a counselor to battered women at a New York City YWCA for the past five years.

She'd also learned all about the dark, evil side of life working there, too. Which was why she was now stranded on this road. Everyone she knew in New York, including her cousins and her immediate supervisor, had agreed it was time for Summer to take a vacation.

Burned out. Stressed out. Angry. Bitter.

Those were the words they'd used to describe her.

And that didn't even begin to touch the surface.

Summer took a long breath, tried to imagine a peaceful scene somewhere in the tired recesses of her mind, while she waited for the old truck to pull up beside her. But somehow, she didn't believe deep breathing would get her through this acute, aching depression.

And neither would God, she decided.

Then she looked up and saw her rescuer.

He was young, probably only a few years older than Summer's twenty-seven years. He was pretty in a rugged, rough-cut way. He had vivid gray-blue eyes that flashed like heat lightning. And he had crisp, curly light-brown hair that seemed to be rebelling against the humidity.

Warning flares went off in Summer's weary mind like fireworks on the Fourth of July.

Putting the rickety old truck into Park, he said, "Need some help?"

Summer decided that was an understatement, but she hid that behind what she hoped was a serene smile. "Kinda looks that way, doesn't it?"

"Want me to look under the hood?"

"No need," she said, ignoring the homesick delight his Texas drawl caused along her skin. "It's the radiator. Probably finally busted for good."

He got out and walked to the raised hood anyway. Since he was a man, Summer figured he didn't trust her word on car maintenance. Had to see it for himself. Probably thought just because she was a blonde, that she didn't have any brain cells. Never mind that she had been a double major in college. No need for this handsome interloper to know that just yet.

He turned and wiped his hands down the sides of his worn jeans. "Yep, looks like you're right. It's too hot to even touch right now."

Summer noted his solid build and laid-back swagger. "I told you so," she said with a hint of sarcasm to hide the hint of interest she had in him.

He ignored the sarcasm, his gaze filled with his own interest. "Where you headed?"

"Athens." She didn't feel the need to give him any more information.

"I live there," he said. Then he extended his hand. "Mack Riley."

"Summer Maxwell," she said, taking his hand and enjoying the strength of his touch a little too much.

He pulled his hand away with a quick tug, making her wonder if he'd felt that little bit of awareness, too. "Summer?"

"Yes," she said, thinking she saw recognition in his beautiful eyes.

"Pretty name." He hesitated, then said, "And just who are you visiting in Athens?"

"My grandparents," she replied, mystified by his suddenly odd behavior. "I wanted to surprise them."

"Oh, I reckon they'll be surprised, all right,"

he said as he shut the car's hood. "Who are your grandparents? I might know them."

"Jesse and Martha Creswell," Summer said, thinking he probably did know them. Everybody knew just about everybody else in the small town of Athens, Texas.

He stepped back, gave her a look that shouted confusion and surprise. "Well, how 'bout that."

"You know them?" she asked, echoing her thoughts.

"I sure do," he replied. "Good people. C'mon, I'll give you a ride into town, then we'll send a tow truck to get your car."

"I'd appreciate that," Summer said, sending up a prayer that he wasn't dangerous. She knew better than to get in a car with a complete stranger, but he seemed normal, and he knew her grandparents. But just to test that theory, she put her hands on her hips and asked, "Will I be safe with you?"

He laughed, shook his head. "I'm not on any Top Ten Most Wanted List, if that's what you mean."

Oh, but he could be on a Top Ten Hunk list, Summer decided. His smile was criminal in its beauty.

"Okay," she retorted as she started locking up the car. "I just had to be sure. 'Cause my grand-daddy, he shoots first and asks questions later."

"I hear that," he said, helping her to latch the convertible top. "I do believe Jesse would have my hide if I let anything happen to you."

"So how well *do* you know my grandparents?"

"I met them when I first moved here."

Why did she get the feeling he was being evasive? Maybe because he wouldn't look her in the eyes. And maybe because she'd learned not to trust people on first impressions.

"Am I missing something here?" she asked, determination causing her to dig in her heels.

"Do you have suitcases?" he asked back, misunderstanding the question, maybe on purpose.

"Oh, yes, I do." She unlocked the trunk.

He laughed as he looked down at the beat-up brown leather duffel bag. "How'd you ever get that in this poor excuse for a trunk?"

"You'd be surprised just how much this trunk can hold."

He nodded, grabbed the considerably heavy bag without even a huff of breath, then tossed it in the back of his truck. "Well, I guess that's it then."

"I guess so," she said as she rounded the truck to get in. Once he was all settled behind the wheel, Summer stood at her open door, glaring at him. "Except the part you're leaving out."

He lifted his brow. "Excuse me?"

"You're not telling me the whole story here, are you, Mr. Riley? And I'm not going anywhere with you until you do."

"Call me Mack," he replied, a look of resolve coloring his eyes. He cranked the truck, motioned toward the seat. "And I don't understand what you're talking about."

Summer had learned all about deceit on the streets of New York, from working with women who lived through the worst kind of deception and deprivation. She could smell it a mile away. "I think you know more about my grandparents than you're telling me. And I want to hear the truth, all of it."

He let out a long sigh, as if he didn't know how to handle such a direct statement. "I said I know them. Can't that be enough for now?"

"Nope," Summer replied, smiling sweetly. "You might not be dangerous or a wanted man, but you're being mighty quiet about my grandparents. And I want to know why."

He looked up and down the long road, then nodded. "I guess you deserve an explanation. Get in and I'll give you one, I promise."

Mack Riley stared over at the assertive, no-nonsense woman sitting in his truck. She was a looker, no doubt about that. He'd heard enough about Summer Maxwell to know, though, that all that long blond hair and those bright-blue eyes couldn't hide the fact that she was also very intelligent and sharp.

Too sharp. And right now, not too trusting, either.

What was he supposed to tell the woman? That he knew her grandparents on a first-name basis. That he also knew her rich, jet-setting parents, through conversations with Jesse and Martha, and through having met them on the rare occasions they decided to drop in and check on Summer's grandparents. That he recognized her now, from the many pictures of her growing up that Martha had displayed in her living room. And that he knew enough about Summer herself to fill a book and his own needy imagination.

Mack wasn't ready to open up and have a heart-to-heart with this intriguing woman. Not yet. So he did what he'd always been so very good at doing. He tried to avoid the issue.

"I'm waiting," Summer said, causing him to glance over at her.

He tried to deflect that in-your-face-look. "Honestly, I don't know what to say, or where to begin.

Okay, I do know your folks—real well. Is that a crime?"

"Oh, no," she said, folding her arms as she stared at him. "The crime would be in you withholding information from me. And I think you are. You said you'd explain things. So start talking. Just tell me—is one of them sick? Has something happened, something terrible, that I don't know about?"

Mack made a turn onto yet another long highway. "They're both just fine," he said. "But…a lot has happened over the last few months. When was the last time you talked to them?"

"I saw them at Uncle Stuart's funeral," Summer replied, her blue eyes going dark. "They invited me to come home for a visit. I told them I'd think about it. I did, and so here I am."

"That funeral was over two months ago," he said, reasoning that she might not know all that had happened since then after all.

"Yes. But they both seemed fine, in good health. Of course, we were all upset about Uncle Stuart."

"So you didn't call ahead, to let them know you were coming?"

She squirmed a bit. "No. I didn't want them to

worry since I decided to drive across the country. I wanted to take my time, do a little sightseeing."

Mack got the feeling she hadn't noticed the scenery on her long trip home. Maybe she'd just needed some down time.

He could understand that.

"Well, they'll be surprised, that's for sure."

Then he witnessed some of that famous temper Martha had told him about.

"Listen, mister, I'm getting very bad vibes here. You're scaring me. If there's something I need to know about my grandparents, good or bad, then you'd better spit it out."

Mack stopped the truck in front of the old two-story white farmhouse that had been the Creswell home for many years.

Summer looked up at the house. "Oh, we're here."

"Yes," he said, hating to be the one to break the news to her. "But…there is something you need to know."

"I knew it," she said, her expression grim. "Something bad *has* happened, right?"

Mack looked at the house, then back to Summer Maxwell, deciding he'd have to be up front with her. There was just no other way. "Depends on how you look at things," he said, his fingers tapping on the steering wheel.

"Because?"

"Because, well, Summer, your grandparents no longer own this house."

"What?" She opened the door of the truck and ran around to stand in the tree-lined yard, her gaze moving from him to the house and back. "What do you mean?" she asked as she turned and stomped back to him.

Mack got out of the truck, dread filling his heart. "I mean, your grandparents decided to sell out and move. Your dad bought them this fancy patio apartment in a new retirement village about a mile up the road."

"He did what?" Summer shouted, her vivid eyes flashing a fire that only added to her obviously fiery nature. "I can't believe this! He sold their *home?* How could he do that? Memaw and Papaw have lived here for over fifty years."

"I know," Mack said, wishing he could soften this news for her. "I know all about this house."

"Oh, yeah. And how come you know so much about all of this?"

Mack glanced at the house, then down at his scuffed work boots. Then he lifted his head and looked straight into Summer's fighting-mad blue eyes.

"Because I own it now," he said. "Your daddy sold this house and the surrounding land to me."

Chapter Two

Summer blinked. "I'm sorry. I don't think I heard you right? Did you say *you* own this house now?"

Mack Riley nodded, shifted his feet, let out a long sigh. "I bought it fair and square about a month ago."

Summer blew at the wispy bangs slanting across her face, one hand on her hip as she wondered whether just to let him have it and get it over with, or wait and attack her father instead. "Fair and square? *Fair and square?* Yeah, I'll just bet my father sold it to you fair and square. How in the world did he get them to agree to this?"

Mack stepped closer, holding his hands out palms up, as if to protect himself. Which wasn't a bad idea right now, by Summer's way of thinking. "Your grandparents seem happy with the arrangement. In case you haven't noticed, this house is old and in great need of repair, and…well, your grandparents are in about the same shape."

She advanced. "And just who are you to be telling me about my own grandparents?"

He stepped closer, no fear in his eyes. More like defiance and that resolve she'd seen earlier. Which only made Summer even more mad.

"I'll tell you who I am," he said. "I'm about the only one around here who does know about your grandparents. You see, I talk to them on pretty much a daily basis. Your father and mother call every now and then, and you…well, you said yourself you haven't seen them or talked with them since your uncle's funeral. So that leaves me. And believe me, I think they are better off in that retirement village. At least there, they're among friends and near qualified people who can help them."

Summer couldn't believe he was standing here preaching to her! "Oh, well, excuse me. Since you obviously know so very much about my shortcomings, and since you are such a saint for watching over my grandparents, I guess that gives you every right to just bully them out of their home."

"I didn't bully anybody," he retorted, his voice low and full of frustration. "I liked the house and knew it was where I wanted to live. So I bought it."

"Fair and square, of course."

"Yes. I made them a good offer and they took it. It's that simple."

Summer stomped to the truck to get her duffel bag. "Oh, there is nothing simple about this. This…this isn't right. But then, I should have known a man in cahoots with my wayward father wouldn't understand the implications of something so horrible."

"Hey, hold on," Mack said, taking the bag right out of her hand with surprising ease. "I'm not in cahoots with anyone. I just moved here and needed a place to live. So I bought this house from your father. End of story."

Summer tapped her platform sneaker against the aged wooden steps of the house, her blood boiling just like the radiator on her car had been doing earlier. She could almost feel the hot steam coming out of her ears. "Oh, I think there is much more to this story, and I intend to find out the whole truth."

Such as, how had her father become the spokesperson for her grandparents, and if the house was in such bad repair, why hadn't James Maxwell forked over the funds to renovate his in-laws' home? It just didn't make any sense. But lately, nothing much in her life had made any sense.

She turned and headed to the house, then stopped, hitting a palm to her forehead. "Silly me. I can't stay here *now*. Not with you." Then she plopped down on the steps and looked up at him. "I don't have anywhere to go."

Mack had never seen a more dejected sight. A beautiful, uptown blonde in worn jeans and strange shoes, sitting on the broken steps of a hundred-year-old farmhouse, her eyes brilliant with tears she refused to shed, her expression bordering on outrage, and...her hands trembling slightly as she dropped them over her knees.

All of his protective instincts surfaced, reminding him that he'd come here to find some peace and quiet, not get tangled up in a family squabble. But he had to help her, even if she was fighting mad at him, and the world in general. If for no other reason than to get her off his doorstep.

Thinking she didn't look so bad sitting there, however, he said, "Look, you know there's plenty of room in the house."

"I can't stay here with you," she repeated, gritting the words between her clenched teeth. "First, I'd rather eat nails than do that, and second, this is a small, old-fashioned town. I wouldn't want my grandparents to hear any rumors."

"I admire your stand," Mack said, daring to sit down on the bottom step. "But even if you did want to stay here, the house is being renovated. There's very little furniture and the plumbing is barely working. I'm not even living here full-time myself right now. How about you get a room at that motel out on the highway?"

"How about that?" she said, hitting her hand on her knee. "Great, just great. I look forward to a visit home and I get to stay in some fleabag motel. That should help my burnout and stress level a lot."

Mack could recognize all the signs of her type-A personality. She was a live one. And she looked just about ready to explode into a doozy of a meltdown. The dark circles under her pretty eyes only reminded him of a time when he'd felt the same way. But he sure didn't know how to help her. Or maybe he was just afraid to help her.

Then Mack lifted his head and glanced over at her. "Hey, what about your parents' house? They're in Mexico, last I heard. Won't be home all summer."

Summer groaned, laid her head in her hands. "Go to my parents' house? Oh, that's just peachy.

I hate that overblown facade of a house. All that modern art and fake-rustic country-French charm? Like I want to stay at that overpriced country club of a house!"

"It's a nice house," Mack said, thinking it had probably set her parents back a cool million, at least. "And it's safe—"

"Oh, I know all about the gated community and the exclusive homeowner's policy, and the golf course and the country club. My mother fairly gushed about it…last time I bothered to talk to her."

"What is it with you and not talking to your relatives?"

She laughed, the sound bubbling up in her throat like a fresh waterfall hitting rock. "I guess my grandparents didn't let you in on all the family history, after all. We're a bit…estranged, my parents and me."

"Oh, yeah? And why is that?"

Summer pushed at the thick blond hair cascading around her face and shoulders. "Oh, I don't know. Maybe because they never had any time for me when I was growing up, so now I make it a point never to make any time for them." Then she gave him a hard glare. "And besides, that's none of your business."

He knew he was heading into deep water, but he didn't get it. "Your parents seem like nice folks. The times I've been around them—which is few, I'll admit—they seem to be happy and fun-loving. I wish I had their kind of carefree energy."

She gave him a harsh frown. "And I wish they'd use some of that fun-loving, happy, carefree energy on staying in one place. Just once, I wish they'd settle down and actually notice that they have a daughter."

"You have issues, don't you?"

"More than you can imagine, buddy."

"So what are you gonna do?"

She kept staring at him long enough to allow Mack plenty of time to get caught up in the blue of her eyes. "I want to see my grandparents, make sure this is really what they wanted."

"It is, I promise."

She jumped up, pointed a finger in his face. "I don't believe in promises, understand? I've been promised so many things that didn't work out, it's sickening."

"Well, I keep my promises, and I'm telling you, Jesse and Martha are doing better than ever."

"I need to see them," she said again, her voice going all soft and husky. "I can't explain things with my parents—it's a long story and it's something I have to come to terms with. But…I can tell you that I love my grandparents, and I came home to see them. So can I please just do that, go and see them?"

That gentle plea melted Mack's defenses with all the slow-moving force of butter meeting honey on a biscuit, and he knew he was a goner. "Want me to take you to Golden Vista?" At her puzzled, raised-eyebrow expression, he added, "The retirement community where your grandparents live."

"Golden Vista? That just sounds depressing."

"It's a nice place. I think your father invested heavily in—"

Summer shot around him, her long-nailed fingers flailing out into the air. "Oh, I get it now. My father invested in this fancy retirement home, so he's just making sure he covers his assets, right? By forcing my mother's parents to go and *live* there? He just gets lower than a snake's belly with every passing day."

Mack didn't know how to deal with so much bitterness and anger spewing from such a sweet-looking mouth. Although there was a time when he'd been the same way, he reminded himself. But not anymore. "I don't think—"

"I'm not asking you to think," she countered. "Just give me a ride to this…Grim Reaper Vista."

"It's Golden Vista," he said, hiding a grin behind a cough. At least she was entertaining—in a Texas twister kind of way.

"Whatever. Just get me to my grandparents. I'll handle things from there."

Mack could only imagine how this bundle of blond dynamite would handle things.

Not very well, from the looks of her. There was sure to be a whole lot of fallout and carnage left along her pretty, pithy path.

Just one more thing for him to worry about.

One more thing he really didn't need to be worrying about right now.

"So this is Golden Vista?"

At Mack's nod, Summer looked around at the rows and rows of compact wood and brick apartments set against the gentle, rolling hills of East Texas. "It looks like some cookie-cutter type of torture chamber or prison."

Mack grinned over at her, which only made her fold her arms across her waist in defiance. She didn't want to like him. In fact, she refused to like him. He was the enemy.

"It's not a torture chamber and it's certainly not a prison," he said as he guided the truck up a tree-shaded drive. "The residents here aren't in a nursing home. It's called a retirement village. It's a community, completely self-contained. And very secure. It has lots of benefits for people like your grandparents, looking for a place to retire."

"I'll just bet. Retired, as in, shuffleboard in the morning and bingo in the afternoon. My grandparents are probably bored to tears!"

"I'm telling you, they love it," Mack replied. "They can come and go as they please, and Jesse and Martha do just that. They have a new car—"

"Courtesy of my generous father, I reckon?"

"Uh, yes. It's a sturdy sedan."

"And I guess they just love it, too, right?"

"They seem to. I see them gallivanting all over town in it."

"My grandparents do not gallivant."

"Oh, yes, they do."

"Oh, that's right. I forgot you know more about their lifestyle than I do, because I haven't bothered to keep up with them."

"That about tells it like it is," he said, but he held up a hand at her warning glare. "Look, as you so sweetly pointed out, it's none of my business, your relationship with your folks. I can only tell you what I've seen in the last few weeks since I moved here. They were lonely and they're getting on in years. That farmhouse is kind of isolated out there on the edge of town. I've visited them several times since I moved into the house, just to let them see how the renovations are coming along, and they seem very content at Golden Vista."

"I can't picture that," Summer said, remembering how her grandfather loved to plant a big garden, just so he could give his crop away to half of Henderson County. And her grandmother—she loved to cook and quilt, can vegetables and sew pillows, make clothes and crafts. How could she do all those things cooped up in some cracker box of an apartment?

Summer dropped her head into her hand. "I just have to talk to them."

Mack stopped the truck, then pointed toward a huge, park-like courtyard in the middle of the complex. "Well, there they are, right over there."

Summer looked up to find a large group of senior citizens milling around in Hawaiian shirts and straw hats. Tiki torches burned all around the festive courtyard, while island music played from a loudspeaker. The smell of grilled meat hit the air, reminding her she hadn't eaten since breakfast.

"What in the world?"

"It's a luau," Mack said. "They have these theme parties once a month. Last month, it was Texas barbecue, and I think next month is Summer Gospel Jam—"

"I've heard enough," Summer said, opening the rickety truck door with a knuckle-crunching yank. "I'm going to get to the bottom of this mess."

"Yes, ma'am," Mack said, his grin widening.

"Do you find this humorous?" Summer asked as they met in front of the truck.

"Kinda," he said, then he turned more serious.

Probably because she had murder in her eyes. "I'd advise you to stop grinning."

He did. "You don't like change, do you?"

She lifted a brow. "I can handle change just fine, thank you. What I don't like is when people manipulate my perfectly respectable, God-fearing grandparents. Especially when it's my own parents."

"I don't think they were manipulated," Mack said as he pulled her toward the feisty-looking group of old people. "I think they just got tired of the upkeep on the house and farm, and they decided to relax and have some fun."

"It's just horrible," Summer retorted, not buying his explanation at all. "You're laughing about a situation I find very serious."

"Well, maybe you just take things way *too* seriously."

She stopped, blocking his way toward the party. "My poor, hardworking grandparents are trapped in this...this one-foot-in-the-grave travel stop. And I refuse to believe—"

"Summer? Is that my sweet baby, Summer?"

Summer stopped in midsentence, then turned to stare at the stout woman running...well, gently jogging...toward her. "Memaw?"

"It's me, suga'. Land's sake, we didn't know you were coming for a visit. C'mere and give your old granny a good hug."

Summer took in the hot-pink flamingoes posed across the wide berth of her grandmother's floral muumuu, took in the bright yellow of the shiny plastic lei draping her memaw's neck, then glanced down at her grandmother's feet.

"Memaw, are you wearing kitten-heeled flip-flops?"

"Ain't they cute?" Martha Creswell said as she enveloped Summer in a hug that only a grand-mother could get away with. "And take a look at my pedicure," she said as she wrapped her arms around Summer. "My toenails are sparkling—Glistening Party Pink, I think the beautician called it."

Her grandmother's tight-gripped hug just about smothered Summer, but the sweet, familiar scent of Jergens lotion caused tears to brim in Summer's eyes. She pulled away to smile down at her petite grandmother. "Oh, Memaw, what have they done to you?"

"Not a thing," Martha replied, laughing out loud. "Honey, I'm fine, just fine. But wait until you see your grandpa, sugar. He's been on that new diet, don't you know. Trim and slim and wired for action."

"Wired for action? Papaw?" Summer had a bad feeling about this whole setup. A very bad feeling.

Chapter Three

Summer looked her grandmother over from head to toe. Martha Creswell looked healthy and happy. Memaw had always been on the voluptuous side, but now she fairly glowed with energy and good health.

"Have you been taking your blood pressure medicine, Memaw?"

Martha patted her on the arm. "Of course, darling. But the doctor tells me I'm doing better than ever." Then she held up her arm like a weight lifter. "Pumping iron and water aerobics. I've lost fat and gained muscle."

Summer wondered at that, but she couldn't argue with her grandmother. Before she could pose another question, Martha pulled her along. "I see you've met Mack here." Then Martha stopped in midstride, causing her colorful muumuu to pool around her legs. "Oh, my. That means you know about the house."

Summer held her grandmother's arm. "Yes, I had to hear about it from *him*." She shot a scowl toward Mack. "Why didn't y'all let me know?"

Martha shook her head. "It happened kind of fast—"

Summer interrupted her with a loud hiss of breath. "I knew it. Daddy pressured y'all, didn't he?"

Martha looked confused. "Well, no, not really—"

"Summer, my little pea blossom!"

The loud voice announcing her grandfather caused Summer to whirl around and brace herself for another hug. "Papaw!"

Summer took in the Hawaiian shirt and khaki Bermuda shorts, the stark white socks and strappy leather sandals, just before her grandfather picked her up off her feet and whirled her around.

"It is so good to see you, suga'."

Her breath cut off, Summer settled back on her feet to look up at her lovable grandfather. "Papaw, what's going on here?"

He waved a hand in the air. "A luau. You hungry?"

Tears misted in Summer's eyes. That wasn't exactly what she'd meant. "Yes, but—"

"Then come on over here and let's get you a plate. We got grilled pork and chicken, and fruit and vegetables for miles—most from my garden out back—"

"You still have a garden?"

Martha piped up as they escorted Summer toward the curious crowd. "He sure does. Everyone here calls your Papaw the Garden King. He's in charge of the garden for the whole village. Came in and took over the one they had planted. Made that puny garden spring right to life."

"That's nice," Summer said, raising her eyebrows at Mack Riley's triumphant I-told-you-so smile. "I'm glad you still have that, at least."

Her grandmother stopped right before they headed into the throng of vivid floral polyester and orthopedic shoes. "Honey, we've got lots to tell you, but that can all wait until later. Right now, I want you to meet some of our friends here at Golden Vista. We just love it here."

Summer blinked back her tears. "I'm glad, Memaw."

But she wasn't so glad. She was fast going into sensory overload, her unresolved resentment at her parents ever-building inside her tired, steamed bones. Since the night she'd broken things off with Brad, she'd longed to be back here in Athens, at home, safe in the house she'd loved all her life, with the grandparents who'd taken her in without questions or judgment and given her unconditional love.

She'd suffered right along with April back in the spring, when April's father, Stuart Maxwell, had passed away, and Summer was still feeling the effects of that and her ugly breakup with Brad Parker. Uncle Stuart had always been larger than life and so much a part of Summer's world, that her grief had been overwhelming at times. But, she reminded herself as she took in the colorful decorations and the festive tiki-themed party plates and cups, her cousin April was happy now. Happy in Paris, Texas, near Reed Garrison, the man she'd always loved. They were getting married in September.

Reed, who'd always been the boy next door, would soon be April's husband. And April would be moving into his house. They had grand plans for the Big M Ranch. They were going to turn it into some sort of vacation resort, because April wanted it to be filled with happy people, and she also wanted to honor her mother by showcasing her artwork there. The Big M certainly would make a lovely, peaceful vacation spot, but even that was changing way too fast for Summer to comprehend.

Summer wanted to be happy for her cousin, but lately, she'd been in a blue fog of regret and resentment, causing even her best intentions to go sour.

Which was why she'd taken this leave of absence to drive home. She'd needed some time to think about her life. In spite of the stress of her job, she didn't like feeling bitter and resentful all the time. She wanted to be happy again.

But now she had to worry about her grandparents.

And *him,* of course.

The man who'd stepped in and bought her grandparents' home right out from under them.

She cast a glance toward Mack Riley, trying to stay unaware of his rugged, craggy good looks and his gentle, smiling gray-blue eyes. But she was very aware, because the man looked at her with all the intensity of a lone wolf out on the prowl. A wounded wolf, she decided.

How she knew this, Summer couldn't picture. But she could almost see that something inside him that drew her to him. She'd seen that look in enough hurting people in the city. And it reflected that empty, unsettled spot deep inside her own soul.

"So you met Mack?" her grandfather said, echoing her grandmother's earlier question. "A good man, this one. Salt of the earth."

"Yes, we met," Mack said, answering for both of them. "Summer wanted to see you two right away, though."

"That's so nice of you, to drive her over here, Mack," her grandmother said, her smile beaming with maternal pride and matchmaking sparks. "Wasn't that nice of him, Summer?"

Summer didn't comment. She couldn't. She felt a huge suffocating lump in her throat. Mack was right. She didn't like change. Not at all. And she certainly didn't like being put on the spot. She was spinning out of control, and she suddenly felt lost and all alone.

This was too much, all at once, out of the blue like this. She wanted to go back, way back, to her childhood. To her room on the second floor of that old house. To frilly pink curtains blowing in the wind, to the fresh smell of line-dried sheets and gardenias from her grandmother's garden beside the back door, to the secure knowledge that they'd have biscuits and gravy and fried chicken for dinner, and some sort of fresh fruit cobbler for dessert on Sunday, right after church. She wanted to go back to family picnics down by the stream, and her grandparents laughing and each holding one of her hands as they walked down the dirt lane toward the blackberry bushes and the plum trees.

But she couldn't go back.

Summer looked up as Mack came to stand beside her. "Are you okay with all of this?" he asked, his eyes gentle and seeking.

"Do I look okay?" she managed, her voice grainy and strained, her eyes burning with tears she wouldn't shed.

"You look just fine. Maybe a bit tired and travel-weary."

She let out a struggling laugh. "I am that. Travel-weary. Very travel-weary."

Martha heard her comment. "Well, you're home now, darling. You're home and you're safe."

Summer almost did cry then, but the look of sympathy in Mack Riley's eyes stopped her cold. She wouldn't have that nervous breakdown today, after all. Instead, she flared her nostrils. "Where's the beef?"

Martha pushed Summer toward three very curious women who'd been watching them. "Summer, I want you to meet Lola, Cissie and Pamela. Lola is our director here at Golden Vista. Cissie is her administrative assistant and office manager and Pamela is our activities coordinator."

"So wonderful to meet you," blond-haired Lola said, extending her hand to Summer. "Your family has done so much for Golden Vista."

"Yes," Cissie said, her short red hair glistening in the sun. "We just love your grandparents. And your parents are always so helpful when they come to visit."

"Really?" Summer asked, surprised to hear that.

"Oh, they love to cart the residents around," Pamela answered, her blue eyes twinkling. "They take them all over. Road trips, shopping excursions."

"Well, you just never know," Summer replied, amazed that her parents even bothered.

"C'mon, now," her grandfather said, tugging her toward the table full of food. "You need to eat more."

"But ain't she still as pretty as a summer day?" Martha asked, her gaze trained with glee on Mack.

Mack lifted his chin. "Is that how she got her name?"

Martha nodded. "It suits her, don't you think?"

"Perfectly," Mack said, his eyes locking with Summer's.

Summer suddenly lost her appetite.

* * *

Mack couldn't eat another bite. These fun-loving senior citizens kept filling his plate with piles of food, and he gratefully ate every morsel, maybe because he had a lot of nervous energy and eating seemed to help curb that, maybe because he couldn't stop staring at Summer Maxwell, and wondering what would happen next with this volatile, intriguing woman.

Who knew she'd be so…pretty.

Summer had the look of a leggy California blonde, but she had the brash nature of a purebred Texan. She wasn't going to take anything lightly. Especially him moving into her grandparents' house.

Mack wanted to explain things to her, but he held back. It probably wouldn't matter anyway. Once he had her settled, wherever she decided to land, he wouldn't have any excuses for seeing her again. She'd visit with her folks, get some rest, then go back to her life in New York.

He'd certainly heard all about that life from her grandparents. A loft apartment with her two cousins in Tribeca, a stressful job as a social worker at one of the toughest YWCAs in the city, a social life that went bad more than it turned out good.

He still remembered Martha's words to him just last week.

"Pray for my granddaughter, Mack. Summer is hurting so much and I can't get through to her. She needs to remember to lean on the Lord, but she thinks everyone has let her down, even God. My daughter Elsie, she doesn't understand Summer the way I do. Those two are as different as night and day."

Night and day. Maybe that's how he and Summer would be, too. Two very different people forced together under awkward circumstances. She'd never forgive him for buying Jesse and Martha's house. He'd never be able to make her see that he'd needed a place to heal because he'd been let down a lot, too.

Summer found a quiet spot away from the party. Pulling out her cell phone, she checked to see if she had any messages. None. Quickly, Summer text-messaged her cousin Autumn in New York.

U won't believe. GPs in retirement home. No house. Not sure what 2 do now.

She hit Send and let out a sigh.
"What are you doing?"

Summer whirled to find Mack Riley leaning on a gazebo post, his cool gray-blue eyes trained on her.

Finding a bravado she didn't feel, Summer tossed her phone back in her tote and said, "I'm checking for messages, not that it's any of your business."

"Okay then." He turned to go, his hands up in the air.

"Wait," she said, regretting her rude nature. "I'm sorry. Look, it's just been a long day and I'm really tired."

"Want me to take you home?"

She raised her brows. "And where would that be?"

He shrugged, gave her a smile that made little flares of awareness shoot off in her system. "You have several choices."

"Really?"

"Yeah. You can go to your parents' home. You can stay here in one of the guest apartments they keep for family, or I can stay here in an apartment and…you can have the house, keeping in mind, of course, that the house is barely livable right now. But you could sleep there at least."

Summer felt as if a soft wind had slipped up on

her and knocked her flat. "You'd do that for me? Give up the house, I mean?"

"Only temporarily," he said, grinning. "But, yes, if it would make you feel better, I'd be glad to do that. I go back and forth between Golden Vista and the house and sometimes spend the night there, but I'd stay away if you decided to stay at the house."

Summer thought about his offer. It was so tempting, but then, the house wouldn't be the same. Nothing was the same. Mack owned it now, for whatever reasons. She couldn't bear to stay there without her grandparents.

"I think I'll just stay here at Golden Vista for now," she said, her voice hoarse with frustration. "But…thank you for the offer."

He pushed off the post and came toward her, that predatory look in his eyes. "Want me to take you to the office, so you can get a key?"

"Sure." She wanted a long soak and a soft bed. "I'm so tired." Then she stopped. "I forgot about my car. I need to call a tow—"

"I already did that."

"You did?"

"Yeah. While you were having another slice of pineapple upside-down cake."

"I only had one slice, but it was a really big one."

"Yeah, right. You have quite an appetite."

She smiled then. "I can pack it away."

"It looks good on you."

Summer wasn't one to blush easily, but she did now. "I like to walk," she said by way of explaining herself. "I walk all over New York. Especially in Central Park."

"It's a nice park."

Surprised that he'd been there, Summer realized she knew nothing about this man who'd moved to Athens and intruded in such a big way on her life. Or rather, the life she'd left behind. "When were you in New York?"

"Years ago," he said as he looked off into the setting sun. "A lifetime ago."

"And I lived here a lifetime ago," she retorted.

"But we're both here now."

"Yes," she said. "Isn't it funny how things happen that way. You just never know—"

"No, you don't," he replied as he guided her back toward the covered walkway. "I never dreamed I'd wind up in a small Texas town, working at a retirement complex."

The warm, fuzzy feelings Summer had been experiencing turned cold and harsh. "You work *here?*"

He nodded, looked sheepish. "Maintenance

man and groundskeeper. That's why I stay here sometimes. Sorry."

"Why didn't anyone tell me that?"

"Didn't seem important. Besides, you and your grandparents were too busy having a good time."

She regarded him as if he'd turned into roadkill. "So that little news flash sort of slipped your mind."

He shook his head. "I didn't think it would matter one way or another."

"You're just full of surprises, aren't you?"

"You wouldn't believe," he said, his smile open and pure. And challenging.

Summer wanted to believe. She wanted to think that Mack Riley was just a nice man who'd become friends with her grandparents. But she'd learned not to accept things at face value. Especially pretty words coming from handsome men.

Something else was up here. Something that didn't sit well with Summer. And she intended to find out what that something was.

Chapter Four

"Are you all settled in, honey?"

Summer turned from putting clothes in the white chest of drawers to answer her grandmother's question. "I think so. This is a really nice apartment."

Martha beamed her pride. "Yes, the Golden Vista is so accommodating to family members. They have two of these efficiency apartments, I think. And they keep them open to anyone who wants to come and visit. We've even got Internet hookup, so you can use that laptop thing I saw you unpacking."

Summer tried to muster up some enthusiasm as she glanced around the homey L-shaped apartment. "I've got wireless, but that's convenient."

Martha rushed across the sitting room/kitchen combination. "What's wrong, darlin'?"

Summer never could hide anything from her shrewd grandmother. "Nothing, Memaw. I'm just tired…and all of this is a bit overwhelming, I guess."

"I told Jesse we should have called you and told you about selling the farm, but it was kind of spur of the moment. Then once we got here, well, we're always going and doing." She shrugged, shook her head.

"It doesn't matter," Summer said, finishing her unpacking with a slam of the last drawer. "I haven't exactly been faithful in the calling-home department."

Martha came to stand next to her, her arm going around Summer's shoulders as they stared at their reflections in the oval mirror over the dresser. "But we always knew you were there if we needed you."

Summer looked down at her petite grandmother, love pouring over her. "Why didn't you… call me? I mean, if you needed money or a place to live—"

"Oh, honey, we're all right, money-wise. Your grandfather, Lord love him, he saves money with a frugal vengeance. And whether you want to believe it or not, your parents have always helped us out. They just don't make a big fuss about it."

Summer scoffed, then laughed. "Oh, not like they make such a big fuss about everything else? The trips, the houses and cars, the celebrities they hang out with."

"They're not as bad as all that," Martha said, a touch of censure in her voice. "They just like to enjoy life. I do wish you'd make your peace with them."

Summer walked into the compact kitchen, then stood staring at the stark white counters and cabinets. A wistful ache pulsed through her heart. "Oh, I'd love to do that, if I ever saw them."

Her grandmother gave her a knowing, gentle look. "Didn't they visit you last time they were passing through New York?"

Summer raised her chin. "Yes, in the airport restaurant at JFK. That was a charming visit, let me tell you."

"But they did make the effort, right?"

"Right," Summer replied, her defenses up. "So I guess they should get the Parents of the Year award for that little layover?"

"No, but you could cut them some slack," Martha said, a twinkle in her eye.

"Okay, I'll try, for your sake at least," Summer retorted. "But…it's just too hard to explain."

Martha pursed her lips. "Well, I can't squeeze blood from a turnip, so let's change the subject. Tell me what brought you home for this special visit."

Summer wanted to pour out her heart to her grandmother, but the day had just been too full of surprises for that. She needed time to think, to comprehend all the things that were going on around her. She needed time to absorb all the country charm of Golden Vista. Right now, it was screaming just a bit too loudly for her to fully appreciate it.

So she turned to her grandmother, determined not to put one speck of worry on those loving shoulders. "I just wanted to see y'all, is all."

Martha came around the counter and took Summer into her arms. "Well, I'm so very thankful for that. I pray for you every day, honey. I pray for you to find love and happiness, and I pray for all of you girls to be safe up there in that big, scary city."

"Well, only two of us are left," Summer pointed out. "April is staying in Texas. We've got a September wedding to attend, Memaw."

"Oh, that's so precious," Martha said, clasping

her hands together. "April and Reed belong together." Then she hugged Summer again. "I hope you find that kind of happiness one day."

Summer allowed her grandmother's sincere love to envelop her like a warm blanket. She closed her eyes and sank against the soft security of her grandmother's embrace, sending up her own thanks to the God she was so mad at right now. "I love you, Memaw."

"I know, darling. And I love you right back." Then Martha let her go, but held onto her arms, her eyes going big. "So…what do you think about our Mack?"

"Mack Riley is a pushy, overbearing, overrated gardener," Summer wrote in an e-mail to her cousins later that night.

Well, actually he's not so overbearing, and he seems to be a good groundskeeper, but I don't like the man. I didn't like him on sight, even though I must admit he's easy on the eye. Attractive in a rugged, outdoors kind of way. But I'm not interested. Not one bit. Even if the man did give me a ride and call a tow truck for my car. I'm not so helpless that I couldn't have handled that myself, but it was nice to have someone step up and do something thoughtful. But then, that same man now lives in my grandparents' house. And that's just not right. Never mind that Me-maw and Papaw act as if they're on some sort of permanent vacation. I think they're just putting on a good show. I can't imagine that they'd actually be happy in this overblown old folks' home. I came home expecting to find everything the way I'd left it. But everything has changed so much. Too much. I don't know if I can handle this. Or Mack Riley.

Summer finished the e-mail, hitting the send button with a defiant punch to her mouse. She pushed away from the tiny kitchen desk and glanced up at the clock over the sink. It was past midnight, but she didn't think she'd be sleeping any time soon. A deep fatigue pulled at her, making her wish for a long rest.

"If I could just be in my bed at the farm," she said out loud to the quiet, efficient apartment. This little cracker box was clean and comfortable, but it didn't feel right. Nothing felt right.

Her gaze fell across the little white Bible lying on the coffee table. A wave of guilt hit her, making her look away. "I don't want to talk to You right now, Lord."

But the Bible's gold-etched cover drew Summer. She plopped down on the floral love-seat and grabbed the Bible, thumbing through it at random. The pages finally stopped at 1 Corinthians, Chapter 13. "Love is patience; love is kind; love is not envious or boastful or arrogant or rude. It does not insist on its own way; it is not irritable or resentful."

Summer closed the book, then stared down at the cover. "I guess I've messed up in that department." But then, she didn't believe in a perfect kind of love. Love only caused pain and heartache.

She got up and went to the curtained glass-paneled door that opened to a small outside patio. Maybe some fresh air would calm her frazzled nerves. Tentatively, so as not to wake up any of the old people sleeping all around her, Summer opened the door and stepped out onto the rectangular patio. Putting her hands in the pockets of her jeans, she took a deep breath and willed herself to find some of that love and peace she'd just read about.

"Nice night."

Summer jumped at hearing the deep, masculine voice a few feet away from her. Squinting, she saw him there in the moonlight. Mack Riley was sitting in a large white wooden swing underneath an arched rose trellis.

Summer's peace was shattered and frayed. Gone. "You scared me," she said, her gaze taking in the circular pavilion centered between the apartments.

"Didn't mean to do that."

"Don't you ever go home?"

"I do. But I told you, I'm renovating the house right now. It's a mess. I have an apartment here, too, remember? I stay over sometimes when I've got an early day ahead. Just until I get the house finished, though."

Great, Summer thought. She'd have to see him night and day, hovering around all over the complex. Maybe she could keep busy and avoid him. "So that line about allowing me to have the house all to myself was just for show then?"

His foot stopped pushing and the swing creaked to a halt. "What do you mean?"

"I mean, you knew you had an apartment here when you made the offer. And here I was thinking you were being so gallant."

"I told you I stay out there at the house sometimes, and here sometimes. If you'd decided to stay there, I couldn't have done that. So, yes, I was trying to be *considerate*."

She shifted then shrugged. "It doesn't matter. Forget it. I'm all unpacked here and things are just dandy. So how many apartments does this place have?"

"All told, over a hundred. That's just the first phase though."

Summer leaned against the wooden porch rail. "Well, I didn't realize there were so many senior citizens in Athens, Texas."

"They come from all around, looking for a good climate and a safe environment near the big medical centers. It's a long-term answer to retirement."

"I'm so glad you've got it all figured out."

"I'm just here to do my job."

She wondered about that, about how he'd wound up here of all places. But she'd save that for another day. "So what are you doing sitting out here in the dark?"

"Taking in the night air." He patted the space on the swing next to him. "Want to sit with me?"

"No, I don't. I came out here to…take a breath before I go to sleep."

"Uh-huh. You couldn't sleep either, right?"

She put her hands on her hips. "And how do you know that? Were you spying on me through the windows?"

He pushed his feet against the flagstone platform underneath the swing, causing the swing to creak as it moved back and forth. "No, I most certainly wasn't. I didn't even know you were in that particular apartment."

"Yeah, right. You're the yard boy, and you did take me to the office to check in and get a key. You probably know every nook and cranny of this place."

"I wasn't spying on you," he repeated, a hint of irritation in his words. "I don't have to resort to spying to be around pretty women."

"Oh, and I guess you know lots of pretty women."

He got really quiet after that. Satisfied that she'd shut him up, Summer stared off into the distance, the buzz of hungry mosquitoes reminding her it was summer in Texas.

"Not anymore," he finally said. "I used to know lots of women, back in Austin. But I'm on a self-imposed bachelor's hiatus right now. No women, no complications. And I'm happy as a clam about it."

"Well, that's nice. I'm glad you're so happy. So you decided to give up women for…senior citizens?"

"I like old folks, and the pay is good."

"That's wonderful, a real win-win situation. I

guess somebody had to take care of all these flowers and shrubs."

"Yep. Don't you feel closer to God in a garden?"

"Not really." Summer turned to go inside, where she'd be farther away from Mack Riley.

"Hey, I don't bite."

"I'm not worried about that. I'm just tired."

"So come and sit with me. Relax and enjoy the night."

"I can't relax with you around. Don't you get it? You're not exactly on my A list."

"How can I remedy that?"

"By going away."

"I was here first."

"Then I'll go away," Summer said, her hand reaching for the door.

He was there, his hand holding hers. "Look, I'm sorry about…the farm. I lost my own grandparents when I was young, so I know it's tough seeing yours in a different place. Grandparents represent home and love and all that stuff. I hate you had to come back and find all of that gone. But…your grandparents are still right here, and anyone can see they love you."

Summer refused to look at him, refused to acknowledge the heated warmth of his hand over hers, or the sincere kindness in his words. "Well, there is no place like home, unless of course some-one comes along and takes it all away."

"I didn't take anything. I received a very nice old house and some land, and gave your grandpar-ents a chance to rest and have some fun in a good place."

"How can I ever thank you?"

"By forgiving me. By understanding that I'm not at the root of all your problems."

"No, but you're right there in the thick of things."

He dropped his hand away, but she could feel his fierce gaze on her. "How'd you get so sarcastic and cynical, anyway? Does living in New York do this to a person?"

Summer managed to open the door even though her hands were shaking. "No, but dealing with bat-tered women does. I've seen it all, Mack. I don't believe in love or faith anymore. I've learned that I can depend only on myself."

"Well, you're doing a lousy job of that, too, if you ask me."

"I didn't ask you, but thanks so much for your compassion and understanding," she said, just before she slammed the door in his face. Then she made sure all the curtains and blinds were closed and shut. If only she could shut her mind down and close it up tight, too.

But she couldn't. So Summer lay in the crisp white sheets of the comfortable bed and thought about Mack Riley out there in that swing. And she thought about what he'd said to her. After pouting with each toss and turn, she wondered if maybe he wasn't right. Maybe she wasn't handling things so well on her own.

She punched her fluffy pillow. "And that ain't the half of it, buster." She would never tell him the whole sordid story. Summer was having a hard time dealing with all the details of that herself. Which, she imagined, is why she'd tucked tail and run home to Texas. She just couldn't face her cousins or her co-workers right now. She'd failed everyone, including all the women she'd tried so desperately to help.

"But I'm not telling you a thing, Mr. Mack Riley—Mr. Golden Vista Poster Boy, Mr. *This Old House* and *Curb Appeal* all rolled into one."

She couldn't give him the satisfaction of being right, of course. And she wasn't ready to set him straight by giving him all the intimate details of her sad life. So she slammed at her pillows and told herself she was just fine, thank you. Then she got up and checked her e-mails, pouring her troubles out to her cousins until she was exhausted and bleary-eyed.

But Mack Riley still stood out like a thorny blackberry bush in her buzzing, confused brain. And she had to wonder if there wasn't more to his story, too. That nagging inside her gut told her to keep digging, to find out what flaws lay beneath that outdoorsman appeal and lethal smile.

Everybody had secrets. Mack Riley was no exception.

Chapter Five

Summer woke up to the smell of bacon frying and coffee brewing. Her stomach growled hungrily. Rolling over, she glanced at the clock. Eight o'clock. After tossing and turning for part of the night, she'd finally fallen into a deep sleep. Stretching, she had to admit this bed was comfortable and this little apartment had wrapped her in a cozy cocoon.

Now the sun was streaming through the white blinds of her window. Time to start her day. "What now, Lord?" she asked as she rolled out of bed. "Do I go make crafts or play a mean game of Scrabble in the rec room?"

Right now, she just wanted to find that coffee.

After taking a quick shower and blow-drying her hair until it was just damp, she put on fresh jeans and some lip gloss, then headed up the carpeted hallway toward the dining room. It was crowded with a variety of senior citizens, some smiling and chatting, some sitting alone, cranky and cantankerous.

Since Summer felt like the latter group, and since she couldn't find her grandparents, she poured herself some coffee and grabbed a fiber-filled banana bran muffin, then headed to the brooding corner of the room.

"Who are you?" a white-haired man asked as she passed his table. He wore a Texas Rangers baseball cap and a big scowl.

Summer tried to smile. "I'm Summer Maxwell. I'm here visiting my grandparents."

"Who are they?"

"The Creswells—Martha and Jesse."

He nodded, then leaned forward. "Hey, wanna go out with me Saturday night?"

Shocked and appalled, Summer shook her head. "No, thanks. I might not be around that long."

He thumped his chest. "Hmph. Me neither."

Sliding as far away as she could, Summer thought maybe he was just lonely. "You always eat alone?"

"Nah. Sometimes I have family come to visit. When they can find the time, that is."

He looked sad for a minute, until the next available female came by, this one much closer to his age.

"Hey, Gladys. Wanna go out with me Saturday night?"

Gladys was carrying a wonderfully aged Louis Vuitton purse which she held very tightly to her middle. Fingering her double strand of pearls, she gave him a look that would have flattened lesser men, then huffed a breath. "I don't think so, Ralph. Especially since I heard you took out Bullah Patterson last Sunday night."

"We're just friends," Ralph insisted, waving a hand at her. "It was just a gospel sing, not a lifelong commitment."

Gladys kept on walking, her purse held to her side as if she were the Queen herself.

Ralph shrugged, bit into a piece of toast and stared ahead for the next conquest.

"I see you've met Mr. Maroney."

Summer looked up to find Mack Riley standing there with a tray full of food in his hands. Noting that he looked as fresh as a daisy in his clean jeans and faded red T-shirt, she wished she'd bothered to finish styling her hair and had applied a bit more makeup. Too late now. And why did she care anyway?

"Oh, yes. But he's more like Mr. Baloney, don't you think?"

Mack grinned and sat down without an invitation at her table. "I'll protect you, don't worry."

"I can take care of myself, thank you."

"Oh, yeah. City girl. Tough as nails. Right?"

"Something like that," Summer said, thinking she wasn't so tough at all. But she'd give it her best shot, because she also wasn't one for backing down.

"How'd you sleep?" Mack asked between bites of biscuit and gravy.

"Like a baby," she said, hoping she'd be forgiven that slight exaggeration. Then she drained her coffee. "So, what does one do around here all day?"

Mack laughed. "Me, I have plenty to do. Yards to mow and weed, flowers and shrubs to prune, trees for days."

"I get that you are very important and indispensable, but I mean, what do the…mature adults do?"

He stopped chewing, took a sip of orange juice, then chased it with coffee. "Well, your grandparents are in a spin class right now."

"Spin class?" Summer tried to picture her stoic grandfather riding a bike. "I don't get it."

Mack pointed his fork at her. "Maybe you ought to try it. Exercise is good for the soul, you know. It clears the mind, opens the spirit, releases all the toxic thoughts from your inner being."

Summer was thinking some very toxic thoughts right now. "I know what exercise does," she said, her tone a bit defensive. "I mean, I don't get my grandparents being into it."

"They can be into a lots of things now that they are officially retired."

She threw down the rest of her grainy muffin. "Oh, yes, here at Glory Acres, life is just a bowl of cherries."

He lifted a dark eyebrow. "You know, you need to adjust that attitude."

She shot him a scowl worthy of ol' Ralph over there. "And you need to back off."

"Not a morning person?"

She glared at him, those toxic thoughts clouding her mind. "You have no idea."

Mack polished off the last of his scrambled eggs. "Oh, I think I've got a pretty good idea. Maybe being here at Golden Vista will help you relax a little. You seem a bit uptight."

"I'm sure I'll find ways to let off some steam," she said, getting up with visions of messing up his perfect flowerbeds dancing in her head. "Enjoy your breakfast."

He smiled, lifted his fork to her in a salute. "Thanks for chatting with me. You've made my day."

Summer pushed past him, waving sweetly to Ralph as she walked by.

She didn't see Ralph glance over at Mack, sympathy clear in his aged eyes. "Got yourself a live one there, boy."

Mack grinned. "Don't I know it."

"Memaw, I don't know what to do with myself," Summer complained later as she sat out on the big covered verandah with her grandmother. Martha had insisted Summer join her for a mid-morning juice break while they watched Summer's grandfather toiling away at his garden down by the lake.

"Oh, don't worry about that," Martha said, patting Summer's hand. "We have lots to get done around here. In fact, I've already signed you up for a few jobs."

Summer swept her hair off her face. "Really?"

"Yes, honey. Golden Vista needs volunteers on a regular basis. There's basket-weaving, ceramics, crafts to make, trips to the malls in Tyler and

Dallas, or shopping for trinkets in Athens Alley, things such as that."

"I don't do basket-weaving, Memaw." Just the thought of that gave Summer the hives. And she wouldn't dare try to keep up with the old folks at a big mall or the antique alley either. "I need something a bit more challenging and stimulating."

Her grandmother's gaze drifted off to the right, where Mack's fancy riding lawnmower purred away like a giant bumblebee buzzing by. "I can understand, suga', what with you coming from New York City. So I have a plan." Her smile was pure enchantment.

"What is your plan?" Summer asked, wary and weary all at the same time. "I can try crafts, I guess."

Too late. Martha's laughter was triumphant. "I've signed you up to help Mack plan the Village Festival."

"Excuse me?" Summer's heart started a buzz of its own. "What exactly is a Village Festival?" And why would she even want to help Mack Riley plan it?

"Oh, it's going to be so exciting," Martha said, slapping her plump hand against her leg. "It's a big arts-and-crafts show we're going to hold right here on the grounds, on the Fourth of July, for all

of our families and friends. We'll show off all the
things we've been working on—our baskets and
ceramics, whatnots and sculptures, paintings and
photographs, our handmade crafts and yard orna-
ments. We'll sell homemade cakes and pies, candy
and cookies. And we plan to have this big cookout
followed by fireworks. Lots of fireworks right over
the lake down there. It's going to be such fun."

Summer could only imagine. She cringed, but
turned it into a smile for her grandmother's sake.
"But, Memaw, you only just moved here. How do
you know this will be fun? It might be a tremen-
dous undertaking."

Martha nodded in agreement, her ladybug earrings swinging back and forth. "Oh, it is a big
undertaking. That's why I'm on the planning committee, and that's why I think you'd be perfect to
help get things organized and in order. This festival should keep you very occupied."

Summer sank into her rocking chair, full of
panic and fear. She didn't know which would be
worse, sitting here in a rocking chair all summer,
or planning a huge event with that man out there
on the riding lawnmower. "I don't think—"

"Don't worry about it right now, sweetie,"
Martha said, her smile still intact. "Today, we play.
Tomorrow we work."

How many times had Summer heard her dear grandmother say that very thing when Summer was growing up on the farm? There was always work to do, but Martha had managed to make everything an adventure and a challenge. Her grandmother had also instinctively known when it was time to stop and have a little fun. Memaw used to say that there was a time for every season, a time for everything under the sun, straight out of Ecclesiastes. Feeling contrite and a bit sad, Summer glanced over at her grandmother.

And for the first time, she realized that Martha had grown old.

"What's wrong, Summer?" Martha asked, concern etched in the wrinkles of her porcelain skin.

Summer jumped up to hug her grandmother. "Nothing. I'm just glad to be home."

Martha hugged her tight. "I'm glad you're here, honey. And I'm sorry about the house and the farm."

Summer sat down on the cool tiled verandah floor, next to her grandmother's chair. "I'll be okay. I just needed to see you and Papaw. I guess it doesn't matter where we meet up, as long as you're both safe and sound."

"We are that," Martha said, holding Summer's hand in hers. "We're doing just fine."

"Promise me something," Summer said, looking out over the grounds, her eyes drawn to the man on the lawnmower.

"Of course, darling."

"Promise me you'll both be around for a very long time."

Martha's chuckle didn't seem so sure. "Well, honey, I plan on trying to stick around for many more years, but, Summer, you have to accept that when the Lord calls me home, I aim on going."

"Don't talk like that," Summer said, tears pricking her eyes. "I don't want to think about that time."

"Oh, Summer, death is a part of life," Martha replied, her own voice husky and soft. "But you have to remember that God will bring us together again one day in heaven. And honey, in heaven, there are no regrets, no sadness. There is nothing but joy up there."

"I don't want to let y'all go," Summer replied, stubborn as she glared defiantly up at the blanket of clouds moving over the sky. "And I can't picture that kind of joy. Joy always comes with a heavy price, if you ask me."

Martha lifted Summer's chin with one hand. "Don't talk like that, now. Haven't you had joy in your life? Haven't you felt God's love inside yourself?"

Summer thought about the bad relationship she'd just left behind. There had been a certain kind of joy at the beginning, but that had quickly dimmed under a weight of doubt and denial. And what she'd believed to be love had only been a sick kind of enabling, a sure sign of a weakness she'd never dreamed she possessed.

"I don't think I have," Summer replied. "I know I love you and Papaw. That's a perfect love, because I know you've always loved me back, in spite of my flaws."

Martha smiled down at her. "Well, that's exactly the kind of love God feels for us, Summer. He loves us in spite of our flaws."

Summer had to wonder about that. If God loved her so much, why couldn't her own parents be proud of her? Why had they left her so many times for something better just over the horizon? When she thought back over her childhood, she saw her grandmother sitting in the school auditorium, watching her in the school play. Or she saw her grandfather sitting in his pickup truck, waiting for her to finish dance lessons or cheerleading practice.

But she couldn't remember a time her own parents had bothered to be there. For anything important in her life.

She only remembered the excuses, the cards sent days after an event was over, probably sent only because her grandmother had reminded her parents to begin with.

They'd missed out on so much. She'd missed them, all of her life. Why had they left her? What was so wrong with her that they didn't want to be a part of her life?

Shaking her head, Summer wondered if maybe it wasn't time to stop being bitter. Her bitterness had caused her to fall for Brad Parker, because she didn't see that she was worthy of a better man. Brad had honed in on that bitterness to use her, to taunt her, to have control over her. What a fine example she'd been to all the women she'd tried to help. Her shame dimmed the warmth of the sun, made this beautiful day dark and dreary. Summer lifted her face to the sun and wished she could find some of its warmth down in her soul. Maybe that was the reason she'd come home. To find some warmth again.

But not if she kept obsessing about the past and her mistakes.

"You're mighty quiet down there," Martha said, her fingers playing through Summer's long hair.

Summer turned to smile her first real smile since she'd come home. "I'm okay, Memaw. I'm going to get past the past."

"I like that attitude," Martha replied. "How do you plan on doing that?"

"Several ways," Summer said, hopping up to brush off her jeans. "I'll start with trying to make my peace with God. And…I reckon I can help you plan that festival. I need to stay busy."

Martha lifted out of her rocking chair, her grin as wide and beautiful as the Texas sky to the west. "That is the best news. We're going to have so much fun, honey. It will just be a big ol' blast."

Summer doubted that, but being here with her grandparents was the best way to heal her wounds. The recent ones, and the ones that had been festering for most of her life.

That is, if she could just avoid getting too close to Mack Riley. She'd lighten up on the grudges and the old hurts, but she wouldn't open up her heart again for a man.

Not in this season. And not for many seasons to come.

Chapter Six

Mack had seen the two women sitting under the shade of the verandah this morning. What a pretty, heartwarming picture they made, Summer with her long hair, curled up like a child at her grandmother's feet. He could almost sense that little lost girl inside her.

He'd been lost like that once, lost inside self-doubt and too many temptations. But now he was safe here in Athens. He loved the simplicity of his life here, loved his job at Golden Vista. He enjoyed renovating the old farmhouse and hoped to turn the place into a good, solid home. The work both there and at the retirement complex was hard and constant, his duties changing with the season, his need to help out being fulfilled each time one of the residents called him to change a lightbulb, or find a lost cat. He stayed busy, but he no longer experienced the stress and burnout he'd felt back in Austin.

That seemed like a lifetime ago, his job as a landscaping architect for large corporations. He'd moved up the ranks from working exclusively for one firm to becoming his own boss. He'd been a self-made man with a whole team of people working under his supervision. He'd made good money and moved in some very elite circles. But he'd lost his soul somewhere along the way. And after years of struggling and fighting and trying to please everyone else, he'd lost the only woman he'd ever loved, too. That she didn't love him back enough still sat sour and flat against Mack's gut.

So he could feel for Summer Maxwell. He could sympathize with her need to find home and hearth again, after experiencing a crisis of sorts in her busy life. He'd left the illusion of finding a family of his own behind, while she seemed to be running back toward it. But Mack couldn't deny the love he felt for his "adopted" family of senior citizens. They'd taken him under their wings and nurtured him until he'd become a part of their little community. He wanted it to stay that way.

And he hoped with all his heart that Summer

Maxwell wouldn't change the status quo. He did not need the complication of having to deal with an overbearing, hostile female in his life. Even one with long blond hair and big beautiful blue eyes.

Mack finished putting away his gardening tools, then strolled down to the vegetable garden he'd helped Jesse rework. Summer's grandfather was out there as usual, toiling away, a straw hat on his near-bald head.

"You still at it, old man?"

Jesse looked up with a grin. "I can outlast you any time, *young* man."

Mack put his hands on his hips and eyed the lush okra and squash, the butter beans and tomatoes, the black-eyed peas, the bushes thick with blackberries and blueberries. There was a whole variety of vegetables and fruits here, enough to feed all the residents and then some. Just thinking of a dish full of hot blackberry cobbler with ice cream made Mack glad he'd moved here.

"You've done a fine job, Mr. Jesse."

Jesse stopped to mop his brow with his white handkerchief. "It ain't bad, if I do say so myself. But I can't take all the credit. Everyone's helped out." He waved a hand down one of the neat, long rows. "And I couldn't help but notice somebody's been hoeing weeds for me. That person wouldn't happen to be you, now would it?"

Mack grinned, shook his head. "I'm not talking."

"That's what I thought," Jesse said as he gathered up his own tools and called it quits for the day. "I appreciate it, son. My old back ain't as strong as it used to be."

"No big deal," Mack replied as they walked together toward the building. "I had some extra time on my hands."

"How's the house coming?" Jesse asked, trepidation and wonder mixed in his voice.

"I'm taking it a room at a time. New wallpaper, paint. I'm putting in all new appliances—" Mack stopped at the faraway look in Jesse's eyes. "I'm sorry. I shouldn't go on and on like that about the house you lived in for so many years."

Jesse held up a hand. "Now, Mack, we sold the house to you. It's yours now, even if I do miss the place now and again."

Mack stood back as Jesse carefully cleaned his tools then put them inside the storage area next to Mack's. Mack locked up the shed, then turned to Jesse. "Are you happy here, Mr. Jesse?"

Jesse puffed out his chest. "Sure I am, son."

"I mean really happy?" Mack asked.

"I guess I'd probably be happier back at that old farmhouse, but life changes just like the wind. I have to go with the flow and hope God has something better just around the bend for me."

"How do you know whether you made the right decision?"

Jesse stared over at Mack, his aged brown eyes filled with a knowing light. "I pray, son. Each and every day. I pray for the Lord's guidance."

Mack nodded. "I do that, too, but sometimes I still have doubts. And I guess, what with your granddaughter showing up all in a huff—"

"Is that what this is about?" Jesse asked with a chuckle. "You're worried about Summer?"

Mack raked a hand through his hair. "Well, she hasn't exactly taken a shine to me living in your house."

"*Your* house," Jesse gently reminded him. "And Mack, there's something you should know about my sweet granddaughter."

Mack was all ears. "Oh, yeah? And what's that?"

"She's a bit high-strung," Jesse said, bobbing his head and laughing softly. "Dramatic, her grandmother used to say. Everything always becomes an issue with Summer. You should have seen her in high school. She was always fighting for some cause, trying to save everything from historical buildings to lost puppies. Her grandmother and I appreciated her enthusiasm and her passion, but I tell you, sometimes we got just plain tired out from listening to her rant and rave. But we love her anyway, 'cause she has a heart about as deep as the Trinity River, and she has this wonderful capacity to love. I think that's why she went into social work. She wanted to save all the hurting people of the world."

Mack could understand what Jesse was saying. But still he worried. "And what about herself? It seems to me, from the little time I've been around her, that Summer needs to take care of herself before she can help all those other people."

Jesse put a hand on Mack's back as they reached the side door to the complex. "Well, that's probably the very reason she came back home to Athens. She's come home to rest and take care of herself. And her granny and me, we aim to help her all we can."

"She sure loves you, too, that's for sure," Mack said, not missing the hint of a warning in Jesse's tone. "I hope she finds whatever she's looking for."

Jesse grinned again, then patted Mack on the

back with a surprisingly strong force. "Oh, I think she will, son. I sure think she will at that."

Summer collapsed against the soft floral cushions of her bed, a moan escaping her lips. "I am beat."

She turned over, looked up at the pristine white of the ceiling. The ceiling fan over the bed whirled around and around in a nice, steady cadence that almost put Summer to sleep. She didn't want to move.

Her grandmother had managed to keep her busy all day long. After taking a tour of her grandparents' roomy apartment and seeing some of their antique furniture from the farm tucked here and there, Summer had obediently followed Martha out to the garden where they'd picked butter beans, peas, cucumbers and tomatoes. Then they'd taken the vegetables inside to be washed and passed out to both residents and workers alike, with everyone singing the praises of her grandfather's green thumb. Along the way, Summer had stumbled onto some interesting old people.

"This is like being at camp all year long, Memaw," Summer had told her grandmother at dinner, which was served promptly at five. After that, the residents were left to their own devices for snacks and other refreshments. They all had small refrigerators and stoves in their apartments.

The dining hall was long and pretty, with colorful high-backed chairs and windows on all sides to show off the thriving flower beds and the feisty ducks and squawking geese prancing around out on the small private lake.

Martha had preened and smiled during dinner, waving to friends as she described each under her breath to Summer.

"The Butlers—she's his second wife. They've only been married ten years, I think both were widowed before. Five children and seventeen grandchildren between them. They do a lot of visiting back and forth between all the families. But when the youngest grandkids come here, mercy, those boys do get a bit rowdy.

"The Gaddys—old money from Tyler. Two grown children who live far away, spending their inheritance already, I imagine. Mrs. Gaddy has her hair done once a week and her nails done every two weeks—right here in the beauty parlor. She has a poodle named Chloe."

"Y'all have a beauty shop?"

"Yes, and a spa, too. You could benefit from a massage and facial, you know."

"And pets?"

"Yes, a lot of the residents have pets, dear. Of course, your grandfather and I didn't want another one after old Sawtooth died."

Summer remembered Sawtooth. The big tabby had gotten that name because of his sharp teeth and his tendency to bite anything that moved. Summer had loved him completely, and the big cat often slept at the end of her bed.

"I miss him," she said, remembering the day her grandfather had called a couple of years back to tell her that Sawtooth had gone on to kitty heaven.

"We do, too," Martha said, still waving to anyone who'd look up. "This is my granddaughter, Summer," she told several of the residents sitting nearby.

And so the dinner had gone, with Summer eating the tender baked chicken and steamed vegetables sitting before her, then devouring the chocolate Texas sheet cake that followed. Memaw had reminded her they'd be having blueberry pancakes for breakfast tomorrow.

A girl could get used to this, she decided.

Until she'd looked up to find Mack Riley sitting at a table with three senior women.

Flirt, she'd thought at the time. But she had to admit Mack had been a perfect gentleman, getting up to help the women with their plates, bringing them fresh glasses of tea and coffee, and always, it had seemed, managing to cast a glance her way.

Then he'd actually gotten up and come to visit their table, much to Summer's dismay.

"Mack, so good to see you," Martha said, waving him down into an empty chair. "Isn't it good to see Mack, honey?"

"Wonderful," Summer said, saluting him with her water and lemon. "Don't you ever go home?" she asked him, causing both her grandparents to lift their eyebrows in shock.

"I'm going back out to the house this weekend," he said, obviously not offended at all by her pointed question. Then he really sprang something on her. "Hey, how 'bout all three of y'all come with me on Saturday?" He looked at Summer's grandfather. "Jesse, I sure could use your advice on a couple of the construction problems I'm having, and Martha, well, I was hoping maybe you could offer me some suggestions on decorating schemes. And the blueberry bushes are bursting with fruit. I can't possibly pick all those berries by myself."

Then he'd looked at Summer, silent and assessing. "And I'm sure you'll have a few suggestions, too, right?"

Summer rolled over on the bed now, remembering the challenging light in his eyes. "Oh, yeah, buddy, I have a few very direct suggestions, but none of them have anything to do with curtains or cushions."

Of course, her grandparents had jumped at the chance to help Mack. They were so enamored of his lethal charm, they couldn't see past the noses on their lovable faces.

"While we're there, maybe we can get a plan going for the festival, too," Martha had suggested. "Time is a wasting. We only have a few weeks."

So Summer's Saturday was already booked, thanks to Mack's thoughtfulness and her grandmother's eagerness to keep her busy. "Thank you very much," Summer said into the silence of her little apartment, raising her hand in a wave of frustration.

On the one hand, she found it incredibly sweet that Mack had thought to include her grandparents in on the renovations of what used to be their house. It would cheer them up and give them something to keep them active and needed, even if the whole plan was a bit strange.

On the other hand, she had to wonder if Mack wasn't just buttering them up to help with the transition of losing their home and having to move to Golden Vista, maybe to appease his own guilt some, too. And she still wasn't sure what his motives were toward her.

Probably wanted to torment her and aggravate her, just to pass the time away.

"Well, I can handle you, Mack Riley. I've swept the floor with men twice as ornery as you."

What about Brad? that inner voice asked, the tone inside her head accusing and taunting.

"Brad is history," Summer reminded herself, pushing back the awful memories of their last few days together. "I learned from my mistake and Brad won't ever bother me again."

But what about how Brad has undermined that bravado of yours?

She thought about all the women she'd helped over the years. Women on the run from abusive husbands and boyfriends. She'd stood up to those men, bringing her expertise and the law down on their pathetic heads. But she hadn't been able to stand up to Brad.

"I'll be okay," Summer said out loud, effectively blocking out that dark pain. Then she got up to turn on her laptop. "Time to e-mail an update to the cousins."

She opened her mail to find replies from both April at the Big M in Paris, Texas, and Autumn in

New York. And—she couldn't help it—she looked for e-mail from her parents, too, only to find none there.

Had she really expected a reply from her parents, even though she'd told them she'd be coming home to Athens for a few weeks this summer?

Summer cleared her head of that particular question, then concentrated on catching up with April and Autumn.

"I miss y'all both," Autumn said in her short, precise e-mail.

I'm up to my eyeballs in work, of course. Do y'all know what's going on with my Daddy? He's been acting really strange. I hope everything is okay at the firm in Atlanta. You know Daddy will never retire, so I hope he's not working too hard. April, how are the wedding plans progressing? Summer, what's this about Mack Riley? Who is he? And how in the world did he wind up in Athens?

"Good question," Summer mumbled, grabbing a bite-sized candy bar from the lovely basket one of the residents had brought to her door earlier.

Then came April's reply to both Summer and Autumn.

Autumn, how *is* it there in the loft all by yourself? Or do you have your nose buried in finances to the point that you haven't even noticed we're gone? About your daddy, talk to Uncle Richard, honey. He's okay as far as I know, so I can't speak for him. But you might want to give him a call and check up on him and your mother. I can't wait to show y'all my wedding dress. It's so pretty. And I made the final choice for the flowers yesterday. Your bridesmaid dresses are lovely, too, of course. Satire originals—designed just for my wedding. Summer, this Mack fellow sounds very interesting. Just be careful. You need to rest and regroup. Autumn, call your daddy. Soon.

Summer had to laugh at the way her cousins' messages always fluttered from subject to subject with a stream-of-consciousness flow. But she'd learned long ago how to keep up and respond. She'd have to e-mail April privately later to find out why her cousin kept insisting Autumn call Uncle Richard. Maybe April did know what was going on in Atlanta, but was afraid to tell Autumn. Hmm.

But, right now, she had lots to tell her cousins about Mack.

"I'm on it," Summer typed, thinking Mack

Riley was more an annoyance than a real distraction. An annoyance with a charming country-boy smile and bright, intelligent granite-colored eyes.

Remembering those eyes, Summer answered her cousins.

Mack Riley is just a man who happened to buy my grandparents' house. A man who also happens to work at the Golden Vista Retirement Village. A man who just happens to invite himself to sit down at our table each time we go into the fancy dining room. A man who just happened to invite Memaw, Papaw and me out to the house that used to be ours to help him with renovations. A man who just happens to like to sit out in the big, open verandah and swing on the pretty white wooden swing that I'm sure he probably helped build. But, enough about him. I *am* resting and regrouping. And I'm going to help Memaw plan a big summer festival here at the lovely acres. Just to stay busy. Oh, did I forget to mention that my partner in all of this is... Mack Riley?

Summer shook her head, signed off and wondered how many e-mails would be passing between her two cousins after they read what she'd

written. She knew they'd jump to the wrong conclusion. They'd think she was actually interested
in Mack Riley.

"I'm not, of course," she said as she went into
the small bathroom and got ready for some television and then bed. "I'm not."

But she had to agree with her cousin Autumn
on a couple of things that had been bugging
Summer already.

Looking at her clean face in the mirror,
Summer asked, "Who exactly is Mack Riley? And
how did he wind up in Athens?"

Deciding to forgo television and do some Internet sleuthing instead, Summer poured herself
a huge glass of diet soda and got busy. She knew
how to find out things about people. And she
really wanted to know the scoop on Mack Riley.

Chapter Seven

A few days later, Summer finished helping her grandmother fold clothes in the community laundry room. "Memaw," she said, careful to sound nonchalant, "what do you know about Mack Riley?"

Martha buttoned one of Jesse's Sunday shirts, then smoothed it on the hanger. "Well, I know he's a hard worker and that he's very good at his job." She lifted a hand toward the windows of the long airy room. "Just look at the landscaping around here. It's lovely."

Summer had to agree there. The grounds of Golden Vista were bursting with color. Even in the summer heat and humidity, Mack's gardens seemed to be thriving as the red geraniums fought to overtake the yellow marigolds and pink gerbera daisies. "He does seem to know a lot about landscaping and gardening."

"Well, yes, of course he would," Martha said with a chuckle. "He went to school at Texas A & M for that very thing. Landscape architect, I believe is his official title—or was, at least, when he was back in Austin. He worked for some big company for a few years, then he branched out on his own. I think he was very successful for a while."

Bingo. Her grandmother had unknowingly confirmed what little bit of information Summer had been able to find on the Internet. Who knew that so many Mack Rileys, or at least several variations of that name, lived and worked all over Texas? She'd narrowed her search down to the top two. And one of them had been a landscape architect in Austin, Texas.

A very successful landscape architect, from what Summer could tell. But the Web site for Riley Landscaping and Design needed updating. Nothing had been posted there in the last few months from what Summer could tell. That had been another red flag. Why had he just up and left a lucrative business?

"How long has Mack actually been in Athens?" she asked her grandmother as they walked back to Martha's apartment to put away the few clothes they'd washed and dried.

"Oh, a few months, I reckon," Martha replied. "He was in town for interviews before the board of directors hired him to maintain the grounds here. Then of course, he bought our house and that's when we really got to know more about him." She stopped as Summer unlocked the apartment door. "Why are you so curious about Mack, honey?"

Summer concentrated on getting the key in the lock. "Oh, just wondering. It just seems strange that he'd want to settle in a small town—I mean if he had a successful business in Austin."

Martha laughed again as they entered the cool, spotless apartment. "You can be honest, Summer. I mean, Mack is the only eligible bachelor under sixty-five around here. It stands to reason you'd be interested in him."

"Only because I don't like the way he came in and took your home away," Summer retorted, denial coursing through her heart like a deer on the run. "Other than that, I really don't care."

Martha hung up the shirts and pants, then turned to Summer. "He didn't take our home, honey. We chose to sell it to him."

"After my father coerced you into moving here."

Martha pulled Summer by the hand, bringing her back into the tiny kitchen. "Sit," she ordered with a gentle voice, shoving Summer onto a swivel chair decorated with a hand-embroidered cushion.

Summer sank down, then propped her chin in her hands, elbows on the counter. "Memaw—"

"Listen to me," Martha said in that voice that Summer knew meant business. "Your father didn't force us to do anything. Honey, we're old. You have to face that. We were struggling out on the farm. We didn't want to let things go down, so we decided the best thing we could do was to sell it and put the money in our retirement fund. Mack gave us the asking price without batting an eye. And he promised to maintain the farm and keep it going. He's even offered for us to come and visit anytime we want."

"That's so very considerate of the man," Summer said, wanting to stew over this some more. "But I don't trust him."

"You never did trust anyone very much," Martha pointed out as she poured two glasses of lemonade. "Especially your daddy."

"Well, maybe that's because he was never around when I needed him," Summer said, her hands cupping the cool glass in front of her.

Martha leaned across the counter, her gaze

tender and understanding. "I don't condone how your parents have treated you, Summer. But your mother is my daughter. Elsie always wanted a life of glamour and riches. And she's had that with your father. But she also found something else with James. She loves him. With all her heart."

"Which doesn't leave much room for anyone else," Summer replied. "Even me."

"They do love you, darlin'," Martha insisted. "They just don't know how to prove that."

"Showing up would be a good start."

Martha looked down at the counter, then wiped at an invisible speck of dust. "Well, that's why I called them and asked them to come for a visit."

"You did what?"

"I told them you were here and asked them to come home."

Summer groaned as she got up to pour out the dregs of her lemonade. "I e-mailed them and never heard back, so I figured that was that."

Martha finished her drink then placed the glasses in the tiny sink. "Well, you know the thing about that high-tech stuff—it's so impersonal and distant. Calling them seems to work better for me."

"Funny, calling them never gets me any answers."

"Well, maybe you're asking the wrong questions," Martha replied. "And maybe this need to pick on Mack stems from your frustrations with your parents."

"That's silly," Summer replied, upset that she'd worried her grandmother so much that Martha felt the need to analyze her motives.

"I'm not going to push you on this," Martha said. "But if and when your parents come home, please try, try hard, honey, to mend this great rift. For my sake. For your grandfather's sake. Okay?"

Summer felt about an inch tall. "I never meant to involve y'all, Memaw."

"Honey, we're your family. Of course we're involved. Do you think I approve of how your parents have gallivanted all over the world? I've talked my head off to your mother, but she can't see that being half a parent is worse than being no parent at all. In her mind, she's done the best she could by you."

Summer saw the pain in her grandmother's eyes. "I know they were around *some* of the time, Memaw. I remember having to leave the farm and go with them each time Daddy would come home from the rodeo circuit, but after he gave that up they still traveled. I cried to stay with you and

Papaw forever, but then, I also cried each time they'd up and leave me again."

Martha nodded. "They didn't want you traveling with them, so they didn't mind you staying with us some of the time."

"I would have been a burden, a hindrance," Summer said.

"No, darlin'. Your mother didn't want you exposed to that kind of nomadic lifestyle. There are a lot of things that go on on the circuit that she didn't want you to see or hear. And, she cried, too, whether you saw it or not, each time they left."

"So she was doing me a favor by leaving me?"

Martha came around the counter, her smile as soft as a down comforter. "Think about it, Summer. Wouldn't you have rather been here with us, than staying in a different hotel room each night? The rodeo isn't a pot of gold, and even though they had Maxwell money to sustain them, they still had to live in hotels most of the time. Your mother didn't want you to grow up living like that. She knew that old farm was the right place for you."

Summer felt as if a light had come on in her mind. "I never thought about it that way."

Martha nodded. "Your mother was torn between her duty to you and her love for your father."

"So she chose him over me?"

"No, she chose your safety and well-being over everything else."

"But why couldn't she just stay here with me?"

"She could have. But life out on the road is hard and full of every kind of temptation."

Summer got up to pace the small kitchen. "So she went along to keep my father straight?"

"That...and to help him, encourage him. He became very successful because of her efforts. She turned out to be a very good manager."

"And what about me?" Summer asked, the bitterness back in full force. "How did I become successful, Memaw?"

She was about to say she'd done it on her own, her own way, but Martha held up a hand.

"You became the woman you are today because we all loved you and were willing to make sure you got a stable home life and a good education. You are blessed, Summer. You have a good, solid family backing you and you are a very intelligent woman. You should be very proud of that."

Summer didn't feel so proud. Not wanting to bring her grandmother any more stress, she could only nod. "I have been blessed. I know that. But...

it's hard to think of my childhood without feeling as if...I didn't matter."

"Oh, you mattered, all right," Martha said. "You will always matter. You need to remember that."

Because she was feeling so low, Summer made a confession to her grandmother. "I did a google on Mack Riley, Memaw."

Martha looked shocked. "You did what?"

Summer laughed then, some of the tension flowing out of her. "Oh, that means I did an Internet search on him."

"My, my," Martha said, slapping a hand to her chest. "You almost gave me a heart attack, child. I thought—"

"You don't need to worry about that sort of thing," Summer assured her. "I just want to know the facts on the man. Nothing more."

"Oh, all right," Martha said, doubt evident in her eyes. "Me, I know everything I need to know about Mack. He's a good Christian man and he works hard each and every day. He'd make someone a very fine husband." Her eyes glowed with possibilities.

"Oh, no," Summer said, backing away, her hands up in the air. "Don't even go there, Memaw. I'm not interested in being paired off with Mack Riley."

"Whatever you say, darlin'," Martha said, her

smile prim and proper. "Now, how 'bout we head to that watercolor workshop? I might just paint me a picture full of bluebonnets and Indian paintbrush."

"Oh, you're painting a picture, all right," Summer said as she followed her grandmother to the recreation room at the other end of the building. "But if you try to throw Mack and me together, it won't be a pretty picture."

Martha smiled and kept walking. "You never know, honey, what God has in store for us."

Summer knew. She knew God wasn't interested in helping her seek any kind of happiness or perfect love. She'd seen too much heartache to believe in that kind of faith.

And lately, she'd felt too much of her own brand of heartache to slip up and fall for the first man who just happened by the minute she'd entered East Texas.

Back in New York, Autumn Maxwell read Summer's last e-mail, then immediately sent her own message to April back at the Big M.

What's up with this? I think she's interested. She's sure making a big fuss out of trying to convince us she's not interested. But maybe this is a good kind of distraction for Summer. Or maybe not. It wouldn't do for her to fall for another man so soon after Brad. Especially a man she's not so sure about. Anyway, I'm worried about her. And I'm lonely. I miss both of you. Work has kept me busy, busy, but something's going on there that I'm not so sure about and nobody's talking. I keep hearing gossip about budget cuts and downsizing. But I don't have time to worry about that now. And in the meantime, my daddy is still acting strange. I think he's up to something, but he won't tell me what. April, do you know anything I should know? As usual, I'll be working late into the night. How this company expects anyone left in the firm to function if they do lay people off is beyond me.

Tell me something good, April. Talk to me about planning your wedding with the man you love. What's that like? And in the meantime, I think we need to say special prayers for Summer. She's hurting so much, she can't even begin to heal. A lot of long-held suffering going on there. Well, got to go. The ledgers and spreadsheets on my computer screen are calling me back to work.

Back at the Big M, April Maxwell read her cousin's e-mail, then sat back in her chair to stare at the screen. "I need to call Uncle Richard."

April knew what her uncle was doing, but she wasn't going to be the one to tell Autumn. Uncle Richard had retired from running his own financial firm in Atlanta, Texas. And he'd hired a man from Louisiana to take over. Without telling Autumn.

"He promised me he'd tell her," April said into the night. Wondering how to handle this, she decided she'd call Uncle Richard and remind him to talk to Autumn. Her cousin would be fit to be tied when she found out that her daddy had hired someone else to run the firm without even asking Autumn to come home and take over. His reasoning was that Autumn was happy in New York and he didn't want to force her to give up her life there. But he at least needed to let Autumn decide that for herself, didn't he?

"I'll go talk to Reed," April decided. Reed would understand her dilemma and give her sound advice, just as he always did. And besides, he was going to be her husband in a little over a month— any excuse to see him and be with him until then was good. April smiled, hugged herself, then did a little jig of joy. In spite of all the work she'd had to do to get things here in order after her father's death, and the many tasks required to put together her wedding, April was happy now. Finally. She missed her parents desperately, but she had Reed. They would make a new family here on the land they both loved. She had faith in that possibility.

I just wish Summer and Autumn could feel this kind of joy, she thought. *Please, Lord, let them find their own kind of happiness.*

Mack knew he should get back to work, but the letter he'd received this morning had stopped him in midstride. Somehow, Belinda had tracked him down. And she was asking to see him again.

Mack stood staring down at the white ducks floating near the shore of the small oval-shaped lake. His history with Belinda went back many years. They'd met in college and things had progressed from there. He'd worked for her father a short time after graduating from college, but even that relationship had soured with one of Belinda's whims, and Mack had lost his job. He'd gone out on his own and worked hard to make a name for himself, until Belinda had come back into his life, apparently for revenge since she'd ruined him for good this time. Which was why he'd finally left Austin to start over.

There were so many memories, good and bad. Belinda liked to move in and out of his life, mad one day and glad the next. She also liked to keep him on standby, in case her other relationships didn't pan out. Which they never did, of course. But this time…this time he didn't feel that tug on his heart, that quickening that he usually felt whenever she decided she was ready to take him back.

Mack didn't want Belinda Lewis back in his life. Ever again.

Remembering the last time he'd talked to Belinda, he leaned his head against the warm bark of an ancient live oak, closing his eyes as he sent up prayers for restraint and self-control. *Dear Lord,* he thought, *don't let me cave. Don't let me go back into that roller coaster of a relationship.*

Mack knew just seeing Belinda again might cause him to have a lapse in judgment. So he had to be very careful when he called her. He had to make her see that he wasn't interested. Maybe he should just not call at all. Maybe he'd just ignore her letter. Letting out a long sigh, Mack batted his forehead against the tree.

"Doesn't that hurt?"

He looked up, sheepish and embarrassed, to find Summer standing there staring at him. She looked as fresh as the flowers all around her in her floral shirt and jeans.

"Are you into self-mutilation?"

"No," Mack said, thinking he probably did look pretty strange standing here banging his head against an oak tree. "Just had a rough day."

"Is that your way of waking up your brain cells?"

Her sharp-edged wit woke him up more than any tree ever could. "My brain cells are just fine, thank you. I was having what I thought was a quiet moment."

She sashayed up underneath the shady canopy of the tree, her eyes gleaming. "Around here? You've got to be kidding. With emergency call buttons going off at all hours, and missing wheelchairs, and food fights in the dining room between women bickering over Mr. Maroney, there are no quiet moments. And don't get me started on water aerobics and strength-training classes."

Mack smiled in spite of his worries. "You do have a point." He shrugged, glancing toward the complex up on the hill. "Did…did you need something?"

"No, nothing," Summer replied, her gaze scanning his face. "I just decided to come feed the ducks and geese." She held out a bag. "Old bread from the kitchen. I get all the fun chores, don't you know."

Mack laughed. "I guess you're bored beyond belief, staying in an old folks' home."

"It ain't Manhattan," she retorted as she reached inside the bag and pulled out some bread. "Here." She offered him a slice. "You can help."

"Gee, think my brain cells can handle it?"

She gave him a look that said no, but then she grinned. "It's all in the wrist, I think."

Mack broke up the bread and threw it down on the edge of the shore. The ducks immediately started squawking and quacking as they hurried to get their dinner. Two big white geese soon followed. "Careful," he told Summer over his shoulder. "Some of them are downright mean."

"I can handle the little duckies," Summer replied, laughing as a fat white mama duck waddled up to her. The ducks were docile, but one of the geese decided he wanted the whole loaf of bread.

Backing up, Summer kept laughing, the sound echoing out over the still countryside like a sweet melody from an old song. "Hey, slow down there, goosey-goose."

Mack stood watching her as the goose advanced. Summer's laughter was refreshing and beautiful. But then, he realized as he held the bread in his hand, *she* was beautiful. Her eyes were big and beguiling. Her hair shone like golden wheat at sunset. Mack groaned inwardly, thinking he'd gone all soft and poetic, just watching the woman. But he couldn't stop watching her.

Until the big goose flapped his wings and started seriously chasing Summer.

"Oh!" Summer looked over at Mack as she rushed by. "Hey, do something. I'm being attacked."

Mack shook his head, his own laughter relieving some of the tension he'd felt since receiving Belinda's letter. "I tried to warn you."

Suddenly, Summer was surrounded by quacking, hungry geese, ducks and ducklings. Throwing up her hands, she quickly tossed Mack another slice of bread. "Try to head them off."

"I'm enjoying this too much," he admitted as he tossed bread back toward the lake to create a trail for the chaotic creatures.

Summer did the same, finally throwing whole chunks of bread as she lured the big goose back to the tidbits. "Maybe we should make a run for it before they eat all of this."

Mack grabbed her hand and urged her toward the building. "Hurry."

They stopped at the verandah, laughing as they tried to catch their breaths. Summer looked down at their joined hands, then looked back up at Mack, her eyes shining with mirth. "I've never been rescued from ducks and geese before."

Mack looked back at her and realized he'd made a fatal mistake. He shouldn't have taken her by the hand, because now he didn't want to let go. Ever.

So he just stood there and slowly, ever so slightly, opened the door to his heart.

To let her in.

Chapter Eight

"There you two are."

"Papaw, hi!" Summer turned from staring at Mack to find her grandfather peeking around the corner of the building. Embarrassed, she stepped away from Mack, her hands flying to her hair as she took a breath, then straightened her long locks. Mack looked away, but not before she caught the expression in his eyes that told her he'd enjoyed holding her hand.

And she'd enjoyed holding his hand right back.

"Papaw, what's up?" She tried to sound cheery and innocent, but her grandfather's shrewd gaze seemed to sum up the situation with an acute accuracy.

"You two kids okay?"

"We're fine, Jesse," Mack said, giving Summer

a look that told her they weren't finished. "Isn't it about supper time?"

"That's why I came looking," Jesse said, holding out his arm to Summer. "Your grandmother wants both of you to eat at our table."

"Together?" Summer and Mack both said at the same time.

Summer didn't miss the fear in Mack's one-worded question. She felt that same fear tripping a fluttery path right through her stomach. She wasn't sure if she actually could eat.

"I figure together is better than apart," Jesse said, giving them a curious stare. "It would be kind of dumb for each of us to sit at a separate table, don't you think?"

Summer finally smiled at her grandfather's humor. "Of course I want to eat with y'all. I just thought that Mack—"

"Mack wants to eat with us, too, right, Mack?"

Mack glanced at Summer, his expression full of questions. "I'd like to, yes. That is, if Summer doesn't mind."

"I don't mind," Summer said, thinking it would be rude to refuse. Thinking with her grandparents between them, they shouldn't get into too much trouble. Trying to lighten things, she added, "That way, dear Mr. Maroney will see that I'm not available to sit with him."

Jesse guffawed at that. "Oh, don't worry about Ralph, honey. He only has eyes for Gladys Hanes. But that woman has her nose so high in the air, I'm sure she gets cloud dust stuck in her nostrils."

Summer smiled over at Mack, comfortable now that her formidable grandfather was between them. Not sure what had just happened underneath the verandah, she pushed the warm sensations coursing through her system out of her mind. For now. Better to talk about Mr. Maroney's interesting love life than to try and analyze her own reaction to Mack Riley. "Why isn't Gladys friendly to Mr. Maroney?"

"She likes to play hard to get," Jesse explained. "She's got a bank full of money—thinks every man here is only interested in her checkbook."

Mack nodded at that. "Well, maybe we need to show her that Mr. Maroney means business. He's been pining for her for a long time, from what I've heard."

"Got an idea?" Jesse asked as they entered the cool dining room.

Mack winked, smiled. Caused Summer's heart to lurch and skip. "Flowers always work for me."

She could only imagine what kind of romantic

notions this man would have. And she couldn't
help but wonder what it would be like to have a
romantic interlude with Mack Riley. Or to receive
pretty flowers from him.

"There y'all are," her grandmother called from
her table in the corner by the windows. "Hurry up
now. Roast beef and mashed potatoes, Jesse. Your
favorite."

"And strawberry pie for dessert," Mack said as
he helped Summer with her chair. "How are you,
Miss Martha?"

"I'm great. Right as rain," Martha replied,
clearly tickled that Summer was with Mack. "Just
sit right down and let's wait for grace. The food's
getting cold."

Summer watched as the multitude of old folks
headed into the dining room, some using the wall
railings for support, some sporting fancy walkers or wheelchairs. She wondered how it felt to
grow old. Her uncle's death had her thinking about
things like that a lot lately. Maybe that was why
she'd felt the need to come home just to make sure
her grandparents were safe and sound.

And they were, whether she liked these new de-
velopments or not. They were still in love and still
happy.

Then she looked over at Mack's gray-blue hued

eyes and wondered how it would feel to grow old with someone you truly loved. She looked from his keen gaze to her grandmother's loving face. Martha smiled over at Jesse, her eyes bright with tenderness. Summer's heart swelled at that display of love. She'd seen so much violence, so much hurt with the women she'd dealt with back in New York, it was endearing to actually witness true, abiding love. She thought of Brad and how he'd treated her, and then she wondered if she even deserved that kind of love.

"What's wrong?" Mack asked after one of the residents had said grace.

Summer hadn't realized her feelings were showing on her face, but Mack had certainly noticed. "Nothing," she answered. "I was…just thinking about my grandparents." She looked over at Jesse. "I'm so glad you two still have each other, Papaw."

"Me, too," Jesse said, his fork in the air. He glanced over at his wife. "And Martha is still as pretty as the day we met."

"How did you two meet?" Mack asked, his eyes on Summer.

Martha put down her dinner roll. "Oh, I was walking home from gathering eggs."

"Gathering eggs?"

She nodded, buttered her roll. "Times were tough back then. Our neighbor shared her eggs with my big family. Two brothers and a sister, me being the baby. Anyway, my mama had sent me to fetch eggs—"

"And I came barreling around the curve in the road," Jesse interjected, a grin on his face. "Driving an old International pickup."

"Scared me so bad, I dropped my basket of eggs."

"Eggs went everywhere," Jesse said. Then he leaned forward. "But, son, to tell you the truth, I don't remember anything about any eggs. I couldn't take my eyes off her pretty face."

Mack took a long drink of iced tea, then put his glass down, his gaze moving over Summer's face. "I think I can understand that concept, sir."

Jesse's grin grew even wider. "I just reckon you can at that."

"That's a nice story," Mack replied. "I hope one day I'll find someone like that."

"You just might," Martha said, mashed potatoes on her fork and a gleam of hope in her eyes.

Summer thought it was mighty warm in this dining room, but then most old folks stayed cold. Maybe they had the air-conditioning set on a toasty temperature. Or maybe she was just having a really strange reaction to the man sitting across from her. The man who kept searching her face with those incredible gray eyes.

Wanting to break the electric hum she felt coursing through her system, she said, "It seems all we do around here is eat."

"Yeah, we like it that way," Jesse replied, rubbing his stomach. "Kinda spoils a man. This food is almost as good as your grandmother's cooking."

"Eat, sleep and be merry," Martha chimed in, her tea clinking with fresh ice. "Of course, we have lots to keep us busy, too." Then she clanked her knife against her plate. "How are the plans for the festival coming, by the way?"

"Haven't worked on that," Mack said.

"Still in the thinking stages," Summer said at about the same time.

Martha looked from one to the other, surprise registering on her face. "Well, what's the holdup?"

"More bread?" Mack asked as he passed the basket to Summer, clearly uncomfortable with this subject.

"Thanks," she managed to reply, her fingers just brushing his. His skin felt as warm as the hot buttered rolls.

"Haven't y'all even had a chance to discuss the festival?" Martha asked, her tone all innocence.

"No," Summer and Mack said at the same time.

We've got to stop doing that, Summer thought. She didn't want everyone to get the wrong idea about them.

"We could do that right after dinner," Jesse suggested. "I know we were planning on organizing this bash when we go out to the farm this weekend, but why wait? We don't want to spend all day out there hashing out the details, right?"

"Good idea," Martha said, patting her husband on the cheek. "You two could come back to our apartment."

Mack eyed Summer. "What do you want to do?"

She wanted to run out of here as fast as she could, but that wouldn't look right. "I guess it wouldn't hurt to get a plan into action."

"Okay, then." Jesse clapped his hands together in glee. "Me, I've got a plan of action that involves this piece of pie."

Summer had to laugh at her grandfather's antics. And she had to admit it felt good, sitting here having a quiet dinner with her grandparents and Mack.

It felt so right. Too right.

Which could only mean it was all wrong.

* * *

"No, no, I think that's all wrong."

Summer got up to find more paper, her arms slicing through the air.

"So...we don't want a pony ride at the festival?"

Mack watched as she paced the confines of her grandparents' apartment, watched and wondered how such a high-strung woman could possibly ever sit still.

"I'm not saying we can't have ponies," she replied, her voice low since her grandparents had headed off to bed about an hour ago. "I'm just saying that I don't think it would be wise to put the ponies right smack in the middle of the yard. You know how ponies are—they'll trample the grass and mess up things."

Mack nodded, winced. "Oh, right. I guess that wouldn't be so smart. We could put the ponies down by the lake, on that level bit of ground away from the buildings."

She nodded as she brought him another cup of coffee. "And downwind."

"Okay, so far we've agreed to a dunking booth, a cake walk, a candy booth and activity booth for the kids, and face painting."

Summer sank back down on the floral loveseat across from the matching chair where Mack sat.

"Plus the arts-and-crafts displays from all the residents. In spite of our many disagreements, we've accomplished a lot."

"We only had two really heated arguments."

"Hey, I don't care what you say, I don't think balloon darts are a good idea with so many residents around with cataracts and bifocals."

"I guess that would be asking for trouble. No sharp instruments for the residents, then." He tugged at his hair. "And I guess the sack race was a bad idea, unless we can figure out how to put sacks around walkers."

She laughed, tossed down her pen. Made him swallow and take in a deep breath. He wished she wasn't so attractive. He wished he could keep his eyes off her.

She looked over at him. "So what did you and Papaw decide about Mr. Maroney?"

"Oh, that." Glad to be on a safe subject, Mack gave her a sideways look. "We're going to suggest he sends Miss Gladys some flowers, as I said earlier. Something simple, but effective."

Summer sat up in her chair, a teasing light in her eyes. "What kind of flowers do you send to women, Mack?"

Mack had to swallow again. "I like all kinds of

flowers, but…it would depend on the woman, of course."

"Of course."

She wasn't making this easy. But then, he had a feeling that Summer wasn't the kind of woman to make anything easy. High maintenance.

She kicked at his shin with her sandaled foot. "So what kind of flowers would you send to me? I mean, if we didn't have this…problem of you taking over my grandparents' house…and if I actually liked you."

"Thanks, I think." He mulled it over, squinted for a couple of seconds, then said, "I'd send you forget-me-nots."

"Oh." That seemed to slow her down, make her stop and think. She stared at him for a long time. "Why?"

"I think the name says it all. I wouldn't want you to forget me, ever. And I know I'll never forget you."

"Oh." She glanced at the clock, got up, back at full throttle. "Look how late it is. I'd better get back to my apartment. Lots to do tomorrow— paper angels to make, lace doilies to knit. You know, that sort of thing. And I really want to visit the gift shop. I've heard the art and jewelry in there is very good and reasonably priced."

"Okay, I get it," Mack said. "Time to go." He started clearing away their cookies and coffee. "Let me clean up these dishes and I'll walk you back to your apartment."

"You don't have to do that."

"No, but I want to do that."

"I know the way. Second door to the right and straight on till I reach number 220."

"I'm right around the corner, so I'm going that way anyway."

"Oh, okay then."

Mack grinned as he made sure everything was back in place and all the lights turned off. He checked the door to make sure it would lock behind them. "Your grandparents must have really been tired tonight."

"They did seem to beat a hasty retreat."

They walked silently down the carpeted hallways until they reached Summer's door. He could smell the citrus fragrance of her shampoo. "I'll get our ideas typed up."

"I can do that," she said, taking the notes from him.

"I don't mind."

"I said I'd do it."

"Okay, okay." He backed away, sure that she wanted him gone. "Guess I'll see you tomorrow."

"I might be busy."

"Okay, well, if I run into you—"

"You know this can't possibly work, don't you?"

Mack lifted his brows toward her. "I think we can pull off this festival, if you'll just quit being so bull-headed."

"I'm not talking about the festival. I'm talking about my grandparents throwing us together. I don't think it's going to work and I just want you to know that right up front."

The impact of her words hit Mack hard in the gut. "I never even considered…." He stopped, leaned a hand against the wall. "Okay, maybe I did consider what it might be like with us…you and me. But hey, I can understand if you aren't inclined toward the same thing—I mean, you and me, us—together." He stalled out and started to sweat.

"You could never understand," she said, all traces of a smile wiped from her face. "No one could ever understand. And I can't hurt my grandparents by giving them false hope."

Mack's disappointment felt like liquid heat inside his body. It burned him, but it also cleared his head. "I wouldn't want to give anyone false hope. Especially you."

"Oh, so you feel exactly the same way?"

Not sure how to respond, he asked, "What way?"

"That this is a bad idea? That we should just stick to the plan?"

"Absolutely," he replied, nodding his head while his heart bobbled and plunged. "Stick to the plan."

"Good then." She nodded, turned the key in the lock. "It's better this way—that we understand each other and keep things cool between us. I didn't come here looking for love, Mack. I'm sorry."

"Me, either," he said, meaning it, but regretting it at the same time. "No looking for love. Too much else to worry about."

She shifted, opened the door a fraction of an inch. "I'm sorry my grandparents seem so bent on pushing us together."

"Me, too." He was sorry about a lot of things.

So he turned and walked back down the silent hallway.

And heard the slamming of her door.

Chapter Nine

Saturday morning dawned bright and beautiful, much to Summer's dismay. She was hoping it would rain so she wouldn't be forced to endure going out to the farm with her grandparents and Mack.

"Great," she said as she finished her coffee. "Sunshine. Lots and lots of sunshine." Maybe the heat would be intolerable. Maybe they wouldn't be able to stay all day.

She stood at the window, watching as Mr. Maroney clipped fresh flowers from one of Mack's many beds. With deliberate precision, the white-haired man leaned over, first sniffing at the pink roses before choosing a nice fat blossom for his Gladys. Then he moved with stiff, stooped grace toward a cluster of orange daylilies, choosing a fluffy flower to go with the roses. Not a perfect match, but endearing all the same, Summer thought. How sweet that such a grumpy old man would go to that much trouble for the woman he obviously adored.

Summer wondered if a man would ever be that kind toward her. Then she thought of Mack again. He was kind and sweet. But he was also the source of much of her woe these days. He'd come to town and messed up the status quo.

But you weren't here to keep him from doing that.

Summer turned from the window, determined to get through this with grace and manners. But just the thought of spending this day with Mack Riley in the house that used to be her own made Summer simmer with pent-up rage. That rage pushed any kind feelings she might have had for Mack right out the window. She needed to focus on her anger, to stay true to her misgivings. She needed to remember that Mack Riley wasn't a friend. He was a foe, right up there with her no-show parents.

Then she felt guilty, even comparing him to her parents. Mack was a nice man, on the surface. And her parents were nice people, on the surface. But Summer didn't take people at surface value. There had to be something bad underneath all that charm and good-ol'-boy work ethic. Summer wished she *could* stay mad at the man, but it wasn't possible. Not after the way they'd laughed and then held hands the other night.

Of course, since then she'd explained how things had to be between them. Nothing serious. No developing, blossoming love. No good could come of it.

No good at all.

Then why did she feel so dejected this morning? And why was she dreading seeing him again? This feeling was about much more than her anger about the house and her grandparents living here at Golden Vista. Her feelings this morning were bittersweet, because she was torn between enjoying the way Mack did things to her head, and the way her heart hurt because he'd taken over what had once been a part of her life. And there was something else, some unnamed emotion that Summer couldn't pinpoint, just on the edge of her consciousness. She suspected that emotion had to do with her nonchalant, absent parents and her recent breakup with Brad. But she wasn't ready to delve too deeply into that right now.

Feeling like a teakettle about to boil over, she hurried to get dressed, throwing on a pair of old baggy olive shorts and a lightweight, sleeveless white cotton shirt. Then she headed down the hallway to her grandparents' apartment.

"Come in, honey," Martha called as Summer opened the door. "Mack and your grandfather are out back, loading up Mack's truck."

"We're all riding in that thing?"

Martha shook her head as she gathered her hat and her knitting. "Oh, no. We're going to follow y'all out there in our car, in case we get tired and need to come home early."

"I'll drive y'all," Summer said, grabbing the keys from her grandmother's hand.

"No, now," Martha said, taking the keys back with an amazingly firm grip. "You ride with Mack, keep him company."

"Memaw, I don't want to keep Mack company," Summer said, frustration coloring each word. "In fact, I'm not so sure I even want to go out to the farm."

"But we promised Mack. And I'm dying to see what he's done with the place."

Seeing the disappointment on her grandmother's face, Summer closed her eyes and prayed for patience. "Okay, but I'm warning you—don't do a number on me and leave me stranded out there with that man. You have to stop trying to match me up with Mack Riley."

Martha batted her eyes, clearly confused. "Who said anything about trying to match you two up, suga'?"

"No one has to say anything," Summer replied as she locked the door and they started out the back hallway to the parking lot. "It's pretty obvious that everyone around here thinks Mack and I should just automatically fall head over heels for each other. Even Mr. Maroney had suggested just that, and he's been busy trying to go steady with Miss Gladys. He shouldn't waste his time trying to match us up, too."

"So you're saying we should all mind our own business?"

"Something like that," Summer replied, nodding her head. "Mack and I don't need your lovable but overbearing interference."

Martha pursed her lips. "I just want you to be happy. So does Mr. Maroney. I think he wants everyone to be happy, especially since Mack's been giving him tips on how to win over Gladys. What's the harm in that?"

"There is no harm in Mr. Maroney courting Miss Gladys, but there is a lot of harm in everyone trying to throw Mack and me together."

Martha was the picture of sweet innocence and firm intensity. "Why?"

Summer stopped her grandmother at the door, lowering her voice. "I just came off a very bad relationship, Memaw. I'm not ready to take on another man right now."

Concern marring her expression, Martha looked over Summer as if searching for bruises and scars. "What happened? You never talk about that side of your life. Is there anything I can do to make you feel better?"

Summer shook her head, wincing at the memories. "Coming here has made me feel better. That's part of the reason I took this leave of absence from my job. I needed—"

"You needed to heal," Martha said, pulling Summer close. "You came home. You knew where you'd find your strength. Everyone knows Texas is one of the best spots on earth to get on with life."

Summer hugged her grandmother tightly, then leaned back. Martha had no idea just how much Summer needed to rest and heal, and yes, to get on with life. "Yes, but I can't get over Brad if I've got all these notions in my head about Mack Riley."

"You have notions?" Martha asked, obviously glad to hear that bit of news.

"I do each time you push us together," Summer

replied, then she waved her hands in the air. "But, that's not the point. The point is—I'm not interested in Mack Riley. I'll help at the house, I'll be nice to the man, and I'll work on the festival with him. But that's it. I have to go back to New York and my job after the fourth, anyway."

"Okay, darlin'," Martha replied, a bit too quickly. "I guess we'll just have to settle for that."

"Good," Summer said, wondering if her grandmother was even listening to what she was really saying. And wondering if she was trying too hard to convince both herself and her grandmother that she didn't have feelings for Mack.

"Good," Martha echoed, a serene expression on her face.

Summer decided her grandmother wasn't very good at hiding *her* true feelings. Which meant Summer had to make it very clear to all involved that she wasn't going to fall for Mack Riley.

He wouldn't fall for her. Mack kept telling himself that as they pulled into the long drive to the farmhouse. After Belinda and her bag of tricks, Mack had made a solemn promise to be careful in the love department. He'd gone back to the strong values and firm foundation his parents had instilled in him, and he'd turned his life over to God.

That meant no roller-coaster, topsy-turvy relationships. The next time he fell in love, he wanted it to be slow-paced and solid, a forever kind of perfect love, like that of his parents and of Jesse and Martha. He needed to stick to the plan, as Summer had suggested.

But he wished he knew the plan. Was he destined to spend the rest of his life alone? Mack thought about how close he and Belinda had come to marrying and having a family. He'd always thought that would happen, but Belinda had only wanted him on her terms. She wanted a man who could move in the high society she was so used to. She wanted a husband who could showcase her own beauty and help her to keep moving up the social ladder while he catered to her whims and demands. Mack had failed miserably at being that man.

He glanced over at Summer, wondering at the paradox of her life. She came from a wealthy Texas family. She was considered a socialite by any standards. She'd had privileges in her life, yet she'd turned away from all the free handouts and set out to make her own way in life, far away from the traditions of Texas.

"Why'd you move to New York?" he asked, needing to understand her.

Summer jumped in the passenger seat as if he'd said "Boo." Pushing at a few stray bangs, she shrugged. "My cousin April got this idea that we needed to conquer the Big Apple. She was running away from a lot of bad things, so after a trip there to celebrate our graduating from college—we're all just a couple of months apart in age—she convinced Autumn and me to come with her. Autumn had already graduated, but she was working with my uncle as a CPA in Atlanta—Texas, that is." She shook her head. "Autumn had this ten-year plan… which she had to modify just a tad after April got this urge."

Mack grinned at that. "So New York City beckoned?"

"Yes. April can be pretty persuasive. I think Autumn came along just to look out for April and me. And I sure was up for an adventure. I mean, my parents were never around a whole lot, and I needed to prove myself, I guess. I had my degree in social work and what better place to get down and dirty? New York is full of broken, hurting people. So, we all packed up and headed out. At first, our fathers footed the bill because they all figured we'd be back in Texas in about a month. But we slowly weaned ourselves off that and did things on our own."

"Do you enjoy your job?"

She laughed at that. Waiting for Mack to park the rickety old truck in front of the farmhouse, she shook her head. "There is no way to enjoy helping battered women. It's a tough battle. But I do enjoy the satisfaction of seeing these women start all over from scratch. It's good to see someone who's been so hopeless and full of despair turn around and find a new beginning. So, I guess I find it fulfilling, yes. But unfortunately, not all of my cases have a happy ending."

Mack saw the darkness pass through her blue eyes like clouds over water, and wondered if she took those lost causes to heart. "How do *you* deal with all of that?"

She opened her door. "Lately, not very well." Getting out, she slammed the door shut and left Mack sitting there.

He wondered what she'd seen up there in the big city. Wondered if the days and nights of so much tragedy and violence had left her frayed and damaged. Maybe that was why she was so prickly at times. He knew she was tough. He'd seen that from the beginning. But he wondered if she wasn't tender, too. Too tender to hurt. Too tender to accept false hope.

And yet, he wanted to see her hopeful. He

wanted to wipe that cynicism right off her pretty face. It didn't help that she'd come home for some peace and quiet, only to find her old way of life completely changed. It didn't sit well that he'd contributed to her pain and her disappointment. Maybe today would give her some sort of closure and peace. He hoped so.

He watched her as she slowly made her way toward the house, her head down as if she couldn't bear to look at the place. He got out of the truck to follow her. "I'm glad y'all came," he said as they waited for Jesse and Martha to pull into the driveway. "I like coming out here to work on the house, but it sure gets lonely."

"I can swing a mean paintbrush," she said in response, her gaze slowly moving over the scaffolds holding up one side of the two-story house. "What's going on there?"

"Just reinforcing the structure," Mack explained. "I've had contractors out here all week working on that. They'll replace boards and shingles and paint the outside once the new windows are in."

"New windows? What's wrong with the old ones?"

"I wanted better insulation," he explained. "I plan on keeping the original design, but I also need to keep the utility bills down. Just being practical."

"Probably a good idea. I remember chilly nights here during the winter. Memaw would pile the quilts on my bed."

"That's what Jesse told me. And hot, humid summers, kind of like today."

She pushed at her hair. "I hope my grandparents don't overheat."

"I won't let that happen."

She turned to him then, her eyes devoid of any anger or doubt. "You care about them."

"Of course I do. I never knew my grandparents."

"What about your parents?"

"They still live in Austin. They're fine. I don't get back there much."

She shifted her sneakers in a mound of dirt, her thumbs hooked in her baggy pockets. "I did a search looking for information on you on the Internet."

"Oh?" He should be angry, but knowing Summer the way he did, he reckoned it fit. But he didn't have anything earth-shaking to hide or reveal. "And what did you find?"

"You owned your own company? Landscaping?"

"Are you asking me to confirm that?"

"If you want. I did it only because I was just trying to protect my grandparents."

"Makes sense, but why didn't you just ask me?"

"I'm asking now."

Mack shook his head. "You just don't trust me, do you?"

"I'm trying. I want to be angry at you, but you're too nice for that. Or so you seem."

"But you don't believe in nice?"

"I've seen nice overplayed, yeah."

Mack turned as Jesse pulled the shiny new sedan up underneath an old oak tree. "Maybe later, we can go for a walk and I'll tell you everything you need to know."

"Maybe."

Feeling as if they'd reached a truce of sorts, he headed off to unload his truck. But Mack couldn't help but wonder what Summer would do if she knew the true story of his life in Austin. And he wondered if he'd have the courage to tell her that story. Would she accept him the way he was now, or would she turn away because he'd once let a woman walk all over him to the point that he had no pride left? He wanted Summer to like him, but more than that, he wanted her to respect him.

She had to admit the old house was coming along very nicely. Summer stood in the empty living room, memories swirling around her in the dust balls that glowed in the morning sun. Everything was different now.

The long paneled room had a new coat of shiny varnish on the walls, making it seem more light and airy. The long row of windows facing the back of the house boasted double-paned insulation. That would work with the new heating and air-conditioning system. The fireplace, which had housed a horrid-looking gas heater, had been restored and polished clean, its walnut wood gleaming. The hardwood floors had been sanded and refinished. The whole room shone with a bright hope that made Summer think of a loving family and future generations of children. She had to wonder if Mack had someone special in mind to share this big house with him.

"You're bringing this place into this century, at least," she told Mack with a grudging appreciation.

He turned from clearing away some clutter. "You approve—finally?"

"I didn't say I approve. But I can certainly appreciate what you're trying to do." The easy banter between her grandparents carried from the kitchen, making Summer smile. "I just hope your two helpers don't waste more paint than they put on the walls in there."

"They're having a blast," Mack said as he tossed some old boards and wallpaper into a huge wastebasket he'd brought in from the back porch.

Summer couldn't argue with that. Her grandparents had such sweet spirits. They could roll with the punches and make anything exciting and fun. She wished she could be that way. But she'd been shifted and shaken too many times to actually see the potential in bad situations. She longed to be…settled. Just settled.

"Hey, don't look so sad," Mack said as he came walking past her, paintbrush in hand. He lifted the brand-new trim brush to her nose, tickling her with the silky fibers.

Summer crinkled her nose, then smiled. "Is that my cue to get to work?"

"You don't have to do anything," Mack retorted. "But you can keep me company upstairs."

She grabbed the brush from his hand. "No, I came to work. I need to stay busy. What are you working on?"

"The master bedroom," he said over his shoulder.

She watched as he made his way up the stairs. Did she dare go up there with him? They'd be all alone. And even though her grandparents were right downstairs, Summer felt vulnerable and exposed when she was around Mack. Maybe because of the way he'd looked at her there on the verandah the other night. Maybe because her emotions were at war right now—trying to hate him and like him at the same time.

"You coming?" Mack asked, leaning his head over the sturdy new oak railing.

Summer glanced around, couldn't find any excuses to keep her busy down here. "Yeah, I'll be right there."

She hurried up the stairs, but when she rounded the top landing she saw movement down below out of the corner of her eye. Glancing down, she just caught a glimpse of her grandparents bobbing their heads around the open arch between the kitchen and the front hallway. They quickly ducked back into the kitchen, but Summer didn't miss the keen interest in their expressions. Or the hopeful looks in their eyes.

"I must be crazy," she mumbled. "I should just walk out of here right now, right this minute."

But she didn't have anywhere to go. Her home belonged to someone else now. Her heart was battered and broken. Her spirit was depleted. She was a weary traveler who needed a place to stop and rest her head.

She looked up and saw Mack waiting there for her, the sun shining through the windows behind him, peeling, tattered rose-hued wallpaper surrounding him. And suddenly, Summer wanted to peel back all the layers that made up Mack Riley. She wanted to explore those layers, so she could figure out what made this man tick. He seemed so sure, so secure, in his life and in his faith. He seemed like a simple man who only wanted a simple life. No hidden agendas, no past dysfunction holding him back, no pain or loss in his life.

He'd promised her he'd tell her all about himself.

Summer intended to make sure he honored that promise.

Chapter Ten

"That was a very good lunch."

Mack put down the remains of his fried chicken and potato salad, then looked over at Summer. She'd been awfully quiet during their meal out on the back porch.

"Thanks," Jesse said, grinning. "I got up at four o'clock this morning to cook this chicken."

"Hmph," Martha said, hitting him on the arm with her napkin. "You were still snoring away at four this morning. The cook at Golden Vista prepared this chicken."

"Blabbermouth," Jesse retorted, sticking out his tongue at her. "But a mighty cute blabbermouth." He winked at her, then offered her an oatmeal cookie. "Have some dessert."

"Think I might." Martha took the cookie, then

stretched back in one of the old kitchen chairs Mack had set up out on the porch. "Mercy, I might need a nap. That afternoon breeze sure is pleasant."

Jesse nodded, put down his chicken leg. "Remember how we used to stretch out underneath that giant cottonwood down by the creek?"

"I remember," Martha said, a becoming blush coloring her skin. "We were so young back then. Now...I reckon I'd get stuck and you'd have to get help to get me up."

Mack laughed at their easy banter, the hole in his heart hurting with a splitting pain. He wished he could have that kind of love. He wished he knew where he'd gone wrong with Belinda. But then, he thought if he dug deeply enough, he'd find the answer to that question. And it wouldn't be pretty. She hadn't loved him enough to make a commitment, and he'd loved her way too much to see that for what it was. Nothing like getting the cart before the horse. He'd rushed headlong into that relationship, then gone against all the values he'd been taught in order to win her over. He wouldn't make that mistake again.

Putting those memories away, he glanced over at Summer. He needed to get some things cleared up between them. "Up to that walk we talked about?"

She looked up, her eyes going wide with surprise. She appeared to be lost in thought herself. Looking confused, she busied herself with throwing away their paper plates. "What about that room we left unfinished upstairs?"

They'd painted most of the master bedroom, their quiet work and easy chat a nice reprieve from all the undercurrents swirling between them. But now, Mack could see those undercurrents had returned.

"It'll be there when we get back," he said, and, thinking their *unfinished* business was more important right now, he waited for her to respond.

"Go ahead, honey," Martha said, urging Summer with a hand on her arm. "Your granddaddy and I will go in and rest—the old couch is still in the back den for me and Papaw can take the broken recliner. We'll be just fine."

"Then when y'all return, it's back to work," Jesse said. "No slackers here." He pushed off the table. "You've done a fine job on this old house, Mack. Makes me proud to know I sold it to the right man."

Mack swallowed, looked down at the floor. "Thanks, Jesse. That means a lot to me." When he looked back up, Summer was staring at him, her eyes bright with questions he wasn't so sure he could answer.

"Ready?" he asked, wondering if she'd just turn tail and run the other way.

"I guess so."

He waited until they'd cleared the porch before speaking. "Well, don't look as if you're headed for an execution."

"I'm sorry," she said, pasting a false smile on her face as she waved to her wide-eyed grandparents. "It's just hard being here like this. I'm helping you fix up the house I've always loved." She shrugged. "I'm a bit conflicted, as usual."

"You don't like the changes on the house, or you just don't like me?"

She pushed at her long hair, her eyes following the treeline along the pasture fence behind the house. The heat of summer buzzed past them in the form of bees droning and birds chirping. A pretty yellow butterfly drifted by, its wings fluttering gracefully. "I don't want to like you, Mack. But I do."

He grinned. "Score one for me, then."

"And I don't want to like this house becoming all modern and pretty, because it was beautiful to me just the way it was. But I have to agree with Papaw. You've done a great job."

Mack took that compliment in silence, admiring her direct nature. "What did you love most about this place?"

She gave him a weary look, as if that were a trick question. "My grandparents," she replied without hesitation. "I've always known I could count on them. They're solid and sure. Not like most—"

"Tell me about your parents."

She shook her head, looked out over the rolling hills. "I don't want to talk about them."

Mack respected that, but knew she needed to talk to someone. So he tried another tactic. "My parents are the salt of the earth. We didn't have much when I was growing up, but they took care of us."

"Do you have brothers and sisters?"

"Two brothers and a sister. I'm one of the middle ones."

Her surprise turned to a pleasant smile. "What's it like, having a big family?"

He laughed at that. "Crazy at times. My two older brothers loved to harass me and my younger sister. I learned to be tough at a very early age. It was survival of the fittest."

She let her hand trail over the fence. "Funny, I learned to be tough the first time my parents left me behind."

Mack stopped and turned to face her as they reached the small creek. He put his hands on her arms, to steady her, to force her to look at him. "I can't imagine that—parents leaving a child. I've met your parents, Summer, and I don't get it. They seem like such nice, self-assured people. Really together."

"That's the key word," she said. "*Together*. They wanted to be together with each other much more than they wanted to be together with me." She shook her head. "I think they love me, but they just don't get that I...I needed to hear that, and I needed to have them here so many times, for the everyday things that a child needs."

"You're blessed that you had Jesse and Martha."

"Don't I know it. My other grandparents died when I was just a baby. I wished I could have known them. I always dreamed that they would have taken care of me, too. I could have been doubly blessed." Her smile was bittersweet. "I know I shouldn't complain, but my parents always treated me as if I were a toy. They played with me when they were in town and they put me back in my place whenever it was time to move on to something better."

"I can't imagine that," Mack replied, wishing there was something he could say to make her feel better. "But I guess parents abandon children all the time. We just don't hear about it."

"It happens," she said. "I saw it a lot in New York. And that kind of abandonment is much worse than what I ever suffered, trust me. I had my grandparents. But there are children out there who will never know their real fathers and mothers. In my line of work, it was mostly the fathers. They'd beat up their women, then either leave for good or try to hurt both mother and child. At least my parents are blissfully happy. So happy with each other, they tend to shut out the rest of the world." She shrugged. "I have this thing about fathers who abuse or abandon their own. It's just not right. So I've fought to fix it. Sometimes, I've won. Many times, I've lost."

Mack could see the hurt on her face. It made him want to protect her, to hold her and promise her that everything would be all right. And he wanted to figure out what was driving her. "Did you choose social work because of the way your parents were always dumping you?"

She drew back, her features going sharp with

pain and denial. "Are you trying to analyze me, Mack?"

"No, I'm trying to understand you."

"There's nothing to understand, except that I had a wonderful set of maternal grandparents who loved me and raised me, for the most part. As I said, my other set of grandparents died when I was young, so I don't remember them at all. They left the Maxwell legacy—and all that money, while Memaw and Papaw gave me a sense of home. I suppose when you add all of that together, I grew up knowing I was blessed, but also knowing I wanted to help others— especially children. Memaw and Papaw taught me to always honor and respect my blessings by being kind to others."

"They did a good job," he said, hoping to win back some of her tentative affection. "You don't seem to be the type to let money go to your head."

"Yeah, well they tried, that's for sure. I never rebelled while living here, but I sure liked to show my angst whenever my parents returned home. That's when I'd play the money card, spending huge amounts on clothes and shoes I didn't need, just so I could go on shopping trips with my mom and then ignore her afterwards. I was trying to fill this great void, and so was she, I guess. I've been trying to fill that place for years since. Now, I'm bitter, burned out, tired, confused. I'm a walking mess. I don't know why I thought coming back here could change any of the mistakes I've made—"

She stopped, a hand flying to her mouth. "And I really don't want to talk about any of this with you."

"Because you don't want to like me or trust me, right? Because you think I just came in here and coerced your grandparents? Or is it because I bought this property through your father and you just can't cut him any slack either?"

"You don't know how I feel about my father," she retorted, her face reddening with rage.

"Oh, I think I do," he said, unwilling to back down now. He was tired of trying to justify his actions and his motives. He understood how Summer was feeling all right, but the things she'd held onto from her past had nothing to do with him. And now, just when he thought he could rest and enjoy life, God had thrown this aggravating, enticing, interesting, *conflicted* woman in his path. Was he supposed to help her or just ignore her? This very minute, he could only empathize with her. "I think I understand exactly how you feel."

She held out her hands in the air. "I thought we

came out here so *you* could tell *me* all about your life. How come you've twisted it around on me?"

"I don't know. I just wanted to…to try and figure you out, I guess."

"Well, don't bother." She turned to stomp away, her long hair fluttering out behind her in waves of gold that reminded Mack of that pretty yellow butterfly they'd seen earlier.

"Hey, wait," Mack said, tugging her back around. "You really want to know why I left Austin? Why I came here to this small, sleepy town?"

She slanted her eyebrows, her head going down as she eyed him. "That would be good, for starters."

He stood, his eyes locked with hers, and decided to lay all his cards on the table. "I got burned, too, Summer. I fell for a woman straight out of college. An Austin socialite who was rich and powerful…and so beautiful.

"I went to work for her father, because she insisted I could be happy there, and because she indicated she could only be happy with me there. For years, we had this kind of sick relationship where she guided everything from the clothes I wore to the people I associated with. But it wasn't enough. I tried to convince myself that I loved her, that

I'd do anything to have her as my wife. But the more she demanded, the more angry and bitter I became—with her, but mostly with myself. She'd promise me marriage, then change her mind over some incident or so-called slight. We battled back and forth and I actually left her father's company to start my own. She left me, but then when it looked like I was going to be a success, she came back, telling me how proud she was of me. I fell for her all over again and we got really close for a while. I thought maybe she really did love me. But I was wrong. She got angry over something I said, then she told me I could never support her financially, that I couldn't make her happy because I refused to accept her wealth."

He let out a breath, pinched his nose with his thumb and index finger. "I decided to show her, so I worked hard and kept on making a name for myself. She tried to get me back then, and I hate to admit this, but I gave in one last time. I gave all the way in, Summer, just to have one night with her. Then I hated myself afterwards. I had had enough. I rejected her.

"She went to her daddy and convinced him that I'd wronged her, so he decided to stick it to me real good. All the clients I'd worked so hard to acquire started backing away, one by one. And because of that, I almost lost everything. So I packed up and headed out. I had to get away. I had to start over. End of story."

She stood staring at him, her expression changing from disbelief to understanding. "I can't believe the man standing in front of me would let a woman do that to him."

He let out a laugh, both relieved and in agony that she'd immediately seen his worst flaw. "Neither can I. But then, we do strange things in the name of love, don't we?"

She flinched, as if she knew about that firsthand. "I guess we do." Then she lifted her gaze, her eyes locking with his. "Did you feel trapped when you were with her? Unable to make a decision on your own?"

Surprised that she got it, he nodded, swallowed the bile rising in his throat. "I felt as if I'd lost my soul. What I thought was love was really more about control, her need to control me, both physically and mentally. I won't be controlled again."

He thought he saw a flicker of admiration in her eyes. And maybe something else. A kind of recognition. "You feel safe here, right?"

He nodded. "Yes, I feel safe here. I feel secure now. Maybe I'm hiding out here, but at least I no longer doubt myself or my faith in God. When I left Austin, I promised Him I'd never stray again. I just want some peace and a simple life. That wasn't good enough for Belinda. It has to be enough—it is enough—for me."

He stood there, his soul bare and bruised, and wondered why he'd just spilled his guts to this woman. How could she possibly understand the disgust he'd felt for himself the last time he'd been with Belinda? How could he make Summer understand the whole ugly story about how Belinda had gotten to him one last time?

He couldn't. Some things needed to be kept inside. That part of his life was over now, and he wouldn't look back. He had asked God for forgiveness so many times, he felt raw from the wanting of it. He wouldn't count on Summer Maxwell to help appease his soul.

But when he looked into her eyes, he saw a reflection of his pain there in the blue depths. He thought he saw that understanding and peace he needed so badly.

"I'm sorry you had to hear all of that," he said, hoping she would at least back off now. "But I want you to understand that...I need this quiet time here, working on this house, working at Golden Vista. I need this in my life right now. And I won't apologize for being here, or for turning back to my faith to guide me. Not anymore. I just want to be settled, to be happy again."

He turned to walk past her, back to the house, but then Summer did something that surprised him and sealed his fate. She touched a hand to his face and reached up to kiss him softly on the cheek. "Then it seems we both want the same things, Mack. Imagine that."

Summer was still accepting this new turn in her heart as they rounded the lane toward the house. She had accepted that this man was becoming important to her, even though she'd only known him for about a week. Not one to rush into anything, she also accepted that this relationship would have to develop slowly and surely and firmly. Maybe they'd just become very good friends, or maybe something else would develop. But she wasn't going to hang around here forever. What then?

Then, she decided with a delicious joy, she'd have a friend to visit each time she came home to see her grandparents. That gave her a kind of sweet security as she glanced over at Mack. After their heart-wrenching confessions earlier, they'd settled under the tall cottonwood and discussed so many things, including the upcoming festivities at the retirement center. It had been nice, going back over the plans for the events with him. He really was a good man. Easy to work with, easy to look at, easy to fall for.

One day at a time, she told herself. Don't rush it. Don't count on it.

"I'm glad we got everything for the festival ironed out," Summer told him. "We can give my grandparents a full report and then next week, I'll get started on organizing things."

He smiled at her, his eyes clear of any mistrust or regret. "Are we friends yet?"

"We are," she replied, almost shy now that she'd let him win her over. "Thanks for telling me… about your life in Austin. I know there's more— isn't there always?—but I won't press for the details. From my experience, people can't be pushed too hard to divulge the intimate details of their lives. That has to come with trust, lots of trust. I can see that Belinda hurt you, but Mack, I could never see you as being a weak man."

He blinked, turned away. "But I *was* weak. I figured you could see right through me."

"What I see is a man who's trying to get his life together, a man who works hard, tries to do the right thing, and…a man who adores my grandparents. The pros far outweigh the cons, Mack."

"Same here," he said, turning to look at her.

"You think you've made mistakes. But I see you trying to find your way back from those mistakes. I guess we both are."

"So, can we agree to concentrate on the here and now, just for now?"

"Okay," he said, taking her hand in his. "But, one day soon, I want to hear the rest of your story, too."

"Still twisting things around on me, huh?"

"Still interested in the details," he countered. Then he laughed. "As your grandmother has so graciously pointed out, we're the only two people around Golden Vista who aren't members of the American Association of Retired Persons. Guess that makes us an item of sorts."

"She told you that, too?"

"Uh, yes. I think the whole place is holding its collective breath regarding us. Even Mr. Maroney, who has a serious crush on you."

"They can keep holding their breaths," Summer replied, grinning. "Let's keep them guessing."

"Oh, I think *you* plan on keeping *me* guessing."

She stopped near the back porch. "I'll be leaving after the festival, Mack. There's no guessing about that."

"I know. But we have a few weeks until then.

And since we've agreed to enjoy the here and now...."

She saw the hope in his eyes and felt that same hope reflected in her heart. "I'm in big trouble," she told him.

"I know the feeling," he replied.

Summer placed one foot on the back steps just as the door from the house burst open. She glanced up, expecting to find her overly eager grandparents grinning down on them.

But the two people she saw standing there caused Summer to grab the porch railing to steady herself.

"Summer, darlin', we were beginning to think you two had fallen in that snake-infested creek. Come on up here and let me have a look at you. Why on earth haven't you cut that hair by now?"

"My little girl's just as pretty as she was when she was a squirt running around here, don't you think, Elsie?"

"I sure do, in spite of that uncontrollable hair. Honey, it's so good to see you."

Summer shot Mack a warning look, then lifted a hand in the air. "Mack Riley, meet my parents, James and Elsie Maxwell." Then she turned to the two people staring down at them, her rage warring with her joy in full force as she confronted them. "They're just passing through, I'm sure."

Elsie came bopping down the steps, her strappy sandals clinking on the aged wood, her orange silk sheath glistening in the sunshine. "Oh, no, darlin', we've come home for a good long stay. And we want you to come and stay in our house with us, just as soon as you can get your suitcase loaded and in the car."

Chapter Eleven

Summer looked around the huge house her parents had dragged her into and wondered why she'd let them talk her into coming here. The place was overdone and tacky, a perfect example of too much of a good thing. The mansion was all silver and gold, all swirls and etchings. It was designed in a country-French style that stuck out like an amusement-park phony amid the many ranch-style houses of East Texas.

"It looks like something out of a bad horror movie," Summer said to herself, her words echoing up into the twenty-foot ceiling of the entryway. She let out a sigh, willing herself to be calm and reasonable. At least her parents had come home. It was a start.

Her mother came tapping down the stairs,

her hand moving over the wrought-iron railing as she descended like a queen about to greet her court. "Your things are all unpacked and put away, darlin'." Elsie stopped at the last step to look down on Summer. "Are you going to stand there in the hallway all day, or actually come on inside?"

Summer didn't miss the nervous laughter behind her mother's words. Elsie had always seemed a bit afraid of her only daughter. Maybe because they were so very different. Don't spook her, Summer told herself. Try to make conversation. Try to be kind.

"I'm…getting adjusted," Summer replied, trying very hard to do what her grandmother had asked in a whispered plea back at the farmhouse. Make nice.

"Well, let's go back to the den and find us something cool to drink," her mother suggested, waving her long orange-polished fingers in the air. Elsie prided herself on her impeccable manicures, which always had to match her outfits.

Summer stifled the groan she felt coming and marched up the marble-floored hallway toward the back of the big rectangular house, her mind reeling with the events of the last few hours.

After getting over the shock of seeing her parents, Summer had somehow managed to get through the impromptu tour they'd insisted on taking to look over the renovations on the farmhouse.

But not before she blurted out, "I'm not going anywhere with y'all."

"And why on earth not?" Elsie countered, her green eyes flashing with a dare. "You can't stay in that old folks' home, suga'."

"It's a retirement center," Summer purposely pointed out. "One you and Daddy convinced my grandparents to move into."

"Hey, now," James interjected, "this was a mutual decision. Your mother worried so much about her folks. It seemed like the best solution."

"Best for you, right?"

Summer stomped into the house, leaving Mack to talk to her shocked parents. But her grandmother rounded on her as she headed for the front door.

"Summer, you are missing a chance here."

Summer stopped to stare at Martha, her pulse racing. "How many chances have *they* missed over the years, Memaw? They missed my tenth birthday. They missed my high-school graduation. They missed when I was crowned Miss Athens.

They missed when I went off to college, and they barely made it to that graduation. I don't think I'm missing anything, because they don't seem to care what they've missed."

"You are so wrong there," Martha replied. "Now, honey, I've never asked any more of you than you can bear. And you can bear this. Go home with your parents and spend some time with them. You're an adult now. It's time to stop this childish grudge."

"You think this is a grudge? Memaw, this is more than just a grudge. This is my life. Because of them, I—"

She stopped, unable to tell her grandmother anything more about her life in New York, about her bad choice in men, especially Brad Parker. Summer couldn't tell anyone the shame she felt in that.

"What, honey?" Martha asked, waiting, her words almost echoing Summer's thoughts. "You know you can talk to me about anything, but you need to quit blaming your parents for everything wrong that's ever happened to you. I think you've had a pretty good life, all things considered."

Summer did feel contrite. "I never said I hated my life here, Memaw. In fact, I cherished it. You know that. It's just that...I wish I could understand—"

"Try talking to your mama, then," Martha replied.

"It doesn't matter," Summer finally said, guilt weighing down on her like a sackcloth. "I'll go with them, but only because you asked."

"Thank you," Martha replied.

Elsie rushed inside, her eyes wide with hurt and concern, her face flushed. "Summer?"

"I'm sorry, Mama," Summer said. "I didn't mean what I said. I'll come and stay with y'all for a few days."

"Oh, honey, I'm so glad."

Mack followed Elsie, his face white with worry. "Hey, are you okay?"

Summer nodded. "I'm going to the big house." Her humor didn't make anyone laugh. "I'm going to stay with my parents."

He gave her a look that combined understanding and confusion. "Okay. Need me to take you back to the center?"

"We'll take her after we tour the house," James said, his cowboy boots announcing his entry into the room. He looked relieved to hear that Summer had changed her mind.

Summer noticed her grandfather was staying in the kitchen, away from the fray. Probably wise. And she also noticed Mack's watchful eyes on her as she reluctantly walked through the house with her parents.

"Pretty impressive," her father said, nodding his approval, his snakeskin boots clicking on the hardwood floors.

"Mack, I should have hired you when we were designing and building our house," Elsie cooed, obviously thrilled to be showing off to a new-comer. "Don't you just love a man who is handy around the house?" she asked anyone who might be inclined to agree.

"I know I sure do," Martha said, joining in the gleeful celebration.

Summer stood back, glancing from her parents to Mack. She could see his discomfort and she had to wonder if he felt uncomfortable for himself, or for her. Probably both.

Now she was glad she'd told him some of the history of her relationship, or lack thereof, with her parents. At least he understood her reserva-tions about going to stay with her parents.

"I don't want to do this," she whispered to him as they were leaving the farm earlier.

"Really? I would have never guessed."

"Does it show that much?"

"Like you've just had a root canal. Stop frowning."

"Do you promise to come and rescue me if I shout out?"

"I promise."

The look in his eyes had told her he'd do just that. That brought Summer a comfort she wasn't accustomed to having. A nice, safe security that had given her the courage to go back to Golden Vista and toss her things in her duffel bag while her parents visited with the administrators and office staff.

Martha had hugged Summer tightly as she was leaving. "I'm so proud of you, honey. Use this time to get things sorted out with your parents. It's precious time, Summer. Use it wisely."

I'm doing this for you, Memaw, she told herself now, gritting her teeth with each step. But if she were truly honest, Summer knew she was also doing this for her own peace of mind. Part of that healing process, she supposed. She couldn't get on with her life and make those changes if she was mired in anger and regret. And besides, she had lots of questions for her parents. Lots.

While her mother busied herself pouring fresh

iced tea that the maid had provided, Summer sank into a heavy cream leather chair and again thought back over the afternoon. When she'd seen her parents standing there, her whole world had shifted. It made her remember all those other times she'd seen them, the times her heart had filled with hope that maybe they'd come home for good this time.

How many times had she been disappointed? How many times had her grandmother had to hold her while she cried herself to sleep because they'd left yet again?

Her mother's grating voice brought her back to the here and now. "I invited Mama and Daddy out to dinner tonight. We'll grill steaks by the pool. Oh, and I invited Mack Riley, too."

Summer felt the rush of relief move throughout her body, only to clash with the universal assumption that paired her with Mack at every gathering lately. Somehow, in spite of her firm denial regarding a romance with Mack, knowing that he would be here did make her feel a whole lot better about things. But all of these spiraling feelings were a bit overwhelming. Things were changing again, too fast for her to absorb and accept.

"That sounds nice," she managed to reply to her mother. "We can all have a good, long visit."

"You don't have to be so sarcastic," Elsie retorted, her gold coin bracelet jingling as she clinked ice into a glass.

"I didn't think I was being sarcastic," Summer replied, all of her old insecurities hitting the surface.

"You don't feel comfortable here, do you, darlin'?"

"Should I, Mother?"

"This is your home."

"No, you and Daddy sold the only home I've ever known."

"Summer, this is getting very tiresome."

"I'm just getting started."

"So...instead of spending time with your poor old daddy and me, you intend to taunt us and tease us at every turn."

"Works for me."

"You are so stubborn."

"Guess I got that naturally."

Elsie sank down on the loveseat across from Summer, then propped her feet up on the matching leather ottoman. "If your father were here—"

"Well, he's not, is he?" Summer pointed out. "Couldn't wait to get to the golf course and brag with all his buddies."

"He'll be here for dinner."

"I won't hold my breath on that."

"You are being completely nasty."

Summer decided her mother was right. Lowering her head, she willed her expression to soften. "I'm sorry. I promised Memaw—"

Elsie's hand flew to her coiffured hair. "So you only came here because my mama made you?"

"Something like that."

Summer watched as her mother blinked back tears. Crocodile tears probably. But then when her mother burst into heaving sobs, Summer became really concerned.

"Mother?"

Elsie sniffed, threw up a hand. "I...so wanted us to be friends again, Summer. I...I need a friend right now."

Summer shot out of her chair and fell down on the ottoman, one hand touching her mother's arm. "Mommy, I've never seen you like this."

"I've never *been* like this," Elsie said, tears streaming down her face. "Honestly, I think I'm losing my mind."

Summer felt a strange shifting inside her heart, like clay crumbling into jagged pieces. "What's wrong?"

Elsie looked up at her, mascara smeared around her eyes. "It's your father. He... I think he wants a divorce."

* * *

Summer shut the door to her mother's bedroom, the scent of Chanel No. 5 wafting out into the hallway after her. Taking the tray of herbal tea down to the kitchen, Summer was careful not to make too much noise in the echoing house. The maid took the tray with a wan smile.

Which left Summer to wander around with her thoughts rolling ahead of her like tumbleweeds. Her mother had needed her. Her parents might be getting a divorce.

Not used to being the nurturer to her mother, Summer thought back on their conversation. Elsie had seemed so small and vulnerable, sitting there on the cushiony loveseat, pouring out her heart to Summer.

"I can't tell Mama and Daddy. It would just kill them."

"Why are you telling me?"

"Because I knew you'd understand," Elsie said in a weak voice. "Baby, you do this kind of stuff for a living right? I mean, you counsel people."

Summer was both astonished and amazed at her mother's words. Her mother wanted her to *counsel* them? Her own parents? How in the world was she supposed to do that, when she didn't even begin to understand them?

But Summer had sat with her mother, talking to

her quietly, soothing her battered nerves until she had finally convinced Elsie to drink some chamomile tea and take a long nap. Apparently, James had been acting very strangely lately.

"He's just not himself. He's quiet and moody. I can't seem to please him. I just know he's found someone else. I mean, I've tried to do everything to please him, I've tried to stay young-looking and slim. I've helped him with what's left of his rodeo glory, but that's about all dried up. Maybe he blames me for that, but I can't help the man growing old. He thinks he's a has-been. Maybe that makes me a has-been, too."

"You're not that, Mother," Summer had said. "You're just both middle-aged now. The rodeo days are over. Maybe it's time to accept that and find something else to do with the rest of your lives."

That statement had only caused Elsie to burst into tears yet again. "I might not have a life, if your father leaves me."

"Now I need some counseling myself," Summer whispered, still in shock. Of all the sure things in her life, her parents' love for each other had always been one of the most outstanding. If that love, so unshakable, so solid, so intense, was about to cave, then she didn't hold out much hope for the rest of humanity. She looked up at the huge iron-and-stone cross hanging on the wall in the den and for the first time in a long time, she turned to God. *I really need You now, Lord.*

The doorbell rang. Summer hurried to answer it, afraid it would wake her mother. When she opened it and saw Mack standing there, her heart lurched. She had to catch her breath. It was if God had heard her plea and sent the one man who might be able to help Summer.

"Boy, am I glad to see you," she said. Then she grabbed his arm and hauled him into the house.

"Good to see you, too," Mack said, pleased that Summer seemed so all fired up to get him inside. "I brought your car for you. I'll catch a ride back to the center with your grandparents."

"Good, fine." She marched him down the long hall and into the spacious den. "Sit."

"Okay." He sat down, watching as she paced before the fireplace. Then he noticed the hollow look in her eyes, the frown on her face. And he saw that her hands were shaking. "You really *don't* like being here, do you?"

"It's weird. Especially right now," she said in a low whisper. "Things are…complicated."

Not liking the way her eyes darted toward the stairs, he said, "Want to clue me in?"

"There's something not right here, Mack."

"Yeah, well, that's obvious. But you promised your grandmother."

"Not that," she said, her hands on her hips. "I'm trying, Mack. Really I am. And I think it's probably a good thing I decided to stay here for a while."

Mack was getting dizzy, watching her whirl around, so when she passed close, he grabbed her arm and pulled her onto the couch with him. "What's going on, Summer?"

She sank down beside him. "I shouldn't be doing this. I shouldn't be so happy to see you. But right before you rang the doorbell, I...I asked God to help me."

Mack let out a whistle. "Must be serious, since you said you'd quit talking to God."

"It is serious."

He saw that seriousness in her eyes. He was so close, he could see the flecks of deep blue in her irises. "So, what did God tell you?"

"Nothing yet. But then you showed up."

"I always have had good timing."

"Don't make fun," she said, her eyes bright with a fear that scared him.

"Then talk to me. Tell me what's the matter."

"You can't tell anyone."

"Okay."

She let out a sigh, pushed at her hair, looked away. "My parents might be getting a divorce."

Mack had to shake his head. "What?"

"That's exactly what I said when my mother poured her heart out to me. Not less than an hour ago, we had probably the longest conversation we've ever had in our lives, with her doing most of the talking and me doing most of the listening. Mack, she…she needed me."

Not sure how to respond, he said, "Well, I guess that's a good thing. Even though it's a bad situation."

But Summer shook her head, ran a hand over the grainy leather of the couch. "But why now, when her life is in a major crisis? I don't mind helping my mother, but I just wish she'd needed me…during all the happy times, too." She put a hand to her mouth. "I don't know if I can do this. I don't know if I can be strong enough to help her through this. What am I doing to do?"

Mack saw the panic on her face, felt it in the way she seemed to be slowly shaking. "Hey, now," he said as he reached for her, "it's gonna be all right. Maybe they just had a fight or something."

"I think it's more than a fight," she said, falling into his arms. "I think it's something that's been brewing for a very long time. And I never even knew, because I didn't take the time to find out how they were doing. I didn't want to know the details of their life, because I was so jealous of that life."

Mack pulled her close, unable to stop himself. Summer was one of the toughest people he knew, but right now she seemed very fragile. "It's gonna work out, I promise. You have to hang tough and help your mother. Maybe it's payback time."

"What does that mean?" she asked, her whisper vibrating against his chest.

Mack closed his eyes, let the scent of her citrus shampoo wash over him. "It means maybe your mother will see that she has a daughter who loves her and wants to be close to her, and now, you have that chance."

Summer lifted her head, her eyes going wide. "That's what Memaw told me. That this was my chance."

Mack smiled down at her. "Then I'd say God heard your prayers, Summer. And he's giving you a chance to bridge that gap you've always felt between your parents and you."

"What if I can't cross that bridge, mend that gap?"

"I think you can," Mack replied. "I know you

can. You try so hard to hide it, but I think there is a lot of love inside you. And a lot of faith."

Summer gave him a grudging smile. "I really didn't want to like you."

"I know," Mack said. Then he lowered his head and kissed her, taking in the sweet, slow way she responded. Summer seemed to melt into his kiss, a reluctant sigh escaping as she kissed him back. He could almost read her mind as she finally gave in and let him hold her close. Hesitant. Scared. Longing. And then, accepting and needing to be touched and held. He felt all the same things and marveled at how much trusting someone was akin to accepting faith in God.

Summer pulled back, her eyes wide with a mixture of triumph and trepidation. "And I really didn't want to kiss you."

"I know," he said. "Which is why you're going to do it again, right?"

"Uh-huh," she said as she tugged him close again.

Mack enjoyed the kiss and let it settle around him. Then he opened his eyes, held his head back for a smile—

And saw James Maxwell's scowling reflection in the big mirror over the fireplace, staring him down.

Chapter Twelve

"Mr. Maxwell!"

Mack jumped up, away from the warmth of Summer's embrace. Summer followed, surprised to find her father staring at them with thunder in his eyes. But right now, she was so angry about her mother's revelations and confused by Mack's sweet kiss, she didn't care what her father thought.

"Well, well," James said, the stern expression on his face making him look as dangerous as the bulls he used to ride. "I leave for a couple of hours and what do I come home to? Summer— with a boy. Some things never change, I reckon." He gave Mack a broad grin. "I can't tell you how many times I came home to catch her with some football player or race-car driver. Even threw in a couple of rodeo rookies, I think just to get to me. My daughter has always been good at attracting the boys."

"He's not exactly a boy, Daddy," Summer pointed out. "And you only came home on rare occasions, so how do you know who all I dated?"

James drew back, frowning. "I can see your attitude hasn't changed much either."

Summer got up, rubbing her hands down her shorts. "This is different, Daddy. Mack's a grown man, and…he's a friend. A good friend. And in case you haven't noticed, I'm all grown up, too."

"Oh, I noticed that right off the bat," James said, a soft smile splitting his frown. Then he turned to Mack, a kind of regret and longing moving over his weathered face. "She always did break hearts. Be careful, son. Be very careful."

Summer watched Mack relax, but she was grateful for his hand reaching for hers. "I think I can handle things, sir."

"I sure hope so. She's a lot like her mama. Stubborn and unreasonable and determined to do things her way. Speaking of your mama, where is she?"

"She's upstairs resting," Summer said, careful that she didn't lash out at her father until she'd had a chance to hear his side of the story. "I'm worried about her. She was so tired."

James looked worried, too. "Elsie, resting in the middle of the day? That don't sound right. Your mama usually goes full-throttle until the wee hours. Can't hold her back. Not one little bit, even when I try."

Summer shot a glance toward Mack. He gave her a warning look. Trying to stay neutral for now, Summer said, "Well, you did have a long flight home, and Mama and I had a good talk. She just needed to take a nap."

"Hope she'll be down for dinner," James said, satisfied for now. "It'll be so nice to have the whole family gathered together."

Summer saw the sincerity in her father's eyes and wondered when her parents had gotten so old and mellow. Her father was still a handsome man, tall and sinewy. But he looked tired and there was a darkness around his eyes. His almost-black hair was shot through with shimmers of gray. And he did seem genuinely concerned about her mother.

Summer stared up at him, seeing so much there in the lines and angles of her father's face. And she realized that she, too, had missed out on a lot of things. Simply because she was so stubborn and so stuck in dwelling on the past. She'd certainly had plenty of opportunities through the years to visit her parents, both here in Athens, and around the world. It wasn't as if she didn't have the means to buy a plane ticket now and then. But her pride and pain had always held her back.

Maybe God had brought them all home for a reason.

She looked over at Mack again. "Mack, would you mind if I have a few minutes to visit with my Daddy?"

Mack lifted his brows, then turned to James. "I don't mind a bit. I'll just go outside and check out that nice swimming pool."

"There's extra swimsuits in the cabana, if you want to take a dip," Summer said, hoping Mack would understand.

He seemed to. "I just might do that. It's been a hot day today. Y'all don't worry about me. Take your time catching up." The look he gave Summer indicated that she needed to do just that.

James watched Mack head toward the back of the house. "Nice fellow."

"Yes, he is," Summer said, remembering the way Mack's kiss had sent her reeling. "But Daddy, don't read anything into this. Mack and I are just—"

James held up a hand. "I know—really good friends." His smile was bittersweet. "You know,

I've always hoped you'd find a good man and settle down. I worry about you, suga'."

Summer came around the couch, watching as her father poured himself a glass of mineral water. "Did you worry about me when you were on the rodeo circuit, Daddy?"

James gave her a resigned look. "You know I did."

"Actually, I could never be sure," Summer replied, her bitterness turning to an aching wound that needed to heal. Suddenly, she felt tired. Tired of holding on to this grudge, tired of blaming her parents for everything. Maybe her grandmother was right. It was time to take a chance and find her way back to the fold. "Daddy, can we talk? I mean, really talk?"

James grinned. "I thought that was what we were doing."

Summer motioned to the chairs. "Let's sit down."

"Don't mind if I do," James said. He tossed his black cowboy hat on a nearby table. "Got mighty hot out on that golf course."

For the first time, Summer noticed the way he held his body, as if it hurt to stand up straight. "Are you okay, Daddy?"

"This old back," James said, wincing as he settled into the soft leather. "I guess I shouldn't have played such a vigorous game today. But you know me. I like the competition. Sure don't like losing, though."

Summer waited for him to get settled, wondering if she should ask him about what her mother had told her. According to Elsie, James had become withdrawn and subdued lately. They hadn't enjoyed their travels to Mexico this time, as they had in the past. Elsie implied that James no longer confided in her, that he seemed uninterested in her. She was sure he was either seeing another woman, or on the verge of just flat-out leaving her.

"Why did y'all come home?" Summer asked her father, hoping he might open up to her.

James smiled at her, his eyes as bright and blue as her own. "We wanted to see you, of course. Your mama read your e-mail telling us you were coming home, and right away, she started fretting. And she was worried about Martha and Jesse. You know, selling the house was hard on all of us."

"Was it really?" Summer asked, holding back on the condemnation she'd felt since coming home.

"Yes, honey. We wrestled back and forth with this decision. But I want you to know, we didn't go into this lightly. Your mother and I let Jesse and Martha make the final decision. You have to know, Summer, that they will always be taken care of. Always."

"Why couldn't they just stay at the farm?"

James leaned forward, winced again, his hand shooting to his back. "Well, we all wanted that, even talked about hiring them a companion. But they didn't want a stranger hovering around them all the time. You see, one day about a year ago, your grandmother found your papaw passed out near the pond. He'd had a dizzy spell. Luckily, he just got a bit overheated and he was fine. But that scared Martha and it really scared your mama. That's when we asked them about considering moving to Golden Vista."

Summer imagined her grandfather, all alone and unconscious, and felt a tinge of remorse over her recent outbursts. "I guess I thought they'd be around forever."

James nodded. "I wish we could all be around forever, but time marches on, suga'." The darkness around his eyes seemed to widen with that statement, but his wry smile was intact. "The thing about Golden Vista is I'd invested in the place myself—sold the investment group the land the place is built on, helped design the entire complex. So I knew it in and out, top to bottom. I knew they'd be taken care of there."

Summer sat silently for a while, then said, "Okay, I can live with that. It's taken some getting used to, but I can certainly see that the retirement center is safe and comfortable. They seem to be happy."

"They are," James assured her. "And that's what matters."

"What about you and Mama?" she asked, holding her breath for the answer. She'd never actually considered that her parents might not be happy together. They had always seemed so caught up in each other, Summer couldn't imagine them any other way.

James's face went blank. "What do you mean?"

"I mean, are y'all still happy, traveling around like nomads? Don't you ever just want to find a place to settle down?"

James looked surprised, then sheepish. "It's hard to say, honey. There are a lot of things I want, but wanting don't make it happen. You know, there never was very much money to be made in the rodeo. It was all about being the center of attention, about being a star. I've been blessed with a grand fortune, thanks to the Maxwell holdings. I milked that and my rodeo days for all they were worth. I guess the gravy train is finally drying up."

Shocked, Summer asked, "Are you saying you've lost money? That you and mother are in financial trouble?"

"Of course not," James said, scoffing at the very idea. "Your Uncle Richard has always taken care of our finances and he'd never let that happen, no matter how much we've tried to spend all our dough. I mean, the rodeo circuit isn't what it used to be. I guess I'm trying to tell you that your ol' daddy is a has-been. Washed out and washed up."

"But you had a good career. You should be proud of that. You've got friends all over the place. And you've had a good life, haven't you?"

James nodded. "I have. Being the middle child, I had to find my own way of getting attention. And I did that in my rodeo heyday. But now, well, I'm struggling. I'm asking myself, was my whole life a big waste?"

Summer stared over at her father, wondering about the paradox that made up her parents. They were a constant source of wonder to her, two people whom she loved and resented at the same time. But right now, to her surprise, the love was fast overtaking the resentment. They were home, and that counted in Summer's book now more than it ever had before. That, and her father's admissions.

"Daddy, are you having a crisis of some sort?"

James laughed. "No, I don't think so. I'm just getting old and...well, losing Stuart made me stop and think about my own mortality." He looked over at her, his eyes bright with regret and hope. "I don't want to waste any more time, honey. I'm tired. I want to find some new kind of meaning in my life."

"There's nothing wrong with that," Summer said, beginning to see what was really happening in her parents' marriage. She reached over and touched her father's leathery hand. "I believe you and Mama still have a lot to give, Daddy. I think you can find your way through this if you look for the opportunities ahead."

"And that would be membership in AARP, right?" James said, his tone teasing.

"Well, that does have its perks," Summer replied. "But you could serve on any number of philanthropic boards. You could find some sort of part-time work, maybe helping troubled teens learn about horses and the rodeo."

James looked thoughtful for a minute. "In other words, instead of wallowing in self-pity, find myself something to keep me busy, right?"

"Exactly," Summer said, smiling over at him.

"But what about your mama?" James asked, sounding frightened.

"What about her?"

He leaned forward, lowered his voice. "What if she—what if she's disappointed in me. You know how she loves to travel and entertain."

"She can still do both," Summer replied, amazed that both her parents were having a major self-esteem problem right now. After all those years of marriage and togetherness, they still weren't completely sure about each other. That only reinforced Summer's own misgivings in the love department.

"You should talk to her," Summer said. "Tell Mama how you're feeling. Tell her what you want to do with the rest of your life."

James nodded. "I sure hope I'm just as smart as you when I finally do grow up."

Touched, Summer said, "Maybe we're all growing up, at last."

James struggled to get out of his chair. "Maybe. And maybe the best place to do that is right here at home, huh?"

Summer felt tears pricking at her eyes. "I think so, Daddy."

James pulled her close, hugging her to him.

"I didn't hug you enough when you were little. I intend to work on that some while we're here, honey."

Summer didn't cry. Instead, she felt a surge of joy as her father's strong arms held her close.

Maybe this time, she'd be the one to leave first. And maybe this time, she could leave knowing that her parents still loved each other *and her*.

Mack stood looking down into the blue waters of the pool, his mind still on kissing Summer. His mind on how that kiss had affected him. He'd taken a dip, all right. Just to cool the mixed emotions and sweet longings he felt inside his soul. The water was great, but Mack was still drowning in that kiss. His cell phone rang, causing him to throw down his towel and fumble for it. "Hello?"

"Mack, it's Belinda."

Silence. She'd finally tracked him down. "How did you get this number?"

"That doesn't matter. Don't hang up on me, please."

Mack closed his eyes, held a breath, said a prayer. "What do you want?"

He heard her intake of breath, heard the quiver of her words. "I want to see you. It's really important."

"Belinda, we don't need to rehash things. It's over this time. It's been over for a very long time."

"I know that," she said. He thought he heard a sob, but then Belinda was so good at acting, it couldn't have been a real one. "I know things can never be the same between us, but I really need to see you."

"I don't think—"

"I can't talk about this over the phone," she said, her tone turning to a plea. "I'm sorry to bother you, but I had to find you. I only need a few minutes, to explain."

"Explain what?" Mack asked, confused. His heart was hammering a warning beat, but he couldn't help but feel that old tug again. "Just tell me, Belinda."

"I can't. Not like this. This is too important. I have to see you for so many reasons, and if you won't come here, then I'll just have to come there."

"No." He didn't want her here in Athens. He'd made a good life here and he wouldn't go back into that crazy, Tilt-A-Whirl of a life they'd had together. "Don't come here. And I can't come there, wherever *there* is for you right now. So if you've got something to say, say it now."

"I…I can't do that, not like this," she said. "I'll be in touch."

Mack heard a beep and then silence. "Belinda?" She'd hung up. He sank down on a patio chair, wondering what Belinda would do next. What if she just showed up in Athens? What then? Grabbing his shirt, Mack jerked it on.

"Bad news?"

He pivoted at Summer's question. "What?"

"The way you're staring at your phone, you must have gotten bad news? A leaky pipe in one of the apartments? A gopher tearing up your cabbage roses?"

Mack managed a shaky laugh. "I wish." Then he shrugged. "Just someone I knew once, wanting to get together and share old times."

She lifted her chin. "About old times—just how many hearts have *you* broken, Mack Riley?"

"None, that I can recall," he said, the guilt of his relationship with Belinda weighing on him. But he couldn't bring himself to talk about that again with Summer. "You know how that goes."

"Yeah, I sure do," she said, shaking her head. "I guess we don't need to go into detail right now."

Mack managed to shake off the bad feeling Belinda's call had provoked. "No, not just yet." Then he looked into Summer's eyes. "But one day, I do need to tell you everything." He shrugged. "You know most of what went on with Belinda, but you need to hear the whole story."

He saw the doubt clouding her blue eyes. "Was that her on the phone?"

He gave her a silent nod.

"She wants to see you again?"

"Yes." Seeing the doubt in Summer's eyes, he added, "But I don't want to see her. I told her to leave me alone."

"She must have really messed with your head."

"She did." He got up, pushed a hand through his wet hair. "Can we change the subject, please?"

Summer gave him a knowing look. "So you do have secrets, just like the rest of us."

"A few," he said, hoping she'd leave it at that for now. "Some things are hard to reveal."

He watched as her eyes changed from a cloudy blue to crystal-clear and full of resolve. "I've got a few things I don't want to talk about either. But… we'll save that for another day. I'm not ready to get into anything heavy. I've got enough to figure out with what's brewing between my parents." She sank down on a chaise. "But I did have a good talk with my daddy, at least."

Mack walked over to her, took her hand in his. "You're very brave, taking on a tough situation like this."

"I'm a highly trained professional," she whispered, her voice full of sarcasm, her smile mocking.

"You are a pro, but...this is your parents."

"How do I try to understand and counsel two people I don't even really know?"

Mack didn't know how to answer that. "I guess you start with love. You do love your parents, right?"

She nodded. "I never realized how much until today. They've grown older, Mack. They...I think they might have come home for good this time." She pushed at her bangs. "But what if they came home, only to go their separate ways? I might not ever get to see them in the role I've always longed for. I wanted a set of traditional parents, not some jet-set party animals. Maybe they just partied themselves out, until there was nothing left."

Mack sat down beside her and pulled her close. "I think there's plenty left. You might not be the one to bring them back together, but you could be the one to bring them home for good."

And yourself, too, Mack thought. But he didn't voice that to Summer. He couldn't voice that silent wish he had inside his racing heart, because he wasn't so sure he should even be wishing it. Not after he'd just talked to Belinda and had all those old feelings pulling at him to remind him of his shortcomings.

But it sure would be nice if Summer would stay home this time, too. Here with him.

Summer looked up at him, her eyes telling him that she could almost read his thoughts. "A homecoming," she said with a sigh. "I've always dreamed of that. But not like this. Mack, I have to try and help my parents."

"That's the spirit," he said, proud of her for turning this around. "Whatever is happening with them, I have a feeling they need their daughter right now."

She blinked, her eyes misty. "I've...never felt needed before. Not by my parents. In my work in New York, yes, which is why I poured myself into it, to the point of losing myself completely. But that was so different from this. There I had to be objective and I had to hold everything inside. I don't know if I can do that with my folks."

"You love them. Show them that love, Summer."

"Do you think my love can save whatever is wrong with them?"

"I can't answer that. But it doesn't hurt to try."

Summer shook her head, turned to stare at the shimmering pool. "Funny, I always resented my parents being so in love. Now, I'm praying that they still are."

Mack pulled at her long hair. "I'm praying right along with you."

Summer leaned back into his embrace, smiling as he settled his nose against the top of her head. "I haven't prayed in a very long time."

Mack kissed her hair. "But even when you weren't praying, God was listening."

"Well, I hope He's still listening. I can't bear to see my parents torn apart and hurt. I won't let that happen."

Mack closed his eyes, wished for Summer to find peace and guidance from above. And he also asked God to help him find that same peace. Because he had a feeling that Belinda Lewis wasn't through with him yet. And maybe, neither was God.

Chapter Thirteen

July hit Athens like a steamy blanket being tossed over a drooping clothesline. The whole countryside was limp with lack of rain, parched and damp at the same time. The humidity only made everything look worse. Mack was constantly having to water the grass and the flowers at Golden Vista. How he managed to keep them alive in this heat was beyond Summer.

But then, everything about Mack Riley seemed to intrigue her these days, Summer thought as she made herself a tall glass of water with lemon. The man was good at his job and good with handling the myriad problems that came with dealing with senior citizens. Lost animals, misplaced medicine, loneliness, sickness and ailments, confusion, doctor's appointments and field trips that went from bad to worse—these were some of the things Mack and the rest of the staff at Golden Vista handled on a daily basis. Sometimes death hung over the place like the humidity, and sometimes a resident would not come home after a rushed hospital visit or a frantic call for the emergency ambulance. But in spite of losing yet another old person, Mack always had a ready smile and kind words to help console the family. His patience and understanding surpassed any dedication Summer had ever witnessed before. And he managed to include her in everything, forcing her to stay involved and just one step ahead of her own depression and misgivings.

And the ladies who managed Golden Vista thought Mack had hung the moon.

"He's a pretty thing, isn't he?" Cissie, the office manager, had cooed earlier today while Summer sat in the office with them, going over the details of the festival.

"Easy on the eye, for sure," Pamela, the events coordinator, had replied.

"A dream to work with," their boss Lola had agreed. "We're so lucky to have Mack here."

Then the three ladies had all turned to Summer, their eager expressions and smug smiles just begging for details.

"Are y'all an item?" Cissie asked, her Southern drawl stretched with innocence. "That's what we keep hearing, you know."

"Can't you tell?" Pamela answered, her blond hair falling against her cheeks. "The way that man looks at her—I'd say he's got a bad crush on this one."

"I think you two should get back to the business at hand, which is helping Summer finish up these plans for our festival," Lola said, her glasses perched on her nose. Then she glanced over at Summer, a dreamy smile plastered on her face. "If I was twenty years younger, girl, I'd sure give you a run for your money with that one."

"It's not like that," Summer insisted. "Mack and I are just good friends."

"Yeah, right," Cissie retorted. "That's what Miss Gladys tells us about her and Mr. Maroney, too. But they've taken to sharing just about every meal together. And they sit together on the bus. Yeah, they're *real* good friends."

"I think I saw them holding hands the other day," Pamela added.

"Well, that's sweet," Summer replied, "but you won't catch Mack and I doing that, I promise."

"At least not while anyone's looking, right?" Cissie asked, grinning.

Summer grinned now as she remembered the gentle ribbing. It was hard to have a romantic relationship in such a tight-knit community. Who knew there were so many romantics and match-makers living at Golden Vista?

While Summer had been up to her eyeballs in planning the big Fourth of July festival, she'd also grown very close to most of the lovable residents of the retirement complex. It would be hard to leave all the seniors who talked to her and asked her advice on everything from bursitis to baby showers. Her grandmother had pronounced Summer the unofficial counselor of Golden Vista, reminding Summer that "old people need therapy, too, honey."

Some in the worst kind of way, Summer had discovered. She'd also discovered that sitting and listening to the residents brought her a certain measure of comfort. She was contributing, so she didn't feel useless. That was something she couldn't stand, being idle and listless. She'd actually helped some of them with sickness, mending relationships with estranged family members, or dealing with the loss of a favorite pet.

This morning, Summer sat at the desk in her father's huge, paneled den, and began an e-mail to her cousins, eager to tell them about her life here.

Things here have settled into a kind of routine for me. I get up each day, check on any e-mails from the Y in New York and respond to those first. Then Mama and I do our laps in the pool. Funny, but we've had some of our best conversations after our swims, when we sit down to have breakfast out on the back patio. This is before the heat takes over and we're forced inside. Then I either go to visit Memaw and Papaw and all the other residents at Golden Vista and help out there, or I get together with Mack to finish the plans for the big Fourth of July Village Festival. That's all the talk at Golden Vista.

Word has it that Mr. Maroney is going to ask Mrs. Hanes to marry him that night, just when the fireworks go off. Isn't that so romantic? Those two are so cute, trying so hard to ignore each other. But Mack keeps supplying Mr. Maroney with flowers at every turn, and Mr. Maroney gives them to Mrs. Hanes with such a flourish that the whole village has noticed. He ambushes her when she's on her way back from the beauty parlor, and sometimes he puts the flowers on her table at dinner. She finally invited him to sit with her the other night. Now they share all their meals together.

Oh, and Mack has given me flowers, too.

Wildflowers and daisies, sunflowers that are just bursting with bright yellow blossoms. He's not like other men. Not very traditional—he thinks roses are only pretty when they're fresh-picked with dew on them. Refuses to order them from a florist. But flowers do not mean a thing. We are good friends now, at least. I don't resent him anymore for buying the farm. How could I, when he's got the house in mint condition and now he's working on the yards and fields. The farm looks better than ever.

I'm progressing with Mama and Daddy, too. Although they seem okay, I still can't get to the bottom of why my mother thinks my father wants a divorce. I think Daddy's just going through some sort of change-of-life crisis, and he won't talk to her about it. So she assumes the worst. You know Mama. She flutters around like a ladybug, decorating the over-decorated house, shopping for things she doesn't need, having her nails done, her hair done. She tells me about her day or invites me to join her. But she won't go into detail about things with Daddy too much. They both seem sad at times, but I can't get either of them just to talk to each other. They both confide in me, which is really surprising, but there is so much more to learn about them. So

I guess I'll keep trying. Who knew that I'd come home to so much: my grandparents living in a retirement village, my parents home and somehow different. And Mack as my new best friend. I miss New York and my work, but I have to admit being here has helped me to slow down and regain my strength. And helping the old folks has shown me that we all just want to be loved and needed.

April, I should be in peak condition for your wedding. I can't wait until we all get together to try on our gowns and have that shower we promised you. And Autumn, you'd better make it home for that! And the wedding.

Oh, Autumn, did you ever find out what's cooking with your daddy? Is he still acting strange? What is it with our parents these days, anyway? Love to both of you, Summer.

Summer sent the e-mail then signed off the computer. She had lots to do today. She had to check with the vendors for the festival and talk to the kitchen staff at Golden Vista about the food booths. Then she had to meet with Mack to go over the layout of the booths and how they'd handle parking.

"Honey, are you still here?"

"In the office, Mama," Summer called, still mystified that she was actually living with her parents and getting along with them.

"Oh, good," Elsie said, her silk teal-colored caftan flowing out around her like butterfly wings. "I was hoping I'd catch you before you got busy."

"What is it?" Summer asked, on eggshells these days hoping her mother would have good news instead of bad regarding her parents' marriage.

"Nothing," Elsie said, smiling. "Just that...well, I wanted to thank you, honey, for listening to all my tales of woe about your father."

"Mama, I don't mind," Summer told her. While she worried about her father's odd behavior and her mother's fears, she had at least grown closer to both her parents. "Where is Daddy?" she asked. Her father was usually gone most mornings by the time she got up, even though she still woke up early just as she had in New York.

"He had a meeting with his lawyers or something," Elsie said. "I have no idea what he's up to."

Summer saw the worry cresting in her mother's eyes, and wished her father would just be honest with Elsie. Elsie had on very little makeup this morning. Summer saw the freckles and age spots dotting her mother's skin, but to her, Elsie had never looked more beautiful. "You don't think—"

Elsie fidgeted with removing the dead fronds from the parlor fern in the corner. "Hard to say. We have been talking more lately. I did what you suggested and tried to question your father tactfully about his comings and goings. He didn't exactly tell me anything, just kissed me and told me not to worry so much. But he turned before he left this morning and told me he loves me." She sighed. "He seemed like the James Maxwell I've always loved. Amazing, how one crumb of hope can make a soul soar."

Summer sat looking up at her mother. Elsie stood by the arched windows overlooking the backyard, her reddish-blond hair shining like a halo in the morning sun. "Mama, you are still so beautiful. Daddy has to see that."

Elsie brushed at tears. "I hope he does. Do you think he sees me as old and washed up?"

Summer got up to come and take her mother's arms, thinking her father had pretty much asked her the same thing about himself. "That's silly. You've worked hard to stay in shape and you—"

"I know. I've visited every plastic surgeon known to man, in several countries. But I never had any work done. Maybe I should check myself into one of those private clinics and have the whole nine yards done, from head to toe."

"Mama, changing yourself outside can't fix the pain inside," Summer said. "I've seen some of the richest women in New York, broke and broken, simply because they didn't have enough gumption to leave abusive situations. They didn't want to give up their salons and shopping sprees, their Botox injections and their chauffeurs and mansions. They would rather put social standing before their own health and self-esteem." She turned in her chair. "Mama, you don't need any of that. I can't speak for Daddy, but I really think he's going through a lot right now. He's still mourning Uncle Stuart's death, and I think he's realizing that he can't be young and carefree forever. You should talk to him and just be honest with him. He needs you, Mama."

Elsie lifted a hand to Summer's hair. "You are an amazing woman, do you know that?"

Summer never imagined she'd be so touched by words coming from her mother, but she was. "I'm not that amazing. I just have a job to do."

"And you do it. You did everything to make me proud. You struck out on your own and made a life for yourself, in spite of your mother's shortcomings."

Summer wasn't ready to get down to the nitty-gritty of the past, even though she knew it would help both of them. That confrontation she'd always imagined now seemed petty and mean-spirited. And her mother seemed so frail and small. Fragile. "I'm the one with shortcomings, Mama, trust me."

"Oh, I don't believe that," Elsie said, her smile bittersweet and strained. "I left you so many times. Left you behind, knowing it was so wrong."

Summer's heart hurt with the pain of that confession. "Why did you do it?"

Elsie shook her head. "It's hard to explain, hard to understand. I was so afraid I'd lose your father if I let him get out there away from me. I smothered him with love, and I forced him always to take me with him." She lowered her head. "I should have been smothering you with love, darlin'. I should have put my foot down and told your father that we needed to put you first. I'm so sorry I didn't see that. And the real kicker is I might lose both of you because of it."

Summer's legs seemed to turn to jelly. She sank down on a chair, her eyes locked on her mother's face. "I never thought—"

"You never thought you'd hear me say that?" Elsie asked, sniffing. "Well, this situation with your daddy and me has got me to thinking about a lot of things. I always knew you were safe here with Mama and Daddy, so I pushed any guilt or worries aside, telling myself next time, I'd stay here with you, next time I'd convince your father to settle down. Then next time would roll around and there I'd go, off to yet another adventure. I think it's all finally catching up with me."

"Better late than never, right?" Summer said, her heart sinking with the sure knowledge that her mother was only turning to her because Elsie was so afraid of losing her father. "Is that it, Mother? You think if Daddy leaves you, you'll be all alone? So you're trying to mend fences with me, just so someone will be there with you in your old age?"

Elsie looked shocked, a slight flush rising over her freckles. "Is that how you see me, Summer? You think I'd just use my own daughter that way?"

Summer shrugged, starting to gather her paperwork. "Honestly, I wonder, I mean, here we are making polite conversation, when we both know there is still a huge gap between us."

"I thought we were trying to mend that gap," Elsie replied, hurt causing her to frown. "I thought that you cared—"

"I do care, Mama," Summer said, wishing she'd learn to choose her words more carefully. "But what happens if this rift between you and Daddy suddenly ends? What then? Will you leave with him? Will I be the one left alone again?"

Elsie sank down on a chair, then pushed a hand through her tousled hair. The guilt on her face told Summer what she needed to know.

Summer started for the door, but Elsie grabbed her by the arm. "Summer, I'm trying. I don't know what's going on with your father, but I've never had any reason to doubt his love until now." Her eyes glistened as her voice became a whisper. "I've never been very good at being alone, darlin'."

Summer pulled her arm away. "Well, maybe you should learn to deal with it, Mama, the way I had to learn to deal with it."

Elsie put a hand to her mouth. "Is that how you felt? All alone? But, honey, you had Memaw and Papaw."

"Yes," Summer said, whirling around. "I had my grandparents and I loved them dearly, but I always had to wonder why my own parents couldn't love me the way my grandparents did. No one has ever been able to explain that to me, Mama." She grabbed her car keys. "You know, for the first time in my life, I thought you might actually need me. I thought we were getting some-where. But now I can see that I'm only a substitute for Daddy. I don't want to be a substitute. I want to be first in someone's heart, just once. You just don't get that, do you, Mama?"

Elsie looked up at her, her face white with shock and hurt. "Summer, you've got it all wrong, honey. I love you. Your father adores you. We're here now, aren't we?"

Summer nodded. "For now, yes. But only until something better comes along. Once you both figure out that old age isn't the end of the world, you'll find something to take you away. Then you'll both be out there and gone again. I can't take that this time, Mama. I just can't."

She left, shutting the front door with a soft thud that echoed the thudding inside her heart. Disappointment and resentment coursed through her with a sharp-edged precision, making her insides feel like shredded ribbons. Why had she let them get her hopes up? Why had she even bothered?

Mack could see the mad all over Summer's face as she entered the rec room at Golden Vista. She had that frown that caused her wide lips to jut out and she had that burning look in her blue, flame-tipped eyes. He watched as she headed straight to the coffeepot and poured a generous cupful into her favorite bluebonnet-etched mug.

Mack thought back over the last few days. Summer and her parents had reached a truce of sorts, or at least that's what it had looked like. She hadn't complained much lately about their glittery house or their shallow ways. She'd smiled and told him about her long talks with her mother. She'd delved into the plans for the festival with the same dedication and zeal he imagined she'd poured into her work back in New York. And she'd sat with the residents, getting to know them by name, and offering them kind but sure advice and words of comfort. Everything had been going so smoothly.

And he'd been moving right along, his feelings for Summer growing with the same steady rise as the wisteria vine that moved up the gazebo out in the courtyard of the center. Now he had to wonder what had happened to put that anger back in her eyes.

"Summer?" he called as he strolled across the tiled floor.

She turned slightly, barely acknowledging his presence. "What?"

"Good morning to you, too," he said, treading carefully.

"Hi," she said before taking a long sip of her cream-laced coffee. Then she plopped down at the table where they'd been working on the festival details, her eyes glued to the inch-thick folder of notes and printouts in front of her.

"Want to talk about it?"

"No."

"Did you get up on the wrong side of the bed?"

"No, just in the wrong house."

Mack sat down beside her. "Fight with your mother?"

"No."

Mack let out a sigh. This frustrating woman could become brooding and tight-lipped as fast as a rogue thundershower could slip up on the Texas horizon. "Are you in pain?"

"Yes."

"Do you want—"

"I want to be left alone," she said, never once looking at him.

But Mack wasn't about to let her alone. No, sir. He knew her well enough after all these weeks to tell that when she said one thing, she usually really meant another. "I can't leave you alone right now. We've got a meeting with Mr. Tatum about the tents. He needs to know where to set up."

She waved a hand, still staring at the papers on the table. "Tell him to put them wherever he wants."

"Okay. But we need to decide about the children's games. Do you have enough volunteers for each booth?"

"Plenty of volunteers."

Mack sat drumming his fingers on the table, then decided to take a direct approach. "Summer, what's got this bee in your bonnet?"

She turned to him then, her big eyes going wide. "Is there something wrong with you, Mack? What part of go away do you not understand?"

Mack felt his own anger rising, but he managed to push it aside. For now. "I don't think I'm going anywhere. Not until you tell me what's wrong."

"You *can* go," she said, getting up to put her mug in the sink on the long counter. "Everybody else does."

Mack let that stew for a minute or two. "Are your parents…are they leaving again? Is that what this is all about?"

She shook her head, her shoulders slumping as she leaned into the counter. "Not yet. But they will. They always do. I should have remembered that."

Mack couldn't relate to what she was saying. His parents had rarely left him overnight when he was growing up. But he could relate to being abandoned. He thought of Belinda and wondered where she was right now. She had certainly abandoned him, rejected him, hurt him, so many times he'd lost count. If he let her back into his life, would he only be disappointed again?

"I think I know how you feel," he said finally. "You kind of let your guard down, didn't you? You let your parents back into your heart and now—"

"And now, once things are all better between my mother and father, they will be gone all over again." She turned to face Mack at last. "Why does that hurt so much, Mack?"

Mack pulled her into his arms, wishing he had the answer to that question. "Are you sure about this? I mean, are they about to up and leave Athens or something?"

She shook her head, her face muffled by the cotton of his shirt, her warmth causing him to want to kiss her again. "I just realized it this morning when I was talking to my mother. She's only turning to me because right now, she's the one being rejected, by my father. When things get right with them, I'll be out of the picture again."

Mack could understand her anger and hurt. "That would be tough, but think of how close you've become with your mother. Surely that has to count for something."

She lifted her face, her eyes misty, her determination solid. "Yes, it means I was just a convenient crutch, someone to be used and discarded."

"I don't think your mother thinks of you that way. She seems to really want to make things better between you two. And you did tell me that James and you have become close lately. Can't you trust in that and let things play out?"

Summer let out what almost passed for a sob, except that her eyes were dry. "I'm so tired of being the one who has to give out all the answers, Mack. I'm so tired of being the counselor. Who can I turn to when I have questions or complaints? Who?"

Mack held a hand to her chin. "Me," he said. Then he pointed up. "Me…and God."

Summer shook her head, pulled away. "And what if you and God both decide you can't handle me either? What if you decide there's something better, some other place you need to be, someone else who needs you more? What if both you and God abandon me, too?"

"I would never do that," Mack said, suddenly realizing he meant it with all his heart. "And God never abandons us, Summer. We might turn from Him, but He's always there, waiting for us to come home."

"I wish I could trust that," she said. "I wish I could hold on to that."

"Hold on to me," Mack said. Then he pulled her into his arms and gave her that kiss that he'd been thinking of, regardless of the prying eyes and amazed looks they'd been getting. He had to convince her that he would never abandon her or leave her or let her down.

Somehow, he had to prove that, both to Summer and to himself.

Chapter Fourteen

"Everything's ready," Summer said two days later. She turned to her grandmother. "I hope you have a good time today, Memaw."

Martha danced around, the excitement in her eyes telling Summer that this had been worth all the extra hours. "I plan to, darling. I am the most blessed woman in all of Texas. I have you and your parents here to celebrate the Fourth of July holiday with me and your grandpa, and I have you and Mack to thank for working so hard on making this festival happen. It just doesn't get any better than that."

Summer looked up to see Mack walking across the yard of Golden Vista. "You can say that again," she mumbled, drinking in the sight of him. He was dressed in his usual jeans and T-shirt, but today his shirt sported an American flag across the front. He looked content and clean-cut, the kind of man she'd seen in fashion ads in New York. Those men had only reminded her that sometimes life was fantasy. Not real at all. But this man was the real deal.

Her grandmother touched her on the arm. "You and Mack seem mighty keen on each other, suga'."

Summer couldn't deny it. "We have gotten close. He's a good man."

"Well, amen to that," Martha said, throwing up her hands. "I'm glad you finally figured that out."

"Memaw, now don't go getting your hopes up about Mack and me. He's a good friend. But we both know that I only have a week or so left on my vacation. I have to get back to New York."

"You might as well just stay another month or two. I mean, April's wedding is coming up and we'll all be there."

Summer noticed her grandmother nodded her head toward Mack when she said that. It would be just like her lovable grandparents to insist he come to the wedding with them. Just so they could throw him and Summer together again.

"I'll miss him," Summer said, not realizing she'd said it out loud until her grandmother turned to stare up at her.

"You're in love, aren't you?" Martha asked in a hopeful tone.

Summer tried to find a reasonable answer to that question. "I...I don't know," she admitted. "Does love feel like fifty drums beating against your rib cage every time he walks by? Does it make you want to laugh and cry all at the same time?"

"Oh, yes, ma'am. You've got it bad, I'd say," Martha replied. Then she smiled. "Don't worry, honey. I'm not going to spill your secret. This is for you and Mack to work out."

"Oh, so now that you'd made me admit that, you're just going to back off?"

"I did my part by keeping y'all busy together," Martha replied with a wink. "It's up to you how you handle the rest."

Summer shook her head and laughed. "So this summer will be hailed a success in the matchmaking department, huh? First, Mr. Maroney and Mrs. Hanes—the whole place has been watching that developing courtship. And now Mack and me. No wonder the folks living here are always smiling. You are all a very nosy, but well-meaning bunch."

"We just love happy endings," Martha replied, her expression smug as a bug. Then she turned serious. "You know, honey, a lot of people move in here after losing a loved one. They're lonely and bitter. They think their lives are over. The staff is wonderful about keeping seniors involved. We love all the trips Cissie takes us on, and we love the activities Pamela helps us with. But sometimes, what we really need is companionship. So those of us who are still blessed with spouses try to help the widows and widowers out a bit."

"And the occasional wayward relative, too, apparently," Summer said, love for her grandmother coloring her world in a golden hue of appreciation. "Thanks, Memaw. I know your being here has added a lot to the lives of the other residents. And visiting you here has certainly been the highlight of my vacation."

"I do my part, as I said." Martha whirled around and fairly danced her way out to the gathering crowd in the gardens. "Hurry, honey. This shindig is about to get started."

Summer stood back, wondering how her grandmother had known something she would have never believed herself. She had fallen in love with Mack Riley. When had it happened? They'd argued on just about every aspect of this festival, including everything from what kind of food to serve to what kind of chairs to set out. But in the end, they'd always managed to reach a satisfying compromise on how this day would turn out. Somewhere in all that playful disagreeing and serious getting-to-know each other, Summer had started relying on Mack for more than just planning a big get-together. He made her smile. He made her happy. And she really liked it when he kissed her.

That acknowledgment caused Summer to stop and consider all that falling in love meant to her. This was different from what she'd had with Brad. That had been a kind of obsession, a need to have someone watching movies with her on lonely nights, someone to go out to dinner with, someone to show off to friends. But it had been a facade. And Brad had shattered that delicate illusion when he'd turned nasty on her and made her see that all her words of wisdom and all her years of training could also be shattered in a heartbeat.

That would never happen with Mack. Mack was an honest, hardworking man. He didn't seem to have a dark side. With Mack, she'd seen the kind of man she'd dreamed about. A man much like her late Uncle Stuart and her Uncle Richard. A man very much like her father in that when he loved, he loved with all his heart. All of them, her father, her uncles, and now Mack, had the qualities that brought Summer comfort and security. They all always did the right thing, even when they had their own burdens to bear. Even her rolling-stone father had his good points, Summer reminded herself. She'd learned that in coming home. James had done a lot of behind-the-scenes work to make sure her grandparents were always taken care of. Mack was the same way.

Mack would never let her down, or turn mean on her the way Brad had. Mack was honest. No illusions there.

But what would happen to her newfound feelings for him when she had to return to New York? Would they survive a long-distance relationship? And did she even have the courage to tell him that she loved him?

Summer wished she could just blurt her thoughts out to someone. But everyone was busy outside. She didn't have time to write a long e-mail or make a phone call to her cousins. She thought about her mother, but Elsie had been quiet since their spat the other day. Summer felt guilty now. It would be hard to go to her mother for advice when she'd just condemned the woman regarding Elsie's own problems.

As she was leaving her grandmother's apartment, Summer saw the Bible lying on the coffee table. Then she remembered Mack's words to her about God. Was God there to listen to Summer's fears and dreams? Did Christ forgive those who'd strayed from his fold?

Summer stood by the counter, then closed her eyes as she gripped the cool white tiles. *Lord, I know it's been a while. But so much has happened since I came home. I needed to find peace again. I needed to find my soul again. And I did, here where I was nurtured and loved by my grandparents. And I also found a real love, Lord. I think I've found that perfect love that my grandmother believes in. Help me to accept this, Lord. Help me to heal. And help me to learn to love my parents, no matter what.*

The back door opened, causing Summer to blink and turn on her sneakers.

Surprised to find her father standing there, Summer motioned him in. "Hi, Daddy."

"Hey, yourself." James held his cowboy hat in his hand. "Honey, can we talk?"

"Sure," Summer said, wondering why he looked so glum. "Did you and Mama have a fight?"

"No, not exactly," James replied. "We had a good long talk. I told her about…well, you know."

"About your glory days being over, about the possibility of your permanent retirement?"

"Yeah, that." James looked so uncomfortable, Summer's heart went out to him.

"How did she take it?"

"It was the strangest thing. She almost seemed relieved." He shrugged, stared down at the floor. "She hugged me good and tight and laughed and cried and…well, let's just say that things have improved greatly between us."

"I'm so glad," Summer said, meaning it. But she wondered if this meant they'd be leaving again soon, too.

"I just wanted to thank you," James said. "You kept telling me to talk to her. You know I've never been much of a talker."

"Yes, I do know that." Summer could see now that all those times she'd thought her father didn't care, he simply just didn't know how to express himself. "I understand that now, Daddy."

"Do you, really?"

Seeing the hope in his eyes, Summer nodded. "I've been too harsh on you and Mama. I judged unfairly all these years."

"We did you wrong, honey."

His gentle admission melted Summer's heart. "You're here now. That counts in my book."

James rushed toward her then, grabbing her

up in a bear hug. "I think I'm going to stay for a while. A good long while."

"I'm glad," Summer said, the lump in her throat burning through her own guilt and misgivings.

"You could, too, you know."

Surprised, she pulled back. "You mean, stay here in Athens?"

"Why, sure. Makes sense that all the flock should just come back together. I know it would make your grandparents happy. And your mama and me, too."

Summer turned away, unable to look her father in the eye. "I'd have to think long and hard about that. April has moved back and I do miss her. But I can't leave Autumn up in New York all by herself."

"It is a lot to think on," James said. "What about Mack, though?"

Summer pivoted, lifting her eyebrows. "I thought you weren't so keen on him."

"I like Mack," James said, palms up. "And he seems mighty keen on you."

"It's complicated," Summer said. "I'm not sure."

James nodded, put his hat back on. "Well, that's your call, suga'." He turned, his hand on the screened door. "I just wanted you to know things are better with your mother and me. And that I approve of Mack."

"Thanks," Summer said, touched at his tentative attempts to be a real father to her. Waiting until after James had gone back out, she pushed a hand over her hair and let out a sigh. Then she gathered her things to head out to the party, the sounds of laughter and shouts echoing over the yard and buildings. "Looks like the fun has already begun," she mumbled, smiling.

She looked up to find Mack walking toward her.

"Hi," he said, waving to her.

"Hi." She suddenly felt confused and at a loss for words.

"Everything is in place," he said, a look of admiration on his face. "You did a great job."

"I had lots of help," she replied, putting on her sunshades and floppy red hat. "Thanks for everything, Mack."

He blocked the way from the patio to the yard, his eyes holding hers. "You look great."

"Thanks." She wore baggy denim walking shorts and a bright red-white-and-blue patterned sleeveless blouse. "It's a perfect day, in spite of the heat."

"Yes, it is."

He pulled her close then. "And tonight, I want you with me when those fireworks start going off."

"Okay." She lowered her head, afraid he'd see the truth in her eyes, even through her dark glasses.

But Mack touched her face, forcing her to look at him. "I want you there, because...well, I think the fireworks started the day I found you broken down on the side of the road."

Summer felt tears of joy pricking at her eyes. "I never told you, but my car wasn't the only thing having a breakdown that day."

"You didn't have to tell me. I figured that out pretty much from the get-go."

"And you're still speaking to me?"

"Yes. I like speaking to you. I like being with you. I like watching the way your face lights up when your grandfather tells one of his lame jokes. I like the way you laugh whenever you're with the residents, trying to make paper angels and lace doilies. And I really like the way you've taken them under your wing, offering them friendship and advice. I like to watch your face when you're listening to one of them tell you the same story you've already heard over and over. You never look bored or irritated. You always listen as if the person talking is the only person on earth."

Summer shrugged, blushed down to her toes. "I guess I've made an impression on you."

"You have."

He didn't seem in any hurry to get out to the party. He pulled her away from the door, then tugged her close. "And I especially like kissing you."

"Oh, Mack—"

Her words ended on a sigh as his mouth touched hers. It was a gentle kiss, reassuring and nurturing, promising and enticing. Summer wanted to stay right here in his arms for a very long time. And yet as he kissed her, all of her fears exploded with the calamity of sparklers going off. How could she tell him she loved him, and then just up and leave him?

She lifted her head, her heart fluttering from his touch, all her hopes pinned on his kisses.

"What?" Mack asked, as if he knew she had doubts.

"It's...nothing. I'm just not sure where all of this is going—"

A knock at a door down the way caused Mack to back up. "That's my apartment." He squinted in the sun. "I can't make out who—"

At his hesitation, Summer looked around to find a tall, attractive brunette standing there with a small, brown-haired boy by her side. Probably one of the resident's family members coming to the party.

"Hello," Summer said, hearing Mack's intake of breath behind her as she walked toward them. "Can I help you?"

"I hope so," the woman said, her tone haughty but cautious. "I'm looking for Mack Riley."

Summer turned to where Mack stood behind a column out of the woman's sight. He looked as if he'd turned into granite. "Mack?"

"I'm here," he said, pushing past Summer to face the woman. "What do you want, Belinda?"

Summer had certainly heard that name before. Then she realized what was going on. This was the woman Mack had left behind in Austin.

Belinda Lewis, the woman who had broken Mack's heart, was standing at the door with a little boy who looked exactly like Mack Riley.

"Mack, can we talk, please?"

Mack stared at the woman who had left him twisted and broken, a kind of dull shock numbing his system. Then he looked down at the little boy with her and his heart dropped to his feet. He felt sick inside. Because he knew why she had come here.

He saw Summer moving beside him. "I'm going to go out and find my grandmother."

He heard the disappointment, the acceptance, in her words. He wanted to run after her, tell her this was all a surprise to him, tell her he didn't love Belinda. But the boy was standing there looking up at him with such big eyes, Mack could only nod.

"Can we go inside?" Belinda asked.

"No," he said. "I mean, yes, this is my apartment." He motioned to the small patio. "Let me get the door unlocked."

Belinda pulled the child along. "C'mon, Michael."

Mack watched as the child followed her without a word. The boy seemed shy and scared. Mack felt the same way.

He quickly unlocked the door to his apartment, every fiber of his being pulled taut with an intense dread. Could this be his child?

Once inside his apartment, he headed to the kitchen counter then turned. Belinda was waiting just inside the door. "C'mon in," Mack said, aware that he sounded hollow and winded. He took a deep breath, watching Belinda and the child as they took a couple of steps. "Sit down."

Belinda pulled the boy to a nearby chair. "I

know this is unexpected, Mack, but I tried to tell you—"

"What do you want?" Mack asked, his eyes on the little boy. The child smiled shyly at him, and something inside Mack's shocked system responded to that smile. "Hey there."

Belinda cleared her throat. "I have some things to tell you, Mack. So don't interrupt until I get it all out, okay?" She motioned to the boy, Michael. "Sweetie, see that television over there? I think it'd be okay if you watch some cartoons while I talk to Mack." Then she looked back to Mack. "Is that all right?"

Mack found the remote and flipped the television until he found the public broadcasting channel, which carried children's programs every morning. "How's that?"

"I wuv this show," Michael said of the singing animals on the screen. He plopped down on bent knees in front of the moving picture.

"Good," Mack replied. Then he turned to Belinda. "What's going on?"

She looked frightened. Her hands were shaking. And for the first time, Mack saw the dark circles underneath her eyes. She'd lost weight, too.

"First," she began, taking another breath, "I

wanted to let you know that my father died about six months ago."

"I'm sorry to hear that," Mack said. In spite of how her father had treated him, Mack knew Belinda had loved the man.

"There's more," Belinda said, tears pricking at her eyes. "My mother has remarried and moved to California. I've…been alone for a while now, except for Michael."

Mack took in that information, wondering how Belinda had managed. She and her mother had never seen anything eye to eye, but worse than that, Belinda hated being alone. She sent a glance toward the little boy, making sure he was absorbed in the learning program.

"Michael is three years old, Mack," Belinda said. "And he's your son."

Mack's sharp intake of breath caused Michael to glance around. In a whisper, Mack said, "What do you mean? How can that be?"

Belinda looked embarrassed. "Remember that time after you'd struck out on your own and I came back to you? I wanted us to get back together and get married?"

Mack ran a hand down his face. "I remember. We…we were indiscreet. I thought you were back for good."

"Yes, you thought that. And I used that to my advantage. I threw myself at you."

Mack remembered all of it. He hadn't exactly turned her away. In a moment of weakness, he'd given in to her tempting promises. Just for one night. But that time, he'd been the one to leave. Now he would have to own up to his past mistakes.

"Belinda, are you telling me that you got pregnant that night?"

She nodded, careful not to talk too loudly. "I found out weeks later, but by then I'd found someone else. He seemed to be everything I wanted—he had the clout, the status. We ran in the same social circles. So I married him and made him think the baby was his. We broke up about a year later, after he found out the truth."

Mack swallowed the bile rising in his throat. "Why would you hide my own son from me?"

Belinda shuffled her feet, then crossed her legs, her expensive sandals clicking on the wooden floor. "You know me, Mack. I didn't think you could give me the things I wanted. And I was bitter because of that, so I decided to get even with you by never telling you about Michael. Besides, my daddy forced me to keep the truth from you. He said marriage beneath our family status would be a joke. Better to pretend Michael belonged to my better-suited husband." She laughed, but it sounded sharp-edged and bitter. "Well, now the joke's on me."

Mack watched as she sucked in a sob, his mind reeling with the knowledge that the adorable little boy sitting in front of his television was his. He had a son. "What do you mean?" he finally asked.

"I'm dying," Belinda said, her gaze moving from Mack to the child and back. "I have skin cancer—all those days by the pool finally caught up with me."

Mack closed his eyes, trying to comprehend what she was saying. "Are you sure?"

She nodded, sniffed back tears. "Oh, yes. I'm very sure. I've had three surgeries on spots on my back, but the cancer has spread. I only have a few months."

Mack held to the arms of his chair until his knuckles turned solid white. Then he realized she was wearing a wig that looked so much like her real hair, he hadn't even noticed. "But…you have money and resources and—"

"That doesn't really matter now. Money can't save me. I'm going to California, to be with my mother. She…she loves Michael, but she's not prepared to take him full-time. She'd want visitation rights, but—"

Mack felt his world spinning, felt the whole foundation of his trust and faith being tested. "You mean, you want *me* to take Michael?"

"That's why I'm here," Belinda said. Then she reached for his hand. "I've done so much wrong in my life, Mack. I've hurt a lot of people. Especially you. I was so self-centered. I loved you, but I thought position and money were more important, so I kept stringing you along because there is one thing money can't buy. I didn't want to be alone, so I kept coming back to you until somebody better asked me to marry him. That was a mistake, because he wasn't the better man. Now I don't have time to string anyone along."

She glanced over at Michael. "He'll have a trust fund. I've already met with my lawyers about that. And my mother only asks to visit him and have him visit her. She knows the truth now. She's willing to let you raise Michael, but she really wants to be his grandmother. She'll need him after…after I'm gone."

Mack watched as she held her head in her hands. "I'm so sorry, Mack. For everything. I pushed you that night, and it was wrong. But I don't regret having Michael. I just regret that I never told you the truth."

Mack looked at the woman he'd thought he'd loved. Then he thought about Summer, the woman he'd fallen in love with completely. Belinda had changed. She was trying to make amends before she died. He had to admire her for that, at least.

Then he looked at Michael. His son.

"I have a son," he said. Then he pivoted back to Belinda. "Does he know about me?"

"I've tried to explain things to him, but he's so young. That's why I had to come now. I wanted us to spend some time with you, just in case."

Mack understood what she was saying. He needed to get to know his son before Michael lost his mother. His heart welled up with a father's protective nature. And already, he knew he'd do whatever needed to be done for this little boy. His little boy. He didn't know how to say the words that thanked God and also asked for forgiveness in the same breath. He and Belinda had had a lapse in judgment, but his son wouldn't be punished because of that. Mack loved the boy completely. And he would protect him, no matter what.

Even if it meant he'd have to give up Summer.

He took Belinda's hand. "I can't turn him away. You know that, don't you?"

Belinda smiled. "Yes, I do. I know you will do the right thing, Mack. Because you're that kind of man. At least I knew that all along, in spite of how I treated you."

"And now you're doing what has to be done, for his sake."

She nodded. "About time, don't you think? I just hope I'm not too late."

Mack held her hand in his. "You're not, Belinda. It's never too late to do the right thing."

He just hoped Summer would see it that way too.

Chapter Fifteen

Elsie touched Summer's arm, causing her to jump.

"Mom, you scared me."

"I can see that," Elsie replied, her bright-red lipstick warring with her equally bright-red spangled earrings. "You were so lost in thought. Honey, are you still mad at me?"

Summer turned to her mother, her heart bursting with the need to talk to someone. "It's not you, Mom. I shouldn't have said those things the other day. I know you're trying very hard to make up for the past."

Elsie let out a breath. "Thank goodness. I've been so worried." Then she gave Summer a bittersweet smile. "But something good did come out of our fight."

"Oh, and what's that?" Summer asked, her mind drifting back to where Mack stood talking to Belinda and the little boy.

They'd stayed for the picnic and she'd had to endure watching Mack offer the child everything from a hot dog to cotton candy. She'd had to endure the way Mack looked at Belinda, the way he'd kept her close all day. Now, she watched as he escorted Belinda and the boy to Belinda's car. They were leaving, at last. And she was dying to hear Mack's excuses.

Earlier, he'd rushed by, grabbed her arm, and said, "We need to talk."

Boy, did they ever.

"Honey?"

Summer turned to find Elsie staring at her, her eyes wide with concern.

"Oh, I'm sorry. Just tired. What happened that's so good?"

"Your father and I," Elsie replied, her expression serene and sure. "I told him about our fight and…he finally opened up to me. About why he's been acting so strange."

"He told me that earlier," Summer said, thinking it seemed as if that had been a whole lifetime ago. "I'm so glad he talked to you."

Elsie let out a long sigh. "What I thought was

another woman was just your father's insecurities about growing old. Imagine him thinking I'd stop loving him if he isn't out there seeing and being seen. I never did much care about all the travel and all the parties and appearances. I did care about being with your father. And that's all I care about now."

"I take it from the smile on your face, that he told you he's not having an affair, and that you two aren't getting a divorce."

Elsie waved a hand, her navy silk blouse shimmering in the growing dusk. "No, no. I was only imagining all that. Your father has been depressed, Summer. Since Stuart's death, he's seen his own life differently, I guess. He was afraid I'd be the one to leave him, if you can believe that."

Summer gave her mother her complete attention. "No, I can't begin to believe that. You love him too much." Her words brought a shard of pain etching across her nerve endings. She loved Mack. But she could see him drifting back to Belinda. He'd shown her that today. And she had a feeling there was much, much more to the story.

"I do love your father," Elsie said. "I'm sure he told you this earlier, but...he knows it's time for him to give up the road, honey. He's tired. He wants to settle down and rest some, but he was worried about how to tell me that. He actually thought I'd be disappointed in him. He thought once we stopped traveling around for all his business commitments and all his doings with the rodeo circuit, that I'd get bored and want to leave him. I just can't see how that man got such a notion." Then she let out a laugh. "Of course, I was thinking the same thing about him."

Summer could see it. She'd seen it too many times in her line of work. "People change, Mom. Things change. Getting old can be a very stressful thing. It's hard for some people to accept. I'm so glad you and Daddy have talked things out. You can grow old gracefully, and together."

Elsie wiped at tiny tears. "Yes. Now I'm looking forward to it, darlin'. I'm so glad we had this time with you. I…I was so afraid it was too late—with both your father and with you. Now I have hope, Summer. So much hope."

Summer hugged her mother close. "I'm so glad, Mom. Daddy loves you. You know that. And I love you."

Elsie squeezed Summer, holding her tight. "Oh, honey, you don't know how much it means to hear you say that. I love you, too. And I promise you this. I will always be right here in Athens from now on, if you ever need me."

Summer felt her heart opening to that promise. "What about right now, Mama?"

Elsie stood back, her gaze moving over Summer. "What's wrong?"

Summer motioned toward where Mack was leaning into the car door, saying goodbye to Belinda. "That," she said. "I think Mack's old flame has rekindled the spark with him."

Elsie squinted toward the sunset. "I wondered who that was. I thought maybe it was his sister, or something."

"Or something," Summer said, whirling to go and sit on her grandmother's patio. She'd had enough of picnics and bandstands. She'd had enough of bean-bag tosses and dunking booths. And she'd had enough of watching Mack with another woman all day.

Elsie followed her and settled down beside her. Then the door to the apartment opened and Martha came out onto the porch. "Well, there you are," she said to Summer. Then she searched the crowd out in the yard. "Who is that woman who's been with Mack all day?"

Elsie patted the chair next to her. "Summer needs to talk to us, Mama."

Martha hurried to the chair. "Tell us, honey.

You've looked so lost and sad all day. Did something go wrong with Mack and you?"

Summer looked down at her sneakered feet. "That's his old girlfriend. She showed up first thing this morning." She took a deep, ragged breath. "And I think that little boy might belong to Mack."

Both her mother and her grandmother gasped.

"That can't be," Martha said, staring hard into the gathering twilight. "Mack's never mentioned a child. I mean, Mack is solid. He wouldn't abandon his own child." She looked from Summer to Elsie. "Would he?"

"That's the burning question," Summer said, suddenly realizing her grandmother had voiced the very thing that had been nagging at her all day. Had Mack abandoned the boy? Was Belinda here because of that abandonment?

"I can't believe this," Elsie said, her tone full of regret and condemnation. "And just when I thought you'd found the perfect match."

Summer got up, leaned against the white wooden railing. "Mack and I were tentative at best, Mom. Things were headed in that direction, but let's face it, we had a lot to work through. My work in New York is a big factor. And I'm not sure a long-distance relationship is what either of us want. And now this—"

Martha made a sound of distress. "You have to talk to him, Summer. I'm sure there is a reason for this."

Elsie nodded. "That might not even be his child."

Summer looked out into the crowd. "It's about time for the fireworks. I'd better go check with the pyrotechs and make sure everything is in order. Y'all should find Papaw and Daddy and enjoy the show together."

Elsie took her hand, pulling her back. "Summer, don't let this ruin things. You and I—we've come so far. Don't turn bitter on me again. Promise me that."

Martha took her other hand. "She's right, honey. You came home in a mood, and even though you've never talked about it, I have to believe your work was just about to do you in. You needed a rest. And you do look rested and happy, or at least you did up until now. We love you, Summer. We're here to help you through this. And God will help you, too."

"Thanks, Memaw." Summer shook her head. "This is between Mack and me, but you're right. Only God can give me the answers I need on how to handle this. But I am bitter. And angry. I trusted him. I didn't think he had any secrets." Then she remembered he'd never actually told her everything about his time with Belinda. Was this the rest of the story? "How could he not tell me this?" she asked. "How could he keep something so important from me?"

"This is a biggie," Elsie said. "Maybe he was embarrassed or ashamed. Maybe he was waiting till the right time to tell you."

"Maybe," Summer replied, her soul bruised and battered. She remembered Mack saying there was more, that he needed to tell her the whole story. Was this what he'd kept from her? It felt as if she'd been slapped. But this time, it wasn't by a man's hand. It was by Mack's deception instead. That hurt almost as much as the night Brad had hit her.

Summer willed herself to be strong. She'd kicked Brad straight out of her life that night, and got a restraining order put against him. She wouldn't take any man's abuse ever again, whether it be physical or mental. And if all of this were true, if that precious little boy belonged to Mack, then he'd not only abused her trust. He'd broken her heart. And that was one wound that would never heal.

* * *

Mack stood apart from the crowd, watching as the sun set to the west over the lake. Out in the water, the ducks and geese squawked their disapproval of all the humans milling around the complex grounds. He closed his eyes and held fast to the sounds of the waterfowl, to the sounds of laughter floating out over the still, warm night. He held fast to the picture of family and friends, of friendships and fellowship.

Today should have been a good day. A perfect day. And so it had been to the many residents and guests who'd come to share in the celebration and the fireworks.

But Mack had been miserable all day. Miserable at times, he corrected. At other times, he'd looked down at the trusting face of the little boy who belonged to him, and a kind of piercing joy had shattered his heart, filling it with light and love even as it filled it with regret and remorse.

He had a son.

He was in love with Summer.

Belinda was dying.

In the flash of a summer sun ray, his whole life had changed completely, taking a one-eighty turn that meant nothing would ever be the same.

He'd put off talking to Summer. But it had to

be done. Their whole relationship would have to be put on hold. And Mack was so afraid that their growing feelings wouldn't survive that kind of holding pattern.

"Only one way to find out," he said as he turned to look for her. She'd stayed away, distant and quiet, since this morning. He knew she was imagining all kinds of vile things about him. Some of them he deserved. And some of them he had to explain. If she'd listen.

Then he saw her.

She was walking toward him, her long golden hair flying out in a haphazard ponytail around her head and shoulders. Her shoulders slumped as she tucked her hands into the deep pockets of her baggy walking shorts. Her head was down. She looked defeated. She looked as if she'd already given up on them.

Mack aimed to change all of that. Somehow.

He closed his eyes again, and asked God to give him the guidance he so desperately needed right now. He'd made a big mistake, but Michael wouldn't suffer because of that mistake. Belinda had come to him, all pride gone now, and asked him to take their child. There was no question Mack would do that. He'd love Michael and raise him and he'd abide by Belinda's request. Michael would never suffer because of the past.

Michael would be his future.

Somehow, he had to find a way to have Summer in that future, too.

So he opened his eyes and looked at her.

"Hi," he said, reaching out a hand as she approached.

She took his hand, her whole being hesitant and restrained. "It's time for the fireworks."

He nodded. "And you're here with me, in spite of everything." That gave him hope.

"You said we need to talk."

He squeezed her fingers. "There is so much to say."

She slanted her head, looked up at him. "He's your child, isn't he?"

"Yes."

The silence was shattered with the first bright white and red bursts of color in the night sky.

"So, are you and Belinda—"

"She's dying, Summer. She came here to ask me to take Michael."

He heard her gasp, but it was soon drowned out by the second burst of color in the sky. Greens, pinks and purples this time. Bright and beautiful and arched to the heavens.

Then Summer pulled away, her eyes accusing. "How could you do that, Mack? How could you walk away from your own child?"

Mack's heart dropped like a lead weight, causing him to feel sick at his stomach. She thought… she thought he'd abandoned his own son? Then he understood. Summer had been abandoned so many times by her own parents. Or so she'd believed. Why should she believe anything but that about him. It looked that way, at least.

"Summer, you need to understand—"

"Oh, I understand. I understand that I fell in love with a man who…who left his own child behind to start a new life."

"That's not true."

"Oh, really? Then why haven't you ever mentioned that you had a child, Mack? Did it just slip your mind?"

Anger coursed through Mack's system. Anger and a tiredness that left him searching for breath. In the sky, the fireworks shot out over and over again, breathtaking in their fiery beauty, loud and crashing and stunning in their simplicity.

"I didn't know," he shouted over the boom of the rockets. "Summer, I didn't know I had a son."

She turned toward him, doubt warring with relief on her face. "How could you not know?"

He grabbed her by the hand, dragging her away from the crowds to take her to the one place where he could convince her that he loved her and that he'd never known until today that he had a son.

As the fireworks came to a pounding finale full of starbursts of fire and sparkles of red, white and blue shimmers raining down around them, Mack put her in his truck and headed for the farm.

Summer clung to her side of the truck. She knew Mack well enough to know not to try and talk to him right now. He was taking the asphalt at a high rate of speed, as if he wanted to put some distance between himself and everything that had happened today.

He hadn't known.

That kept crashing over and over in her mind. He hadn't known he'd had a son.

And she had to admit, knowing Mack the way she thought she knew him, that this had to be the truth. He would never leave a child of his behind. Never.

So she waited until he pulled the rickety old pickup into the yard of the farmhouse, her heart bursting like the fireworks they'd just left behind as her childhood home came into focus in the moonlit night.

Mack halted the truck, then came around to open her door. "Get out."

She did, allowing him to take her hand and pull her to the steps of the house. Mack sat down, then he pulled her down beside him. "I'm going to talk, Summer. And I want you to listen. Can you do that for me?"

She nodded, silent and waiting.

He let out a long breath. "Belinda started calling me a couple of weeks ago, just as I mentioned to you. I told her I didn't want to talk to her or see her, but she tracked me down anyway. And now I know why." He stopped, checked to make sure she'd heard him.

Summer nodded. "Go on."

"I knew Michael was my son the minute I saw him. Almost four years ago, Belinda and I had one last encounter. She had me convinced that she'd never leave me again, so I gave in to my need for her." He gave a disgusted grunt. "You know that old saying about hating yourself in the morning? Well, I did.

"This time, I asked *her* to leave. I realized that I couldn't live like that anymore, waiting for her to come back, waiting for her whims to decide what would happen for the rest of my life. So I told her it was over for good this time. I tried to explain why—that I needed a commitment, that I wanted marriage and a family—but she couldn't see things very clearly. She was so angry at me.

"I didn't try to find her after that. I just tried to get on with my life. But she didn't take my rejection too well. She went to her father, complaining that I'd used her and then dumped her. Her father believed her and decided to get even with me for hurting his little girl. He'd never approved of me, and even though Belinda and I were through, I guess he still considered me a threat. Especially since I was becoming more and more successful, which would look good in Belinda's eyes. He thwarted my efforts at every turn. And even though I had a growing business in Austin, one day after I lost a major client because of Mr. Lewis, I just kind of went numb and decided I needed to move on. I think deep down inside, I'd been hoping Belinda would come back to me, but she never did. She married another man and that was that. That's the last I heard of her.

"I left Austin and traveled around the country, working here and there at landscaping firms and doing nursery work when I could. Then I settled here in Athens and tried to put Belinda out of my mind.

"Today, she told me everything. Her marriage

didn't work out. The man she married found out about Michael's true parentage. Apparently, at her father's insistence and to protect herself, she had passed Michael off as her husband's, but he couldn't hack it, so he took off."

He took Summer's hand, his eyes locking with hers. "I didn't know, Summer. You have to believe that. I didn't know I had a child. If I had, nothing would have stopped me from taking responsibility for him. And now, Belinda is dying. She only has a few months to live. Her father's dead and her mother's remarried. She wanted me to get to know my son before it's too late. She wants me to raise Michael. I have to do that, Summer. Now that I know the truth, I have to be with my son."

Summer sat there, listening to him, and felt her soul being turned inside out. He was telling her the truth. Because Mack always told the truth. He'd been honest with her from the beginning, so she had no reason to doubt him now. Still, it hurt so much.

"What about us?" she finally asked, her words raw with confusion and pain.

"I don't know," he said, shaking his head. "It's a lot to ask of you. But I want you to understand. I'm going to have to go to California for a while, to be with Michael and Belinda. Her mother is there, and she wants to be with her mother...at the end. She wants Michael to be with people who can help him when things get tough. I have to go, Summer."

Summer nodded, tears forming in her eyes. "I do understand. You can't turn your back on them."

"No, I can't. But I don't want to turn my back on you, either. I love you. I think I've loved you since the day I found you there on the side of the road."

She laughed through her tears. "I was so broken. So confused. And things sure went downhill from there."

He pushed closer to her, taking her against him. "That depends on how you look at things."

"Well, things aren't looking so good from where I'm sitting."

He kissed her tears. "Look at where you're sitting, Summer. You're home. This is the house you came back to. The people you love will always be welcome here. If you're willing to wait, I will be right back here one day, too."

"With your son," she reminded him.

"Yes, with my son. I hope you can accept that."

She shuddered, turned toward his arms. "But...I have to go back to New York. I have to think about all of this."

"I don't want you to leave," he said, his cheek touching hers.

"I have to leave. You need time to…get through this. And so do I."

He nodded, silent as he just held her there. "So are you saying…there's a chance for us, in spite of everything?"

Summer looked up at him, her heart filling with that perfect love she'd tried so hard to understand. "I think there's a good chance. You see, Mack, you are the kind of man a woman can trust. Because you always do the right thing. And taking Michael is the right thing."

He slumped toward her, the relief in his eyes shining through the moonlight. "Loving you is the right thing, too."

"That's debatable, but I like the sound of it. So you go and take care of Michael and I'll…I'll figure out how to resign from my job and come back here to you. Back to you and Golden Vista. Maybe there's a place there for me, if I can get licensed to be a social worker in Texas."

"I think that's a good idea," he said. Then he took her head in his hands. "You're really okay with all of this?"

"I'm getting there. I was so worried. I thought—"

"You thought I'd left Michael behind, like you were left behind so many times."

She bobbed her head. "I was wrong. I'm glad I was wrong." Then she looked up at him. "But there's something I need to say."

"I'm listening."

"It's about me and my own hang-ups. It's about my work. I see abused and battered women every day, but in my last relationship, I was the one being abused."

Mack's expression changed from loving to protective. "You let a man abuse you?"

"Hard to believe, isn't it?" She sniffed, lifted a hand in the air. "He only hit me once. But that was enough to make me stop and see things very clearly. I had to practice what I preached, so I told him to get out. He left, and he never bothered me again. He knew he'd regret it if he did."

Mack drew her close. "I can back that up."

"You don't need to do that," she said, glad she'd finally told him the truth. "It's over. I've got people watching him very closely. He'd be wise never to hit a woman again." She touched a hand to Mack's face. "But that was part of the reason I took a leave from work and came home. I needed…to find my confidence again. I felt so ashamed, so weak. I'd failed all the women I tried to help."

"You didn't fail," Mack told her. "You did the right thing. You got out of that situation."

"No more wrongs," she whispered. "We were both condemning ourselves for being weak, for being human. But now, we have a chance to make things right."

"No more wrongs," Mack said, cradling her close. "From now on, we work at it until we *do* get it right," he said, moving toward her. "So right. Together."

Summer sank into his embrace, her mind whirling with all the struggles ahead. This did feel right and perfect and wonderful. And she knew that in spite of everything in their way, it would all turn out the way God had planned for them if they just put their faith and their love first. She hadn't done that with Brad—he would never have agreed to those terms, and she couldn't tolerate his abusive nature. And she certainly hadn't trusted in God's guidance with her parents. But all of that would change now.

Now she knew how to accept the perfect love Christ extended to His flock. Now she knew how to accept the love of a good, strong man who had learned through trial and error how to be a faithful

Christian. She deserved that kind of love, even if she didn't feel worthy. But God had shown her she *could* be worthy. She would fight for that honor, for that grace. She would fight for Mack, and her parents and grandparents. And all the residents of Golden Vista.

Summer looked over Mack's shoulder at the house she'd loved and lost. But she still had the heart of this old house. She had her memories and she had all the people she loved here with her.

And now she had Mack and Michael, too. She was home at last, and the view looked perfect.

* * * * *

Dear Reader,

Is there such a thing as a perfect love? Maybe not in this life. But we know we have the perfect love of Christ with us always. That's a lesson Summer Maxwell had to learn in order to find true happiness with Mack Riley.

Mack had failed at love because he tried to be perfect for the wrong woman. Summer had failed at love because she always felt unworthy of receiving love. Together, they had to learn that while human love might not be perfect, it can be complete and fulfilling with a little help from friends, family and especially God.

I hope you enjoy this second book of my Texas Hearts trilogy. Please look for the third and final story in this series, *A Leap of Faith*, when Autumn Maxwell learns that she can depend on faith to help her find her soul mate.

I hope you have God's perfect love in your life to help you through sad times and joyous celebrations.

Until next time, may the angels watch over you—always.

Lenora Worth

REQUEST YOUR FREE BOOKS!

2 FREE INSPIRATIONAL NOVELS
PLUS 2
FREE
MYSTERY GIFTS

Love Inspired

YES! Please send me 2 FREE Love Inspired® novels and my 2 FREE mystery gifts (gifts are worth about $10). After receiving them, if I don't wish to receive any more books, I can return the shipping statement marked "cancel." If I don't cancel, I will receive 6 brand-new novels every month and be billed just $4.49 per book in the U.S. or $4.99 per book in Canada. That's a saving of at least 22% off the cover price. It's quite a bargain! Shipping and handling is just 50¢ per book in the U.S. and 75¢ per book in Canada.* I understand that accepting the 2 free books and gifts places me under no obligation to buy anything. I can always return a shipment and cancel at any time. Even if I never buy another book, the two free books and gifts are mine to keep forever.   105/305 IDN FEGR

Name _____ (PLEASE PRINT) _____

Address _____ Apt. # _____

City _____ State/Prov. _____ Zip/Postal Code _____

Signature (if under 18, a parent or guardian must sign)

Mail to the **Reader Service:**
IN U.S.A.: P.O. Box 1867, Buffalo, NY 14240-1867
IN CANADA: P.O. Box 609, Fort Erie, Ontario L2A 5X3

Not valid for current subscribers to Love Inspired books.

**Are you a subscriber to Love Inspired books
and want to receive the larger-print edition?
Call 1-800-873-8635 or visit www.ReaderService.com.**

* Terms and prices subject to change without notice. Prices do not include applicable taxes. Sales tax applicable in N.Y. Canadian residents will be charged applicable taxes. Offer not valid in Quebec. This offer is limited to one order per household. All orders subject to credit approval. Credit or debit balances in a customer's account(s) may be offset by any other outstanding balance owed by or to the customer. Please allow 4 to 6 weeks for delivery. Offer available while quantities last.

Your Privacy—The Reader Service is committed to protecting your privacy. Our Privacy Policy is available online at www.ReaderService.com or upon request from the Reader Service.

We make a portion of our mailing list available to reputable third parties that offer products we believe may interest you. If you prefer that we not exchange your name with third parties, or if you wish to clarify or modify your communication preferences, please visit us at www.ReaderService.com/consumerchoice or write to us at Reader Service Preference Service, P.O. Box 9062, Buffalo, NY 14269. Include your complete name and address.

LIREG11B

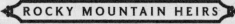

Love Inspired

Raising four-year-old triplets and an abandoned teenager, single mom Arabella Clayton Michaels loves her big family. But when Denver surgeon Jonathan Turner arrives to announce that Arabella's beloved teenager is his long-lost niece, they find themselves becoming an unexpected family....

The Doctor's Family

By *New York Times* bestselling author

Lenora Worth

◆ ROCKY MOUNTAIN HEIRS ◆

Available September wherever books are sold.

www.LoveInspiredBooks.com

LI87692